IT'S JUST NOT GOOD ENOUGH

VIVIEN HEIM

© 2015 Vivien Heim

First published in 2015

www.vivienheim.com

The moral right of Vivien Heim to be identified as the Author of this work has been asserted in accordance with the Copyright, Designs and Patents Act, 1988.

All Rights Reserved. No part of this publication may be reproduced, stored in a retrieval system, or transmitted, in any form or by any means, electronic, mechanical, photocopying, recording or otherwise, without the prior permission of the Copyright owner.

ISBN 978-1-5176-5021-6

Any resemblance to actual persons living or dead or actual events is purely coincidental.

This book is dedicated to every leopard that can't (or won't) change his (or her) spots

... and my wonderful reviewers said ...

Ali felt: "...a real connection to Lucie Hunter. Her trials and tribulations, having to rebuild her life, struck a major chord. But her passion and love for food, cooking and men makes this a thoroughly delicious read."

Dawn said: "IT'S JUST NOT GOOD ENOUGH made me laugh and cry in equal measure. It hit so many chords for me and reaffirmed my faith in the Sisterhood. It also gave me hope that, at whatever age you are, living life and falling in love can happen."

Kate's thoughts were that: "Any woman of a 'certain age', having experienced the highs and lows of life and loves will understand what Lucie goes through in her turbulent year. I found it funny and moving. I think many women will find it gives them hope, because their next adventure could be just around the corner."

Alan thought: "IT'S JUST NOT GOOD ENOUGH is an enthralling tale of the life and loves of Lucie who, supported by her many friends, bounces back from a very bruising love affair. Some readers may find Lucie's frequent, detailed, culinary descriptions unnecessary but, although not a 'foodie' myself, I found them an endearing and necessary aspect of Lucie's character."

Patsy wrote: "This is a courageous story which speaks for all women who refuse to let life pass them by. Vivien's debut novel charts, with devastating honesty, one woman's journey through her emotional hell and out the other side. Live with Lucie, laugh with Lucie, love with Lucie, eat with Lucie - she will become a part of your life!"

Caroline commented: "Lucie has a dilemma. Should she stay with the man who doesn't make her feel loved and wanted? Is this as good as it gets? It's a dilemma which will resonate with many women. It's only when the decision is made for her that she learns to live and love again."

ACKNOWLEDGEMENTS

I can't begin to thank so many people enough - for their help, encouragement, support - and even gentle cynicism on occasions. However, I must make some special mentions.

To Audrey, who never stopped believing in me.

To my daughter Harriet, who's been cheering me on from the side-lines throughout, for making me sit through a photoshoot and for building my website.

To Julian Shakespeare, who made sense of my embryonic ideas to create this wonderful cover. (www.zebrathree.co.uk.)

To everyone at the One Elm, who have been unendingly wonderful to me - supplying me with tea, coffee, lots of laughs and a vibrant place to write.

To my wonderful reviewers, without whom this book probably wouldn't have seen the light of day. So, huge thanks to Alan Bedford, Ali Buxton, Caroline Day, Kate Harrison, Patsy Spiller and Dawn Turner.

And finally to you - my readers. Thank you for reading this, my debut novel. I hope you enjoy it and will look forward to the sequel – oh yes, Lucie's adventures will continue ...

Introduction

I was in one of those delicious transient moments between sleeping and wakefulness when reality gently nudges into consciousness. I'd been sleeping on my back with my right arm curled over my head and gradually became aware of butterfly kisses travelling down the inside of my arm. More insistent kisses and nibbles were lavished on my right breast and then the butterfly journeyed down towards my hip which was nuzzled and licked. Before I could draw breath, the butterfly moved down my belly, a firm hand eased my legs apart and I heard a soft moan as a determined tongue explored me. It usually takes me more time than many men are able - or willing - to wait for me to come but the sheer audacity of what was happening drove me into a fast, hard orgasm and I bucked, gasped and whimpered into blissful release.

As my breathing slowed and I returned to a semblance of normal awareness, I opened my eyes to see him gazing at me and looking incredibly pleased with himself. "A very happy Christmas my love."

"And - and a happy, happy Christmas to you sweetie," was all I could think of saying which, in view of what had just happened, seemed a bit tame.

I leant over to kiss him and as my tongue skirted the inside of his lips, I could taste myself on his mouth. It occurred to me that I really ought to return the favour but as I started to graze my mouth down his neck onto his chest I heard him say, "I think I should wait till later for this," and he firmly pulled me back up to kiss my mouth again. As he was never one to refuse such a generous offer, I drew back and stared at him, raising my eyebrows in amazement.

"You feeling ok?"

He grinned, that wide smile that had initially attracted me and which always melted my heart. "Time for breakfast I think – coming?"

I smirked as he gazed down at me. "Come on you, downstairs. Don't we have people arriving soon who'll be expecting Christmas lunch?"

"Oh shit!" I exclaimed. "Why the hell didn't you wake me earlier?" I threw a pillow at his departing back and scrambled out of bed, almost falling over in my haste, grabbed a sweatshirt and pulled it over my head as I made for the bathroom.

Washing my hands, I glanced into the mirror. An unexpected wave of doubt swept over me. I shook my head to try and clear the negative and destructive thoughts that threatened to engulf me and scowled at myself impatiently.

I looked more closely into the mirror. Panda eyes stared back at me and I swore to myself, for the umpteenth time, to take off my makeup before bed. I made the same promise every time I saw my pillow cases but it was so hard to be that sensible when going to bed turned into a passionate and tempestuous business. And on those nights when I was alone, I found that I just couldn't be bothered anyway, bad habits do tend to linger. I quickly splashed cold water over my face, rubbed the worst of the dark smudges off and ran my fingers through my hair.

"Come on, slowcoach," I heard as I ran downstairs. I passed the open door to the sitting room and glanced in. There, behind the safety of the fireguard was a freshly lit fire, logs cheerfully crackling their welcome. As I walked into the kitchen, I smelled coffee and toast and more cooking scents.

"Mmmm, mmmm – aren't you just the best." I hugged him from the back as he was standing at the sink. He turned round to return the hug.

"Come and sit down," he directed, gently pushing me towards the table. I stared in amazement. The table was beautifully set for Christmas lunch and as I sank into a chair I realised that the delicious fragrance was in fact the turkey beginning to roast. I quickly stood up and almost cannoned into him as he held a glass of orange juice towards me. I took a gulp and felt the hit of champagne.

"Bucks Fizz – my fave – you remembered."

"I listen more than you think." He grinned at me again - that spontaneous open smile that said and meant so much.

"Smug bastard," I teased. I glanced over his shoulder and saw bowls of peeled vegetables all ready to be cooked.

"When on earth did you get up?"

"Oh, an hour or so before I ... errrr ... woke you up."

"I like your early morning calls – very, very unexpected."

"Well, you always said that you wanted to expect the unexpected and, of course, I always aim to please."

"And my dear you do, you so do."

"Go and sit down. There's scrambled eggs to eat before you're allowed to even think about anything else." Obediently I sat and waited as he produced a plate of toast piled high with creamy scrambled eggs festooned with strips of smoked salmon and a decorative sprig of parsley. He brought through another for himself and we sat at a corner of the table, eating in companionable silence.

"Coffee next." He stood to fetch the coffee which was rich and strong, just what I needed. I'd only recently taught myself to truly enjoy black coffee and the novelty still made me feel grown up - after all it had only taken me sixty-plus years to get there.

As I finished my breakfast, he looked across at me.

"Time for your Christmas present I think," he said and stood up. As he walked past me, I caught hold of his waist and pulled him towards me, tilting my head upwards. He looked down at me.

"Kiss," I commanded and he compliantly bent over me. I adore kissing. Too many men prefer to get down and dirty and often the faster the better, so to have found someone who was prepared, more than just prepared, to spend time revelling in old-fashioned snogging was a gift beyond compare.

"Let me go and get your present – please," he managed to say inbetween kisses.

"Hmmm ... well, ok." I pretended to be cross while secretly delighting in his eagerness to please. All negative thoughts had completely vanished. He pulled free and disappeared.

"Why don't you join me?" I walked into the sitting room where he stood, naked, in front of the fire with an enormous, beautifully wrapped box held out at arms' length.

"Well now, is it the box or you that's my present?" I asked teasingly. He stared at me with an intensity that I found disconcerting.

"Both ... either ... whatever you want," and he sank to his knees. I hesitated and then gave him a small smile.

"Box first I think - but you stay exactly where you are." I took the box out of his outstretched arms and sat on the sofa. Dutifully he stayed on his knees and watched as I slowly undid the red ribbon, pulled off the shiny paper and opened the box. The inside was lined with more pretty paper but was empty save for a large red envelope. I blinked - another unexpected - and reached down for the meagre contents. I glanced at him. He was staring fixedly at me, a slightly nervous smile on his lips. I peeled back the flap of the envelope very unhurriedly and pulled out a card, it was a really beautiful card too. The picture was a charcoal sketch of two people locked in a close embrace. I looked at him.

"You did this?" He nodded. "Very good – amazingly good in fact."

I looked again and saw our resemblance on the entwined figures. I smiled as I opened the card and as I read his elegant handwriting, drew in my breath sharply and turned towards him only to be suddenly hit by a jolt from the past - a memory of last Christmas which I thought I'd managed to consign to the past but which occasionally came back to bite me ...

Chapter 1 – Christmas past

Christmas Eve...

"Oh shit," I swore under my breath. I'd set the alarm on my mobile to the sound of harps gently playing but the message was still the same, time to get up. Getting up at six o'clock to get last minute provisions really wasn't my idea of fun, but I'd ordered the turkey and sodding pigs in their sodding blankets because I just couldn't face making them on Christmas morning – who could? Grumpily I got out of bed and pulled on tracksuit bottoms and a baggy sweater. Early morning pee, a splash of cold water, teeth brushed and I was done. It was cold and dark so it hardly seemed worth the effort to do anything else.

I went downstairs to two startled cats blinking up at me as I switched the lights on, threw some cat biscuits into their bowls, picked up my car keys and stepped outside. It was a grey, chilly, sleety morning and I shivered as I got into my cold car. Half an hour later I was in Leamington at Aubrey Allen's, one of the best butchers in Warwickshire. It had seemed such a good idea a few weeks ago when I'd placed my order with them, but of course I hadn't thought through the reality of getting up at unearthly o'clock on an uninviting Christmas Eve morning.

I stood in the queue while the couple in front of me faffed around, discussing if they needed an extra piece of pork, and whether they could be bothered to make cranberry sauce and red cabbage or should they buy them ready made. Bloody hell, I thought, couldn't you have had that conversation before you'd come out? I shifted from foot to foot and coughed loudly in an effort to make them hurry up which, of course they didn't. Eventually it was my turn. "Order number 2713 please."

The woman smiled at me. "You're in the wrong queue. Bit early for you? Don't you worry love. We're not so busy that I can't go and get it for you." Her kindness startled me.

I smiled back. "Thanks so much – it's not the best morning for me."

"I can tell. You don't exactly look Christmassy."

She was so right, but by the time I'd thought of what to say, she'd disappeared, returning in a few moments with a large carrier bag. "Turkey, two bread sauce, two trays pigs in blankets and a small ham – that it?" I nodded. "That's £93.49. Anything else?"

I shook my head, paid, thanked the assistant again, lugged the heavy bag outside and chucked it in the car. Luckily I'd managed to park just outside the shop so I went to the greengrocers next door and bought the rest of the fruit and vegetables I needed, put the full-to-bursting bag in the boot and sank gratefully into the driver's seat.

I drove back into Stratford. I wanted a decent cup of coffee and managed to park close to one of my favourite cafés. They'd only just opened and as I walked through the door, the smell of frying bacon and strong coffee hit me. I sat at a table in the window and gazed out. People were already wandering around doing their last-minute bits of shopping, and it seemed to me that the world was full of couples doing coupley things. I sighed. Maria, the owner of the café, came over.

"The usual?" I nodded and within a minute, a large cafetiere of scalding hot coffee was plonked in front of me. I poured out a cup, allowed myself some cream and sugar as a treat and took a sip. It was hot, strong and sweet - just the way I liked it.

My mobile quacked; I had quacking ducks to tell me when a text came though. I picked up and saw that it was a message from Richard. I smiled. 'Can't make it til later, probably 6. Sorry. Have a good day. Rxxx'

My smile faded. He'd promised to be up for lunchtime. I'd planned to cook a pork, chorizo and cannellini bean cassoulet for lunch - one of his favourite winter meals. I felt my eyes prickling with tears of anger and frustration as I swallowed my disappointment and gulped the rest of the coffee with little enjoyment.

Maria came over. "Are you alright?" There was real concern in her voice.

"Yes, I'm fine." I smiled at her and tried to look more cheerful. "It's just that he's not arriving til later and I'd really hoped he'd ..." my voice trailed off.

Maria frowned. "Bloody men. Unreliable, the lot of them."

"No, no," I protested, "he's not like that. He's just busy, got a lot to do. He's planning to stay up here til New Year, so he needs to make sure all's ok at his place."

"Yeah, ok love." She didn't sound convinced. Frankly, I wasn't that confident I was right either, but I certainly wasn't going to let her know that. I put a fiver on the table for my coffee and stood up, saying a Merry Christmas to Maria who smiled gently at me as I left.

It was now daylight, the sky a pale grey and, as I left the café, more couples walked past me. Why, when I'd been with Richard for nearly five years did I feel so very un-coupley for so much of the time? I wandered round aimlessly for a few minutes, not wanting to go home to face putting the shopping away and do the final tidying for the festivities. I really didn't feel in the mood for any festivities now. One little text had seen to that.

I shrugged and returned to the car. Stop being so silly, I muttered to myself. He can't help being busy. Just make lunch dinner instead. It'll be lovely – you wait and see. I started to smile as I got into the car and drove home.

As soon as I arrived home, I emptied the car, unpacked the food, prepped the lunch that was now dinner and did a final quick tidy. After that I got into the shower and as I stood under the hot water, reflected on Richard's text. He'd said that he'd be up for lunch so why, suddenly, did it have to be dinner? He'd had a full three days at his place, so what hadn't he done that could have been done in good time? Unbidden, more tears prickled my eyes. Enough of this, I told myself sternly. Stop being such a baby. Quickly, I washed my hair and stepped out. Once I'd dried my hair, put makeup on and donned some decent clothes I felt lots better. I smiled at myself in the mirror.

Downstairs the cats mewed at me for fuss. I sat down and petted them and listened to their appreciative purrs, enjoying their unconditional affection. After a few minutes, I gently shooed them off and played Mike Oldfield's Tubular Bells, turning up the volume to lose myself in the music. I glanced at my watch. It was only eleven thirty and while I wondered what to do until six when he was due to arrive, the phone rang.

"Hello?" I barely kept the eagerness from my voice.

"Hi, it's Karen. Fancy a festive drinkie sometime today? Or are you busy with lover boy?" Her voice sounded slightly mocking.

'No, no, he's not here - I'd love to - when's good for you?' We agreed to meet in the One Elm, one of our favourite watering holes in town. I felt much more cheerful.

Half an hour later Karen and I were in the One Elm, lounging in comfy seats by the open fire that had just been lit, sipping a large glass of red each. We'd known each other for some thirty years and been firm friends for over ten. She was a caring, honest and supportive friend and I felt very lucky to know her. We'd seen each other through husbands, divorces, bereavement, jobs, kids and lovers. A cornerstone of our relationship was a searing honesty which often hurt but which was always, always, well meant.

"Well?" She raised a quizzical eyebrow.

"Well what?"

"You know perfectly well what; tell me what's bothering you."

"It's nothing really. I'm just being silly."

"I don't think that you're silly. You look as though you've been crying. Have you?" She suddenly looked serious. "Just because he's the first real relationship you've had since Alex died, doesn't mean you have to let him walk all over you. You've managed perfectly well on your own for goodness sakes. How long's it been now?"

"Oh God, it's been thirteen years." My mind flashed back to the terrible struggle in the early days when my darling Alex had only just left work to set up his own business. We'd never expected him to have that terrible accident and, of course, hadn't bought all the right insurances so I'd had money problems to worry about as well as the dreadful shock of losing him. Our daughter, Susie was only eleven at the time and had taken her father's death terribly hard. I couldn't keep up the payments on our house, which was then far too big for just the two of us, but managed to sell at a reasonable price - just enough to be able to put a small deposit on my current, much smaller, house. Then I was made redundant a year or so later. Still, I had my teacher's pension and that, with a few bits and bobs of work, enabled me to keep my nose above water. I recognised that it was all a bit brinkmanship which made survival a real challenge sometimes but things always seemed to work out, even if it could be quite hair-raising from time to time.

Karen nodded. "Yes, you had it tough but you coped so well. So, why aren't you coping now?"

"I don't know, I honestly don't know. I was devastated when Alex died but I knew I had to keep going, for Susie as much as for myself. And once Susie reached eighteen, I knew I wanted someone special just for me. And, Karen, it feels so right with Richard for so much of the time ... well, it did."

"Hmmm." Karen looked thoughtful. "Well, loving relationships don't make you as unhappy as you've been for the past few months. You've got to stop crying over him. He won't know he upsets you if you don't tell him, but quite honestly, I'm not sure he cares that much. It's a bit my way or the high way, isn't it?"

I blinked at her and then told her about my early start in the cold dark of the morning, the queue, the kindness of the assistant, the coffee, the text and how I'd felt sidelined and sad when I'd read it.

"I wouldn't have minded if he hadn't known. But I mentioned lunch a couple of days ago and he'd agreed that was a great idea. And now ..." My voice trailed off and I felt a tear roll down my cheek. "I'm being so stupid. It's ridiculous to feel like this. He's just busy. He'll be here in a few hours."

Karen smiled at me. "Cheer up. Here's to a happy Christmas." We clinked glasses and sipped. We then talked about her plans for a family Christmas with both her children and their respective other halves who were coming over to her for the day.

"You're so lucky to have your kids living close. Susie's hoping that her contract will be extended for another year. And China's a bloody long way away, isn't it?"

Karen nodded. "Yes, but she's loving it out there and the experience will stand her in good stead - pretty girlies who are also great engineers are in hot demand, you know." I nodded. Of course I was pleased that my talented daughter was having a great time, but there was no doubt, I missed her. By this time we'd both taken off our boots and put our feet on the leather fender in front of the fire as we talked. We wiggled our toes and laughed.

After another couple of hours we left the warmth and geniality of the bar and shivered as we stood outside.

"Happy, happy Christmas darling." I gave her a warm hug.

"And you – make sure it's a good one."

I'd walked down the hill into town to meet Karen and as I couldn't face walking back up, we strolled over to the market square to a waiting rank of taxis. "Come on, let's go home in style."

It took a few minutes to drop Karen off and then for me to get home. As ever the cats were in and wanting to be stroked. "Too busy," I told them as I laid and then lit the fire. I watched as the flames licked the firelighters and kindling wood. Soon the logs started to crackle. I always enjoyed an open fire and smiled as the warmth started to permeate the room. It was nearly four o'clock and I felt pleasantly mellow. I lay on the sofa and closed my eyes.

I awoke with a start to an incessant knocking sound. Groggily, I staggered off the sofa, looked at my watch to see it was just after five o'clock and opened the front door to see Richard standing in the sleety rain, not looking best pleased.

"I've been standing here for ages," he complained. I stood in the doorway, trying to wake up properly. "Come on then, aren't you going to let me in?"

It took a couple of seconds for me to take in what he was saying. I stood on one side. "Of course darling, come on in."

"What on earth have you been doing? You're not exactly looking your best."

I looked in the hall mirror to see that my hair was flattened on one side, one eye's makeup smudged and no lipstick. "Oops. I'll get myself sorted while you bring in your bags."

I grabbed my handbag, joozed up my hair, put lipstick on and rubbed a licked finger under one eye to remove the smudge. "There you are." I lifted my face towards him.

"Better." He smiled and bent to kiss me.

"What would you like to drink? Tea, coffee or something stronger?"

"I'm not feeling terribly well so perhaps I ought to start off with a nice cup of tea."

I went into the kitchen and put the kettle on. "The fire needs rescuing." I heard the clatter of the shovel in the coal bucket that stood on the hearth. "It's almost out - you should have put some coal on along with the logs."

I sighed. "Yes, you're probably right," I called as I made the tea and took it into the sitting room to find him kneeling in front of the fire.

"Think I've saved it," he said as he rose to his feet. I put the mug of tea next to where he always sat on the sofa and raised my arms up towards him; we briefly hugged and kissed cheeks.

"It was a bit of a trek up here. The traffic was terrible. Mind if I just sit and relax for a short while?"

He sat down, pulled out the battered leather footstool, put his feet up, leaned back and closed his eyes. I sat in an adjacent chair and gazed at his lean frame, silver hair and chiselled features. There was absolutely no doubt about it, he was a very, very good looking man and even in repose he had the power to make my heart beat faster. It was strange I mused, as I continued to stare at his relaxed face, how when we were together everything seemed alright - well, for most of the time. Not all of the time though. If I was being brutally honest, cracks were beginning to show but so much was good between us, I felt sure that we could overcome them, given time, a little effort and a willingness to listen and compromise - not qualities he'd demonstrated much in his many past relationships from what I'd gathered.

We'd met through an internet dating website. Although I had specified that my preference was for someone who lived within twenty miles of Stratford upon Avon, I had decided that this was probably too narrow a criterion and so had happily met men from as far as fifty miles away. Richard had initially messaged me and although he lived about eighty miles away, I agreed to meet him. His piercing blue eyes and sardonic smile had made me melt within minutes. There was clearly a mutual attraction so, despite the distance, we'd now been together for close on five years. It was, however, a weekends only relationship which had been perfectly acceptable for the first couple of years but, as time went on, I'd become more and more dissatisfied with our arrangement. I wanted more. More time, more sharing, more commitment - but every time I tentatively raised the subject Richard made it abundantly clear that our 'modus operandi' as he called it suited him just fine.

After about half an hour Richard opened his eyes, yawned and stretched. "That's much better." He smiled warmly at me. "Now, what are we doing this evening?"

I bit back my very slight irritation. Because our weekends-only arrangement meant that, mostly he came up to mine, it seemed that our social life had, more and more, become my responsibility. "Well, I hadn't really thought ..." my voice trailed off as he frowned.

"I'd have thought you'd have wanted to go out to see someone."

"I think that most people are having family time this evening. Shall we just have dinner and then watch a movie?"

"Yes, that'll be fine. Probably for the best as I think I'm getting a bit of a cold."

I gazed at him. Good looking he certainly was but one of his less endearing qualities was an over-riding preoccupation with his health which seemed to get worse with every birthday.

"Man flu?" I teased.

He frowned. "Don't be so silly."

"Let's eat early." I walked out of the sitting room to hide my mild exasperation.

I took down one of my favourite Le Crueset pans. My love of cooking meant that I'd treated myself to a few very expensive pots and pans over the years and always enjoyed using them.

I sploshed in a small slug of olive oil, chopped onion, a leek and a couple of cloves of garlic and added them together with a small pinch of pink salt, which I felt gave many dishes a more intense depth. The smell of cooking filled the room; I smiled as I instantly felt calmer. After a few minutes I added the small pieces of pork tenderloin and some chorizo, gently stirring the mixture and watched as the contents of the pan became red with the oils released from the chorizo.

"Be about half an hour," I called as I opened a tin of cannellini beans and added them to the pan together with a splosh of white wine, stirring for a moment before clamping the lid on. Richard appeared in the doorway.

"Shall we have a drink now?' I looked at him as I poured myself a large glass of Pinot Gris which stood open by the hob.

He opened the fresh bottle of Southern Comfort, his favourite drink which I always made sure was in plentiful supply, and poured himself a large glass.

"Would you lay the table please?" He did so, forgetting to put out the paper napkins as usual. I lit the two festively red candles that I had put on the table.

He grinned at me. "What is it with you women and your bloody candles?"

"They add atmosphere - and romance."

He snorted. "Romance? Hmmm – don't you mean sex?"

"No, I mean romance," I retorted. "Stop being such an old grouch. Just because you're nursing a cold, it's no excuse for being un-Christmassy."

"Ok, ok, I'll be good." He put his arm round my shoulders. I looked up at him and leaned against him. "Come on – food," he urged.

I took our plates out of the oven where they were warming - he hated eating hot food from cold dishes - and served up. While I did so, he put on a CD and Bryan Ferry's voice filled the room. We sat down and started eating. "Mmmm – very nice."

"You're a master of the understatement." I sounded mock-indignant. "It's bloody good – and it's one of your favourites – did you notice?"

He nodded in agreement. "I did. You are a good girl, aren't you?" We continued to eat in comfortable silence, listening to Bryan's soulful ballads.

Once we'd finished, I cleared the table and put the dishes into my very old dishwasher which was, in fact, older than Susie. Every time I put it on I kept my fingers crossed that it would work. I loathe washing up by hand and always teased Richard that if I had to choose between him and a dishwasher, the dishwasher would win hands down.

By this time Richard had gone back into the sitting room and turned on the TV. I sighed again. Not that I minded a good movie but it seemed to me that we had the TV on an awful lot.

"What about Inglorious Basterds?" he asked.

"That's fine." Truth to tell, I really didn't care.

I replenished our empty glasses, picked up a large box of chocolates I'd bought for Christmas and returned with them tucked under my arm. As I gave Richard his glass, he looked at the box and then up at me.

"Should you be eating chocolates? Won't help the diet, will it?"

I felt my face go hot. "It's Christmas - not the best time to diet."

"That's true – but you will start again after Christmas, won't you?"

"Mmmmm," was all I could think of saying.

"Well, open them then."

I looked at him, trying to keep the resentment out of my face. "Don't want to now."

"Oh, stop being childish. Open the bloody chocolates, why don't you." I tore the crackly cellophane and offered him the box. He took one and ate it slowly. I looked at the contents, they were very expensive chocolates that I'd bought several weeks ago and had been looking forward to. Not now though.

"Oh, for Christ's sake, have a fucking chocolate." He sounded really cross. Obediently I took one and put it in my mouth. It was, as I'd expected, absolutely delicious, but all I could taste was guilt, anger and seething resentment.

I'd been a stone or so lighter when we first met, but Richard made it very clear very early that he really liked his women to be on the larger side. When I heard this, I could hardly believe my luck - here was a man who revelled in a woman with curves, lumps, bumps and all. We'd spent many happy times in various restaurants trying out all kinds of dishes so inevitably I gained weight. When Richard noticed, he started to criticise the fact that my jeans and shirts were getting tighter yet in bed he delighted in my body. Such mixed messages I reflected, as my clothes gradually got tighter and tighter and I continued to struggle with diet after diet.

I sat down and stared at the television screen. It was a very good movie and I started to unwind and relax into the drama that was unfolding. We both liked films and I could sense Richard unwinding too. He's just feeling poorly I thought, he wouldn't normally make such a fuss over a silly chocolate. After ten minutes or so I went over to the sofa and nestled against him. The voices of the characters in the movie faded as I relaxed more and more deeply.

"Time for bed, sleepy head," were the next words I heard. I lazily opened my eyes. "It's after eleven. You've been asleep for hours, must have been exhausted."

I yawned. "It was rather an early start this morning."

He gently pushed me away from him and stood up. "You go up and get the bed warm for me. I'll sort things out for you down here." He reached down and pulled me to my feet.

I went upstairs, washed my face, brushed my teeth and then stripped off and crawled into bed. Usually I love the chilliness of a freshly made bed but the cold that evening made me gasp. I wriggled to make my space warm and then moved over to his side of the bed to do the same. Richard hated getting into a cold bed and said that as I didn't have an electric blanket, it was my job to make sure the bed was snug and welcoming.

A few minutes later I heard his familiar footsteps ascending the stairs. I wriggled again, this time in anticipation.

"Over to your side now." I moved over but returned to his side, reaching out to him. He returned my embrace but, unusually, didn't reach for my breasts, which was his normal next move. He coughed. "I'm really not feeling up to par. Would you mind if I slept in the spare room? I don't want to disturb you with my coughing."

"No, of course." I did mind but knew he preferred to sleep alone if he felt even a little unwell. "You get a good night's sleep and you'll feel much better in the morning. All Christmassy and festive. James and Felicity are coming over for lunch so you have to be on good form."

"Yes, of course. I'm sure I'll be much better tomorrow."

He leaned over and kissed me. Not the passionate, I-can't-live-without-you kind of kiss I wanted. More of a friendly, companionable kiss. I kissed him back.

"Night night then." He pulled away from me slightly. "Need my rest. You sleep well. Lots of cooking to do tomorrow."

"Night night." I heard him pad out of the room and close the door behind him.

I stared into the darkness and tried to snuggle down to sleep. It was no good, I was now wide awake. Despite some difficult moments, I had been so pleased to see him and after the hours of lounging against him, wanted more of him. My hand crept down from my throat, round my breasts, down my stomach and between my thighs. I relaxed as I started to rub myself slowly and rhythmically and as my hips moved in time to my hand; I squeezed my eyes tight shut and let my imagination fly. After a few minutes I could feel myself get hot and the familiar deep throbbing pulse that started in the pit of my stomach gathered momentum as I climbed towards orgasm. My hand moved faster and faster as I moaned and writhed involuntarily. A few minutes later I relaxed as the pulse subsided and my breathing started to return to normal. I left my hand cupped between my legs and fell into a deep, dreamless sleep.

.

Christmas Day...

My mobile vibrated and I heard the familiar sound of ducks quacking. I reached out, felt around for it and brought it to my eyes. I had been in a deep sleep when I'd been roused and was still buried under a mound of tangled duvet and pillows. I blinked and pressed the messages button.

'Happy Christmas honey. Di x'. I smiled. I'd known Diana for over ten years. We'd first met when we worked together at a local university where I was teaching part-time and she'd been brought in to deliver a couple of marketing seminars. She spent most of her working week in London where she worked for a very large company, so we got together much less than we used to. She was blonde, petite, pretty, dynamic and very good company. We'd hit it off from the word go and continued to do so. 'And to you – have a great day en famille. L x'. It was quarter to eight - far too early to think about getting up just yet. I snuggled down again and closed my eyes, still clutching my mobile.

It seemed like two minutes later when I heard ducks again. "Oh no, not again," I muttered as I reached out to find my mobile. 'Have a great day. Back in a few days. See you then. PS xx'. Bless them I thought. Pennie and Simon were, to me, the embodiment of romance. They'd met and married within two years of meeting. That was about three years ago and every time I saw them they seemed more and more devoted and in tune with each other. Nothing so strange about that but he was in his 60s and she in her 50s – so love could strike at whatever age I'd told myself, and Richard, whenever he was prepared to listen. 'Happy Xmas you guys, see you for drinkies on your return. L x'.

I yawned, stretched and suddenly realised it was twenty past ten. James and Felicity were due to arrive at about twelve thirty and absolutely nothing had been done. I leapt out of bed and pulled on my dressing gown.

I stumbled downstairs and looked into the sitting room which was empty and smelled of last night's fire. Need to sort that I thought to myself as I went through to the kitchen. That too was cold and empty, as was the dining room. I put the kettle on and realised that there was no sign of Richard. I made myself a cup of tea and fed the cats. I looked again at the time and scowled. It was now nearly a quarter to eleven - two hours to get a whole Christmas lunch prepped and cooked. I picked up the phone and dialled.

"Hello," a pleasant male voice said.

"Happy Christmas James. Listen darling, I'm running a wee bit late. Lunch two thirty to three be ok for you?"

There was a pause and then I heard Felicity's laughing voice. "'Now why on earth are we having a late lunch? Got distracted this morning - or was it a very late night?"

I shrugged, if only she knew. "No, no. I overslept and would really rather have everything sorted for when you get here."

"Of course you did darling," Felicity chuckled. "We could probably do with a bit of a walk to work up an appetite for your excellent food. So, if we get to you for about two thirty then?"

"That's perfect. See you later. Enjoy your walk."

Oven on now I said to myself and turned it up high. I'd put the vegetables in the garden shed so I shivered my way out to get them. I washed the turkey, laid bacon strips over the breast with my usual pink salt and some black pepper and slammed it into the hot oven. Half an hour on high and then turn it down I muttered to myself, and I've got to stop talking to myself, I'm turning into some mad old woman who talks to herself in supermarkets. "So why don't you shut the fuck up," I said out loud.

"Pardon?" I heard a male voice say.

I spun round to see Richard standing inside the back door, all wet and muddy.

"Where have you been? And, what's more to the point, where was my early morning cup of tea?"

He smiled at me. "Went for a run," he explained briefly. "I woke up early and you were sound asleep so I thought I'd get some exercise. We're not going to be doing much today and you know me, I like to stretch my legs every day."

I smiled back more warmly than I felt.

"Well, it wouldn't hurt you to do this occasionally, you know." He sat down at the dining table and looked expectantly at me. "Breakfast?"

I looked at him. Was he kidding? A whole Christmas lunch to get ready and he wanted breakfast?

"I could do you scrambled eggs and smoked salmon."

"No thanks, I think I'd prefer some porridge. We'll be eating a rich meal later, won't we?" He paused for a moment. "Anyway, happy Christmas."

"And to you darling." I kissed him. He kissed me back and briefly stroked my face. I tingled at this tenderness.

"Better get on though. Won't they be here soon? Sorry, I didn't mean to be out for so long but I was so enjoying my run it seemed a pity to stop."

"Of course. I'm glad you're feeling better. By the way, I called James and Felicity and they won't be here til about two thirty so we don't have to rush that much."

"Why's that?"

"Well, I've only just got up and lunch will take quite some time to get sorted, so I called them to ask them to come later."

"Really?' They were ok with that?"

"Of course," I smiled. "They understand the intricacies of Christmas catering."

He raised his eyebrows. "It's just cooking. Hardly bloody rocket science." I turned my back. This was an argument I knew I could never win.

I opened the overflowing carrier bag and started to take out the vegetables. "Shall we breakfast first?" he persisted.

I sighed. "Ok, I'll do it now."

"Do you want me to do it?" He sounded very slightly irritated.

"No, no, I'll do it. I wonder if you'd sort the fire for me please?" He looked more cheerful, he liked doing what he called blokey-stuff as opposed to the day-to-day girlie-stuff that I always asserted was the day-to-day fabric of life.

He went through to the sitting room and I heard the clatter of fire irons. "Could I have a bag for the ashes please?" His voice floated through.

I put down the potato I'd been peeling and the paring knife, opened a drawer, pulled out a couple of old carrier bags and took them through to the sitting room where he was kneeling in front of the cold fireplace. He took them from me and turned back to the fire.

"Off you go then. I know there's lots to be done in the kitchen."

I stared at his back and for a split second I wanted to tell him to take his trainers and his sweaty clothes and fuck right off. I shivered as I thought of how life might be without him. Despite our differences I so wanted this relationship to work and, for much of the time, it did.

I turned away and returned to the kitchen where I finished off the potatoes and parsnips. Parsnips are one of my favourite vegetables and I was looking forward to tasting their creamy sweetness. I'd started on the carrots as Richard came through carrying the bags full of fire debris. He put them in the waste bin and teasingly came towards me, holding out his sooty hands. I dodged away and came up behind him, hugging his back. He chuckled. "Breakfast ready yet?"

I dropped my arms and sighed. "Sure - be less than five minutes." He washed his hands and sat again at the table so, abandoning the vegetables, I started on his porridge. "Bucks Fizz?"

"Perhaps not. We'll be drinking quite a lot with James and Felicity, won't we? I think I'll just have some orange juice."

"Yep, you're probably quite right." I was thinking that I was more than up for a drink.

I'd almost finished prepping the vegetables. "When shall we do pressies?"

"I need a shower - perhaps after you've finished off here and we're both ready?"

"Hmmm – ok." I love giving and receiving presents and it seemed a shame to wait.

I turned down the oven, made sure that all the vegetables were in their bowls, cleared the dining room, washed up and then started to lay out the table to make it Christmassy. Out came the gold chargers and coasters and the large white serving dishes. I love the paraphernalia around cooking and entertaining and it gave me great pleasure to lay a good table. Pity he's not here to share this I thought as I folded the red napkins. But he really doesn't like doing this sort of thing I thought as I counted out the cutlery and serving spoons. And he does all kinds of other helpful, practical stuff which is wonderful I thought as I opened the box of red and gold crackers I'd bought back in October. I stood back and surveyed the table with a self-satisfied smile. It looked festive and welcoming - just the effect I wanted.

Back in the kitchen I double checked that everything was ready and in their right dishes and pans - almost forgot the bacon and chestnuts to accompany the sprouts. I snipped the bacon into strips ready for frying and opened the pack of chestnuts. I looked round again. The kitchen was beginning to smell of Christmas. I made sure that the orange juice, champagne and white wine was in the fridge and opened a fresh bottle of Merlot to breathe. I was never sure why it was necessary to let red wine 'breathe' but always did so – just in case it really made a difference.

Upstairs I found Richard stretched out in the bath. "Thought you were having a shower."

"I thought that a bath would help my muscles relax more. Don't want to stiffen up."

I smiled down at him and sat on the edge of the bath "Well, stiffening up mightn't be so bad."

"I'm nice and clean now. Don't want to get dirty again, do I?"

I stood up and turned away.

"Won't be long - just a few more minutes and then the bathroom's all yours."

I nodded, went into the bedroom and sat on the edge of the bed. It wasn't that I particularly wanted to make love, well, it might have been nice, but it would have been much nicer to have had a different response to my small overture. Stop being a doormat, the little voice in my head told me. How can you expect him to know what's in your mind if you don't say what you're thinking and feeling? I sighed.

Now, what to wear, I thought as I riffled through my wardrobe. Richard was, of course, quite right about my weight. I'd been steadily gaining a few pounds a month over the past six months so there were fewer and fewer clothes that were comfortable. I settled on a pair of black trousers, a black skinny top and a pretty chiffony shirt I'd bought years ago in Mallorca when holidaying with Susie that covered all my lumps and bumps. Richard came through wrapped in a towel. I looked at his hard, lean body appreciatively. For a man in his sixties there was no doubt, he was in amazing shape. He stood in front of the mirror and flexed his muscles. "You lucky, lucky girl." He smiled at me. I realised it was meant as a tease, but deep down he really meant it. I was the lucky one in this relationship, not him. I threw a pillow at him.

"Less of the narcissism – get dressed." He grinned at me and disappeared into the spare room.

Minutes later he suddenly reappeared. "Hey, it's after twelve - shouldn't you be getting ready now?"

"Oh God, yes. Shan't be long. Are you ready?"

"Almost. I'd like to make a quick call to a couple of people to say Happy Christmas, then I'm all yours. Hurry up otherwise we won't have time to relax before they arrive." He disappeared.

I stood under the shower, luxuriating in the hot water as it cascaded over my body, loving the sharpness of the water as it hit me. I washed my hair and then leaned against the coldness of the white tiles while the steaming hot water streamed down my back. I could have stayed like that for ages and as I stretched my arms up to embrace the unending torrent of hot water, Richard looked in.

"Nearly one o'clock." I sighed and reluctantly turned off the shower.

"Here you go." I stepped out and a large towel was firmly wrapped around me. I leaned towards him slightly, tilted my face upwards and planted a soft kiss on his cheek. He smiled down at me. "Go and make yourself beautiful." He gently pushed me towards the bedroom, patting my bottom as I passed him.

I sat on the bed, moisturised and put my makeup on, dried my hair, dressed and then stood to look at myself in the full length mirror. Not bad I said to myself. You could stand to lose a bit, well a quite a lot, but you're looking pretty good nonetheless. I smiled and blew myself a kiss.

As I entered the sitting room, I could see the fire had been lit and the logs and coal were beginning to crackle. The cats suspiciously stayed on their respective chairs. Richard was sprawled on the sofa with some brightly wrapped parcels at his feet. "Oooo – goodies – how lovely." I clapped my hands.

"Now, don't get excited. I really haven't had much time to buy presents. Remember, I said that we were to have a slightly more frugal Christmas."

My excitement evaporated. "Yes, I know." I reached into the bag that I'd left by the Christmas tree and pulled out the presents I'd bought for him.

"One at a time each." He handed me a small box. I giggled and tore the paper. Inside was my favourite perfume, Eternity. It was a 35ml bottle - the smallest available.

"Lovely, thank you." I swallowed my astonishment. Normally he was a very generous present giver so it came as a real jolt not to be given a larger bottle. I leaned across to kiss him.

He took one of my gifts and opened it, a bottle of his favourite whisky. He looked at me. "Thank you, you really shouldn't have." He dropped a kiss on the top of my head.

We continued to exchange gifts and after a few minutes I sat back and considered what had just happened. I had spent much time and thought, not to mention money, in selecting his favourite whisky, a travel book that I knew he would like, a blue and white spotted silk handkerchief, an invitation to the theatre with pre-theatre dinner and an overly sentimental card. Along with the perfume, I'd just received some obscure-sounding herbal teabags, two bottles of glucosamine (for my achy knees) and a funny card. For the first time, I absolutely knew that I hadn't been uppermost in his mind - or his heart - when he'd selected my gifts and that knowledge made me furious and disappointed in equal measure.

I stood up. "Need to check things in the kitchen." I turned away so he couldn't see the hot, angry tears that were threatening to spill down my cheeks. I opened the oven to check the turkey.

He stood, leaning against the kitchen door, his arms folded. "You ok?"

"I'm fine."

"You don't look it."

"I'm cooking and it's very hot." I pushed my hair out of my eyes.

"Can I help at all?" He sounded quite concerned. Hmmm - guilty, not concerned - I thought.

"You look after the fire – oh, and perhaps you could put out some nibbles."

"Will do." He sounded relieved that I'd given him something to do. He opened the larder and took out crisps, nuts and the jar of olives. "Anything else?"

I glanced over. "No, I think that's about it. The smoked salmon on blinis are in the fridge - they can go through as well." I was still seething but because James and Felicity were due to arrive at any moment, tried to sound cordial – I knew it wasn't working though. Silently he filled the bowls and took them through to the sitting room. I heard sounds of coal being shovelled onto the fire.

What I really wanted to do was to scream and shout, throw the fucking turkey at his fucking head and then for him to tell me again and again that he loved me while taking me to bed and making the kind of love we'd made when we first met: hot, torrid, passionate, all-consuming. What I did was fry the bacon until it was crispy and put it to one side, roughly chop the chestnuts and parboil the potatoes and parsnips. I'd just drained the roots, making sure that I kept the water for the gravy, and put them in to roast when I heard the doorbell.

"Happy Christmas." I heard from two jolly voices. Felicity came into the kitchen.

"Happy Christmas my dear." I was engulfed in a warm, caring hug that tipped me into tears. I held onto her tightly. She drew back and looked at me with concern.

"What on earth ..."

"Don't. I'm ok." I went to the sink and splashed cold water over my face. I looked at her again. "Honestly."

James came into the kitchen and put his arm round my shoulders. "Happy Christmas James." I returned his embrace. "Now, what can we get you?" I turned to Richard who'd followed them into the kitchen. "Bucks Fizz, don't you think?" He nodded, poured four glasses and we then stood to toast each other. I'd known James and Felicity for many more years than any of us cared to remember and sharing so much history made our friendship very special.

The atmosphere lightened as we sat in front of the fire and talked. Unbidden, Richard refilled glasses which was unusual as he normally didn't notice when people needed another drink. After another half hour I rose to my feet. "Time to check lunch."

"I'll come and help." Felicity followed me. Now, what's happened?' Truth now."

I shook my head. "Not now. I have no intention of spoiling Christmas. It's ok – kind of. I'll tell you another time."

She nodded. "Whenever you want I'm here, you know that." I gave her another hug.

We took the turkey out of the oven to rest and turned up the heat to make sure the potatoes and parsnips darkened and became slightly crunchy. I put the carrots onto a gentle heat to braise and started to warm a pan for the parboiled sprouts which were to be fried with the bacon and chestnuts. "Oh no, I've forgotten those bloody pigs in their sodding blankets." We laughed as I hurriedly slid them into the oven.

"They'll be fine," Felicity said consolingly.

"They'd better be - I was up at silly o'clock yesterday to get them so we're going to eat them, no matter what."

She grinned at me as she decanted the pre-made bread sauce into a saucepan to heat. "Cranberry sauce?"

I stood still. "Oh fuck." Felicity wasn't keen on my swearing which, she said was getting worse. "Never mind, I'm sure I've got some redcurrant jelly somewhere." Thankfully there was a half jar lurking in the fridge so that went into another pretty dish and put on the table.

As always, there was a flurry to get all the food onto the table so that everything was hot. "Lunch. Come on you two," I called as I lit the red candles at each end of the table.

"Wow," James exclaimed appreciatively, "it all looks wonderful. Well done Lucie."

"Thank you so much." I smiled at him.

"Yes, very nice. You can always depend on Lucie to do well in the kitchen." Richard said. I shot him a glance but he smiled neutrally at me. "Shall I do the honours?" I passed him the carving knife and fork and he deftly filled the waiting plates.

We sat and ate what had turned out to be a very good Christmas lunch. Crackers followed with the usual bad jokes and silly paper hats. "Time for pud." Felicity helped me clear the debris and after filling my ancient dishwasher, I patted it affectionately as I pressed the 'on' button. Felicity laughed.

I'd made the Christmas pudding with Anita, a dear friend I'd first met when we were both pregnant with our respective daughters many years ago, the previous summer. It had become our tradition to share this task in August or September, usually on a Sunday afternoon which we always thoroughly enjoyed. We always made enough for three or four puddings, feeling very virtuous and housewifely as we did so, toasting to Christmas success with chilled wine in the summer sunshine. This year's pudding had been steaming for over two hours and I held my breath as I turned it out, but I needn't have worried, it plopped out of its basin perfectly. I poured brandy over the hot pudding and quickly held a match to it - blue flames flared as I carried it through to the dining room which was dark save for flickering candlelight. Approving applause met me, giving me a warm rush and I placed the dish squarely in the middle of the table. As the flames died down, I brought brandy butter through and served up. "Mmmm, up to your usual high standard," James murmured through a mouthful. I glowed and knew I could now relax after the rigours of Christmas catering.

We sat at the table with coffees and the expensive chocolates I had bought for another hour. Halfway through Richard rose. "Just checking the fire." He returned several minutes later.

"You've been a long time," Felicity teased him.

"Well, tricky stuff, looking after fires. You girlies just don't understand." I looked at him and wondered whether he had really been just checking the fire or perhaps had made a call, or possibly text. I mentally shrugged. There was no point in spoiling Christmas - he was here, wasn't he?

It was much, much later when James and Felicity eventually left. We'd moved into the sitting room and toasted our feet in front of the fire and talked more about inconsequential things. I felt cosy and relaxed, memories of earlier upsets faded.

As they left Richard put his arms round me. "Thank you," he said quietly.

I looked up at him. "For what'?"

"For a really lovely Christmas - you do look after me so well, don't you?"

I returned his embrace. "I do it because I care."

"I know." Surprisingly he sounded rather sad. "Oh, just a second." He disappeared and returned in moments with a white envelope. "For you." I reached out and opened it excitedly, the memory of his disappointing gifts gone. Inside were five crisp £20 notes. I stared at him. "Just a little contribution towards Christmas. I meant to give this to you sooner but forgot." I pushed the notes into the envelope and tucked back the flap. So, this wasn't an amazing, well-thought-out present, just some money. I swallowed hard, not knowing what to say.

"Thank you," was all I managed.

"Well now, a nice cup of tea would be good, wouldn't it?" Returning to the kitchen I sighed deeply. I knew that he would never understand that giving me the money in that way and at that time had so deeply affronted me. I splashed cold water over my face and regained my composure.

I took the tea down and settled myself next to him and as I did so he curled his arm round me. After a while, I heard his breathing deepen as he dozed. He could sleep on a clothes line I thought to myself, and moved my head slightly to glance up at his relaxed features. As his sleep deepened, the arm around me became heavier and his firm embrace lessened. Against my better judgement, I pressed myself into his body, ignoring the fact that debris littered the kitchen and dining room. I could always sort it out later or even tomorrow. I hated coming down to a dirty kitchen in the morning but the peace we were sharing right now seemed far too precious to disturb. I closed my eyes.

A shrill ringtone woke me and at the same time I felt Richard sit up and fumble into his trouser pocket. "Just a text," he said.

"Who from?" I asked as he looked at his black iPhone. He didn't answer.

I leaned away from him. "Julie?"

He nodded, his eyes fixed on the screen - not at me.

"Well, read it then." My heart was pumping so loudly I felt sure he could hear it.

He turned towards me as he put the phone back into his pocket. "No. Not now." He pulled me towards him. For a moment I considered resisting but as I sat staring at him he kissed me - a lingering, passionate kiss. The kind of kiss we'd exchanged in the early days. He actually had a mild aversion to kissing and often joked that snogging was mainly for teenagers - I absolutely disagreed with him.

My breathing started to quicken as he pressed me into his body more firmly. One hand reached for my breast, which he gently caressed and as my nipple hardened he laughed softly. "Mmmm, time for bed?" he whispered.

"Why not here?"

"You know I'd rather be in comfort, don't you?" In the past I'd occasionally suggested making love in different locations both indoors and outside, but every time his answer had been that he really would prefer the comfort of bed, which usually meant that our love-making was confined to night-times.

He disentangled himself from me, stood up and pulled me to my feet. Still holding my hands he took a step towards to the door. "Shall we?"

I smiled up at him and as I passed him stood on tiptoe to kiss his cheek.

"I'll follow you," he murmured. "Won't be a minute."

As I walked upstairs I thought I heard a click, the kind of sound a mobile makes when the message box is opened. I paused on the stairs and listened. Nothing. Don't be silly, I thought to myself, he's just putting the guard in front of the fire. I quickly stripped off, leaving my underwear on, he preferred a partly clothed body to complete nakedness, and slid into bed, wriggling slightly to make the bed warm.

Moments later Richard appeared. "Now, where were we ..." His hands reached out for me and we locked in a tight embrace. We'd been together for nearly five years and knew each other's bodies very well. Perhaps too well, I sometimes thought, as more and more I recognised a certain predictability in our sex life, but whenever I had suggested any variations, they'd been met with a gentle yet firm rebuff.

As we kissed, nibbled and stroked each other we gazed into each other's eyes. As I stared at him I could see his passion rising as he could mine. I couldn't sustain it, I closed my eyes and threw back my head as he entered me, gasping and moaning at the piercing sweetness as he fucked me rhythmically. I clung to him, my cries getting louder as we moved inexorably towards orgasm. Suddenly, with a soft groan he came and collapsed onto me.

I opened my eyes. Oh shit, shit, shit I thought as he rolled off.

"You carry on without me." His eyes were closed.

I stared at his profile for a few moments and then turned onto my side.

Richard breathed deeply and moved. "You ok?"

"Yes, I'm fine." I wriggled a little to get more comfortable.

"Fidget," he sighed. I settled onto my side and closed my eyes. I heard Richard's breathing deepen and he started to snore, light little snores rather like a small animal which I actually found very endearing.

I lay still with my eyes closed but sleep eluded me. The more I tried to be sleepy and peaceful the more I thought of the money, the text and the disgusting mess waiting for me in the kitchen. It was no good. Very slowly I inched my way to the side of the bed and slid out. I tiptoed to the door, picking up a clean pair of knickers and a sweatshirt on the way, listening to Richard's continuing soft snores.

The kitchen was just as bad as I'd remembered so I set to work quickly. I emptied then refilled the dishwasher and as it purred, poured hot, soapy water into each pan. My mother had always said that a few hours soaking saved much scouring and I'd taken her advice seriously for many years. After half an hour I stood back and surveyed the scene. The dining table was bare save the red candles waiting to be relit at some time and apart from the pots waiting to be scrubbed out, the kitchen was pretty civilised.

I heard footsteps and Richard appeared. "What on earth are you doing?"

I turned and smiled. "Look - all done and dusted."

"Very good - are you coming back to bed?"

"I honestly don't feel that tired at the moment. You go back, but I think I'm going to stay up for a little while."

He blew me a kiss as he turned on his heel and I listened as he returned upstairs.

I went through to the sitting room and stirred the embers of the fire. There's enough heat left for another half hour I thought as I turned the TV on, threw a couple of cushions on the floor and settled down. I stared at the screen and started to flick through the channels in an effort to find something to hold my attention. Suddenly, I heard the familiar sound of Richard's mobile ringing, it stopped and I heard his voice, clearly in conversation with someone. I froze and quickly pressed the mute button, trying to hear what was being said but all I could catch were murmurs. I got to my feet and quietly inched the door open but as I stood in the hall, his voice stopped. Dammit to hell I thought. Who the fuck was calling him after midnight on Christmas night? Of course, deep down I knew the answer but as I slumped wearily against the wall, my eyes prickling with yet unshed tears, I also knew that I wasn't going to make a fuss. Not tonight.

I padded back into the sitting room, sat down on the pile of cushions and turned the volume up on the TV to hide the sound of my uncontrollable weeping. It was an hour later when I was all cried out that I stole back upstairs and crept into bed. Richard was fast asleep and the sound of his heavy breathing helped me finally to sleep.

Boxing Day...

I was hot, sweaty and panicky. Scorching sun was beating down on me but I couldn't move because I was ensnared in brambles which became tighter and tighter as I struggled frantically to free myself. With a start, I awoke to find myself entangled in the duvet with one pillow resting askew on my head. I pushed everything away from me and looked down. No wonder I was hot, I was still wearing the sweatshirt I'd put on last night to go and clear up Christmas. I stumbled to my feet and went into the bathroom to have a pee and try to wake up.

Returning to the bedroom, I realised that Richard wasn't there; his side of the bed was tidy and cold. I looked out of the bedroom window to see his car on the drive and felt a surge of relief and then annoyance with myself. Of course he was still here, why wouldn't he be? As I turned away the memory of last night hit me - the text he'd ignored and then read when I was out of the room, the late night conversation, my feelings of fury and despair, my tears ...

I quickly dressed in grey leggings, a black sweater and flung a red scarf round my neck, put on bright red lipstick and looked at my reflection – not bad I thought. I could hear the television on as I stood on the landing and shook my head. Surely I'd turned it off before coming to bed?

I walked downstairs slowly and opened the sitting room door. Richard was sitting on the sofa with a mug of tea in his hand watching the news. He looked up at me and smiled briefly.

"Want a refill?" I asked. For some reason his stillness was unnerving.

"Please." I took the empty mug from him and as I waited for the kettle to boil and sub-consciously braced myself for whatever was to come. "Breakfast?" I called.

"No. No thanks, not now." I made the tea and returned to the sitting room, handing him his tea, and then sat down.

He looked at me. "Well."

"Well what?"

"Well, I think we have to talk." I sat motionless and listened as he spoke, the mug of tea getting cold in my cupped hands. "Well, you know I'm troubled about a few things about us and our possible future. I'm concerned that you're just not losing weight, probably putting it on in fact, and that you're not as fit as you were. It seems to me that you're just not bothered about how I feel about this. I really don't like the fact that you stay as fat and unfit as you are rather than try to do something about it. I mean," he continued as I sat with my mouth open, "I try not to nag you but I do feel I have to keep reminding you about this. And that's not the only thing of course. You never seem to know when the next bit of work is coming, you have to take in lodgers in the summer - it's all a bit ad hoc isn't it?" He paused and looked at me. I went hot and cold and took a deep breath but before I could say anything he resumed. "And you told me last week that you were still paying a mortgage? Well, at your age that's ridiculous, it's just not good enough ..."

I stood up, shaking with fury and fear. "Just where the hell's all this come from?" I tried to keep my voice steady. "You dare to come up here - eat, drink, go to bed with me and then talk to bloody Julie." I stopped, appalled yet proud of myself. I'd swallowed down so many insecurities and suspicions over the past few months that now I'd started I was terrified I wouldn't be able to stop.

Julie and her husband, Patrick, had known Richard for many years and about eighteen months ago poor Patrick had unexpectedly dropped down dead with a heart attack. Very naturally, Julie had been shocked and traumatised by this and, naturally, Richard had offered his support. However, this support had transformed itself into seeing her pretty much every week which made me uneasy and anxious. I had raised this twice before but each time Richard had snapped angrily at me, saying that they were just good friends and that I was being irrational, silly and downright selfish to have any doubts about his trustworthiness, which had only served to fuel my misgivings even more.

"It wouldn't be so bad if I'd met her but she doesn't want to see me so you do what she wants and never what I want ..." I wished that my voice was steadier. Tears were threatening to erupt and I was desperate to remain calm. "And, well, it's just not reasonable or fair. How would you feel if I behaved like this, saw someone else and always excluded you from what was happening?" It was no good, the tears came and I stood crying helplessly.

'"Oh for God's sake." He sounded disgusted. "More tears. How convenient. Typical bloody women's games."

I stared incredulously at him through the mist of tears and wiped my nose on the back on my hand. Was this the man who, in the beginning, had been so caring and tender towards me? Was this the man who had seemed concerned and compassionate? Was this the man who'd been helpful and understanding when things went wrong for me? And was this the man who'd said that leopards could change their spots and promised that his philandering days were over? As I struggled to make sense of what was happening, I was becoming dimly aware of my new reality and the pain went through me like a knife.

He stood up. "I can't cope with this - and I don't want to cope with this. This is doing my head in. I'm going to go." He pushed past me and walked upstairs. I followed him into the spare room to find him packing. He looked up. "We both need time and space to think. I don't want to hurt you. I do care for you ..."

At this I stepped forward. He raised his hand to ward me away. "No, no. I need to get away. Go home. Be by myself and think about what I really want."

I stood aside and he walked past me, holding his bags and I watched as he opened the front door. He looked up at me. "You need to think too." His voice was softer and gentler.

I looked down at him and my tears flowed again. "I do love you."

"I know." And then the door closed behind him.

I slid down the wall, ending up sitting on the landing and cried so hard I really thought my heart was broken, and that nothing could ever mend it.

After, I didn't know how long, I rose stiffly to my feet. I felt exhausted, all cried out, and slowly made my way downstairs. I looked into the sitting room and stared at the Christmas tree I'd so painstakingly decorated and the cards pinned up neatly on their tinselly gold streamers. Very calmly I walked over and ripped down the streamers, watching as they tore into spikey shreds. I sat on the floor and slowly unpinned the cards, piling them up neatly. The torn tinsel went into the waste bin and I looked up at the tree. Again, very slowly, I took down all the silver and gold tree ornaments, fetched the bags I normally kept them in and put them away. The naked tree looked forlorn and sad. Just the way I feel I thought as tears threatened to spill again. Fuck that, I thought, how dare he, how fucking bloody dare he treat me like that. I pulled the tree through the front door, ignoring the sharpness of the needles pricking my hands and dumped it by the bins. There, I thought, that's the end of Christmas.

I went back into the sitting room and shivered. I suddenly felt cold and, I realised, very thirsty so made a scalding hot coffee and sat on the sofa. As I drank, tears ran down my cheeks, I could taste salt through the bitterness of the coffee. I was still cold so piled kindling on top of a firelighter, lit it and went to get some logs which I heaped on the spitting flames. I crouched in front of the fire as the flames licked upwards. It's bloody, bloody Boxing Day I thought; I can't put this shit onto anyone else - not today. I shivered again and lay on the floor as close to the fire as I could and stared into the flames.

A little while later, I don't know how much later, I realised that I was hungry, starving in fact. Opening the fridge door, I gazed at the leftover turkey and vegetables. Far too healthy I said to myself and reached in for the remains of the Christmas pudding which I quickly microwaved, then piled vanilla ice cream on top. I picked up a spoon and returned to the sitting room. I really didn't taste what I was eating but nonetheless ate most of the contents of the huge bowl while I mindlessly watched happy programmes showing happy people and, as I did so, I felt icily alone.

I heard ducks quacking and looked up. No doubt that was him texting to say he was sorry. Sorry? Would sorry ever atone for the pain today had given me? Probably not, but I knew I was prepared to do almost anything to make things work. 'I'm sad that we might be over. Sat at home now getting slightly drunk. Its far too complicated to work things out now. I'm worn out. Rx'. I stared at the words and they started to blur as yet more tears flowed. I had no idea how to respond but after a few moments of contemplation texted back. 'It would be so much better if we were able to work things out together than apart. Let's talk very soon. I love you. Lxx' and as I pressed the send button, I wondered whether those last three little words were wise. Sod it, I thought, they've gone now.

It must have been about four o'clock when I felt able to move and all I did was go into the kitchen again to make a pile of cold turkey sandwiches topped with cold bread sauce with a sprinkling of salt and took them through with a very large glass of red. I threw more logs on the fire and settled down again and as I ate and drank I felt calmer. I lay on the sofa and fell into a deep sleep.

27th December...

I woke up in the weak winter light of the morning and it took me a few minutes to remember the events of Boxing Day. I felt like crying again so before the tears started, I made myself step under the shower which I ran as hot as possible. I started to feel a little better when I washed my hair and as the hot water cascaded over me it seemed to wash away some of my tensions. I wrapped a large towel around myself and padded into the bedroom.

I looked at my watch. It was just after nine which meant that I could make a call without being too anti-social. I picked up my phone and while I was debating whether to call Richard or not, it rang. I jumped and pressed the answer button. "Hello sweetie."

"Di? How great to hear from you. I was about to call you." In my haste the words fell over each other.

"Hey, are you alright?"

"Yes. Well, no. Not really." I started to cry yet again.

"Right. Are you up? Are you dressed? That doesn't matter anyway. Get yourself over here right now."

"But," I said weakly, "aren't you busy?"

"No, I'm not. And even if I was this is much more important. I'll make us lunch. Be here in an hour?"

I felt a huge sense of relief - relief that someone understood without my having to say anything and relief that someone was going to look after me, if only for a few hours. "That's just lovely, thank you so much. I'll get dressed, put a bit of slap on and then be with you."

Di lived about thirty five miles away from me but as the roads were clear, it took me less than half an hour to get there. As I raised my hand to ring the bell, the door opened and I was engulfed in a warm hug. "You silly thing," she said affectionately. "Stop crying, you'll ruin your makeup."

We went through to her immaculate sitting room which was tastefully decorated in shades of cream and gold. "Nice. Very nice." I surveyed the Christmas baubles in two matching glass vases on each side of the fire and the twinkling lights on the slender Christmas tree. Di had a great talent for understated elegance which I'd often tried to emulate and, to my irritation, never succeeded.

"Tea or coffee?" she asked, looking into my face. "No, no. Something stronger is called for I think." She disappeared into the kitchen and returned with two large glasses of champagne.

"What are we celebrating?" I didn't think I had anything to celebrate.

"To life my dear, to life, whatever it may bring and to never ever letting the bastards grind us down."

I raised my glass. "Absolutely Here's to life and ..." My voice cracked and unbidden tears came.

Di looked aghast. "Oh, I'm so sorry. I didn't mean to upset you, not any more than you already are."

I managed a small smile. "Don't be silly. It's not you, it's me. Me and the mess that's my life." We sat down clutching our champagne and both took very large swigs. As she put her glass down I continued and then held my empty glass towards her. "More please."

"Bloody hell - you must have really needed that."

I settled more comfortably on the sofa, took my boots off and started talking. She sat in silence as I told her about the getting up early on Christmas Eve, the overly expensive shopping trip, the coffee, the Christmas Eve text, the trying to make Christmas perfect, the chocolates, the Christmas morning jog, the not having Bucks Fizz, the porridge, the calls, the texts, the thoughtless presents, the envelope with money in it, the so-so sex, him talking to Julie, the out-of-the-blue Boxing Day argument - it all spilled out amidst hot tears and sobs. After an hour we sat in silence.

Di took a deep breath. "Well, I could tell you that things will blow over, that everything will be fine, that you'll live happily ever after." I looked at her warily. "But that's not true, is it? I mean, it really, really won't." I looked away and blinked. She might have been right but it absolutely wasn't what I wanted to hear.

"Just how much longer are you going to be a doormat?" Her voice rose. "Because that's exactly what you are, and you know it. And behaving like this isn't really you at all." She got to her feet. "Time for coffee I think, and then we're going to get this mess sorted out once and for all."

I followed her into the kitchen and looked out at her beautifully ordered garden. The sun was trying to shine through and the early morning clouds had dissipated leaving a pale blue sky.

"Can we go for a stroll please?" I asked.

"Yes, of course. Coffee can wait."

We donned our boots, coats and scarves and left her house. She lived close to a large playground and we walked across the road and up a small hill to reach it. We kept in step as we skirted round some children playing with their bright, shiny, new bikes.

"Want to know what I think?" she asked quietly as we strolled past another happy family.

I took a deep breath. "Yes – no – yes, of course I do."

"I'm going to say it the way I think it is. I think we're way past pussy-footing around. I get very angry when I see you getting upset so often. It breaks my heart to see you in tears like this." I opened my mouth but she ignored me.

"For a start, you need to stop being such a bloody wimp."

"No, I'm not," I said hotly, and then paused. "Yes, I am, aren't I?"

She nodded. "'Fraid so - now you listen to me. The truth of the matter is - it's over. I've seen you hurt far too many times to believe anything else. It seems to me that your spells of happiness get shorter and shorter and the periods of pain and disappointment get longer and longer. I know that he can be incredibly kind and generous and certainly has been in the past, but over the last few months there's been less and less of that and more and more disapproval and unkindness. Seems to me he criticises you much, much more than he compliments you and that's just not right. And that's often about stuff you have little control over, you know, work and stuff like that. Anyway," she continued as I listened silently, "so what if you're overweight? It's your body and maybe if you felt a bit more cherished and appreciated, you wouldn't eat as much."

I swallowed - this was so hard to listen to. I took a deep breath. "Now look Di ..."

"No, you look," she sounded quite cross. 'You've asked me and I'm going to tell you." I fell silent. "The worst thing is this Julie woman. It's just not bloody fair and well you know it — she does too, come to think of it. You say that you're uncomfortable about the amount of time he spends with her and he just says that you're being silly. You're being silly?" Her voice rose indignantly. "Bollocks!" She stopped and faced me. "You do know he's probably sleeping with her, don't you?" Her voice was very gentle and she hugged me as I started to cry again.

"You really think he's having an affair?" I could barely say the words.

She nodded. "Of course he is. That's why he's behaving like this. He knows he's doing wrong and the best way to deal with that is to make you wrong," she sounded thoughtful, "and then, when you're in the wrong, it justifies him doing this shitty stuff."

It felt like someone was repeatedly hitting me in the solar plexus, I doubled over in pain and gasped for breath. It wasn't that Di was saying anything I hadn't already thought, but hearing the words out loud made me feel as if I'd been kicked by a mule.

I continued to weep. Did I really love him and that was why I couldn't bear the thought of losing him? Or was it fear? Fear that at my age he was as good as I was ever going to get. Fear that no-one else would want me because I was fat and didn't have that much money. Fear that I would be on my own for the rest of my life.

Di rubbed my back and let me cry but after a few minutes she stopped rubbing and patted me. "Ok, enough. I'm so sorry but I had to say this. But you know all this anyway. You know you do." I looked at her, tears still streaming down my face.

"God, you look dreadful," she said with a smile.

I summoned up a returning smile. "I know."

She nodded. "Shall we go home?"

"Yes please." We fell in step again and strode back, this time in silence.

Di opened her door and as I sat on the bottom stair to take off my boots I heard my familiar ducks quacking. She frowned. "Leave it, please leave it." But it was too late as I'd eagerly taken my mobile from my pocket. 'I'm so sorry I keep upsetting you, don't mean to. Let's get together over New Year. Rxx'

As I read it out loud, Di sighed. "He gives you just enough to keep you sweet doesn't he?" She looked at me grimly. "It's up to you, but, at the end of the day, it's almost certainly not going to end well. But you'll probably continue to take his nonsense until you reach your own point of no return. Please, please promise me though that you won't let it drive you down any further."

It was late that evening when I returned home to accusing looks from the cats. Di and I had talked more. She'd tried to persuade me to take a harder line with Richard. "If you don't," she warned, "he'll go on and on with this rubbish, probably because it boosts his ego and makes him feel young again - shades of clubbing and pulling the birds just because he can. It's going to blow up soon though. It has to. I don't see how it can go on like this much longer."

I'd hated listening to this. I was hoping beyond hope that she was wrong. That he would stop seeing Julie. That he would want to be with me more. That he would openly acknowledge his love and devotion to me. That he would commit. That we would be happy together ...

The next few days...

I'd always found the days inbetween Christmas and New Year slightly odd, not quite usual but not out-and-out celebratory. I'd decided to try and be as normal as possible but not being able to sleep properly didn't help. Every morning Di's words resonated in my head and when I looked in a mirror, I saw pale, blotchy skin and huge, dark shadows under my eyes.

One morning when I'd just made a large mug of tea, I heard ducks quacking and grabbed at my mobile. 'Tried to skype you yesterday. You must have been out partying. Miss you mummy. Susiexxxxxx' I started to cry again. Even though I was so pleased that she was enjoying her amazing life, I missed Susie so much. I missed her presence, her smile, her wit, her wisdom. 'I'm fine darling. Hope you had a great Christmas. Miss you lots. Let's skype very soon..xxxxx'. I knew I couldn't face talking to her, forcing cheerfulness and trying to avoid explaining what had been happening.

I suddenly felt impatient with myself - my indecision, my uncertainties and my willingness to so readily accept Richard's bad press about me so, after showering, I got dressed and made sure that I put makeup on with care. The grey clouds looked threatening so I decided to drive into town and managed to find a parking space in the One Elm's small car park. As I crossed the road to walk to the shops, I started to feel happier and more like me.

I wandered round to see if I could find a bargain that would cheer me up. I found a beautiful dark blue dress but when I tried it on, it was tight, too tight, across my hips. It was the same story with several other things I found, and each time I struggled with a pair of trousers or blouse that I liked, I found myself feeling more and more depressed.

Eventually, I went into Maria's café and ordered a baked potato topped with cheese. While I waited for my order to arrive I drank a large coffee with cream and sugar. I knew that I ought to be sensible but wanted, no needed, the hit of carbs and the pleasure, no matter how short lived, that eating brought.

I wandered round for a while longer before returning to my car and wondered briefly whether to go into the bar for a drink but decided against it. As I opened the driver's door, Kyle, the father of one of Susie's friends appeared and enveloped me in a bear hug. "Lucie, great to see you. How are you? Good Christmas?"

I hugged him back. "Not bad thanks, Kyle. And you?"

"Excellent. All the girls came over, we had a blast. Coming in for a drink?" He let go and looked at me. "My God Lucie, are you ok? You don't look it, that's for sure."

"I'm ok Kyle. Think I'm going down with a bug so I'm going home. Probably a hot toddy and an early night will knock it on the head."

He looked at me closely. "You're not ill, you're upset. You're coming in with me. Come on. I'm not taking no for an answer." He pushed the car door shut, took my arm and steered me through the door.

A wave of warmth and noise hit me. Two of Kyle's daughters were sitting at a table so I joined them to a chorus of hellos. Both girls were excitedly chatting about their latest news which made me smile. Moments later, Kyle brought over a champagne cocktail. "Get that down you. And there's another one waiting for you." He sat down and grinned at me. "Silly cow," he said warmly. "Want to talk about what's bothering you?"

"No, no thanks. Tell me, how business?"

Kyle leaned back. "How long have you got? Like everyone else running their own show, it's been a struggle but I'm really optimistic about next year. Got a few good contacts who I'm pretty sure will lead to contracts. And you know what it's like, once business starts to pick up, it kind of gathers momentum."

I nodded in agreement. "That's exactly the way it seems to work. This self-employed malarkey can be really hard, can't it? I know that it tends to be feast or famine as far as I'm concerned. But isn't it funny how, when it all seems awful, something pops out of the woodwork?"

He laughed. "Yes. God knows why it works like that, but it does. The last few months have been desperate but I've got a good feeling about next year."

"That's great," I said warmly, finishing off the champagne cocktail. A moment later, a second glass was put into my hand.

"Drink up," I was admonished, so I did. The next hour or so passed in a haze of champagne cocktails and laughter but as the evening progressed, I realised that I really shouldn't drive, so cheekily asked if I could leave my car until the following morning to which the answer, luckily, was yes.

I was woken by the sun streaming in and as I moved I realised that in my slightly bombed state, I'd fallen into bed fully clothed. I yawned, stretched and realised that I felt better than I had done for several days. Lazily I reached over to the bedside table and groped for my mobile to see if any more texts had been sent. It was nine thirty and there was just one text from Di. 'Thinking of you. Keep your chin up and smile lots, it suits you. Di x'.

I smiled as I tapped out: 'Can't thank you enough - bless you. See you soon. Have a great day. X'

The rest of the day passed in a haze of cautious happiness as I walked down to the One Elm to collect my car, went to the supermarket to replenish the fridge, tidied up, went for a short walk and then lounged on the sofa with the cats, mindlessly watching old black and white movies.

I'd slept well, much better than I thought I would. I awoke to a bright, sunny day with high, grey wisps of clouds that showed how windy it was. I looked at my mobile and saw, to my surprise, that it was just after eight thirty. I'd slept for close to eleven hours. I went into the bathroom and looked in the mirror. The dark shadows under my eyes had all but gone and I looked calmer, refreshed and altogether much better. It was amazing what a few hours' sleep could do, I thought. I stepped under the shower and let the hot water completely wake me up.

As usual, I did my hair and makeup and then looked in my wardrobe to find something that fitted. Must start and, more importantly, keep to that bloody diet, I muttered to myself as I looked at the jeans that I couldn't get into - not yet, anyway. I decided on brown leggings, a long brown sweater combined with a long cream scarf. That with a couple of long pearl necklaces and I was done. I stood back, considered my reflection and smiled.

The cats greeted me and purred their thanks when I gave them their breakfasts. I switched on the kettle and put two thick slices of white bread into the toaster. As I made the tea, I heard the familiar quacking sound. 'Shall we have dinner in your favourite place tomorrow evening? Will you book a table? Rxx'.

I raised my eyebrows in amazement; it seemed that Julie might be fading into insignificance. 'Lovely. Of course I'll book a table. 7 be ok? Lxx'.

'Looking forward to seeing you. I'll be up about 6. Let's have a peaceful new year. Rxx'.

Even though it wasn't me who'd made Christmas unpeaceful, I so wanted our relationship to work, I knew that I'd continue to take otherwise unacceptable comments from him. I sighed.

I spent the day shopping for New Year and general domesticity before talking to Di and reassuring her that I was much better and happier. I then spent a blissful hour skyping with Susie who was bubbling with her news. Clearly she'd had a great time over Christmas with some new friends and a couple of colleagues and I smiled as she told me about an impromptu party that she'd thrown in her very small flat. By the time darkness fell, I was in a calm and reflective state of mind and slept very well that night.

I awoke early the next morning and, rather than get up, stayed in bed and read. The next time I checked the time, I saw that it was almost twelve. I giggled to myself, it felt very self-indulgent. I made my usual morning tea, fed the cats and laid the fire ready for lighting later after which I returned to my book and read for another couple of hours.

Better get ready I thought to myself and made my way upstairs. I peeled off my nightclothes in the bedroom and as I did so, I caught a glimpse of myself in the full-length mirror. Normally, I avoided looking at my body but this time I stood and gazed at myself. I saw a tall woman with good shoulders, pretty hands with well-manicured nails, upper arms that definitely met the bingo-wings benchmark, breasts that missed the nipple-between-shoulder-and-elbow criteria but not by that much, a waist that of course could have been smaller but was a waist nonetheless, too-broad hips and a much-too-big stomach. I scowled at myself but continued the inspection. Chunky thighs, big-ish calves, reasonably neat ankles and feet with immaculately varnished toenails. I stood sideways. Large arse and, oh God, that belly - but, I said to myself as I turned away, not that bad for a woman in her sixties. I glanced back. He was right. I was fat but, I told myself, that really wasn't what defined me as a person. I defined me - my wit, my integrity, my honesty, my determination, my caring, my humour, my tolerance - that's what I was about.

I walked into the bathroom feeling much better, enjoyed a scalding hot shower and then took more care than usual with my hair and makeup. I pulled on a pair of winter white trousers that still fitted and a pale blue sweater and then rooted through a tangled pile of ear-rings to find a pair of large silver hoops. I stood back and surveyed myself in the mirror. Yes I said to myself, you're ok, you really are. I turned on my heel and walked downstairs.

At precisely six o'clock Richard's silver 4x4 pulled onto the drive. I breathed deeply as I checked myself in the hall mirror and opened the front door. He sat still for a moment and I wondered what he was going to do and then, to my relief, he opened the door and got out. I joined him and, as he reached into the car to pick up his bag, put my arms around him.

"I'm so, so glad to see you."

He looked down at me and a small smile appeared. "Me too, me too." He returned my hug. "Let's go in. I'm so tired, haven't been sleeping at all well."

He slumped onto the sofa and, unasked, I made him a cup of tea. When I put it down, I curled up next to him and put my head on his shoulder as he wrapped his arm around me. "I'm so glad you're here," I whispered. "I hate us fighting, us being apart, us being unhappy ..."

"Sssh, no more talking. Not now." He cupped my chin in his hand and, to my delighted astonishment, kissed me with passion and conviction. I melted as I returned his kiss.

Half an hour later we stirred and agreed that it was time to leave. "I just need to freshen up and I'll be with you. Ten minutes ok?" He got to his feet.

"Perfect - I've been so looking forward to this evening."

"Yes, me too," he said as he went upstairs.

Was it my imagination, or did he suddenly sound bone weary and sad? I looked up at the now empty stairs and shivered; what was it Di had said? '...you'll continue to take his nonsense until you reach your own point of no return...' I nodded to myself. She was right, I thought to myself. I'm not strong enough to walk away from this man; I'm going to have to see it through to the end, whatever the end may be. I closed my eyes as the now-familiar pain washed over me.

I heard Richard's footsteps on the stairs and quickly stood upright, making sure that there was a smile on my face.

"Just need to pop upstairs for a second. Shan't be a moment." I stood on tiptoe and gave him a light kiss on the cheek.

He raised his hand and touched my cheek for a moment, gazing into my eyes searchingly. "You really do love me." He sounded disbelieving.

I gazed at him. "I do, of course I do. You know I do." I stared at him, willing him to say those three little words back to me. He said nothing but continued to look deep into my eyes. I moved closer so he could feel my body down the length of his. With a small groan, he enfolded me in his arms so tightly I could hardly breathe and held me that close for what seemed like a long, long time.

I ran upstairs to freshen up and pull on my comfortable Uggs. As I came downstairs, he looked at my feet and gave a wry smile. "Not all that glamorous are they?"

"They're warm and comfy - and we're walking down and back. And it's dark. So shush ..."

He laughed and held up my jacket so I could slide my arms through. Goodness me, I thought, he hasn't done that for quite a while. As I did up my jacket, I turned my head. "Thank you."

"More than welcome. You deserve more ..." His voice faded.

"Ok, ready," I said brightly. I was frightened that this might be a precursor to another in-depth, Julie-fuelled conversation and didn't want it. Not now. Probably not ever.

We walked down the hill into town towards the bright Christmas lights that always gave me such delight. "Oh look. Aren't they lovely? We're so lucky, Stratford has such great lights."

He looked at me. "You're a real child about this, aren't you?" His voice was warm and affectionate.

I grinned up at him. "I just adore seeing the town like this, all bright and welcoming. It reminds me of when Susie was a little girl and her joy and excitement at Christmas-time."

He looked thoughtful. "Yes, I see what you mean. I'd not thought about it like that. Now I come to think about it, Lou got all over-excited about Christmas lights too." Louisa was his daughter and she, like Susie, lived and worked abroad.

"Kids love Christmas and it's nice to act like kids again, even though we're all grown up."

He laughed and put his arm round my shoulders as we gazed up at some particularly fetching snowflakes that were suspended halfway across the road. "Let's just get to our table. A small drink and then we'll see what the chef can do for us."

We walked into the warm geniality of the One Elm and found, to my delight, that our reserved table was my favourite. The gods are looking after me tonight I thought, and smiled to myself. Richard looked across at me and smiled back. Within a minute we were sipping large glasses of warm mulled wine while we read through the menu.

"I can't decide between the venison or roast cod. Cod's much healthier ..." He sounded thoughtful.

"Well, not really. Any game is really low in fat so I would have thought that they'd be much of a muchness."

"Hmmm, you're probably right, and venison is a great dish when it's done well."

I looked at the menu again. "Looks terrific, well worth a try, don't you think? I'm going for the winter couscous with shallots and parsnips. I adore parsnips. And I'm going to see if they'll pop a piece of chicken on the top."

He looked at me. "You always do that," he sounded edgy. "Why can't you just order from the menu instead of having to ask for something special just for you?"

"They never usually mind, and of course I'll ask them if it's alright."

He sighed in exasperation. "Ok, ok," he spread his hands out, "you'll just do what you want to do, as always."

The waiter came over to take our order and I considered changing my request but then realised that would be pointless. If Richard was going to be irritated with me, then he was going to be irritated with me, no matter what. We placed our orders and, as I'd anticipated, there was absolutely no problem with my having some chicken with the winter couscous.

"I don't know how you get away with it."

"With what?" I widened my eyes innocently.

"With expecting to be treated differently from everyone else in the restaurant. Why do you do it, Lucie?" He was beginning to sound really cross.

"Well, I just fancied some chicken with the couscous. I don't expect to be treated differently from anyone else and I really don't see why that would be a problem because ..."

He shrugged. "Let's not fight about it. If you're happy asking for special treatment, then there's nothing more to be said about it."

I put my hand on his arm. "Darling, there's no need to fight at all, is there? Let's just relax and have a nice meal."

He smiled. "Yes, of course. I'm just a bit tired and edgy, I'll be fine."

Our orders arrived and I breathed a sigh of relief. As expected, both dishes were excellent and as we finished we simultaneously sighed contentedly and laughed.

"Another mulled wine, don't you think?" I asked. He nodded. As we sipped our wine, he continued to visibly relax and I felt myself doing the same. It was as if we'd gone back to the time when we were truly in tune with each other and could finish each other's sentences.

It was another couple of hours later that we started to make our way back up the hill. "I don't want to upset you when I talk about money, you know." His voice was very gentle. "I just worry about you, how you're coping and how we'd manage if we were living together ..." I barely contained my gasp of amazement. In all the nearly five years we had been together he'd never talked about the real possibility of us living together and here it was now, out in the open. For a few seconds, I couldn't speak so I simply held his hand tightly.

As I opened the front door, I anticipated the usual late night cups of tea and casual chats and was amazed that, as the door closed behind us, I was enveloped in a bear hug. "Bed - now." His voice was hard and tense. I stood with my mouth open. "Well, are we going to have a debate about this?"

I shook my head. When I was on the second step, I turned to see him staring up at me. I opened my arms. "I can't make it without you. Please hold me."

He stepped forward and we put our arms around each other, his head nestled on my breasts. "I can hear your heart beating," he whispered.

A few moments later we were in bed and as I turned towards him, he kissed me deeply and tenderly. He nibbled my neck, my shoulders, my breasts and, as I reached down, felt his hardness. I laughed softly and very gently curled my hand around him and started to play with him very, very slowly. He moved his hips to match the rhythm I was setting and I arched backwards, pushing my breasts towards him.

"More ... please more," I whispered and he obediently lowered his mouth to nip and suck my nipples while his hands clutched at my hips. I could hardly keep my hold on him as I squirmed in an effort to press our bodies together as closely as possible. I felt myself getting hot - aching to feel him inside me. I lowered my head so that my mouth was closer to his ear. "Fuck me - fuck me right now." He almost growled, and then drew away from me, leaving me spread-eagled and panting for more.

He knelt above me and gazed down at me. "Again - ask again - beg me ..."

Shamelessly I stared up. "Fuck me - Richard, please fuck me." He lowered himself onto me. I trembled as I felt him penetrate me and, as I'd asked, he fucked me slowly and deliberately until I yelped and whimpered into blissful orgasm. A few moments later he came with an explosive sigh and collapsed onto me. Exhausted, we curled around each other and, as our breathing slowed, started to drift into peaceful sleep.

New Year's Eve...

It was still dark when I awoke with the kind of headache from which, thank God, I rarely suffered but when they did come, made me feel sick, giddy and barely able to stand. I could hear Richard's deep, regular breathing next to me so crept out of bed as silently as I could. I put the bathroom light on and closed my eyes. The pain of the light was excruciating. With my eyes half closed I fumbled in the cupboard for a couple of painkillers. I really didn't want to disturb him, so tiptoed into the spare room and collapsed on the single bed. I pulled the duvet up and inhaled his scent from when he had slept there on Christmas Eve which comforted me as I tried to ease the tension enough to get back to sleep.

"Lucie, Lucie, are you ok?" I opened my eyes and the brightness of the day hit me.

With a groan I closed my eyes. "Close the curtains please."

"What's wrong Lucie? You look dreadful."

I mustered a small smile. "I've got the mother of all headaches. I've taken some painkillers so I should be fine very soon. I'm only here because I didn't want to disturb you. Just please close the curtains, the light hurts my eyes." I half-opened one eye and watched him carefully close the curtains.

"What can I do for you?" He sounded really concerned.

I closed my eyes and smiled. "Darling, I'm ok. It's just a headache but it really hurts. Best if you let me sleep through this. Perhaps I could have a drink with a couple of painkillers please?"

"Yes, of course." He was so much better when asked to do something practical. I heard his footsteps recede as he went downstairs.

A few minutes later he reappeared. "Tea. I made you tea. Thought it would be better than coffee."

I opened my eyes and blinked in pain. "Thank you. That's perfect. Can I have the painkillers please?"

He disappeared and returned in moments, holding two white tablets and then sat on the side of the bed, watching me. "I was going suggest we went out but you're clearly not up to that, are you?"

"'Fraid not. Not at the moment, anyway. Where were you thinking of?"

"I don't know. Just thought it would be nice for us to have a day out, go for a walk somewhere."

"It would, it really would, but you're going to have to give me a couple of hours to get rid of this." I smiled as he gently kissed my forehead.

"You sleep," he whispered. "Hope you feel better very soon."

Some time later I awoke with a start to see him standing next to the bed. As I opened my eyes I could feel the pulsing throb deep in my head. "Those bloody ducks have been having a field day." He held out my mobile. I looked at the screen but the words were blurry and my head hurt even more as I tried to concentrate. "Shall I read them?" I nodded. "There's lots - from Karen, Di, Anita, Fran, Chrissie, Susie, Hannah and Simon – who's Simon?" His voice rose slightly.

"Simon's Pennie's husband." Even in the midst of my pain I was amused by the irony of his apparent jealousy. "Please don't bother to read them now - I'll answer them when I get up." I didn't want him reading texts from Karen or Di, not after the recent days I'd spent with them.

"It's gone eleven - seems a shame to waste the day ..."

I squinted up at him. "I agree. I really don't want to spoil your day and this wretched headache doesn't seem to want to go ..." I paused, willing him to say that he would stay with me, even though that probably wasn't what he wanted to do.

"Well," he said slowly, "would you mind very much if I went out for a walk? Probably stop somewhere for a bite of lunch as well. I'll only be a few hours and that'll give you the chance to get better without worrying about me."

I closed my eyes wearily. "Of course, that's fine. No point in both of us missing a lovely day."

I could sense his relief. "Ok, that's good. I'll be off in ten minutes or so. Anything I can get for you before I go?"

"Perhaps another cup of tea. And a glass of water. And some more painkillers. And could I have a piece of toast? Just plain toast. A little food might help ..."

"Yes, of course." The words floated back as he disappeared.

I could feel tears prickling yet again. It would have been so wonderful if he'd opted to stay in with me, sit on the side of the bed and talk to me, make lunch, share lunch, cuddle the pain away - I'd so hoped that he would, especially after the passion and connection of last night's love making.

He returned a few minutes later, carrying a small tray on which there was a mug of tea, a large glass of water, a plate with a slice of toast and two painkillers. I struggled to sit up. "That's lovely darling, thank you so much." I surveyed the tray and noticed that the toast was lightly buttered.

"Is that it? Or do you want anything else?" I could sense his slight impatience.

"No, no, that's great. Now you go off and have a good walk."

He bent to drop a kiss on the top of my head. "You get better, see you later," and he was gone. I drank the tea and swallowed the painkillers, ignoring the buttered toast; the thought of anything fatty made me feel nauseous. I lay down again and closed my eyes.

It was almost dark when I opened my eyes again. Cautiously I moved my head. The pain was still there but as I stood up I knew it was receding. "Richard?" I called, "Richard, are you there?"

There was silence. I reached for my mobile and saw that it was after three thirty.

I went into the bathroom and stood under the shower. My head hurt much too much to be able to wash my hair but the warm water refreshed me. After I'd pulled on leggings and the biggest, cosiest sweater I could find, I looked at myself. My face was white with huge dark shadows under my eyes. I reached for my makeup bag and found some lipstick; I knew that I couldn't bear to wear any eye makeup.

Still feeling fragile, I carried the tray downstairs. It was by now completely dark so I switched on as few lights as possible to avoid too much brightness. I went through to the kitchen and made another cup of tea and some toast which I nibbled at. I was starting to feel much better.

I looked into the sitting room where both cats were curled up on their respective chairs and purred as I stroked them. The fire had been cleaned out and laid ready for lighting. As I held a match to the paper and kindling I smiled to myself. That's lovely, I thought, really kind and thoughtful. I sat in front of the fire, looked through and replied to my texts. All were from dear friends which made me feel cared for and very, very lucky.

I realised that, amongst all the texts, there was nothing from Richard. Where the hell was he I thought but mildly texted 'Just got up and feeling so much better. Thank you for sorting the fire. Where are you? Lxxx'. An hour later, there was still no reply to my text and I was beginning to feel edgy and nervous. I wanted to send another one but common sense prevailed - mustn't be seen as needy, I said to myself.

It wasn't until six when the sound of ducks heralded a text. 'On my way back. Be about an hour or so. Rxx'. I stared at it disbelievingly. He'd been out for over six hours without a word. What the fuck I said to myself, what the fuck is he playing at? I replied 'Dinner 7.30-ish ok? Lxx' and sat back. Within a minute his reply came 'Great. Thanks. See you later. Rxx'.

I went into the kitchen to see what I could rustle up. The left-over turkey was looking very sad and a bit suspect so I threw it away. I took some spicy sausages out of the freezer - sausage and mash I thought. I peeled some potatoes and a half-swede that was lurking in the vegetable drawer and put them on to boil, finely sliced an onion and gently fried it in a pan to form the basis of onion gravy, mashed the cooked potatoes and swede with black pepper and a generous lump of butter. I tasted it - yummy I said to myself. I'd reserved the water and poured it over the cooked onion to soften it still further and then added a dollop of whole grain mustard into the mix before adding my old standby, Bisto granules. I knew they were a real cheat but couldn't resist using them. By this time it was about six thirty so I put the sausages into the oven on a low heat. The house smelled of warm and welcoming food, just the way I liked it. In the sitting room, I stacked more logs and coal onto the fire to make sure that everything was ready for Richard's return.

Just after seven I heard Richard's car pulling onto the drive. He's nothing if not punctual, I thought as I opened the front door to welcome him. He looked tired but happy.

"Had a great day on the Malvern Hills," he said as he pulled his muddy walking boots off. "There were lots of walkers out there. Lucie, you'd have loved it. Such a pity you were too ill to come with me."

"I know - it would have been lovely but it was after three when I managed to get out of bed."

"How are you feeling?" He sank onto the sofa with a contented sigh.

"Much, much better. Still got a vestige of pain but I can see straight and felt well enough to cook your dinner."

"Good job too. Man needs a decent dinner after all that exercise."

"What would you like to drink? Tea, coffee or something stronger?" It was my normal question and usually made him smile.

"Hmmm - I'll start off with a nice cup of tea and then move onto something stronger I think." I made a cup of tea and returned to find him with his feet upon the footstool and his eyes closed, and smiled to myself as I quietly put the tea next to him and then tiptoed out to finish off dinner.

A quarter of an hour later, everything was ready so I returned to the sitting room where Richard was still dozing. I sat next to him, leaned over and gently kissed his cheek, he murmured and moved. I kissed him again. "Time for dinner, sleepyhead."

He opened his eyes, stretched and smiled up at me. "You are a good girl, aren't you? You look after me so well."

"Do my best," I said over my shoulder as I returned to the kitchen.

A couple of minutes later we were eating dinner. "Nice, very nice," Richard said through a mouthful of mash. "Very tasty."

"Good, glad you like it." In the past, I had talked about recipes and how I had prepared food, but Richard had made it abundantly clear that these were conversations he would rather not have. He was very happy to eat good food and discuss the pros and cons of dishes in restaurants, but cooking at home didn't interest him.

As we finished dinner, he looked across at me. "Shall we have a quiet night in? Everywhere'll be heaving and you're still not feeling great, are you?"

My heart sank. I knew what a quiet night in would mean. We'd watch lots of TV and then go to bed. I nodded. "You're right. I'm still feeling a wee bit fragile. Shame though, to stay in on New Year's Eve, don't you think?" I stared at him, willing him to make a suggestion to do something exciting - anything different would do.

"Well then, we'll find a couple of movies to watch and relax in front of the fire. Ok?"

And that's exactly what we did. Two movies later, we'd moved on to Jools Holland's New Year's Eve and I stared at happy people partying as I sat in front of the dying embers of a fire while the man I loved dozed on the sofa. Occasionally I looked across at him and reflected on what Di and Karen had said but tried to banish their words. I love him I thought and don't want to be without him.

At midnight I moved across to the sofa and sat next to him. "Happy New Year my darling." I leaned towards him and kissed him.

He opened his eyes and blinked. "God, I'm tired. Happy New Year." He returned my kiss. "Time for bed I think, don't you?"

As usual, Richard went into the spare room where he kept his bags, to undress. My bedroom was full of my clothes, makeup and shoes so of course it was sensible that Richard kept his belongings out of my very feminine space, but there were times when I wished it wasn't so. I wanted our things to be intermingled together - a mark of our entwined lives but, very rationally, Richard had decided against this.

A moment later, I heard the sound of his mobile and stood stock-still in shock. It was after midnight and he was getting a text? Both our girls had texted us earlier in the evening to wish us a Happy New Year and so I knew it couldn't be Louisa. There was only one person it could be: Julie. My heart pounded and I felt sick. I thought about joining him but knew that I couldn't face the argument that was bound to ensue.

I slowly got into bed, staying on my side. Richard came in and as he got into bed he frowned. "Bloody hell, it's cold. What's happened to my bed-warmer?"

"She's on strike. Tell me, who was that on the phone?"

He sank back and looked at me. "You know who it was. Look, I'm not encouraging her, you know. You're my partner, not her. I just want to be her friend. You know, be there to help when she needs me."

I snorted. "Can't you see what she's doing?" My voice was shaking. "You can't be so stupid that you can't see."

"Oh, not again," he sighed wearily. "I can't stand this. Between the two of you, I don't know whether I'm coming or going. I thought we were going to have a nice relaxing time and all you want to do is pick a fight ..."

"I'm not picking a fight, I'm not - but surely you can see how much this upsets me?" I sat up and looked down at him.

"You know I care ..." he started.

I turned towards him. "Kiss me. Make love to me ..." I was stopped as he pulled me down and we kissed. Not passionately, but with a tenderness and depth that brought tears to my eyes.

Very gently, he kissed my neck, my shoulders, my breasts and pushed his body into mine. I reached down but, to my astonishment, I found he was completely unready for any sort of action. I held him gently with very real affection but he pulled away. "I'm so sorry Lucie ..."

"Hey, it's not important. I don't care, not at all. I just want to be with you ..."

"It's important to me," he interrupted. "It's embarrassing."

I held him close. "You silly, of course it doesn't matter. What matters is that we're together and we love each other. You're just tired. Let's just curl up and go to sleep."

He didn't return my hug; instead he lay back and stared at the ceiling. "I think I should sleep in the spare room. I'm sorry Lucie, but I'm feeling very tense and need to unwind." And with that, he got out of bed and left, closing the door softly behind him.

I turned on my bedside light and stared at the closed door. What had I done wrong I asked myself, as all the old doubts and fears crowded in on me again. I'd really thought that after the caring and passionate love-making of the previous night, the issues between us had, to some extent, been resolved, but clearly I was wrong. With a deep sigh I turned off the light, lay down, closed my eyes and tried to sleep.

.

New Year's Day...

"Tea, here's some tea for you." I heard his voice as from a great distance as I struggled to wake up. I opened my eyes to see Richard standing next to me, a cup of tea in his hand. "I was beginning to worry about you - you just wouldn't wake up. How are you feeling?"

I smiled up at him. "Much better thank you. What's the time?" I sat up to take the mug from his outstretched hand.

"It's just after twelve. I tried to rouse you at ten and then again at eleven but you were completely zonked out. You sure you're feeling ok?"

"Honestly, I'm so much better." I shook my head and then grimaced. "Well, I am much better. There's still a tiny bit of pain left, but nothing I can't handle." I sipped the tea.

Richard sat down next to me and gently stroked my hair. I held my breath. "You must have been exhausted. All that pain you were going through." I nodded while wondering whether he was talking about my headache or all our arguments.

"Well yes, pain is pretty tiring, but I think it's on the way out now. So, what shall we do today, do you think?" I look at him expectantly.

"I'm sorry." His voice was very soft.

I raised an eyebrow. "What for?"

"Well, about last night. I was unreasonable. But that kind of thing hits hard, you know. It's not the kind of thing us blokes find easy to deal with ..."

I interrupted him. "Hey, stop. We were both tired, I wasn't that well, and anyway, these things happen occasionally, don't they? Please don't worry, there's nothing to worry about."

Richard reached up and touched my cheek. "You're so understanding - I probably don't deserve you ..."

"Stop. Stop that right now. It's the first day of the New Year; let's start as we mean to go on. I'll get up in a few minutes, make some brunch and then we'll go out. How does that sound?"

He must have been holding his breath because I heard him exhale. "That sounds good Lucie, very good indeed."

"Good. I'm going to get up and sort myself out before cooking. Is that ok?" He nodded in agreement. "So why don't you go and relax and then you can join me in the kitchen while I'm cooking."

"Ok boss," he said with a smile as he dropped a kiss on the top of my head.

After showering, dressing and taking more painkillers, I started breakfast and a few minutes later sausages and bacon were sizzling in a pan, baked beans were in a saucepan, eggs were beaten and waiting to be scrambled, tomatoes, mushrooms and a couple of slices of black pudding were gently cooking in another pan and bread was in the toaster waiting to be toasted. Brunch is such a messy meal to cook I thought, but it's so great to eat. I realised that I was very hungry.

Ten minutes later we were sitting at the table enjoying our meal, at the end of which Richard sat back and sighed. "You're a really good cook Lucie. I know I sometimes tease you, but make no mistake, you are. Thank you, that was good, very good indeed."

I beamed at him. "Well, thank you kind sir. You know I enjoy cooking and it gives me such pleasure to cook for appreciative eaters."

He looked at his watch. "It's getting on for two - it'll be getting dark soon. Shall we just go out now?"

I hated leaving dirty dishes but I knew that he was right, if I cleared up it would be another half-hour before we left. "I'll just pile everything into the sink and then I'll be with you. Five minutes. Ok?"

True to my word, in five minutes I was standing in the hall with my coat, hat and boots on. He smiled approvingly. "Walk down to the river?" I nodded and we set off, chatting about inconsequential nonsense, the way we had way back in the beginning.

The river was dark grey and fast flowing due to the recent rains. We stood at the side of the theatre gazing down at the ducks battling their way upstream towards some children who were throwing bread into the water. Richard put an arm round me and as I leaned into him, I heard what I thought was a stifled sob. I looked up to see that he had tears in his eyes. "Darling, what's wrong?" I asked in alarm.

He looked down at me with real sadness in his eyes. "Oh God, Lucie, I just don't know ..."

My heart started the familiar pounding and the pain in my head suddenly tightened. Oh no, what's he going to say now - I closed my eyes in anticipation of yet more pain.

"I love you." I stared at him, wondering if I had heard him properly. He looked deep into my eyes. "I love you Lucie. I don't particularly want to, but I do. You're often moody, you're a financial liability, you never know when and where work is coming from," I opened my mouth to say something to stop the flow of disapproval and as I did so, he bent and kissed me, "but I love you. I don't know why and ..."

I put my hand over his mouth. "And I love you Richard. And because I love you and you love me - well, that's all that matters."

He looked at me with a small smile. "Ever the optimist, aren't you? Life's much more complicated than that, you know ..."

"Stop, please stop. Isn't it enough that we love each other? Can't we talk about this another time? Can't we just hold this precious moment close? Do you realise that this is the first time in nearly five years that you've told me that you love me?" He enveloped me in a tight embrace and sighed. I felt him take a breath as if to say something and I knew that I wouldn't be able to bear anything more so I reached up to bring his face to mine and kissed him.

We looked into the murky water and simultaneously shivered. "You're cold." He sounded solicitous. "Do you think we should go back?"

I shook my head. "Let's go for a drink and then we can go home. What about the Dirty Duck?" I love that pub which was just along from the theatre and decorated with countless signed photographs of famous actors both past and present. We walked in step to the pub and, luckily, found seats next to the fire.

Richard stood at the bar and then suddenly looked horrified. "I've forgotten to pick up my wallet." He looked across at me. I started to giggle and then found I couldn't stop. The tears ran down my face as I continued to laugh helplessly. Richard stared at me incredulously and then, to my relief, he joined in my laughter.

"Good job I've brought my handbag, isn't it?" I teased.

He came and sat next to me. "Go on then. Buy me a pint."

I went to the bar and ordered his beer and a slimline tonic for me; I knew that any alcohol would flatten me. I brought the brimming glasses across and as we sat sipping our drinks, I felt happy beyond belief.

We strolled home, arm-in-arm and as we walked through the front door I took his hand and we went up the stairs together. In bed, he held me gently. "You ok? I mean, can you manage this with your headache?"

I held his hand and gazed into his eyes. "I want you so much."

He kissed my face, my neck, my shoulders, my breasts until I tingled. As I returned his kisses, I reached down and he gently pushed my hand away. He continued to kiss my stomach, my belly and then returned up to my face which he held between his hands, kissed me gently as he penetrated me and very slowly and very gently loved me. I held him as tightly as I could, wanting it to last forever. He came with a soft sigh and then drew back slightly and looked at me. "You ok? You didn't come, did you?"

I shook my head. "No. No, I didn't. But I feel wonderful. Really, really - I'm very, very happy." He sighed and lay back with his arm around me and as I curved within his embrace, I closed my eyes.

Chapter 2 - January

I awoke just after eight to find a mug of cool tea on my bedside table. I sipped at it and wrinkled my nose. I really do prefer my drinks to be either very hot or very cold - but it's a lovely thought anyway, I said to myself. I could hear the murmur of the TV downstairs so after I had been to the bathroom, brushed my hair and pulled on a baggy sweatshirt, I made my way downstairs. Richard was in his customary place on the sofa, dozing in front of the news that he insisted on watching several times a day.

I went over to him and planted a soft kiss on his cheek. "Good morning darling."

He blinked and stirred. "Morning Lucie." He yawned and stretched. "I was thinking that I should probably go home today. I've got quite a few things I need to sort out. And you need to try and get some work sorted out, don't you?" He looked up at me. So early in the morning I thought, so early, and he has to make some comment about my work – or lack of it. I stifled a sigh. The truth was that of course I was hoping that he would stay for longer but I'd anticipated this. He'd always made it very clear that he needed his own space and there was no denying that I liked time to myself as well.

I smiled down at him. "Yes, of course Richard. When do you think you want to leave by?"

He scratched his nose and looked thoughtful. "Well, I could either leave straight after breakfast ..." he paused and looked at me, "but you'd probably prefer me to leave later, wouldn't you?"

"Well, yes, that would be nice. Perhaps we could have a couple of hours out somewhere, have a light lunch and you'd still be able to get back in daylight. What do you think?"

He nodded. "That's a good idea. Ok, breakfast - what's on offer?"

I reeled off various suggestions but, as I knew it would be, porridge was chosen. "With no salt," he added.

I went into the kitchen with a wry smile and made his porridge with no salt, as instructed, even though I knew full well that a few grains would add hugely to the flavour.

After breakfast, I gazed out at the tiny garden that we had spent so many summers in, I suddenly wondered why I was so desperately holding onto this relationship.

"Oh God, it hurts," I said out loud.

"What hurts?" Richard sounded concerned. I spun round, not realising that he was now ready and had returned to the kitchen.

"Nothing. Just a slight headache. Nothing to worry about at all." The words tumbled out of my mouth.

"Hey, what's wrong? You sound really strange. You sure you're ok?" He held my shoulders while he looked searchingly into my eyes.

"No, I'm fine, absolutely fine. Really. I'll go and get ready, shall I?"

He shrugged. "Up to you. I'll wait for you in the lounge." He always used the word 'lounge' which I hated; lounges are in hotels or airports I used to tell him. As with many of our discussions, there was no convincing him. What was it that Karen had said? 'My way or the high way' - if that was the worst thing we disagreed about, there were no problems. But, of course, there were.

Upstairs, I had a quick shower, did my hair and put makeup on. As I reached for my jeans I scowled at myself. Not yet I said to myself as I reached for black leggings, black boots, a red shirt, a heavy grey cardigan and a black and red scarf. Once I was ready I looked in the mirror, gave a small twirl and smiled to myself, I quite liked what I saw. Once downstairs, I picked up my handbag and went into the sitting room with my car keys in my hand.

"I'll drive because you'll be driving home later, won't you? Now, where shall we go?" I made a point of driving when he visited me because, as I frequently told him, he had driven the eighty-plus miles to come up to see me. "I know exactly where we can go - lovely pubs, tea rooms and a few shops. Ready?"

We listened to some soul music as we drove to the pretty little Cotswold village of Stow-on-the-Wold, such an odd name I always thought. As I parked, I noticed that the clouds were beginning to break and pale blue sky was emerging. We strolled round the square, looking at a few shops but soon felt chilly. "Time for a coffee I think," Richard suggested. A few minutes later we were sitting in the warmth amidst the soft chatter of a tea room that smelled of coffee and freshly baked cakes. A pretty young girl came over to take our order and I confined my request to a large coffee with my normal glass of water.

"Cake to go with your coffee?" we were asked.

I instinctively looked at Richard. "No thank you," we both replied.

"Lucie, we probably need to talk, don't we?" He looked at me but I couldn't read anything in his expression.

"Yes, we probably should." I was surprised at how calm I felt.

"I mean, we do have problems, don't we? And that makes me nervous about the future."

Future - he said future I thought.

I straightened up and took a deep breath. "I don't think that we can solve everything all in one go and I know that you probably don't agree, but I honestly feel that now we're being more open with each other about our feelings, well, there's nothing that can't be sorted out. I have to admit that, at the moment, money's tight for me but you know that I've never ever been one to sit back and do nothing. I'm always chasing work and ..."

"Look Lucie, I know perfectly well that you try to get work," he interrupted, "but all too often it doesn't pan out that well, does it?"

"I can only do my best." I was beginning to feel pre-judged and not in a good way. "I'm contacting everyone I know to see what part-time teaching's available. I don't want a full-time job partly because I think I'd be seen as too old to be taken seriously and also because that would mean I'd have to let go of other potential opportunities." I paused for a moment. "But, you've always known this, haven't you, so why is it such an issue now?"

We were interrupted by our coffees arriving. I took the opportunity to marshal my thoughts and properly confront what I had been avoiding for so long.

I took a very deep breath. "You know what's killing me?"

He looked at me. "What?"

"You know exactly what." I was amazed that my voice was steady. "I can't stand it that you're seeing Julie so often ..."

I watched Richard's reaction closely; he looked uncomfortable and slightly embarrassed. "Look, I'm helping Julie partly in Patrick's memory and partly because I just want to be there for her. She's going through a really hard time and I think you ought to be more understanding."

I stared at him with my mouth open, hardly able to believe what I was hearing. "What?" I tried to sound more reasonable than I felt. "Do you think you're being fair to her? Don't you think that by seeing her as often as you do, you're giving her the wrong impression? That you might be up for some sort of a relationship with her? Doesn't she know that we're together? Surely she must have other friends she can call on? Can't she see the effect this is having on us, well on me, and doesn't she care about that?" I stopped to draw breath, amazed at my temerity.

Richard stared at me. He was unused to my speaking out as vehemently as I had just done. "You think I'm being unfair to her?" he asked, barely audibly.

"Yes, yes I do." I suddenly sat back. Oh my God, he's more worried about her than he is about me was the thought that flashed through my mind. "I honestly think that you seeing her is poisoning us. Tell me, how would you like it if I was to spend as much time with another man as you spend with her?"

He blinked as if he was returning to me. "Well, I wouldn't like it, not at all."

"Well, there you are then." I felt cautiously triumphant. "Please, please Richard, for my sake, for our sake, stop seeing her. Or if that's not possible, don't see her as much. Every time you do, it hurts me - you have no idea how much." I felt tears on my cheek and tried to blink them away.

Unusually, Richard didn't show irritation or frustration at my tears. Instead he reached into his pocket and passed me his handkerchief - the blue and white spotted silk handkerchief I'd given him for Christmas. I wiped my eyes, wishing that I could control my emotions better. As I passed the handkerchief back to him, he laughed. "Best look in the mirror I think."

I repaired the damage my tears had wrought as best I could and then looked at him. "Please can we stop now?"

He looked at me closely. "You've gone very pale. What's wrong?"

"It's just this headache. It's back. And would you mind driving please?" My vision was blurred with little flashes, a sure sign of an impending migraine.

He held out his hand. "Give me the car keys then." He sounded slightly annoyed but when I swayed as I got to my feet, he grabbed my arm. "Lean on me, I'll look after you." Those were the words I'd wanted to hear for so long but I was acutely aware he was only talking about my feeling ill, not about how our future could be. I took his arm and let him lead me from the tea shop to the car. He gently settled me into the passenger seat and drove us home.

The cats greeted us as we pulled onto the drive. Richard smiled as he helped me out of the car. "They're always here, those two." He closed the front door behind us. "I can see that you're ill. Why don't you go to bed? I'll get you a drink and painkillers and then I'll leave you in peace so you can rest and not worry about me."

I would have so much preferred him to say that he would stay until I was better, that he wanted to stay with me always, but I took his outstretched hand and allowed him to guide me upstairs. He closed the curtains, very gently undressed me and then put me to bed. "Back in a moment," and he disappeared. Moments later he returned with a mug of tea, a glass of water, a plate with two plain biscuits and two painkillers.

I looked up at him. "You're such a sweetie. Thank you so much."

He sat on the side of the bed. "Shush, you rest. I'll leave now and ring you later, probably tomorrow morning so I don't disturb you if you're sleeping."

I held up my arms for a goodbye hug. "I love you," I whispered into his shoulder.

A few minutes later I heard the front door close. I wanted to wave him off so I got out of bed, opened the curtains a crack and saw him sitting in his car with his mobile held to his ear. I groaned. Nothing had changed I thought as I closed the curtains and fell back into bed.

The next few days passed drearily. I knew it was too early in the New Year to get in touch with my existing contacts about potential work which I found very disheartening. I spent hours scrolling through websites, searching for work that looked interesting or well-paid but all I saw were call centres advertising for customer service advisors. I'd once worked in a call centre and whilst it certainly had been an experience, it wasn't one I was keen to repeat.

As usual, Richard drove up on the Friday evening in time for dinner. I'd thought long and hard about what to cook and decided on a chicken, leek and ham pie which he declared was 'very nice'. We then watched a movie and went to bed later than I would have liked.

I usually found it a bit of a challenge to be enthusiastic in bed after so long in front of the TV and that evening was no exception. His kisses, cuddles and caresses seemed perfunctory and as he penetrated me, I feigned passion in an effort to keep up with him but all too soon he had come leaving me to satisfy myself. I reached into the drawer next to the bed for a new purchase that had been delivered a couple of days before, a pale blue rabbit. I switched it on and as it purred enticingly, I pushed it deep inside me. I kept up a slow, steady pressure with my hand and the familiar deep pulse gathered momentum until I arched my back and moaned as quietly as I could while Richard snored softly beside me. Afterwards I lay and thought more about our relationship. I realised that things weren't perfect but we were compatible on so many different levels, I felt I could cope with what clearly wasn't ideal.

After breakfast, we enjoyed a leisurely walk down the hill and mooched round the sales. There was nothing that particularly tempted either of us until Richard found a James Galway CD I'd been searching for. As he presented it to me with a pleased smile on his face, I felt a surge of love that almost brought tears to my eyes. "Thank you so much."

"You're more than welcome. I know it's something you've wanted for ages." He was always gently amused by my reluctance to buy on the internet, much preferring to find what I wanted in what I called 'proper shops'. I hadn't told him about my latest acquisition from the internet though; some things were best kept to myself.

We both enjoyed lunching at the One Elm and, half an hour later, were at our favourite table looking through the menu. After some debate, Richard settled on the roasted cod while I decided on Caesar salad, with chips of course, at which Richard raised an eyebrow. "Need carbs in this weather," I said mock-defensively.

"It's up to you Lucie, it's up to you. I'm tired of trying to support your dieting." I shrugged and defiantly ate the chips along with the salad.

I quickly changed the subject and we talked about possible theatre productions that he might like to see. I was thinking of my Christmas gift to him, but it was clear that he was thinking of future plays we could enjoy as well which gave me a warm, tingly glow.

It was cold and dark as we strolled home. "Time for a fire, I think," Richard said as I opened the front door, almost falling over the welcoming cats.

"Great. Coffee?" I went through to the kitchen. I knew that Richard wouldn't want a large meal that evening so quickly prepped onions, leeks, a stick of celery and a potato for leek and potato soup while the kettle came to the boil. The fire was starting to crackle as I returned to the sitting room and sank into my usual chair.

Richard piled some coal and another log onto the fire and then sat back on the sofa with a satisfied sigh. "I do like a good fire."

I smiled across at him. "Boys always like playing with fire. And you always manage to get us nice and warm."

"You talking about the fire or something else?" he unexpectedly teased.

"Well, my darling - now let me think. Hmmm … well, the fire of course."

"You cheeky little mare. Why don't you come over here?" I didn't need asking twice. As the words were out of his mouth I was beside him on the sofa. He put his arm round my shoulders and pulled me towards him. "You're a bad girl, aren't you?" I lowered my chin and gazed up at him through my fringe.

"And aren't you glad I'm bad?" I made my voice low and throaty. This was a game that we'd very occasionally played in the early days of our relationship but hadn't for some time and I wondered what his reaction would be. He stared at me and then lowered his mouth onto my neck. I leaned back as he softly bit me. "Bad girls need to be punished," his voice was husky, "and you've been a very, very bad girl, haven't you?"

I stifled a giggle. "I have, I have," I whispered, "and I'm very, very sorry. What are you going to do with me?" I couldn't believe that he fell into his role so seamlessly. As soon as the words were out of my mouth, I was pulled across until I was face down over his knee and held down firmly as I struggled very half-heartedly to get free. "Naughty girls need to be spanked," I heard and then four or five stinging slaps were administered across my bottom. A game it might have been but it still hurt. I yelped at each blow and was close to the point of tears when he stopped and pulled me up to kiss me with a demanding lust that took my breath away. A moment later I was on my hands and knees in front of the fire as he pulled my trousers and knickers down and I then felt him push into me. I gasped and tried to match him as he thrust faster and faster until he collapsed over my back with a sigh. It was a wham-bam-thank-you-ma'am best and I hugged the memory of his mindless passion as I felt him slip away from me leaving me kneeling front of the fire. As I rose to my feet slightly unsteadily, I looked into the mirror above the fireplace to see my face was red and blotchy from the heat. I pulled up my knickers and trousers as elegantly as was possible and, nonchalantly sauntered to the door. "Time for soup I think, don't you?"

The rest of the evening passed peacefully. We enjoyed the soup, watched a movie and then went to bed. "Lucie, I'm very, very tired," Richard said as we nestled under the duvet. "Let's just sleep, shall we?" I nodded my agreement against his chest and we drifted into sleep.

The next morning I awoke alone. After going to the bathroom, I checked the spare room which was empty apart from Richard's open bag and clothes strewn on the chair. I stood on the landing and could hear his voice in conversation. "Oh God, not again" I whispered and, as I debated whether to stay upstairs or not, his voice stopped. A moment later he appeared in the hall and then vanished in the direction of the kitchen. A few minutes later I saw him again, this time holding two mugs and as he looked upstairs and saw me he looked startled. "What are you doing just standing there? Do you want your tea upstairs or are you going to join me?"

"I'll join you." I took the mug from his hand and reached up to kiss him on the cheek. As we settled in front of the fire he'd relit, I took a deep breath. "I thought I heard your voice. Who were you talking to?"

He looked at me warily. "You know who I was talking to, don't you?"

I nodded. "I think so but I'd rather you told me."

"I don't always tell you because I can't stand all these scenes. I keep telling you that there's nothing in it yet you keep badgering me."

"I think she's playing a very nasty little game and I can't believe that you don't see it. It's so unkind to pretend that you don't." I took a deep breath. "Well, what did she want this time?" My voice was very steady.

He stared into the fire. "Well ..." he started and then paused. "I don't like what she's doing either, you know." He looked across at me.

"Well, tell her to fuck off then." My voice was less steady now.

"I can't do that," he said softly. "She's in a really bad place at the moment."

I stood up. "Just don't ask me to be sympathetic. She doesn't care about me and how I feel, so why should I care about her?"

"That's not very nice, is it? You're normally so kind and understanding ..."

"I am to people who treat me with just the tiniest degree of consideration," I interrupted, "but tell me exactly why I should care about someone who so obviously doesn't give a flying fuck how I feel?"

Suddenly Richard looked very annoyed and whilst I normally backed down in the face of his anger decided not to - not this time. "I know that you'll do what you want to do. You've always made it perfectly clear that you don't take orders from anyone. I do wonder why you do what she wants and not what I want but that's up to you. You must understand that this hurts me; I just don't think you appreciate just how much. Richard, I love you. How can you do this to me?"

He stood up and took a step towards me. I stayed where I was. He reached out and pulled me towards him, burying his face into my neck. "I'm so, so sorry." His voice was muffled.

I pulled away slightly and looked up at him. "What exactly are you sorry about Richard? Sorry about seeing her, sorry about hurting me - what?"

He stared into my eyes. "This can't go on, can it?" My heart was beating so loudly I was sure he could hear it. I shook my head. "I'm going to have to tell her. We have to give us a proper chance. It's not going to work like this, is it?"

"No darling, I don't see how it can. Believe me, I'm trying to be fair and I honestly don't think that I'm being unreasonable. I know that you wouldn't tolerate it if I was spending a lot of time with someone, would you?"

"No, no I wouldn't. I need to go and see her and explain things to her."

I bit my lip. I wanted to say that he could surely send her an email or a text. That he could speak with her on the phone. That he could send her a letter. That he didn't need to see her again – not ever.

"I have to leave this to you. Richard, I trust you. Please, please don't betray that trust."

"I won't. I promise. Look, I think I ought to try and get this sorted out now, today - don't you?"

I blinked. "I guess so."

Richard hugged me very tightly and then opened his arms. Within ten minutes I was watching him put his bags into the car, start the engine, wave to me and go.

I sat down in front of the fire as both cats joined me and while I ran my hands over their warm, furry bodies and listened to their contented purrs, I wondered just how much longer I could bear this roller-coaster of emotions I'd been enduring for the past few months. But he said that he was going to go and get it sorted, I told myself. And you have no choice; you just have to trust him.

It was on the Tuesday that David, a colleague of mine from some years before, called me, asking if I could take him to hospital for a check-up. He'd suffered from bowel cancer the previous year and undergone surgery, chemotherapy and radiotherapy and that day was due to get the results of yet more tests. His daughter usually took him to his appointments, but her baby son had a snuffle and she didn't want to expose her dad to any infection. As I drove him towards the hospital, it reminded me of all those days when my mother had to wait in hospital corridors for her treatment, she'd died many years ago of breast cancer. Luckily we didn't have to wait very long and as his news was cautiously optimistic, we decided to pop into a village pub on the way home to have a celebratory drink. We sat at a table near a roaring log fire and caught up with each other's news.

"So, what's happening with you and Richard?" David asked out of the blue. "Is everything really alright?"

I smiled at him. "It would be so helpful to get a male perspective on what's been happening."

He leaned back and nodded. "But before you start, perhaps we should have a refill?" He held up his glass and I went to the bar, returning a few moments later with brimming glasses. He took a large mouthful of beer. "God, this is wonderful stuff, isn't it Lucie? I wasn't allowed this throughout all those bloody treatments and now I can." He looked at me. "Now, shoot."

And I did. I told him everything and as I did, he sat still, occasionally taking a sip of beer. When I'd finished, we sat in silence for a few moments.

"What an arse. Lucie, why are you putting up with this shit?" David was nothing if not a plain speaker.

"But, I love him." Even to my ears, it sounded pretty feeble after telling my sad story.

"And that means that you have to put up with his crap?"

"He's trying to get this sorted out. He's seeing Julie and he's going to tell her that she has to back off ..."

David snorted. "He's just gone for another shag." I flinched. "You're not stupid Lucie. It's obvious what's happening. Why are you in denial?" He looked at me intently. "You're usually a strong, smart woman. Stop being so fucking spineless and tell him to ..."

"Oh, stop!" I interrupted. I couldn't bear to hear any more and as I opened my mouth to continue defending Richard, David leant forward and put his hand over mine.

"Now you listen to me. You asked me for my opinion and I'm giving it to you. Whatever you think, he's spending time with someone else. I presume that you're not ok with this?" I nodded. "Well," he squeezed my hand, "let me ask you this. If someone you knew and cared for told you the story you've just told me, what would your advice be?"

"I'd tell them to tell him to ..." my voice trailed off and I sat gazing at David with tears in my eyes.

"You need to grow a pair." David was smiling. "This isn't doing you any good at all, you know. But maybe you feel you have to see this thing through to the bitter end?"

I stared at him. "Di said just the same thing."

"Hmmm, two great minds thinking alike. Well, all I can say is what I think and that's what I think. Get rid Lucie - you're worth better than this." He sat back and I suddenly realised how tired he was.

"I'm so sorry David. I didn't mean to burden you but really appreciate your advice. I don't think that I'm strong enough to take it at the moment, but I might have to eventually. Now, let's get you home."

On Thursday evening, Richard rang for our usual mid-week chat. He sounded very tired and strained and as we chatted about inconsequential things, I wondered what was wrong. "It's my bloody roof. I woke up this morning to find water actually dripping onto my bed. I've had a look but can't find what's wrong. I need to get this sorted out really quickly. And I noticed that snow's forecast for the weekend." He sighed.

"That's awful. Look, if you need to spend time at yours this weekend, of course, that's fine. I can come down to you. It'll make a nice change."

"We'll see. You know I'd much rather come up to you than you come down here."

I bit back a retort. I knew perfectly well that Richard disliked my staying with him and that had always saddened me.

It came as no surprise when Richard called me on Friday afternoon to say that water was still dripping through and that he needed to stay at home. "And Lucie, I'll be busy trying to fix this dam' leak so I won't have any time for you, you'll just be bored down here. Better that you stay at yours in the dry and warm."

In the face of this logic, I had no choice but to agree and so, for the first time in several months, I had a weekend on my own. I met Karen in town for a coffee, visited Anita and her husband John who gave me lunch and lots of laughs, went for a walk with Simon, Pennie and their lovely Labrador, talked interminably on the phone to other friends and Skyped Susie. It had been, I reflected on Sunday evening, a very pleasurable weekend.

I awoke on Monday morning to find that Richard had been right; there was a sprinkling of snow which turned into several inches over the following days. The cats tiptoed outside, making small pathways across the garden which became tracks as the days passed. Much as I wanted, and more to the point, needed work I was very grateful to be able to stay at home. I'd always been a very nervous driver in the snow.

"You're such a wuss," Richard teased me during one of our telephone chats, "and you usually drive pretty fast, don't you?"

"I know, I know. It's not logical but I can't help it. Driving in the snow scares me." We both laughed and for those few moments, I was really calm and happy.

As Richard had managed to find and mend the leak in his roof before the snows came, he said he wanted to come to Stratford at the weekend and arrived, as usual, on Friday. Despite the snow, I had managed to get to the supermarket without mishap and brought plenty of food and drink, just in case the snow worsened.

I'd prepared a huge pot of beef stew that Richard judged as 'up to your usual high standard' which made me smile. It was unusually early when he looked over at me. "Time for bed, do you think?"

"Yes, sure," I replied, thinking that perhaps he was feeling particularly tired.

He smiled as he came into my bedroom and saw me on his side of the bed, got into bed and turned towards me. "We haven't really talked over the past few days, have we?"

I froze. This absolutely wasn't the time I wanted an in-depth discussion on the state of our relationship. "No, but let's not talk, not now ..."

I propped myself up on my elbow and looked down at him and as he returned my gaze, I leant over and kissed him gently on the forehead, his now-closed eyes, his cheeks and then his mouth. I moved down to his chin, very tenderly scraped my teeth along his jaw and felt rather than heard his soft sigh. I nibbled down his throat onto his chest, gently bit his nipples and then let my tongue trace downwards to his belly button. I was intent on giving him a blow job but felt his hands pull me back, so I straddled him instead and as I lowered myself onto him I stared deep into his eyes. He gripped my hips so tightly it hurt, but I barely felt any pain as we set a rhythm that got faster and faster until he bucked, groaned and then relaxed with his eyes closed. He was almost asleep.

I turned off the bedside light and tried to settle down again but needed my own release. On my own again I thought to myself as I ran my hands over my breasts, felt my nipples harden and then reached down to start a gentle but steady pressure which inexorably led me into the familiar throbbing pulse deep within me. As my hands moved faster I felt a cascade of sensations which took me by surprise as ripples of pleasure engulfed me. I wanted it to last forever but all too soon I felt the final few spasms ebbing away and as my breathing slowed I felt hot tears trickling down my face - rarely had I felt so alone.

I awoke the next morning to see a watery sun in a pale blue sky. After breakfast, we sat over coffee, watching the cats carefully pick their way across the garden, trying to avoid the snow. "They're fair weather cats. Bit like me."

Richard laughed. "Well, you're certainly fair weather, but we are going to walk into town, aren't we?" He looked across at me expectantly.

"Certainly are." Although given a choice I'd have braved the conditions and driven down.

I showered and then stood in the bedroom wandering what to wear. Riffling through a drawer, I found a long red cashmere sweater that I'd treated myself to years ago. To my delight it fitted and, teamed with black leggings and a red and black scarf, made a stylishly cosy outfit.

The roads and pavements were almost clear in town and I breathed a sigh of relief. We spent an hour or so mooching round bookshops which reminded me of the early days when we were so much more at ease with each other than we seemed to be now. I found a book on Victorian cooking which Richard bought for me.

"I like giving you little presents," he said in the face of my mild protestations.

"And I love it that you do." I gave him a warm hug as he smiled down at me. Pity he didn't think like that when it came to choosing your Christmas presents the little voice in my head said. That's so bitchy I said to the voice. But it's true, the little voice insisted. Shut up, you just shut up - the little voice fell quiet.

Half an hour later we were sitting at our favourite table in the One Elm, relishing the muted noise of people enjoying themselves. We looked at the menu and, as always, discussed the pros and cons of various dishes. I was particularly taken by the house pâté followed by fish pie while Richard favoured a pint of prawns and then onglet hanger steak.

"I wonder if chef would let me have her recipe for the pâté," I mused out loud while we waited for a server to take our order.

Richard smiled indulgently at me. "Don't you have enough recipe books at home to be able to make pâté if you want to?"

"Well, yes, I do but you know me. I love talking about food and I'm always up for learning new ways of doing things."

"So, pâté isn't just pâté?" Richard teased.

"No, not at all," I said thoughtfully, "any more than a white rose is a red rose or a Smart car is a Rolls. You know, in broad terms they are, but there are so many variations and subtleties to be taken into account ..."

"Yes, of course." There was an edge of impatience in his voice.

"Hey, I really enjoy talking about food. Maybe even more than I enjoy eating it, which is saying something."

"Well, you certainly enjoy eating." Richard leaned across and patted my stomach.

We were interrupted by the server coming over to take our order which arrived very quickly. The pâté was, as I'd expected, absolutely delicious. "You must try this." I offered Richard a small piece of thin toast topped by pâté.

"Very nice."

"It's got undertones of smoked paprika I think." I nibbled another piece.

"Really? You can taste that? It just seems like a nice pâté to me."

"Yes, I'm sure I can taste paprika. And they've used white pepper, not black."

Richard leaned back and gazed at me benevolently. "You're just an addict, aren't you? You just love food; it must be in your genes."

I smiled back. "Probably. My mother was an amazing cook and I learned so much from watching her. I remember being about five and helping her make mayonnaise. It was pure magic, seeing this fabulously tasty stuff grow from egg yolks and olive oil. You know, cooking's pretty scientific, you need to understand what happens when different things are put together ..."

My voice trailed away as Richard looked bored. "Anyway," I said brightly, "tell me about how you sorted the roof." Then, while he explained the intricacies of mending the hole in his roof, I looked as interested as I could.

The fish pie was excellent, as I knew it would be, and Richard pronounced that his steak was 'very good'. Replete, we sat back and ordered coffee.

"Just nipping to the loo." Richard rose to his feet.

"Excuse me?" I heard a male voice and looked up. "Excuse me?" the voice said again. I turned round to see a pleasant-looking man at the table behind ours looking at me.

"Yes?"

"Well, I couldn't help overhearing you." He smiled - a wide, disarming smile. "You obviously know a lot about food."

I looked at him. "Well, I guess I've been cooking for a long time, and eating for longer."

He laughed. "Well put, very well put." He held out his hand. "Phil, Phillip Ellis. I'm involved in cooking and I'm about to launch a foodie magazine. I've just been let down by one of my contributors and I'm looking for a food critic. If you can write half as well as you can talk about food - well, you'd be ideal."

I stared at him in amazement. "You want me to write you an article about food?"

He scratched his nose thoughtfully. "Oh, more than that. I'm looking for regular articles on recipes, crits on local and not-so-local eating places - you know the kind of thing I mean?"

I continued to stare at him.

"Look," he glanced towards the men's room, "I can see you're with someone. I'm not trying to hit on you," he paused. "Not that it would be such a bad thing to do ..."

I gasped; it had been a very long time since anyone had flirted so openly with me.

"But," he continued, "I'm seriously looking for someone. Here's my card." He took out his wallet and passed me a silky white business card which was embossed with dark claret lettering. "You get in touch with me and we'll talk. I'm really serious - this isn't a chat-up line ..." He suddenly stopped talking and as Richard returned, stood up and went to the bar to pay his bill.

Richard stood next to me and looked across at Phil. "What's happening?" He sounded indignant. "I turn my back for a moment and you're talking to a complete stranger. Or do you know him?"

I gazed up him, still holding the business card. "I think I've just been propositioned." I couldn't stop a giggle.

Richard scowled and took a step towards the bar. I quickly reached up and held his sleeve. "Oh, for goodness sake, Richard, don't be silly. He just wants me to write articles on food for his magazine. If I'm good enough. Which I seriously doubt ..." I waited, hoping that he would be pleased for me.

Richard snorted. "You silly cow. He just wants to get into your knickers, that's all. Writing articles indeed. For God's sake, grow up."

I looked across at the bar and saw Phil watching me. He gave a small, almost pitying, half-smile, raised his hand in farewell and left.

We finished our drinks and then made our way up the hill. It was getting dark and the snow crunched beneath our feet as I held onto Richard's strong arm. Once home, he quickly laid and lit the fire. I went upstairs to find a cooler top and after pulling it over my head, took Phil's card out of my wallet and pushed it deep in my knicker drawer.

The fire was crackling when I went back into the sitting room and Richard was, as usual, sprawled on the sofa but with his mobile in his hand.

I wanted to shout at him and ask why the hell he was holding onto his mobile but of course I didn't. I walked into the kitchen and whisked eggs for an omelette. He followed me into the kitchen silently, opened the new bottle of Southern Comfort that I'd bought for him and poured himself a large glass. He sat at the table while I poured the egg mixture over the cooked potatoes and onion I'd prepared and watched as the omelette start to cook. After a minute I scattered the grated cheeses over the half-set mixture in the pan and as they melted into the eggs, quickly sliced tomato and onion onto our plates, drizzling olive oil and lemon juice over them.

I brought the plates to the table and Richard looked up. "Looks good. Always looks good though." I smiled my thanks.

As we finished our meal, Richard sat back. "We really must talk, you know."

The words jolted me as they'd done many times before and I braced myself for yet more criticism. "Ok, what do you feel you need to say this time?"

"This time?" Richard looked puzzled.

"Yes, this time. You keep telling me what I'm doing wrong but you never ever talk about positive things. You know, where we're heading, what plans we ought to have for the future ..." my voice faded as I looked into his eyes which were cold and flinty.

"You know what I'm worried about. I sometimes feel that talking to you is like pissing in the wind. You don't do anything to reassure me that things will improve. You simply bleat on and on about love. Love? You can't live on love, you know ..."

"You can't live without it either," I said softly. "Without love, why would one bother?" I stood up and looked down at him. "I love you. You know that. I want us to talk about ways forward. I don't think that I deserve being told all the time how useless I am. Yes, there are issues that need to be addressed but it's not fair to keep beating me over the head with them ..." I stopped as I heard Richard's sharp intake of breath.

"You think I'm unkind to you? That I don't care about you? Christ, Lucie, I've stuck around for the past five years. I've not gone even though there've been times when it would have been so easy to walk away from all your issues and problems. Doesn't that say a lot?"

So, everything's your fault is it? The little voice in my head was back. And he's so kind to stay with you despite the fact that your work is erratic, although you never give up and always manage to get something. And he's so caring that he considers your feelings all the time, doesn't he? And he's so sensitive about your struggles with your weight, isn't he? I listened to the little voice and this time didn't tell it shut up.

"If you're determined to make everything my fault then so be it, but actually that's not true and you know it. I know that you think I'm unreasonable about Julie but, as I've said before, you seeing her as much as you do doesn't feel kind at all. In fact, it feels very cruel. You know how much that hurts me but you just carry on."

"And what about that bloody man at lunchtime?" Richard's voice was clipped. "You took his fucking card, for God's sake. Probably still got it for all I know. And you give me earache because I'm trying to help a friend? How childish is that?" He was almost shouting. Richard was a tall, strong man and when he raised his voice, I always found it scary and intimidating regardless of the fact that he'd never ever raised his hand to me in anger. This was no exception. I caved in.

"I'm sorry. I know that you've known Julie for a long, long time and she's going through a bad time. I just wish ..." my voice trailed off and I sat feeling a myriad of conflicting emotions. I was furious that Richard didn't take me seriously, felt self-centred for putting me and my emotions over someone who had lost her husband so tragically, frustrated that I found it so difficult to articulate how I felt, childish because Richard so often treated me as a child and pathetic because I had always found controlling my weight so tough.

I stood up, picked up our empty plates and took them through to the kitchen. "I'm exhausted. Would you mind very much if I crashed out? I know it's early." I looked at my watch and saw that it was nearly nine. "And you said that you were tired too? Let's go to bed Richard. I don't want us to fight. I want us to be happy." I held out my hand wanting him to take it.

He looked up at unsmilingly. "You go up. I'll join you a bit later. I'm feeling tense. I want to try and unwind first."

I gazed down at him. "Ok; I'll go up now. Unless you want me to stay with you?"

He shook his head. "No, I might even go for a short walk. Just round the block. I need to clear my head, Lucie. I can't think straight any more."

I looked down at my hand that was still outstretched, dropped it to my side and as I moved closer to Richard to kiss him, he raised his hand slightly. "Not now Lucie, just leave it will you?" It felt as if he'd slapped me and as I made my way upstairs I felt weary and defeated. So often passion had overtaken us and there had been no time to take my makeup off before going to bed, but that evening I went into the bathroom and very carefully removed every scrap. I looked at my reflection. It was like gazing at a stranger who looked sad and old and I watched as tears ran down her face. I went into the bedroom and got into bed. And this is the man who said 'let's never let the sun go down on an argument' is it, the little voice in my head said. I rolled over onto my stomach and pulled the pillows over my head to drown it out.

I must have been completely wiped out because the next thing I remembered was Richard getting into bed and automatically moved towards him. This time he didn't turn away from me but pushed me on my back and rolled on top of me. I was still half asleep and as I felt him try to push himself into me, I instinctively winced and pressed my hands against his chest.

"Wait, please wait. I'm not ready." I protested.

He pulled back slightly. "Use some lube then." His voice was hoarse and impatient.

I reached across to the bedside table where there was a tube of KY, smeared some on my fingers and quickly rubbed myself. Richard pushed himself into me and thrust faster and faster until I heard him groan as he collapsed across me. He was asleep within seconds. I lay beside him listening to his deep, regular breathing and, despite myself, gradually fell sleep.

I didn't expect to find him next to me in the morning, and I was right but there was a cup of cool tea on the bedside table next to the open tube of KY. I took the tea through to the bathroom and poured it down the loo. I showered quickly, pulled on a pair of black leggings and a bright pink sweater, applied a little makeup and made my way downstairs.

Richard was on the sofa and looked up as I walked into the sitting room.

"Thanks for the tea. I'm going to make some fresh. Would you like a cup?"

"That would be very nice Lucie, thank you." He sounded slightly subdued.

I took the mugs through, put them both in the dishwasher and made fresh tea in clean mugs, it seemed really important to have clean mugs.

As I returned to the sitting room, Richard stood up. "Lucie, I'm sorry."

"What about?" There seemed so much for him to apologise for.

"Well, about last night." He looked embarrassed. "I didn't mean to hurt you."

"It's ok. It was just a bit of a surprise but it's ok. I'm still talking to you."

"God knows why."

"You know Richard, whatever you say, love really does matter." I sat down and looked up at him.

He cleared his throat as he resumed his seat on the sofa. "The snow seems to be clearing so the roads shouldn't be too bad but I really don't want to get home late."

"I understand completely. So, when do you think you ought to hit the road?"

"Probably lunchtime." I watched him carefully. He looked slightly ill at ease.

"Doesn't give us very long, does it?"

"Well, no." He was looking more uncomfortable.

As we finished our breakfast, I looked at my watch. "It's just after ten thirty. Not much time left at all, is there?" I looked at him steadily.

He looked back at me. "I really am trying to sort things out Lucie. I can't bear hurting you. Of course I care deeply about you ..."

I took a deep breath but remained silent. I knew if I started being pedantic, it would end up in yet another pointless argument. After all, what was in a word? As long as he felt what I called 'love' then I thought all would be well.

"But there are things that bother me. And you know me; I need to have things clear in my own mind."

"I don't know what I can say to you. You want 'assurances that things are on the up'? I know that the work which always comes my way is often last-minute which isn't always comfortable but that's just the way it is for me. I've managed since Alex died and I'm really proud of that. No, no, please let me finish ..." Richard had looked as if he wanted to speak but I was determined to finish what I'd started. "I never stop being open to possibilities. Remember that man yesterday? The one you said just wanted to get into my knickers? Well, had it occurred to you that maybe, just maybe, that might be a real opportunity? But no, no - you just have to be suspicious of anyone who thinks that I'm worthwhile." I took a deep breath.

"I don't always look at the negative." He sounded defensive. "If this is a genuine chance to do something worthwhile, then good for you, but I don't think it's the case in this instance. But don't you see Lucie that I can't possibly make any real commitment until I'm sure that we could afford the lifestyle that we both want. I have no intention of diminishing my life by being with you ..."

"Stop. Just stop right now." I was shaking, partly with fear but mainly in fury. "Can't you hear how awful that sounds? You want a balance sheet and profit and loss account of my circumstances and then you'll make a decision as to whether I'm a good enough bet? Really? So, everything comes down to money, does it?"

I stood up and looked down at him. "I've never hidden the fact that I often struggle with work but something always seems to come along just when I need it. My God Richard, I never stop looking for opportunities and all you can say is that I'll probably devalue your life?" By this time I was almost shouting with anger. I paused and took breath. "You know I love you," I said more softly, "and you know that I believe that if two people love each other, there's nothing they can't do. It saddens me beyond belief that you don't trust me."

"I do trust you," Richard interrupted, looking startled.

"No, no, you don't. You don't trust me when I say that I'll get work. You don't trust me when I say that I'm coping financially. You don't trust me to make sensible decisions. And I'm not sure that you trust me when I say that I love you." I took Richard's face in my hands and stared down at him, wanting so badly for him to refute what I had just said but he remained silent.

"I love you." I bent to kiss him. For a moment, it was like kissing a statue and then he stood up, held me close and kissed me back with tenderness and passion. We stood holding each other close for what felt like a long, long time.

We sat at the table, gazing out at the snowy garden. It was almost as though we could read each other's minds as we talked about trivial things, deliberately avoiding anything that could lead to further disquiet and upset. I looked at my watch and saw that it was now nearly one. "Darling, it's nearly one o'clock and I absolutely don't want you to leave but you said that you wanted to be home in daylight."

Richard stretched. "Yes, I did say that, didn't I?" He looked across at me and smiled gently which made me feel warm. "I really don't want to leave you Lucie."

"Well, don't. You know I'd much prefer you to stay."

"No, I ought to get back. And you've probably got things you want to get on with." He stood up and dropped a kiss on the top of my head as he walked past me and I heard his footsteps go upstairs. Minutes later he returned and, after giving me a gentle hug and a promise to call later, he was gone.

I stayed at the table, holding the now-cold mug in my cupped hands. It seemed to be becoming our norm to have emotionally helter-skelter times together. I just hoped that he would reflect on what I'd said, and believe me when I said that with mutual love and understanding would come the answers that would allow us to be happy together.

The next few days saw the lingering snows disappear fast and even the side roads were clearing day by day, much to my relief. I was delighted to receive an email from a school in Leamington, asking me to undertake some A-level coaching in February and then later that day a college asking if I wanted to cover for someone's maternity leave from March. It was, as I knew it would be, a slow start to the year but work was starting to come in.

Thinking of Richard's Christmas present, I looked on the Royal Shakespeare Theatre's website to see what was on and saw that a production of Richard III was starting in a couple of weeks' time. Richard III I thought and smiled; his namesake. Tickets were always much more expensive at weekends so I chose a Thursday performance in the second week of February. Better check with him I thought as he was never one to enjoy unexpected surprises.

Early the next morning I rang Richard's landline and, to my surprise, there was no answer so I left a brief message. I assumed that he was in the shower or perhaps had just popped out to his local shops but after an hour it was obvious that wasn't the case. I called again and again there was no reply. I called his mobile. It rang several times and then went to voicemail so again I left a message. I didn't know why but a dull feeling of foreboding washed over me as I continued to try both his landline and mobile at ten-minute intervals.

About two hours later I heard ducks. 'Sorry. Am in London. No problems. Rxx'.

I re-read the text. No problems? Was he trying to be funny? After everything we'd said and he'd promised - I was sure he was with Julie. Against my will, tears prickled my eyes and trickled down my cheeks. My fingers hovered over the keys. 'I'm sure you're having a great day in London. With Julie? And here I was going to ask you to the theatre. Lxx'.

A few moments later his reply came. 'Yes, am with Julie. No problems. When do you want to go to the theatre? Rxx'.

I sat and stared at the screen. Why, when he continued to see another woman should I love him I asked myself but I knew the answer, he was now a habit that I found too hard to break. 'Thurs 21 Feb. 7.30. Richard III. Fancy it? Lxx'.

'Yes I can be free on that date. Sounds nice. Rxxx'

It wasn't the response I wanted and even though the very last thing I wanted to do was to have a celebratory evening out with him, I mechanically went onto the RST's website to book tickets and reserve a table at the theatre restaurant. 'Tickets booked. Happy Christmas. Lxx'. There was no reply.

Later that day, I received a text from Karen who had recently returned from a winter holiday with her mother. 'Think I can leave work early. Are you up for making me a cuppa? Kx'.

I smiled. 'Great, be good to see you. Kettle's on. See you soon. Lx'.

Half an hour later I saw Karen's red car pull onto the drive and as I opened the front door she held out a bunch of yellow roses. "Thought you'd like these. I know that you like yellow flowers."

"They're beautiful, just beautiful. So thoughtful, bless you darling. Come on in."

We went through to the kitchen and while I found a vase and arranged the roses, Karen put the kettle on. I glanced up. "Maybe something stronger?"

Karen grinned. "Great idea. I've had a really stressful day."

"There's a bottle of red that's only been open since yesterday."

"That'll do." She poured out two glasses as I put the finishing touches to the flowers and took the vase through to the sitting room.

We sank onto the sofa and toasted each other. "Good Christmas?" I asked.

"Lovely," she replied and told me about her Christmas. As I listened, I reflected on the sharp contrast between the relaxing and fun times that Karen had enjoyed and my chaotic days. "And what about you?" she asked after we'd laughed about her son's new kitten's antics.

"Oh Karen, it was difficult, makes me want to cry just thinking about it."

She looked at me sharply. "I'm so sad to hear that. I'm sorry I've been away for so long. Tell me all about it." And she sat silently while I told her about my Christmas.

"What a dickhead." She sounded angry. "What a bastard. And he's still seeing that woman?" I showed her the texts.

Karen leaned forward and took my hand. "Now listen to me. This is getting out of hand."

"But he's told me that he's trying to explain everything to her and make her see that by seeing him, she's damaging our relationship," I protested. "And Karen, I love him. It's so hard to think logically isn't it?"

She looked at me steadily. "If it were me, love or no love, I'd want to tell the lying, cheating bastard to fuck right off." I smiled at her. "But, I don't think that you're able to do that. Not yet anyway. So, you're going to have to see this through to the end. And even though, deep down, you know what the end's going to be, you're hoping that something will happen to bring him to his senses. And of course it might, it just might ..."

I sat very still absorbing what she had just said. "You're probably right. I'm so hoping that he'll see a way forward for us. I can and it seems so clear to me - it's bewildering to me that he can't ..."

"Or won't."

"Won't? What do you mean, 'won't'?"

"Well, if he's starting to get really involved with this Julie, he won't be open to anything else, will he? I mean, like so many men, he's led by his dick and from what you've said about his past, he's allowed his little friend to call the shots a fair few times."

"Little? Not a word he'd use." We giggled.

"Yeah, well, not many of them would." We nodded wisely in agreement. And then we relaxed and chatted about Karen's work for a while. After an hour and another glass of red, I stood up.

"Fancy something to eat?"

We walked into the kitchen and I looked in the fridge to see what I could find: a small piece of steak, a few leftover boiled potatoes, an onion, a couple of sad-looking carrots and half a chilli. While Karen peeled and diced the vegetables, I sliced the steak into fine strips and took some peas and sweetcorn out of the freezer. "Stir fry I think, don't you?" I shook some soy sauce over the meat and added a little olive oil. "Ten minutes should do it." After a quick marinade, I took out my trusty wok and stir-fried the vegetables and steak, watching as everything sizzled and then ladled the food into bowls which we ate in front of the fire.

"Delicious, really yummy." I had to agree.

By ten o'clock we were both talked out and she left, saying that our next dinner would be at hers very soon.

The following day I prepared for the coaching classes I'd been asked to deliver in February. As always, I found work completely engrossing and the time passed quickly. I'd been sitting at the computer for so long that I had to unkink my back as I stood up but felt proud and very satisfied with what I had achieved.

Richard arrived on Friday evening but looked tired and worn. We had dinner at home that evening and when, eventually, we went to bed he seemed pre-occupied. Sex was hurried and perfunctory leaving me disappointed and unsatisfied. On Saturday after breakfast, we walked into town, looked round some shops, lunched at the One Elm and then strolled home. We watched a movie and then went upstairs.

I was already in bed as Richard undressed and went to the bathroom. I really don't want more of the same I thought to myself so curled up on my side of the bed and closed my eyes. I heard Richard come into the bedroom but didn't move as I felt him get into bed. He leaned over. "Lucie, are you awake?" I lay still, keeping my breathing slow and steady. After a few moments, he moved to his side of the bed and I heard his breathing deepen as he went to sleep. I lay still, my eyes wide open, wondering what the next day would bring.

On Sunday, after breakfast, we read the papers; as it was a dull, cold day. we decided to stay in. I love lazy Sundays in front of the fire but sensed Richard's disquiet so it came as no surprise when he announced that he wanted to get back in daylight. As I watched him leave, unusually, I felt a strange sense of relief.

.

Chapter 3 - February

Susie's birthday was in February and, when she was a little girl, her birthday celebrations had brightened an otherwise dull month. Ever since she'd left home I'd found February very gloomy and this year was no exception.

The first half of the month was fairly dismal apart from work which always made me feel more uplifted and positive. It wasn't just the money which of course was the prime motivator for working; it was the feeling of doing something worthwhile and helpful.

I was kept very busy with the coaching sessions for the school in Leamington Spa; the staff were very welcoming too which made it much more of a pleasure to be there. I particularly liked Annie, a part-time arts teacher. She told me that she was on a dating website and had met several perfectly nice men, but no-one who had matched her ideal. "But it's great fun going out with lots of different people. I'm having a great time." As I heard her story, I reminded myself how lucky I was to be in a relationship, albeit a slightly rocky one.

Late one afternoon, Roger the senior maths tutor, came over to me as I was photocopying some handouts for my first class of the following day to ask how everything was going for me. I looked up from battling with the recalcitrant machine I'd been struggling with. "Well, apart from wanting to kill this bloody copier, things are going well. They're great kids, aren't they?"

"They're not bad. Some need a nudge in the right direction, but on the whole they're ok."

"I think so. It's a real pleasure working with them. I'm going to miss them."

"Why? Are you leaving us?" Roger looked surprised.

"Well, yes, I think so. Far as I know, I'm just here for the month."

"Hmmm, we'll have to see about that." He sounded reflective. "I've been hearing some very positive things about you. Seems like the groups really like you and are making good progress very quickly. Don't be surprised if you're asked to stay on til at least Easter."

I beamed at him. "That would be great. Really great. I like it here a lot."

Roger smiled. 'Well, that's good news. I'll let the head of department know that you're up for extending your time with us." He paused. "By the way Lucie, would you like to join a couple of us for a drink this evening? If you're likely to be here for longer, it'd be good to get to know the team."

"Good idea. Yes please, I'd love to."

We agreed to meet at the Saxon Mill, a restaurant just out of town, so I left the school at five thirty, feeling very virtuous having prepared all of the following week's classes and arrived at the pub just before six to find Roger sitting there alone. "Where are the others?" I asked as I sat next to him.

"They'll be along later. Now, what would you like to drink?"

Much as I'd have liked a glass of Merlot, I knew that one would inevitably lead to another and as I was driving, decided not to start at all. "A slimline tonic with a few drops of Angostura Bitters please."

The next time I glanced at my watch it was nine thirty, no-one had joined us but we hadn't stopped talking. We'd talked about school, the students, our respective subject areas, our kids and a bit about our personal lives. I learned that Roger was divorced, had three grown-up children two of whom lived and worked in London where their mother was based, and that the youngest boy had learning difficulties and was still living at home with Roger. "It's really hard sometimes but he's a great kid and we rub along pretty well most of the time." I looked at him with new respect as I heard his story.

"Hey, where are the others?" I asked after a while.

Roger looked slightly uncomfortable. "I didn't think you'd have come if it was just me."

I leaned across and lightly tapped his hand. "You idiot - why wouldn't I be up for having a drink with a work mate?"

He looked relieved. "I don't know but I just thought you might not. I mean, you're in a relationship, aren't you?"

"I think I am."

Roger looked surprised. "What do you mean?"

"Oh, it's a bit of a sad story and would take far too long to explain, maybe another time." We chatted for a little longer and, just before ten, I stretched and looked at my watch. "Time to go - I'm teaching first thing."

Roger stood up and walked me to my car. "You take care," he suddenly sounded serious. "You're really nice - I'd hate to see you hurt."

"I'm fine Roger. See you tomorrow morning."

It was about ten thirty when I arrived home. I picked up the phone to see if there were any messages. There was one from an agency asking me to call them about a potential contract and one from Richard. "I'm ringing for our usual chat but you're not there. Where are you? If it's not too late when you get back from carousing give me call. Who are you with anyway?"

I debated for a moment whether to call him or not. Part of me wanted to make him wonder and perhaps worry about what I was doing and who I was with, but the other part of me wanted to behave properly - behave in the way I'd want to be treated. I rang his number and within a few seconds he picked up.

"Hello? Richard? How are you?"

"Where've you been?" He sounded annoyed.

"I'm fine thank you darling. I've been out with some colleagues for a drink. We had a very nice time - talking mainly about work of course."

Now, why not tell him you've been having a drink with just one colleague? I ignored the little voice in my head and we continued to talk about our respective days.

True to our usual arrangement, Richard arrived on Friday evening. I was determined that we would have a good weekend and tried to think of something different from our normal routine. "Lucie, I'm a bit tired. Let's stay in and relax," was his response when I suggested that we take in a movie. I stifled a retort and cooked dinner, salmon on a bed of potatoes, onion and vine tomatoes with some mange tout which, as usual, he pronounced as 'very good'.

Most of the weekend followed the same pattern as so many previous weekends which made me feel exasperated and sad in equal measure.

Sunday morning brought our usual cups of tea and late breakfast of porridge. "What do you fancy doing today?" Richard asked as we sat over our third cup.

I'd arranged to meet some girlfriends that afternoon at the Welcombe, a large, luxurious hotel a couple of miles out of town set at the foot of the Welcombe Hills. It was a late Christmas treat that we'd organised several weeks ago and something that I'd been looking forward to.

"Remember that I'm meeting the girls for afternoon tea?"

Richard frowned slightly. "No men allowed then?"

"No. It's for us girlies. I'm sure I mentioned it a couple of weeks ago - didn't I?"

"You might have done. I'd forgotten if you did." Richard was unsmilingly. "Why do you women insist on meeting up so much without partners? Bit sexist isn't it?"

I sighed. We'd had this conversation several times before.

Richard regarded me unsmilingly. "Seems that you think more about your girlfriends than me."

"Oh, for God's sake, don't be so ridiculous. It's just afternoon tea with some friends." I was going to add something like 'so why don't you go for a walk and then join us towards the end of the afternoon' when he stood up.

"Well, it's obvious that you don't need me around this afternoon. Think I'll clear off and leave you to it."

I sat with my mouth open in astonishment. "Where the hell did that come from? All I've said is that I'll be out for a while. Why's this such a huge deal?" My heart was thumping.

"I just think if I go, you'll have time to get ready and have a nice afternoon. I understand the girls are important to you and certainly don't want to come between you." And with that he left the room.

I sat at the table in absolute bewilderment. It seemed that more and more we were ricocheting from one extreme to another. Sometimes we were able to be soft, loving and relaxed and then, within a heartbeat, at complete odds. I leaned forward and put my head in my hands and was like that when I heard Richard's footsteps returning. I looked up to see him fully dressed.

"Have a good afternoon with the girls." He kissed the top of my head lightly.

I stood up and tried to hug him but he'd stepped back. "I don't understand this at all. You could stay, go for a walk and then join us towards the end of the afternoon. We could have the rest of the morning together. You could stay tonight. Richard, what's happening?"

"There's stuff I need to do at home anyway and if you're out this afternoon, I'll give you a bit of space. That's all. No problems, Lucie." No problems, the little voice in my head said in my ear. Really? Now, why is he so eager to leave? Is it any excuse to go? Any excuse to make you in the wrong? I stepped towards him and held up my arms, as I did so he embraced me briefly. "Lucie, it's ok. It just seems silly for me to be hanging around while you get ready and then go out when there's stuff I could be getting on with at home. Have a good time with your girlfriends. I'll give you a ring later – see if you're back"

I rang Anita who promptly invited me round for a drink, so I hurriedly got ready, and within half an hour was sitting at her kitchen table while she and her husband, John, listened patiently as I told them what had happened.

"Lucie, just stop it," John said. "This has gone on for long enough and well you know it. You're worth so much more than this. Why are you putting up with him?" There was little love lost between Richard and John so I felt I had to take what he was saying with a pinch of salt. Then Anita chimed in.

"John's right, you know ..."

"I know," I interrupted, "and bless you both for being there for me but, I'm so tied into him and just can't let go ..." My voice faded away and I sat silently as they both looked at me, Anita with a worried frown and John with a slightly cynical smile.

"We're always, always here for you. You know that. Whatever, whenever. You do what you have to do but just know that we'll always support you." I blinked back tears as I hugged her.

A little later I drove her over to the Welcombe where we all congregated and, as I'd expected, had a wonderfully relaxing and cheerful afternoon, eating tiny sandwiches and delicate cakes, drinking Earl Grey tea and catching up with each other's news. I'd managed to sidestep talking about Richard; it was too raw and painful to share.

The following week, my students were away on an educational visit to France for a few days, so effectively I had the week off which was a welcome break. Of course, it was less welcome financially, but it was good to have time to refresh my CV and look for other work.

On Monday morning the agency called to tell me that they wanted to put me forward for a contract to support students at the local university for a couple of weeks with study and research skills and did I want to consider this? Of course I did, I told them emphatically and they agreed to set up a telephone interview as soon as possible. The university called on Wednesday afternoon and it was agreed that I should start off with them for one day a week after Easter to give support to first year students who were struggling with their assignments. I had always relished this kind of work and was delighted to accept their offer.

It was Valentine's Day on Friday. As soon as I awoke I sent Richard a text even though I'd posted a slushy card to him the previous day. 'XxXxXxX' was what I sent him at six thirty. Half an hour later I received 'Is that all I get? No poems? No hearts? Rxxx' swiftly followed by 'Don't waste time making up a poem, get on with some work! Rxxx'. I sat back and then tapped 'Too early for poetry. Just big hugs and xxxxes'. Even on Valentine's Day he had to mention work I thought and sighed.

When the post arrived later that morning, there were only bills and a couple of pieces of junk mail, nothing with hearts and flowers from Richard. I knew that he didn't particularly like occasions like Valentine's Day, saying that they were just money making opportunities but he'd sent cards in previous years which had made me feel loved and special. So, nothing this year I reflected as I tore up the junk mail and dumped it into the recycling bin.

I'd found a rather swish bottle opener in November, meaning to give it to Richard as part of his Christmas presents but had forgotten to do so, and had decided to give it to him as a Valentine's Day gift, but was so angry and disappointed, I flung it back in the drawer. Nevertheless, I went to the supermarket, as I usually did, on a Friday to buy a bottle of Southern Comfort together with food that I knew he liked. I'd hoped and half expected that he would suggest eating out to celebrate Valentine's Day that evening but nothing had been mentioned so I picked up a piece of cod loin, some chicken, chorizo, olives and assorted fruit and vegetables together with a large loaf of artisan bread and a couple of interesting cheeses. As I unpacked and put away the food I wondered what else I could do to reassure him that, given love and understanding, all could and would be well with us.

Richard arrived just after seven that evening and as I drizzled olive oil over the cod on a bed of parboiled potatoes, cherry tomatoes with strips of chorizo and put it in the oven to roast, prepared a rocket, cucumber and red onion salad and laid the table, he lounged against the kitchen door sipping his usual Southern Comfort on ice watching me. "You really like cooking, don't you?"

I looked up and saw that he was smiling indulgently at me. "Love it. Really love it."

He laughed. "Well, you're certainly an advertisement for good food."

I was beginning to feel as though I was being provoked into an argument and was determined not to rise to the bait so quickly changed the subject. "Darling, there's a bottle of Prosecco in the fridge. Would you open it and pour us a couple of glasses please?" I spoke quickly so he didn't have the chance to say anything else.

After dinner, we sat and watched a DVD that Richard had brought up with him, and then went to bed. Richard came into the bedroom and smiled as he looked down at me on his side of the bed. He slid under the duvet as I shifted slightly to give him room to join me. His hands moved over my body and as I wrapped my arms around his neck we kissed, not particularly passionately, but affectionately. He lowered his head to softly nibble my nipples and as I draped one leg over his hip and pushed myself towards him, he penetrated me and we rocked gently together until, a minute or so later he came with a sigh.

"You ok?" he asked as he lay back. I knew what that meant; I was on my own again.

"Yes, I'm fine thanks." He closed his eyes and I heard his breathing deepen. I lay and stared into the darkness.

It was a drizzly morning that Saturday but despite that, we walked into town for our customary mooch around the shops before enjoying lunch at the One Elm. Our conversation was light and as it had been many years before. It was dark when we strolled back up the hill. As I opened the front door, I saw that the post had been delivered and as I picked the sheaf of bills and junk mail up, saw a red envelope. I carried the envelopes through to my desk, sat down and started opening the post, deliberately leaving the red envelope til last. When at last I opened it, of course expecting it to be from Richard, I was amazed to see that the card, which was slightly slushy hearts and flowers, was anonymous. Richard always signed his cards and I now saw that the handwriting, although similar, wasn't his. I re-read 'For a very beautiful and very fanciable lady X'. I was holding the card with a small smile on my face when Richard joined me.

He reached down and took the card out of my hand. "Who the hell's been sending stuff like this to you?"

I looked up at him. "I have no idea Richard, none at all. Probably a joke from one of the kids I've been teaching."

"And how did anyone get your address?"

"Again, no idea. But it's not hard to find these things out, is it?"

He stared down at me, blue eyes hard and flinty. Before he could say anything, I stood up. "Don't make this into something it's not. It's just a silly card, probably sent as a joke. I have no idea who it's from and, quite frankly, I don't care. So please, don't let's have an argument about something that means nothing to me." I dropped the card into the wastebin next to the desk.

"Now, tell me - who was that card from?" Clearly, he wasn't about to give up.

"Oh for goodness sake, I've already said that I have no idea. It's just a silly card, probably from one of my students who thinks it's funny to send a card like that to a teacher." I stepped close to Richard and put my arms round his neck. "You ought to be flattered."

He stared down at me unsmilingly. "Why?"

"Because I'm with you and someone else thinks I'm nice. But you're the one I truly care for, you're the one I love, you're the one I go to bed with ..."

I felt his arms tighten round me and nestled my head under his chin. We stood like that for what seemed like a long time and gradually felt myself relaxing into him. He was the first one to break the embrace.

We sat at the table with a glass of wine and I talked about what I was planning for my students the following week. "You know, they're good kids. They find some subjects very hard, mainly because they can't see the relevance to their world. And it was so nice to learn that I'm getting positive feedback which will probably mean I'll be there til Easter."

Richard leaned back reflectively. "Yes, that is good. But it's all very last minute, isn't it? I mean, it's difficult to plan ahead. Holidays and things like that."

I sat very still. "So what are you saying? That what I'm doing isn't good enough?"

He looked at me and gave me a small smile. "No Lucie, I'm not saying that. But I am saying that your work and income makes it hard to plan. That's all."

I knew I needed to change the subject otherwise we'd end up in yet another argument that would inevitably spiral out of control. "So, what shall we do this evening?" I said as brightly as I could. After a few minutes' discussion, we agreed that we would stay in and watch a movie. I stifled a sigh of exasperation - another weekend that seemed set to follow the same old same old routine. So, I made some soup which used up the half cauliflower I had in the fridge with some blue cheese that should have been Roquefort but worked just as well. As we ate the soup with crusty bread, Richard smiled across at me. "Very good Lucie, very good. This is one of your best ever soups." I smiled my thanks for the compliment.

I decided to treat myself to a hot scented bubble bath as Richard wanted to watch a horror movie so went upstairs and unexpectedly felt tears in my eyes. You only spend weekends together the little voice in my head said, so why is he downstairs while you're upstairs? Bit silly, isn't it?

After washing my makeup off, I stared at myself in the bathroom mirror. I was sad beyond belief that the relationship I thought was so stable seemed to be slipping through my fingers. Equally I was furious that Richard was treating me in such a cavalier manner and, perhaps even more than that - that I was allowing it to happen. I was exhausted with the conflicting emotions that I'd been enduring for what seemed like an awful long time.

It was pouring with rain on Sunday morning and as we sat over breakfast, we agreed that it wasn't a day to be out and about. "Let's just light the fire, get the Sunday papers and relax," I suggested.

"Hmmm. Well, I've got quite of lot of things to do at home so perhaps I'll nip back. I'm coming up again on Thursday for the theatre anyway."

I knew that if I confronted Richard about why he wanted to leave so early and how that made me feel, we would inevitably have an argument and I felt far too weary to bear that, so I kept quiet as he went upstairs to pack.

A few minutes later he was downstairs. "Bye then. See you on Thursday." He gave me a brief hug and kissed my cheek. I hugged back and kissed his mouth.

"Bye darling. Drive safely. See you on Thursday - looking forward to it." I watched him put his bag into his car and reverse off the drive we'd spent so long building together. I waved him off and once he had turned the corner went back into the house.

"Fuck it, fuck it to hell," I whispered aloud as I laid the fire before grabbing my umbrella to walk round to the local newsagent, buy the Sunday papers and a huge bar of chocolate. I lit the fire and made a very large pot of coffee. I felt angry and disappointed, and as I tried to read the papers, my emotions wouldn't let me concentrate.

I did manage to finish off the preparation needed for next week's work though, before talking to Di and Anita on the phone and Skyping with Susie. I then visited Pennie and Simon for tea and shared a bottle of wine in the evening with Karen. As I lay in bed that night, I realised that the time without Richard had been full of friendship, care and laughter, a far cry from our normal days. And what does that tell you, the little voice in my head muttered. Shut up, you just shut up I told the voice. We're going to be alright, we're going to be alright ... and clinging onto those thoughts, I fell asleep.

The next week, my students were back from their time in France and full of excitement about their experiences, so Monday was spent talking about their trip and by Tuesday morning, I was just about able to refocus them onto the business in hand. They were a very likeable group and took their studies seriously which meant that working with them was a real pleasure.

On my return home on Tuesday afternoon, I spotted a red envelope along with a couple of pieces of junk mail. I opened it and saw that it was a funny, slightly rude, Valentine's card from Richard in which he'd simply written 'Richard X'. I smiled wryly as I read it. I don't know what made me do so, but I looked at the postmark and saw that it was yesterday's - the 17th. Clearly, he'd only sent me a card because I'd sent him one and presumably felt slightly guilty. I sat holding the card, staring at his small, neat handwriting until the words began to blur. I then stood up, slowly ripped the card into small pieces and threw them into the recycling bin.

I was only required to be with my students on the Wednesday morning and as there were no meetings, decided to go home at lunchtime. I called Felicity on the way home and we agreed to meet in Maria's café for a coffee. I found a space in a nearby car park and made my way to the café and while waiting for Felicity to join me, decided to text Richard. 'Hello darling. How are you today? So looking forward to tomorrow. Lxxx' and as I waited for a reply, Felicity joined me. While we waited for our sandwiches and coffee to arrive, my phone quacked. Felicity frowned - by her own admission she was a Luddite and hated the way mobiles intruded into everyday life. 'I'm fine. Giving Julie and her friend a lift from Gatwick. Rxxx' I stared at the screen in disbelief.

Felicity looked across at me. "Lucie? What's wrong? You look awful."

I continued staring at the screen and then passed the phone over to her. She read it and then gave it back to me. I looked at her. "What the hell's he playing at? He knows how much I hate him even being in contact with her and he just doesn't stop. In fact, I think he's seeing her pretty much every week now."

"It might be perfectly innocent, you know. I mean, he's known her for years and ..."

"And what?" I interrupted. "Felicity, I feel such a fool. He's doing something that he knows hurts me, that I don't like and yet he keeps on doing it. And, stupid cow that I am - I put up with it ..."

"Why do you put up with it?"

"Because I love him. I must do, otherwise I wouldn't tolerate all this, would I? And at my age, well, it's really hard to meet people. Remember, I dated a lot of men before Richard came along."

The arrival of our sandwiches and coffee interrupted us and we sat in silence for a few moments. I sipped my coffee, ignoring the sandwich which looked very appetising. "This is really good," Felicity said as she ate her chicken salad baguette.

I looked at my pastrami and coleslaw sandwich and then took a small bite, it was indeed delicious but I couldn't face it. "I'll ask Maria to put it in a doggy bag for me. I just can't face eating at the moment. Sorry."

"You've got to stop this. You know it's doing you no good and, quite frankly, all we keep hearing is the same old thing. I'm not being unkind - well, maybe I am a bit, but you have to decide whether you can put up with him the way he is or get out. This constant wondering, guessing and worrying is draining you of all your get-up-and-go. You're always tired - you look tired, you sound tired."

I sat with my head bowed over my coffee, trying to stop my tears. "I know you're probably right but I can't give him up. I'm in too deep. I keep hoping that he'll see what a great thing we've got between us and then we'll be able to talk about our future." I looked up at her. "You know what loving like this is. It's ..."

"Loving like this shouldn't hurt the way it's hurting you. Love can be bittersweet of course, but you're being ripped apart and it's horrible to watch."

I sat upright. "I've just come to a decision," I paused. "I'm going to put a time limit on this. I'm going to do my very, very best to make this work. I know that it might not, but I really believe that it could, and I think it's worth a real go."

"And just how long are you going to let this continue?"

I blinked. "Well ..." I looked at her pleadingly and she looked back at me steadily without saying anything. "The summer. The end of the summer."

Felicity looked sceptical. "Well, of course, it's up to you. But I think it's crazy going on like this. Lucie, just ask yourself, if he's behaving like this now, what on earth would it be like if you ever got to live together? He'd be calling the shots all the time and you'd find yourself having to accept whatever shit he dished out."

I gasped. Felicity wasn't known for her bad language and I knew that she must have been very irritated to have used the sh-word. "You just be careful what you wish for. Are you really sure that he's what you want?"

"I don't know Felicity ..."

"I rather think you do. Now, eat that bloody sandwich, will you?"

It was nearly four o'clock when I arrived home and, as always, was greeted by my furry companions. I lit the fire and sat in front of it, with a cat on either side. I looked at Richard's text again and started to feel the tears threaten. Stop it, stop that right now - it's time to fight back. 'Really? How nice of you. Can't she afford a taxi? Lxx'. There was no reply.

I tried Richard's landline at six, seven and eight o'clock, each time there was no reply. It must have been close to half past ten when my landline rang, it was Richard for our normal chat. After the how-are-yous I took a deep breath. "Tell me Richard, why did you go and meet Julie from her flight?"

"She asked me to," was his neutral reply.

"And you do what she asks?"

He started to sound angry. "Look, I keep telling you. I'm helping her because she's in a bad place. You know Lucie, I'm a nice bloke and like helping people. And I feel it's right to do this in Patrick's memory. Stop being so selfish. You're being really silly about this. Julie's just a friend. I don't know how often I have to tell you ..."

"I tried you earlier this evening," I interrupted.

"Yes, well, Julie insisted on giving me dinner as a thank you."

"Was her girlfriend there?"

There was a pause. "Erm, no. No, we dropped her off before getting to Julie's place."

I sat in silence, holding the phone tightly.

"Lucie, are you still there?"

"Yes, I'm here," I said very softly.

There was another pause. "Look, talking over the phone probably isn't the best thing to do at the moment. I'll see you tomorrow. What time should I get to you?"

For a split second I actually thought of telling him not to come up. Not tomorrow, not ever.

I paused. "About four thirty ok for you? The table's booked for six."

"Four thirty's good for me. See you then. Night night Lucie."

"Night night." I clutched the handset for several more minutes before putting in gently onto its rest.

I awoke early the next morning and immersed myself in work which always made me feel better. The day passed quickly as I worked with the students in the morning and attended a staff meeting in the afternoon which, luckily, finished early so I was able to get home just before three thirty.

Richard arrived just after four thirty and seemed in good spirits. He gave me a warm hug and kiss. "You go and get ready," he urged as he did so. "You've been working all day and I've just been relaxing." He patted my bottom gently.

Slowly I walked upstairs. I felt a mass of contradictory emotions, from shaking fury to the warm rush of love that always swept over me when I first saw his car pull up onto the drive. I stepped under the shower and quickly washed my hair and after I'd blasted it dry, put on my makeup with care. I was getting dressed in an ankle-length black dress with black high heeled boots and a red and black scarf when Richard came upstairs. "I heard you in the shower, so waited til you'd finished before bringing you a drink." He held out a glass as he looked me up and down.

He stepped towards me. Normally I would have melted but being readily compliant clearly didn't work so perhaps, I reasoned, a different tactic would.

I put my hand on his chest. "Easy tiger," I smiled, "you wouldn't want to mess up my makeup, would you?"

"I might want to do just that." He pulled me towards him.

I kept my hand pressed against his chest. "Later. Let's go and see what your namesake's been up to." He looked down at me disbelievingly; he wasn't used to any kind of rejection from me and was visibly surprised. I gazed at him and kissed the end of his nose. "Come on darling. Time to go," and with that I left the room and walked downstairs.

It was a cold clear evening so we walked down to the theatre and by six we were seated at our table, looking at the menu. Richard decided on smoked mackerel and capers, roast shoulder of lamb with winter vegetables and steamed chocolate sponge served with vanilla ice cream. I chose beef carpaccio, confit of pork belly with a butterbean and chorizo cassoulet and salted caramel tart served with banana ice cream topped with pecans. As we placed our order I asked for a bottle of champagne. Richard raised his eyebrows. "What are we celebrating?"

"Christmas," I said briefly and then raised my glass. "Let's toast Christmas."

He smiled and raised his glass in return. "You silly girl." There was real affection in his voice. As each course was brought to the table, we agreed that they were all beautifully presented and absolutely delicious.

The production was, as usual for the RST, breathtakingly good and we agreed on the walk home that we had both thoroughly enjoyed it. "Lovely evening, really lovely."

"Yes, it was. Thank you for my Christmas present."

I smiled up at him. "My pleasure darling. Shall we have a nightcap before turning in?"

When I returned a few minutes later, Richard was sitting in his customary place on the sofa, watching the news. I stifled my irritation as I handed him his Southern Comfort. I would so much rather have cuddled up together but I could see he was engrossed so I settled myself in my usual chair. After half an hour or so I could bear it no longer and stood up. "Think I'll go up."

He looked up and smiled. "You go and warm the bed. I'll be up in a few minutes."

I smiled back with more warmth than I felt and blew him a kiss.

True to his word, he came upstairs a few minutes later and as I lay in bed, dutifully warming his side, I heard him undressing in the spare room, his dressing room as he called it. He smiled as he came into the bedroom and reached for me, stroking my body with more tenderness and care than he had shown for many weeks which made me quiver and ache for him. He followed his hands with his mouth and kissed, licked and nibbled his way down my throat, to my breasts, then down to my belly and hips. As he kissed his way back towards my face, he gently tweaked my nipples which made me sigh with pleasure. I held his face in my hands and kissed his cheeks, his forehead, his chin and finally his mouth while slowly arching my body into his and as I did so I realised, to my surprise, that he was soft. I reached down and gently held him but despite my ministrations he remained unresponsive. "Oh shit," I heard him mutter in frustration.

I wound my other arm around him and held him close. "Hey, it's all ok."

"No it's bloody well not." He sounded angry and pushed my hand away, falling back on the pillows. I leaned towards him and tried to hug him but he lay still, it was as if he was now a million miles away from me.

"Just leave me alone will you." He turned away from me.

I stared at his hunched shoulders and reached out to touch him only to see, to my bewildered astonishment, him flinch from me. "For Christ's sake, leave me be."

Obediently I raised my hand from his shoulder and slowly retreated to my side of the bed, lying on my right side, still facing his back. Unbidden tears rolled silently into my pillow as I closed my eyes.

I woke at about four on Friday morning, still facing his back and crept out of bed as quietly as I could. I curled up on the sofa and wondered how best to deal with Richard's volatility. By six, I was incredibly cold and stiff so spent the next ten minutes standing under a steaming hot shower which made me feel lots better. I tiptoed into the bedroom, grabbed a pair of black leggings, a white sweater, a pair of warm socks and stole back out. I dressed in the warm bathroom, then realised that I hadn't picked up my makeup so sneaked back in. As I reached for my makeup bag I sensed Richard's eyes on me and looked down to see him gazing up at me.

I stayed where I was, watching him and a few moments later he looked at me. "You ok?"

"I'm fine thanks." I didn't feel fine at all but there seemed little point in making waves this early in the morning.

Later, Richard joined me in the kitchen and as we ate breakfast together I felt surprisingly calm and relaxed. I made us coffee and as I handed Richard his, he leaned across and held my hand. "Thank you," he said quietly. "You're so good to me, aren't you?" He was still holding my hand. I raised my eyebrows in puzzlement. "You give me a lovely evening, make me a nice breakfast, put up with my nonsense ..."

"What nonsense?" I asked, my heart thumping. I really didn't want an in-depth you're not fit enough, you don't make enough money, Julie-fuelled conversation right now.

"Well, you know ..." He looked embarrassed. "In bed. Last night, you know ..."

I breathed a silent sigh of relief. "Oh that. Don't be silly. You were just tired. We both were, weren't we?" I squeezed his hand and then leaned across and kissed his cheek. He'd said earlier that he wanted to go home and return on Saturday morning so after we said out goodbyes and I waved him off, I made my way to school.

I arrived home just after two to hear a Robin-Hood-like fanfare on my mobile which heralded an email. I read a brief email from Karen. 'Just been given two tickets for a preview at The Swan for tonight. Fancy coming with me?' One of Karen's friends worked at the theatre which meant she occasionally received tickets and, very generously, she often invited me.

'Love to. Thanks so much. Fancy a lite bite here before we go?'

'Great. I'll be with you just after five'.

I smiled as I went into the kitchen to see what I could see in the cupboard to make us an early dinner. I found some penne pasta and some shreds of cheese in the fridge. Mmmm, cheesey pasta bake I said to myself. On further investigation I unearthed a few florets of cauliflower and broccoli so I blanched them and then put them into another dish which I topped with some shredded mozzarella and grated cheddar. Yummy, I said to myself as I cleared the kitchen.

It was just after five when Karen's small red car pulled onto the drive. I opened the front door and we hugged warmly. I put the two dishes of pasta bake and vegetables into the oven to cook through and put the kettle on. Half an hour later we were enjoying the comfort food that I'd prepared earlier. "This is delicious, thank you."

I smiled "My pleasure. It is good, isn't it? So simple, yet so scrummy."

It was a cold night but as the skies were clear, we decided to walk down to the theatre. "Let's nip into the Dirty Duck for a drink," I suggested. We were fortunate to find seats by the open fire and sat by it, nursing our respective glasses of red.

Karen looked across at me. "You ok?"

"Yes, yes of course I am."

"Hmmm, so tricky Dickie's stopped being a dickhead then?"

I laughed. "Well, he's still seeing Julie but keeps assuring me that there's nothing in it. And Karen, I feel I don't have any other choice than to believe him. I know that it probably sounds ridiculous in the face of how he's behaving, but I care so deeply and so many things are good between us ..." my voice faded as I remembered the non-events of last night.

"What? What's wrong?"

"Well. Well ..." I started and then paused. Karen waited patiently. "Well, you know how sex has been a really important part of our relationship?" She nodded silently. "Well, it's not as good as it was. In fact last night he couldn't get it up at all. And for the last few weekends, it's been, well, not so good. Pretty crappy actually." I looked at Karen who was staring at me with concern in her eyes. "It's getting more and more predictable. And, on its own, I can cope with that. But add to that him seeing Julie. Him still criticising me most of the time. Him picking a fight at the slightest opportunity ..."

"Blimey. Have you heard yourself? It sounds awful. Being criticised. Being nagged. So-so sex. What the hell's keeping you with him?" She looked at me intently. "And this nonsense with Julie? That's ok is it? How can you love someone who keeps seeing someone else?"

I looked down. "I don't know how I'm managing that one. It's that that's killing me."

She stared intently at me. "Well, I've said it before – I think you should just tell him to fuck off." She drew a deep breath. "Just what will it take to make you realise what's happening?"

"You think he's actually cheating?" My heart was thumping loudly.

Karen leaned back reflectively. "Possibly. Probably. Almost certainly I'd say." She watched as tears came to my eyes. "You know what's happening Lucie. You're not stupid. Why should he bother to make an effort in bed with you when he's getting it from someone else? You know what men like him are like. It's all about the thrill of the chase. Something new. And ..."

"Stop. Please stop," I interrupted. "I can't bear the thought of him with someone else."

"Ok, ok. I understand that you love him. God knows why, but you do. And I know that he gives you enough, just enough, to make you think that this could come to something significant. Just because I don't doesn't mean that you don't. I do get that." She finished her drink and looked at me. "Now, drink up and let's go and see what this play's all about."

We were watching a preview of Arden of Faversham which is all about a wife cheating on her husband. As both Karen with her ex-husband and I with my present partner well understood what cheating meant, it seemed all the more poignant. The production was loud, active, raunchy and very, very bloody and by the end of it we were both emotionally spent.

"That was amazing. Thank you so much for inviting me," I said as we stepped outside, our breath showing white in front of our faces.

"My pleasure. Seems kind of appropriate that we saw that together, don't you think?"

We strolled back to mine, chatting about this and that when Karen suddenly said. "I don't suppose you remember Nick, do you?"

I did indeed remember Nick. He'd been in Karen's life for just over a year and led her a merry dance. I had only met him a few times but he'd seemed a slightly supercilious, arrogant, albeit good looking, young man. The last time we'd met he'd been rather drunk and extremely rude to everyone, including me. Their relationship had ended just before Christmas when Karen inadvertently saw some texts he'd been exchanging with a model in London that were explicit in the extreme, after which she kicked him into touch with absolutely no right of reply.

"Well, ages ago he gave me a present of a subscription to a foodie mag. You know 'Olive'?" I nodded. "Anyway, I keep getting it and wondered if you'd like to have it. I thought it might amuse you to have something from someone who'd been so rude to you. I'm sure it would irritate him, don't you think?"

I laughed. "I'm sure it would. And I'd love to have it. Sure you don't want it?"

Karen shook her head. "No. I don't want anything from him but I'd love you to have it. It would make me laugh to think of him paying for something for you."

"Suits me. Thanks darling."

As I opened the front door, Karen disappeared in her car. "Here it is." She waved a magazine over her head.

We sat over a cup of coffee and a chocolate biscuit apiece while I flicked through the pages. "Sure you don't want this? There are some great articles and recipes, you know."

"No, no. You can share anything you think I'd like. I don't want anything from that little shit in my house." Another hour passed as we drank more coffee, ate more biscuits and talked. After she left, I sat for a while longer, reading an article on game cooking which I found fascinating. When I glanced up I saw that it was after midnight. Too late to call Richard I thought and grimaced. I knew that he would probably have tried me earlier in the evening and would be wondering where I was. Serves him right, maybe then he'll understand why you get upset when you can't reach him. I yawned and walked upstairs, collapsed onto my bed and fell asleep almost instantly.

I was woken by the landline ringing and as I groped for the handset, I glanced at my watch and saw that it was six thirty. "Yes? Hello?"

"Lucie? So you're home now are you?" Richard's voice sounded tight and clipped.

I struggled to wake up properly. "Good morning Richard. You ok?"

"No, I don't think I am. Where were you last night? I called you several times. Didn't you check your voicemail?"

"It's six thirty," I protested. "Isn't it a bit early? And what do you mean, so I'm home now?"

"Exactly what I say. I called you last night at about eight thirty, then nine, nine thirty and ten. Either you were out or not answering the phone, which was it?" He still sounded angry.

"I don't play games by not answering the phone Richard. I was out ..."

"Who with?"

I gasped at the sheer cheek of what he was saying. "Now you just wait a minute. Yes, I was out and no, I didn't check my voicemail. I was invited to a preview of a fantastic play at the Swan and had a great time thank you. And before you ask, I went with Karen. Ok?" I was getting crosser and crosser as I spoke. "She came here to eat, we went to the theatre, drank coffee back here and talked. Then I crashed out. Anything wrong with that?"

"Oh - I'm sorry Lucie, but when I couldn't get through to you I started to get worried about you ..."

He has the nerve to be worried about who you were with after all the times he's spent with Julie, the little voice said in my ear. I nodded in silent agreement and waited for him to say something else.

"Lucie? You still there?"

"Yes. Yes, I'm here Richard. I'm really sad that you were worried. It makes me feel that you don't trust me and I've never ever done anything to let you think that you can't trust me, have I Richard?"

"No. No, of course, you haven't Lucie. I'm sorry. It was just when I couldn't get through to you ..."

"You just had to think the worst of me."

"No, Well, yes ..." There was a lengthy pause. "Do you want me to come up?" He sounded very tentative.

"Why not? Why wouldn't we have the weekend together? Or have you made other plans?" I was amazed that my voice was steady.

He sounded startled. "No, of course I haven't. I'm looking forward to us having a nice weekend ..."

"Good. When are you thinking of getting up here? Or would you like me to come down to you for a change?" I knew what the answer would be to that question.

"No. I'll come up to you. About lunchtime ok with you?"

"That's fine Richard. I'm going to put my head down and get some more sleep but I'll be bright-eyed and bushy-tailed by lunchtime. I've got to go to the bank and get a few bits and bobs, so shall I meet you in town? The One Elm? About twelve thirty?" I usually waited for him to say what we would do. It felt very good to take charge if only over something as trivial as where and when we would meet.

"Yes, that's fine with me." He sounded slightly subdued.

"Lovely. Well, I'm going to have a doze now. See you later. Drive safely." And with that I put the receiver down.

Later I sat at the table with tea and toast and 'Olive' propped up in front of me and was soon absorbed in an article about a new Italian restaurant that had recently opened in Cheltenham when the phone rang.

"Hello darling," I said, thinking that it was Richard.

"Well hello," a male voice said.

I blushed, realising that it wasn't Richard. "I'm so sorry."

"Don't be. It was rather nice to be called darling."

I searched through my mind, wondering who I was talking to. "It's Roger. Look, I'm sorry to call you on a Saturday, but ..."

"Roger. Of course. Everything alright?"

"Well, no. I'm sorry to disturb you but I knew that you'd want to know …"

"Know what? Roger, what's wrong?" I was beginning to feel very nervous.

"It's Tracy." Tracy was one of my best students, the best in fact. She was a pretty, bright, bubbly girl who looked like a stereotypical dumb blonde but was in fact as sharp as the proverbial knife. "There was an accident last night. Tracy wasn't driving but the lorry hit the passenger side of the car. She was trapped for over an hour and was pronounced dead when they managed to cut her free …" His voice faltered.

"Oh Roger. I'm so, so sorry" I could barely speak through the sobs that were threatening to break free. "Such a beautiful girl. With so much potential Oh God, her poor parents …"

I heard Roger clear his throat. "There was another reason I called this morning Lucie." He paused. "Her mother called us and said there were some books to be taken back to school. I was wondering whether you'd come with me. As her tutor, I'm the one who has to go. I know that Tracy really liked and admired you and I just thought …" His voice faded.

My mind flashed back to that dreadful day when the police had knocked on my door to tell me about Alex's fatal accident. How devastating that had been, how hard a struggle it had been to support Susie both financially and emotionally, how frightened and alone I had felt for so long and how those feelings still occasionally returned and troubled me all those years later.

I swallowed my sobs. "Yes. Yes, of course I'll come. When are you planning to go?"

"I thought about eleven thirty. She lives … lived … in Leamington. I need to call her Mum to make sure she'll be in. Lucie, thank you so much. I know you're the best person to see her."

"It's fine. Don't worry Roger. Just give me a call, probably on my mobile, and I'll be with you within half an hour." I tried to smile but my mouth was trembling too much to respond.

As I put the phone down I burst into tears and sobbed helplessly. I was crying for Tracy and her mother who had to endure the loss of her precious daughter so soon after losing her husband, but I was also crying for myself because I missed Susie so much and because I was in a relationship where I loved so much more than I was loved.

I continued to sit at the table, staring into my half empty mug of tea disbelievingly while thoughts whirled through my head. It must have been an hour later when I stiffly stood up and carried the crockery through to the kitchen while the cats weaved around my legs. I tipped some kitty biscuits into their bowls automatically and shivered as I thought of anything happening to Susie. I suddenly needed to be in touch with her so I sat at my laptop and sent her an email. 'You just popped into my head my darling. Trust all is well with you. Missing you loads. xxxxxxxxxxxxxx' and as I hit the send button I blew her imaginary kisses. I know that she was some seven hours ahead of me and, being the weekend, she was probably out and about, but just sending the email made me feel much better.

I looked at my watch. It was coming up to nine. Roger had rung back and we'd agreed to meet in a local hotel car park at about one so I knew that I had to leave Stratford by twelve thirty and still needed to get to the bank and sort out a few errands. I went upstairs to repair the damage that crying had wrought on my makeup. It seemed that I'd had to do this more and more recently but this time it was for Tracy whose bright, young life had been snuffed out. Half an hour later I was standing in a queue at the bank.

An hour later I had managed to get all my errands done and found myself standing in the market square, wondering what to do. It was far too early to meet Roger and as I wandered aimlessly down the high street, decided to spend some time down by the river. I bought a coffee on the way and managed to find an unoccupied bench in front of the theatre and sat, gazing in the dark water. After what seemed only a very few minutes, I looked at my watch and saw to my horror it was now well past eleven so quickly called Richard's landline. There was no reply. Oh no, he's left already I thought as I then tried his mobile. As I expected, there was no reply. He's driving, of course he won't pick up I thought. I left a voicemail, explaining briefly what had happened and that I had agreed to go and see Tracy's mother in the afternoon, that I didn't know when I'd be home, but that I'd leave a key out for him so he could let himself in and relax. As I finished the voicemail, I grimaced. Richard liked our weekends to be as uninterrupted as possible.

As I made my way towards my car, my mobile rang, it was Richard. "Hello darling."

"Lucie? What's happening?" He sounded slightly annoyed.

"Well ..." I explained the happenings of the morning.

"That's very sad. Tragic. And of course you must go and see her mother. How long will you be?"

"I have no idea. Probably a couple of hours but I can't say for sure."

"I'm parked at the side of the road about fifteen miles from home."

"Shall I leave a key out for you?"

There was a pause. "When did you know about this?"

"Well, Roger first called me at about eight. In fact, I thought it was you."

"Oh for God's sake Lucie. Couldn't you have called me then?"

"I'm sorry Richard. But I just didn't think ..."

"That's your trouble Lucie. You just don't think." He now sounded very cross.

I felt completely wrong-footed and foolish. Of course he was right; I should have called him sooner.

"So, what do you want to do? Shall I leave a key out for you?" I asked again, feeling indignant yet slightly timorous at the same time.

"I'm wondering whether I should come up today. I mean, you don't know how long you'll be. You'll probably be very upset and won't want to do much. I think I'll just go home"

I stood still, clutching my mobile tightly, tears prickling my eyes, made my way to the car and drove very slowly to meet Roger.

I pulled into the car park of the Chesford Grange just before one and saw Roger standing on the steps of the main entrance looking sombre. He smiled as I walked towards him. "Lucie. Good to see you." He held out his arms.

I leaned forward and gave him a brief peck on the cheek. "You too Roger. We're a bit early. Shall we have a quick coffee?"

We sat and talked about Tracy while we drank our coffees. It was very clear that we were both tremendously affected by her death.

"I just can't imagine anything worse than losing a child. I've not seen Susie for nearly a year and although we email and Skype regularly, I miss her terribly. But to know I could never ever see her again - well, it just doesn't bear thinking about."

Roger nodded grimly. "I know exactly how you feel. No matter what sacrifices are needed, we do them willingly and lovingly don't we?" I nodded. "And we have to remember that Barbara lost her husband fairly recently as well."

As we walked outside I took a few deep breaths and tried to prepare myself for what I knew would be a very heart-rending couple of hours. "I'll drive, shall I?" Roger opened his car.

I could see piles of marking on the back seat and smiled. "Typical teacher's car." I settled myself in, closed the door and Roger set off.

We turned a corner into a quiet suburban street and Roger pulled up outside number thirty one. "Here we are. Ready?"

"As ready as I'll ever be." I got out of the car and took more deep breaths. As we reached the front door, it opened and a petite, dark haired woman who had obviously been crying, smiled wanly at us. Roger cleared his throat. "Mrs Fraser?"

She nodded. "Barbara. It's Barbara."

Roger held out his hand. "I'm Roger Townsend. I'm ... I was ... Tracy's personal tutor." He cleared his throat again. "And this is Mrs Hunter - Lucie. She taught Tracy economics."

Barbara stood back. "Do come in, please." She led us into an airy living room. "Would you like a drink? Tea? Coffee?"

There was a slight pause. "I'd love a cup of tea," I said and Roger nodded his assent. "May I come and help you?" I turned to Roger. "Won't be a minute," and I followed her into an immaculate kitchen where she put the kettle on. As we stood, waiting for the kettle to boil, I touched her arm. "I can't tell you how sad I am. Tracy was a remarkable girl. You must have been so proud of her." And with that her tears flowed. I put my arm round her shoulders. "Let me make the tea. Please." She sat at the small round table in the corner of the kitchen and stared at her outstretched hands.

I made the tea, took a cup in to Roger who followed me back to the kitchen where we all sat at the table. After a few moments she looked up and swallowed hard a couple of times, and then we started to talk and cry together. We talked about Tracy, about her husband who had died nearly three years ago of pancreatic cancer, her work as a care worker in a local hospice, her parents who lived in Cornwall, Tracy's older brother who lived and worked in Melbourne and then back to Tracy. We drank more tea as we talked and darkness fell.

Roger stood at the sink and washed the mugs while Barbara and I remained at the table. "You've both been wonderful," Barbara said warmly. "Thank you for coming over."

"It's the very least we could do - and wanted to do ..."

"Absolutely," Roger added over his shoulder as he continued to wash up.

"I think I'm hungry and I really don't want to eat alone. I don't suppose ..." Barbara's voice trailed off as she looked at us.

"Well, I'm starving. I'd love something to eat. What about you Roger?"

A few moments later I was buttering some bread as Barbara opened a large cake tin. "I made this cake for Tracy. She loved my chocolate cake." She had tears in her eyes.

"I know Barbara. It all feels far too much to bear ..."

Somehow, we managed to make some sandwiches and slice the cake while Roger made tea. We then sat at the table. I realised that I really was hungry and tucked in. Barbara nibbled at one sandwich and then started to eat more. "I really was hungry." There was a note of surprise in her voice.

After we had finished the sandwiches, Barbara cut three slices of the cake and we sat looking at our plates for a few moments. She broke off a small piece and slowly ate it, Roger and I followed suit. The cake was moist and richly chocolatey. "No wonder Tracy loved this - it's very, very good," I said. Barbara smiled and we talked for another hour about Tracy.

More tea had been drunk and after we'd washed up and were taking our leave, Barbara hugged us both. "I can't thank you enough. I didn't know how I could ever get through today and you've just made it possible."

"Do call me if you ever want to talk, won't you?" I said firmly as I gave her a final hug. "You will, won't you?" Barbara nodded and then waved as we drove off.

"That was terrific - the way you listened and helped her. I know that you made a huge difference to her."

"That's very kind of you Roger but there were two of us, remember?"

"I was pretty redundant," he said reflectively.

"But you made great tea," I teased.

We arrived back at Chesford Grange where Roger got out of the car, came round to the passenger side as I got out and engulfed me in a warm embrace as I stood up. "I don't suppose you can stay for a drink can you?"

I pulled away as tactfully as I could. "That sounds really nice Roger, but I think I ought to be going now. Sorry, perhaps another time."

He looked disappointed. "I understand of course." He let me go but kept hold of my hand. "Lucie, you know if you ever need to talk, I'm always here for you."

I gently pulled my hand away. "Thanks. 'Bye Roger."

I got into my car and as I drove away I could see Roger standing by his car, watching me. See, the little voice in my head said, there are other people who think you're nice, even if Richard doesn't. You shut up, I said to the voice fiercely. He does care. He does love me. You just wait and see. The little voice fell silent as I drove home.

I called Richard's landline as soon as I arrived home. "Hello darling," I said eagerly as he picked up.

"Lucie. Nice to hear from you. How did it all go?"

"Emotional. Very emotional as you can imagine. I'm so sorry it's late but we just couldn't get away any sooner. In fact, we stayed on for a bite of tea as Barbara couldn't face eating alone. Well, that's understandable, isn't it?" I didn't know why but I could feel myself talking faster and faster.

"You ok?" Richard interrupted. "You sound a bit strange."

"I'm fine. Fine but very tired. It was a very odd afternoon. I mean, it brought back all sorts of stuff to me like when I was told about Alex's accident. Then of course, it made me think about Susie ..."

"Yes of course."

"Why don't you come up tomorrow for about eleven and I'll make us brunch?"

"That a really good idea. You sound weary Lucie. Why don't you have an early night so you're bright and chirpy tomorrow?"

"Yes, goodnight Richard."

I was woken by ducks quacking and eagerly reached for my phone thinking that it was Richard. It wasn't - it was Barbara. 'Wanted to thank you again for coming over yesterday. Can't tell you how much it helped. Barb x'

'I'm so glad to have been with you Barb – here for you whenever you want. Lx'

I looked at my watch and saw that it was just after six thirty. I realised that Barbara probably hadn't slept and shivered as I thought of Susie. It was much too early to think of getting up so I snuggled down again only to be disturbed minutes later by another text. 'Morning Lucie. Thanks so much for coming with me yesterday. You made a very hard job so much easier. Roger'. I thought about sending a reply and decided against it but as I settled down and drifted into a doze, was smiling.

A couple of hours later I heard harps and lazily reached over to press the snooze button but the second time they played, I sat up and turned the alarm off. I yawned and stretched as I slowly got out of bed and padded into the bathroom. After my usual hot shower I dressed in black leggings, black boots and my latest purchase, a bright pink sweater that I'd fallen in love with a few days ago and been amazed to find that what purported to be a baggy sweater was indeed, even on me, a baggy sweater, so how could I resist it? I dug in my makeup drawer to find a bright pink lipstick which completed the look.

After I had given the cats their breakfast and made my first cup of tea of the day, I tried Richard's landline which, after a few rings, went to voicemail. Perhaps he's in the shower I thought as I left a brief message. Half an hour later there was no reply to my message and I wasn't sure why but I had a slight feeling of unease. I was about to call again when I heard ducks. 'On my way. See you at 11. Rxxx'.

'Lovely. Brunch will be ready. Drive safely. L xxx', but I did wonder why he hadn't called me after hearing my message.

True to his word, Richard arrived at eleven on the dot. "Hello darling. Wonderful to see you." I wrapped my arms round him.

He returned my embrace. "Good to see you too Lucie. It felt very odd not seeing you on a Saturday."

"It was, wasn't it," I agreed as we went into the kitchen and he sat at the table with a sigh. "Cup of tea or some Bucks Fizz?" I asked as I started to cook the sausages.

"Oh, tea, I think." He stretched his legs out and watched me in the kitchen. "I do like watching you cook." I handed him a mug of steaming tea.

Twenty minutes later, brunch was ready. "Would you open this please?" I passed Richard the icy cold bottle of Cava and poured some orange juice into two glasses.

Brunch was delicious and two glasses of Bucks Fizz later I was feeling very mellow. "Let's go and sit by the fire." I stood up.

As Richard walked past me, I leaned towards him slightly. "You're tipsy," he said accusingly but with a smile.

"No I'm not." I smiled up at him and tilted my head for a kiss.

He looked down at me. "I think I'd better carry your drink, don't you?"

I gazed up at him. "Don't you think you should kiss me?" He bent and kissed me briefly so I reached up to hold his face while I kissed him more insistently. He accepted but didn't return my kisses and then moved away to carry the drinks through to the sitting room leaving me standing by the table.

"Fucker," I said to myself very softly. "Bastard. What the fuck's he playing at?" I stayed where I was for a few seconds while the mellowness the Bucks Fizz had given me disappeared, leaving me feeling bleak and exasperated. "I'm going to make some coffee. Would you like a cup?"

"Please." His voice floated back to me.

I made the coffees very strong and carried them through to the sitting room. I put Richard's down next to him and sat in the adjacent chair. "Thanks Lucie."

"Pleasure." I looked outside, it was cloudy but there was no sign of rain. "Shall we go out?" I stopped to think for a moment. "Let's drive over to Broadway. We can have afternoon tea in one of those quaint little tearooms. What do you think?"

So, ten minutes later we were driving through the country lanes to the very picturesque Cotswold village of Broadway. Luckily the car park had plenty of spaces and we spent a very pleasant hour or so strolling up and down the high street both window shopping and dropping into a gallery. Richard found a book on famous walks which he bought. "Perhaps there'll be one that you'd come with me on," he teased me as we strolled down the road. We were just making our way back towards a tea shop when I noticed a pale lilac-with-a-tinge-of-grey dress topped by a matching bolero jacket displayed in the centre of a smart dress shop window. I stood and gazed at it.

"I think it would suit you." Richard looked thoughtful. "Just a moment." He disappeared into the shop and before I could gather myself together, reappeared seconds later holding a large bag which he held out to me. "You deserve a treat."

I hugged him. "Oh my darling – thank you so much."

He smiled down at me. "It's a pleasure. I like making you smile." For that moment, I couldn't have been happier.

It was dark by the time we went into a tea shop and ordered tea and cakes.

"That was very nice." Richard took his new book and leafed through it.

"It was," I agreed through a mouthful of very scrumptious lemon gateau.

He laughed. "You are a hopeless case, aren't you? You just can't resist all this." He gestured towards the contents of the table. I remained silent. I knew that he wanted me to lose weight but the more he talked about it, the more I defiantly ate.

Half an hour later we were back in the car, making our way home. As I pulled onto the drive, Richard glanced at his watch. "Are you working tomorrow?"

"I am. And it'll be a difficult day." He raised his eyebrows. "You know - because of Tracy."

He nodded. "Of course. Yes, it's hard for her friends."

"And the staff. Tracy was a terrific girl and a very good student. We were all very fond of her and ..." my voice trailed away as I remembered yesterday.

Richard put his hand on mine. "I know. It's not easy for you. Trouble is you get too involved."

I looked at him, my eyes brimming with tears. "I'm sorry. I don't mean to cry but it was so tragic. And I keep thinking of Susie ..." I leaned against him and let the tears flow. I knew I wasn't crying just for Tracy. I was crying for everything in my life that was giving me pain and, to my unending sorrow, Richard figured large in that - and not even a beautiful new dress would heal that.

After a few minutes my sobs abated. I felt exhausted with all the different emotions flooding through me. I looked at Richard who still had his arm round my shoulders. "Thank you darling."

He smiled at me gently. "Let's go in, shall we?" I nodded.

I gave Richard the key. He opened the door and ushered me in. "I'll make us some tea. You go and sit down."

"Think I need a wee," I said over my shoulder and as I made my way upstairs I heard him chuckle.

After going to the bathroom, I went into the bedroom and sat on the side of the bed staring out of the window. It was now drizzling and cold and, by the light of the street lamp opposite, I could see droplets of rain on the window. I heard Richard's footsteps on the stairs and he came into the room. "Tea," he said as he put the mug on the bedside table. I looked up at him as he sat beside me.

"It's been really hard for you, hasn't it?" I felt his arm round my shoulders and leaned against him with a sigh and kissed his cheek. He turned towards me and kissed me gently while his other hand stroked my breast lightly.

I forgot all about drinking tea. I wanted to hold and be held. I wanted to touch and be touched. I wanted to caress and be caressed. I wanted to tease and be teased. I wanted to want and be wanted. I wanted to fuck and be fucked.

I kissed him deeply and ran my hand down his chest to his belt and flicked the buckle open. He pulled away from me slightly and I tried to follow him. "Just a moment," he whispered as he stood up and shrugged off his jacket. I stood opposite him, pulled the pink sweater over my head and dropped it on the floor. He mirrored my movements and tugged his black jersey off. We continued to strip until we stood looking at each other in our underwear, I knew he preferred me to be partially clothed so had left my bra and knickers on. He shrugged off his underpants and slid into bed. I walked round to his side as unselfconsciously as I could and ran my hands down my body, from shoulders to belly and back again. Even though he was under the duvet, I could see that he was slowly wanking. I leaned over, kissed him and then strutted back to my side of the bed. As I slipped under the cover I very gently scratched down his chest, following my fingers with my mouth and as I did so, I heard him sigh.

I reached down to cover his hand with mine and together we caressed him. I leaned over and started to kiss my way down his body - as I did so he gently but firmly pushed me away. In the past he'd told me that he wasn't keen on giving or, in particular, receiving oral sex but as I loved both, I continued to try and convince him that we were missing out on a lot of fun. I found myself on my back as Richard pushed himself into me, setting up a firm, insistent rhythm which culminated, as I knew it would, a few moments later as he came with an explosive groan.

As he rolled off me and lay back on the pillow with a contented smile, I could feel myself trembling slightly but didn't know if that was in sadness or frustration. I moved and heard him say, "Just going to close my eyes for a moment, you carry on without me." I squeezed my eyes tight shut for a moment and then opened them again to see him blithely dozing. As I started to get out of bed I felt his hand on my arm. "You ok?"

I glanced backwards. "Yes, I'm fine. Just going to freshen up." He smiled and nodded as he closed his eyes again.

I went into the bathroom, stepped under the shower and let the hot water rain on me. I was still aching for release so I set the stream of water slightly cooler and directed it between my legs. The sensation was unexpectedly electrifying, so to prolong the breath-taking moments, I played the powerful jets up and down my body from my throat, across my breasts, down my stomach and back to my crotch. I felt the familiar heavy pulse deep inside me that gathered momentum and, as I leaned against the cool white tiles, my legs trembled and I shuddered into bittersweet spasms of pleasure.

I stepped out from the shower, wrapped a large towel around myself, stared at my reflection in the steamy mirror and sighed. I so wanted everything to be good between us and hoped that the now, almost perpetually predictable sex, wasn't a harbinger of something worse to come.

I returned to the bedroom, curled myself round him and dozed for a while. He woke, yawned and stretched. "I'm sure that you need an early night. I think I should leave you to have a proper rest." I looked at him and saw gentle concern in his face.

"I'd much rather you stayed. We've had so little time together."

"I know, but we'll have more time next weekend." He looked down at me. "It's no problem Lucie; I just think you need to rest."

It wasn't what I wanted to hear but silently watched as he got out of bed and pulled his clothes on. He looked down at me and smiled. "You stay in bed and try to sleep." He bent over me and dropped a kiss on my forehead. "You look exhausted. Don't bother to see me out. I'll call you tomorrow." I heard his footsteps go downstairs, the front door open and close and then his car started up. As the sound of his car faded I turned my head into the pillows and wept.

As I got ready for work on Monday morning and drove into the school, I felt a heavy sadness sweep over me. The staffroom was eerily quiet, given that all members of staff were there and felt surreal beyond belief. Normally the school was alive with laughter and chatter but that morning all that could be heard were soft footsteps and hushed voices. Somehow, we all managed to get through the day and as I was packing up my bag late in the afternoon, Roger came over to me.

"Well, that was a day and a half, wasn't it Lucie?" He looked tired and strained.

I nodded. "It was dreadful Roger. It's so hard for teenagers to come to terms with one of their own dying, isn't it? I used to think that I was immortal at that age."

Roger gave a wry smile. "Me too, me too." He moved his shoulders slightly. "I had a call from Barbara. She told me that there'll have to be a post mortem. Of course that's no surprise is it?" He moved slightly closer to me. "Lucie, we have to go through her locker. Would you mind helping me on that?" He looked as if he was in real pain. I put my hand on his arm.

"Yes of course I will Roger. When shall we do it?"

He looked relieved. "I'd rather not do it now. Is first thing tomorrow morning ok for you?"

I wasn't planning to get in particularly early on Tuesday but nodded my agreement. "Of course. That's fine. I'll be in bright and early - quarter past eight-ish ok for you?"

"That would be perfect Lucie. Thanks."

I took my hand away from his arm. "See you tomorrow Roger. Bye."

Richard called in the evening and we chatted for a few moments about our respective days. For those few minutes it almost felt like the early days when we teased each other and laughed. As I settled down to sleep an hour later I was smiling.

As promised, I arrived at school the next day just before eight fifteen and met Roger in the main lobby. Grimly we unlocked and emptied Tracy's locker into a box and then took it back to the staffroom. There were school books which we kept and several personal items which we carefully boxed up ready to return to Barbara. We'd just finished when I heard ducks. 'Morning. Off to London for the day. Speak this evening, have a GOOD day, no worries. Rxxx'

My heart pounded. 'Seeing Julie?'

'Yes. NO worries. Rxxx'

I sat clutching the phone, gazing out of the window unseeingly. "Lucie? Lucie, are you ok?" I heard Roger's voice as if from a long way away. I blinked and looked at him.

"Yes, yes I'm ok. Thanks Roger." My voice was shaking.

"No you're bloody well not." As he put his hand on my shoulder I burst into tears. "Oh Lucie, what's wrong? Please don't cry." He sat next to me and held my hand.

After a few moments, I managed to compose myself. "I'm so sorry Roger." I managed a smile.

"So tell me what's wrong. Is it Tracy?"

Wordlessly, I held my phone out towards him and as he read the texts he grimaced.

"I don't know what to say," he said slowly. "I know what I want to say ..."

"Stop. Please stop. I'm fine. It was just a bit of a shock. I thought that he'd stopped seeing her, I really did ..." My voice faded.

Roger looked sombre. "I have to say that I think he's a real shit. And you're crazy letting him get away with this. Christ, if I had a woman who loved me like you love him, I'd never let her go." I looked at him and saw nothing but care and concern in his face and closed my eyes as the pain swept through me. No worries, the little voice in my head said, no worries? What the fuck is he playing at, sending you texts like that when he knows full well how seeing Julie makes you feel?

The day passed in a haze of classes, tutorials and meetings. I made sure that I kept very busy and before I knew it, it was four o'clock and everyone was leaving. The staffroom was empty as I collected my bag and made my way to my car, opened the door and sat down with a sigh. I looked again at my mobile and re-read Richard's texts. I couldn't believe that these were the actions of the same man who had delighted me with such a beautiful gift only a couple of days ago. I felt strangely numb and drove home in silence, unable to bear even the sound of the radio.

The next day I arrived at school bright and early and the morning passed in a flurry of activity. By twelve thirty I had finished off everything that needed to be done, including preparation for the following week and felt very virtuous.

I drove back into Stratford and rather than go straight home decided to park and meander round the shops. I enjoyed a cup of coffee at Maria's café and then drifted through an arcade where I was startled by a large white Basset running in my direction. He stopped in front of me and as I wondered what he wanted, I saw a slender blonde woman walking towards me. "Albert, you bad dog," she exclaimed as she bent and took his collar. She straightened up with a smile. "Hope he didn't alarm you too much."

"Not at all, I like dogs." I bent and stroked his silky head and as he looked up at me he gave me a warm doggy smile as his long tail gently waved.

The woman smiled at me, clipped a leash onto Albert's harness and gently led him towards a nearby shop which had white painted furniture and interesting-looking ornaments artfully displayed in the window. I followed her in and saw that it was crammed with painted furniture, retro china and glassware, candlesticks and pictures – a real Aladdin's cave. I spent a few minutes looking round and suddenly saw a delicate heart-shaped box that I really liked, so paid for that before returning to talk to Albert who, by the time, was happily settled in his basket.

"I'm Kate." I shook her outstretched hand, introduced myself and was invited to take a seat on a small sofa by the door. "I'm intending to sell clothes as well as furniture, I'm sure there's a market for vintage as well as modern stuff. And I've not found many places in Stratford that have both."

I pricked up my ears. "Tell me more. I'm always on the lookout for unusual schmatter."

Kate smiled at the old-fashioned word and joined me on the sofa. We continued talking for over an hour while Albert peaceably snoozed in his basket, only looking up when we laughed. "It's a real coincidence, Albert running into you," Kate said thoughtfully. "I need to get out and about a couple of times a week to do some buying. I don't suppose you'd be interested in minding the shop occasionally would you?"

"I'd love to, really love to."

Kate made a celebratory cup of tea so we could toast to our new business relationship. "You realise I can't pay much, don't you?"

"It's not the money Kate. I'd just like to help out as and when. I really admire what you've done here and would love to be a small part of it. I'm flattered that you've asked me. I'm looking forward to working with you - and Albert of course." We laughed as Albert looked up and wagged his tail when he heard his name.

We continued to chat. "I'm so pleased you've said yes." She took the mugs through to the tiny kitchen at the back of the shop. "It's important to have people I can trust working here."

I beamed. It felt wonderful to have such fulsome praise and I carried on smiling for the rest of the day. I liked the idea of a wide variety of different work. Alex had always said that a self-employment philosophy should include lots of eggs in one's basket so that if one customer disappeared, there were always others. I wholeheartedly agreed with him and apart from instantly liking Kate and Albert, felt that adding another string to my bow could only be useful as well as hugely enjoyable.

That evening, when Richard called I told him about the afternoon with Kate. "And you think it's a good idea to work in a shop, do you?" Richard asked.

"Well yes, I do. It'll only be occasional and it'll be a laugh and ..."

I heard a sigh on the other end of the phone. "Lucie, what the hell are you doing? Can't you see this is just a waste of your time? She'll only pay you a pittance and it's bound to distract you from other work that ..."

"I don't think it's a waste of time," I interrupted. "I think it's worthwhile, I'll be helping Kate out, I'll meet new people and it'll be fun ..."

"Fun? Is that all you think about?"

I fell silent and listened as he told me exactly why I shouldn't consider doing it and why I should be chasing 'proper' work. Every time I tried to justify myself, I heard cold, hard logic so that in the end I felt childish and foolish. "But of course, it's your decision Lucie. You must do as you think fit," he said eventually.

By this time, I felt completely deflated and irrational. "I know that what you say is right," I realised that I sounded defensive, "but I honestly don't think it'll distract me. In fact it'll be better for me than sitting at home worrying ..."

"Up to you." There was a note of finality in his voice.

We said our goodbyes and as I put the phone down, I burst into tears. The earlier feelings of warmth and happiness had disappeared and as I drifted into sleep, I felt dismally dejected.

I was still feeling down on Thursday morning so decided to call Richard and try to smooth things over. There was no reply from his landline and as I sat holding the handset, the all too familiar feelings of disquiet and anger started. I tried his mobile and that rang out too. I decided not to bother to leave a voicemail on either. I went into the kitchen to make breakfast and watched my hand tremble as I reached for the kettle. I sat at the table eating toast slathered with butter and my homemade marmalade and sipped my tea, debating what to do next.

I jumped as my landline rang, it was Richard. "Lucie? Did you call me earlier?"

"Yes I did. Are you ok?"

"Yes, I'm fine. What can I do for you?"

I sat back; it wasn't the tone I wanted the conversation to take. "I just wanted to talk to you. I woke up feeling bad that we'd argued last night. I hate it when we fight."

"Me too - but Lucie, I'm a bit busy at the moment. Let's talk later, shall we? Bye." And he was gone.

I sat motionless, completely stunned. I didn't know whether to cry, throw a plate against the wall or call him back and tell him that finally and at last I'd had enough of being treated so shabbily. I did none of these. Instead I pulled on a warm sweater and boots, got into the car and mindlessly drove fast, far too fast, towards - I didn't know where. An hour later I'd travelled over sixty miles through meandering country lanes and found myself in the small riverside town of Upton-on-Severn. I was thirsty and found a small pub by the river's edge; luckily there were spaces in the car park. I sat outside in the cool, damp air, drinking hot chocolate and gazing into the cold water for over half an hour, after which I went for a long walk along the river bank trying to fathom out how I could make Richard see just how good we could be together and how to stop him seeing Julie. Nearly an hour later I realised it was beginning to get dark so I returned to the pub for a coffee before driving home more slowly.

I lit the fire, poured myself a large glass of Merlot and looked at my mobile which I'd deliberately left in my bag on silent. There was a text from Richard that he'd sent at eleven. 'At Julie's. Helping put up shelves, build bookcases, etc. Talk later. Rxxx'. I stared at the screen. After everything I'd said, he was still seeing her. By my second glass I was getting angrier and angrier but the third glass saw my anger dissolve into frustrated and bitter tears.

Just before eight thirty I heard ducks. 'Have had a very busy day. Just had dinner as thanks. Had a glass of wine so will drink coffee for a while. Should be heading home in about an hour. All is well!!

Rxxx'. All was well? As far as I was concerned all was bloody well not well. I didn't return his text - I saw no point in doing so.

I slept badly and awoke feeling almost as tired as when I went to bed. Two large cups of tea helped as did a plate of velvety scrambled eggs on thick white toast. It was just after nine when my phone rang.

"Hello? Lucie?" Richard sounded cautious.

"Yes, good morning Richard."

"Good day yesterday?"

"Well, since you ask, no, not particularly" I took a deep breath. "I slept really badly last night, things going round and round in my head. You're giving me incredibly mixed messages so I really don't know where I stand with you. You insist on knowing all the details of my finances so that YOU can make a decision about our future. Aren't couples meant to share in this kind of discussion together?" I stopped, feeling breathless.

There was silence and then, "Well, where's all this come from?"

I'd started and there was no going back now. "You've seen Julie three times in as many weeks, twice at her flat - now please tell me why you think I'd be ok with this?"

"But ..."

"No, let me finish Richard. You're always telling me what you think. It's my turn now. I want you to tell me what you'd think and just how you'd feel if I did stuff like this to you?"

"I wouldn't like it," he said very slowly.

"I rather imagine that you wouldn't Richard. I have to ask myself whether these are the actions of someone who wants to be in a lasting relationship. You've been so generous with financial help and some lovely gifts like that dress last weekend which I really appreciate, but real love means taking emotional care of the other person too. Don't you agree?" I held my breath.

"Of course that's part of it, but you seem to think that money isn't important ..."

"I've never said that but we're not talking about that. At least I'm not. I'm talking about you seeing another woman a very great deal which you know I hate. Or do you think it's ok that I'm angry, get upset and cry?" I held my breath again.

"I don't want to upset you. She's asked me to help her on a couple of weekends but I have told her that I always see you at weekends. You see, you do come first."

"It so often doesn't feel like that."

"Well, you do. Anyway, I'm good at practical stuff and I have to say it makes me feel good to help friends in this way. Yesterday I worked from early morning to about seven, when she insisted on giving me dinner. She talked a great deal about missing Patrick and general worries, much of it said between floods of tears. I hope I said the right things to console her." I curled my lip but again kept silent. "I suspect there may be a couple more days of picture hanging and electrical bits and pieces, and I see no harm in helping her out. I hope you can tolerate that."

"Do I have a choice?"

There was another pause. "I've promised her I'd help. So the answer is no."

I could feel tears threatening but swallowed them down. "Well, all I can tell you is that I hate, hate, hate feeling like this. And I don't want to go on feeling like this. I want, need, to feel emotionally secure ..." It was no use; I couldn't hold back the tears any longer.

"I can't talk to you when you're crying."

I dug my nails into my palms in an effort to stop. "I just had to say what was in my head Richard. You seeing her as much you do is going to seriously damage us."

"Maybe you're right. Look, I'll see you later and we'll thrash this out."

We agreed that he would drive up for seven when I would have dinner ready. As I put the phone down I was trembling but whether with anger or fear I couldn't tell.

By seven, the fire was lit, the table laid, a lamb meatball tagine with lemon and olives was gently simmering and the vegetables to accompany the couscous were chopped, seasoned, sweated down and ready.

As usual, Richard was punctual and when I opened the door to welcome him, that warm surge of love that I just couldn't stop, engulfed me. I put my arms round him and leaned into his body, closing my eyes. "Hey, let me in, it's cold out here." He sounded amused.

After dinner, I would rather have gone out for a drink or even gone to bed early but was reconciled to go along with yet another movie night.

"Well, I enjoyed that," he said as the credits rolled.

He started to channel flick, something that I hated. We had so little time together - it seemed ridiculous to be spending time watching TV. I stifled my irritation. "Hey, this looks good." I saw that it was a yet another horror movie.

I stood up. "Sorry to disappoint you darling, but you know that horror movies and me just don't mix."

"You go up and warm the bed. I'll be up soon." His eyes didn't leave the screen.

I slowly got ready for bed and slid under the duvet, deliberately staying on my side. I'd felt so excited on his arrival but now felt small and ignored. I ran both hands across my stomach and then over my breasts, my nipples hardened instantly. I smiled to myself. "So that's what you want," I whispered. I brushed the back of my fingers round my throat, up my face and through my hair. I ran one hand from shoulder to fingertip and back again and did the same with the other arm. I gently caressed from my shoulders to my hips then round and round my breasts, eventually grazing my nipples with the lightest touch. My hips started to rock slightly and I could feel my arousal gathering momentum. I reached into the bedside drawer for my pale blue friend and switched it on, gently rubbing the vibrating shaft between my legs for a few moments before thrusting it deep inside and twisting my legs together. I felt the familiar spasms climb, juddered into release and reached down to gently stroke myself into a second, gentler orgasm. As I switched off the vibrator I started to cry, feeling sadder and lonelier than I had a right to, given that the man I loved was only a few steps away.

I curled up on my side and tried to sleep. I must have managed to doze because the next thing I remembered was Richard in bed beside me, stroking my shoulder. "Lucie? Are you awake?" I heard him whisper. I kept my eyes closed and breathed deeply. A bit late for tenderness, isn't it, my inner voice said as I drifted back into sleep. I had to agree.

I awoke late on Saturday morning to find Richard sitting next to me. "Let's have a nice day today. No arguments, no sniping, just a lazy day together."

"Sounds good," I agreed and we smiled at each other.

After breakfast we ambled round town, ending up at the Dirty Duck where we sat by the fire drinking and chatting companionably. Richard laughed at my pleasure about a new lipstick I'd bought which in turn made me laugh. We moved on to the One Elm where we lunched on their vast surf-and-turf board which I insisted was accompanied by a large pot of chunky chips. I was surprised and relieved that he didn't comment which made lunch a much more relaxing experience than usual.

Much later we strolled back up the hill in the gathering gloom talking desultorily about this and that. As I opened the front door I heard his mobile ring. He reached into his pocket. I closed my eyes in disbelief but to my surprise he didn't answer the call. I opened my eyes again to see him looking down at me. "It was Julie. But I don't want to talk to her. I'm with you," and with that he kissed me. I automatically responded and his kisses became more insistent. "Shall we?"

"Absolutely yes," I whispered back.

"You go up. I'll join you in a moment."

As I walked upstairs I could have sworn I heard little clicks when a text is keyed in, but when I stopped for a moment, I heard nothing. Just my imagination I said to myself as I reached the top of the stairs. Nothing to worry about I said as I opened the door. He's with me, not her I said as I stripped down to my underwear and slid into bed. A few moments later I heard Richard's footsteps on the stairs and he appeared in the doorway. He quickly peeled off and joined me in bed. "Now, where were we?" He leaned over me.

I relished his kisses which were more tender and passionate than they had been for what seemed a long time. I ran my fingertips over his shoulders, down his arms and onto his hands which I then guided across my body. He tried to move towards my breasts but I pushed his hands down my torso to my hips as I gently nibbled on his neck and shoulders. He gripped my hips so hard it almost hurt, and then ran his hands to my back and down my bottom to my thighs, gently pinching as he did so, pulling me into him. I squirmed against him, desperate to feel as much of his body against me as possible and again reached down for his hands, holding them firmly against my breasts, caressing and kneading myself through him, shivering with desire and anticipation. He suddenly pushed me back and before I could draw breath, started fucking me with a force and intensity that made me gasp and whimper.

He came quite quickly but instead of turning away as he usually did, he held me close and continued caressing me. I luxuriated under his touch and minutes later arched my back. "Don't stop, please, please don't stop," I breathed and he obediently continued to kiss and nuzzle my shoulders and neck while softly fondling my breasts and nipples. I felt surges of pleasure engulf me and as the final paroxysms died down I closed my eyes in contentment and snuggled into him.

When I next opened my eyes, I was on my own. I got up, pulled on a long sloppy sweater and after having a quick wash, went downstairs. Richard was sitting on the sofa in front of a roaring fire, watching the news. He looked up and smiled. "You must have been really, really tired. Feeling better now?"

"Yes thank you." I sat next to him and kissed his cheek.

He looked at his watch. "It's getting on for eight. Let's get a takeaway. Then we can eat in front if the fire." I nodded. "Tell you what - I know what you like so leave it to me. You stay here and get things ready. I'll only be twenty minutes or so."

I waved him off, reminding him to get onions and pickles to accompany the poppadums and then put glasses filled with our preferred tipples, plates, bowls, cutlery and a few paper napkins on trays and brought them through to the sitting room. I settled back down in front of the fire, smiling contentedly.

Suddenly I heard a mobile ringing and ran upstairs to where mine was on the bedside table. I picked it up - no-one had called me. I heard ringing again and realised that it must have been Richard's, so went into the spare room to see his mobile lying on the bed, still ringing. As I put my hand out, the ringing stopped and, to my outrage, I saw Julie's name as a missed call. I wondered what to do - normally I would never ever have thought about going into someone else's mobile but suddenly it seemed like fair game. As I stared at the screen, I heard the front door open. I dropped the phone back on the bed, quickly left the room and closed the door very quietly. Looking down from the top of the stairs, I saw Richard smiling up at me holding a large bag. The scent of curry and spices wafted up at me.

"Come on Lucie - lots of your favourite things here." He looked very pleased with himself.

"Coming Richard. I'll be with you in a moment." I splashed cold water over my face, breathed deeply and before opening the bathroom door, flushed the toilet and waited a moment before going downstairs.

Richard had spread a couple of tea towels on the floor and was taking lids off various containers. "Chicken tikka masala, lamb madras, some onion bhajis, a couple of samosas and that potato and cauliflower dish you like so much. Saffron rice and here are the poppadums with onions and pickles. Feast fit for a king. What do you think?" He sat back on his heels with a proud grin.

I managed a returning smile; after all, it wasn't his fault Julie had called.

"Let's eat then." He started to fill our bowls, passing me one. I sat with it in my hands. I really didn't feel hungry now but took a mouthful – it was delicious.

"Richard? Your mobile rang while you were out."

He stopped eating and looked at me more closely. "And?" He sounded guarded.

I took a deep breath. "I thought it was mine but it wasn't and she called again ..."

"She?"

"Yes, she - you've got a couple of missed calls from Julie." I looked at him.

He gazed back impassively. "I don't know why she's calling me now. She knows that I'm with you and I've asked her not to call at weekends ..."

"Only at weekends?"

He looked at me steadily. "Look Lucie, I try to keep her as a platonic friend and she seems to respect the fact that you're my girlfriend. Just how many more times do I have to tell you?" His voice rose slightly.

I sat very still, what else could I say? Yet again I felt small and foolish. "Sorry Richard. It just rattled me a bit. You'd feel the same if you saw a man's name come up on my phone and knew I was seeing him."

He nodded. "Yes, I know." He sounded sad.

As we continued to eat, some of my tension abated. I knew that Richard was still seeing Julie very frequently and that saddened me beyond belief but equally knew that if I continued to challenge him, he would simply lose his temper and that would do neither of us any good. I sighed. Richard looked up. "You alright?"

I nodded. "I'm really enjoying this. You chose just the right blend of dishes. Thank you darling."

He smiled contently and leaned back.

Once we'd finished, I threw the debris away, put the crockery into the dishwasher and after making sure the kitchen was tidy, returned to the sitting room where Richard was piling more logs and coal on the fire and scanning through the TV programme guide. I sat next to him, held his hand and took a deep breath. "Richard, we are ok, aren't we? I mean, deep down, we're alright?"

He stopped me with a kiss that melted me. "Let's not talk now."

Later, as we settled down in bed, Richard dropped a kiss on my cheek and I nestled next to him. "Let's just relax and go to sleep," he murmured. Moments later I felt his breathing slow and deepen and his arm round my shoulders loosened.

We woke at about nine and the rest of the day passed tranquilly. We drove to a little Cotswold village and strolled up and down the high street, stopping for lunch in a tiny pub. It seemed that by tacit agreement we avoided any contentious subjects so chatted about light, inconsequential things that made us laugh and when we returned home, Richard remade the fire and we sat sipping tea and nibbling on beef and horseradish sandwiches. When he left at eight, we hugged each other wordlessly. For the first time in a long time at the end of a weekend, I went to bed in a calmer frame of mind.

Chapter 4 - March

I awoke bright and early on Monday morning still smiling, the memories of last weekend still fresh in my mind. Over breakfast, I read Susie's latest email where she described her trip to Laos the previous week which sounded amazing. I was so glad and happy for her, reading her emails made me feel much closer to her world.

Despite the school still feeling very subdued, the morning flew by. I was on a high as Richard had messaged that morning just to make sure I was ok and was still smiling to myself when I made my way to the staffroom at lunchtime where Roger was sitting by the window. "Well, the morning's gone a lot better than I expected, given what's been happening."

He looked away from the window and gazed up at me, looking slightly embarrassed. "Yes." There was a small silence as he cleared his throat. "Lucie, can I ask you something?" I nodded. "Would you consider coming out to dinner with me?" I took a breath and he hastily added, "As work mates Lucie, as work mates."

"Roger, thank you. I'm very flattered but you know my situation and it's just not possible. But I can't tell you how much I value your friendship." I patted his shoulder. "You're a real sweetie ..."

He stood up. "I understand. Well, I must dash, got a meeting to get to. See you later," and with that he left the room.

I had very little time to reflect on Roger's invitation that afternoon and by the time I'd arrived home and sat down for a well-earned coffee, I really wanted to talk to Richard. I tried his landline but, to my disappointment, it was engaged. I tried again ten minutes later, it was still engaged. And again a further ten minutes later. Perhaps it's out of order I thought to myself, so I called my provider to have the line checked. A few moments later I was told that the line was working and it was engaged because people were in conversation. I tried again twice more - how very odd I thought to myself.

Half an hour later my landline rang. "Hello Lucie, did you have a good day?" Richard sounded jovial and upbeat.

"Hello darling. I've had a very good day thanks. How about you?"

We chatted for a few minutes about our respective days and I was just about to ask him who he'd been talking to for so long when he said, "Oh, by the way, I've booked us a couple of tickets at Warwick Arts Centre to see Two Gentlemen of Verona. It's on Saturday fortnight. Is that ok?"

It had been a long time since he had done anything like this and I was delighted. "That sounds lovely darling; what a wonderful idea, I'd love to see it." All thoughts about the reason why his line had been engaged for almost an hour had disappeared. We chatted for a few more minutes and then said our goodbyes. As I put the handset down, I realised that I hadn't asked him who he had been talking to and then shrugged. Did it matter when he had so clearly been thinking of me? No, it didn't I told myself as I happily cooked myself a cheese and onion omelette and ate it, savouring the contrasting tastes of the sharp cheddar and stringy Gouda that I'd grated over the hot eggs.

The landline rang again. "Hello darling, missing me already?" I giggled in pleasure.

"Hello? Is that Lucie Hunter? It's Barbara – Tracy's mum."

"Barbara. How are you?" I felt slightly embarrassed for a moment.

"I'm ok. No I'm not. You said if I needed anything, you'd be happy to help. Would you mind if we talked?"

"Of course not - would you like me to come over or would you prefer to come to me?" I could hear a stifled sob. "Are you free tomorrow after school? I can be with you by four. Is that ok?"

I heard a sigh of relief. "That's wonderful. I'll have tea and cake ready."

The next day I managed to leave school at three thirty and was about to get out of the car at Barbara's when I saw the heart-shaped box I'd bought from Kate's shop on the back seat. I don't know what prompted me but I picked it up and as I settled myself at Barbara's kitchen table, gave it to her. Her eyes widened. "You can't have known of course, but Tracy collected hearts, there must be hundreds in her room. Thank you so much." She made tea and we sat together as she talked about Tracy's post mortem and arrangements for the funeral. "My brother and his family live in Australia. Of course they want to be here and I want them here, but it means that it's going to be another three weeks which seems like such a long time before Tracy can rest."

I put my arm round her shoulders, trying to comfort her. "I'm so sorry ..." she hiccupped between sobs.

"Don't be silly. She was your darling girl. She'll always be your darling girl." I stopped for a moment to gather my thoughts. "You know, Tracy's at rest now. The funeral's for everyone who cared for her so we can come together and celebrate her life, tragically short though it was. So, it's ok that we have to wait a little while longer for that."

Barbara looked at me through her tears. "You think so? I've been so worried that it's too long to wait."

"Absolutely not," I said firmly. "We can wait. Girls' prerogative to keep people waiting, you know."

A small smile appeared on Barbara's face. "I found myself making Tracy's chocolate cake this morning. It made me feel closer to her somehow. And then I felt stupid. Am I being stupid?"

"No, you're not. Nothing you do is stupid and whatever you do that makes you feel better is good."

I watched as Barbara opened a cake tin and carefully cut two slices which she brought over to the table. It was dark, rich and moist, just the way a chocolate cake should be and I nibbled it slowly, savouring every mouthful. "Delicious. Absolutely scrumptious. Have you thought about doing this for a living?" We continued talking and drinking more tea. The time flew and the next time I glanced at my watch it was nearly ten. As I put my jacket on and prepared to take my leave, I hugged her. "I didn't know Tracy for very long but I liked her enormously. I'm very happy to talk whenever you want to."

Barbara's eyes filled with tears again. "Thank you Lucie. I can't tell you how much that means to me." As I slowly drove home, I reflected how very lucky I was that Susie was well and healthy albeit some five thousand miles away and whilst I would have loved to be able to get together, I was very happy that she was enjoying her amazing opportunity.

It was just after ten thirty, later than usual to talk with Richard and as I picked up the handset, I heard the familiar intermittent tone that signalled a voicemail. It was him. "Lucie? Where are you? This is the third time I've called. Ring me when you're back from wherever you've been."

I rang back and as he picked up, saying an interrogative hello, he sounded slightly edgy. "Hello Richard. I'm so sorry darling, but I went to visit Barbara ..."

"Barbara?"

"Yes, Barbara. Tracy's mother. You remember? Tracy was the student who recently died in a car accident."

"Oh yes, I remember. So, what did she want?"

"She wanted to talk so I went over to hers. We had a really nice evening, talking about all sorts of things. She's worried that it's going to be another three weeks before Tracy's funeral and ..."

"So, why did she want to talk to you? I mean, she must have lots of friends. Why you?"

"I don't know why me Richard. I just know she was incredibly distraught. I guess she feels that she can talk to me. And I'm not personally involved so I don't get as upset as someone who's much closer to her. She's having such a hard time; it seemed such a small thing to spend a few hours with her."

"Yes, of course. I'm sure she appreciated the time with you. Anyway, how's the rest of your day been?"

"Fine thank you. The usual really. How about you?"

"Oh, I went for a long walk up in the hills. Lovely views. You know Lucie, we ought to do more of that. You know how much I like hill walking." And he went on to describe the walk and his subsequent late lunch in a village pub. After a few minutes he said, "So, no other news then?"

"No, no other news."

"Ok. Well, I'll say goodnight then. Have a good tomorrow, won't you. Bye."

I wanted to talk some more but it was clear that as far as he was concerned the conversation was over. "Night darling," was all I managed to say before I heard the click as his phone was put down.

I sat back and stared at the handset. What had just happened was a million miles from the warmth of last night's conversation and, half an hour later as I made my way upstairs slowly, I wondered what had happened to make him so brusque. I fell asleep still wondering and feeling sad that our relationship was blowing hot and cold, I so yearned to reach a place of calm.

The rain lashed down all through the next gloomy day. By lunchtime, I'd finished and as I was picking my way through the carpark, trying to avoid the worst of the puddles, I saw Roger by his car. He saw me and smiled slightly diffidently but warmly. "Hello Lucie. How are you?" He came over and held his umbrella over both of us.

"I'm cold and wet, but apart from that, I'm fine. How are you?"

"I'm ok. I've just had a meeting with a local company I've been talking to for some time who've finally agreed to take four of our lot on work experience next term. Isn't that great news?"

"Fantastic news. Well done you." He looked so pleased I couldn't resist giving him a friendly hug. "That's a wonderful contact for the school. You should be very proud of yourself."

He grinned and returned my hug. "I am, I am."

I could feel his embrace becoming a little more insistent and gently disentangled myself. "And quite right too. Listen Roger, I'm absolutely delighted and you must tell me all about it - but not now. I'm sorry but I am in a bit of a hurry. See you next week. Ok?"

It was still raining when I arrived home. I shivered as I put the kettle on and boosted the central heating. I'd curled up on the sofa when I heard ducks quacking. I thought it might be Richard and eagerly picked up but saw that it was a text from Di. I read and then re-read it, after just over three years in a job she loved, she was being made redundant. I quickly sent her a reply. 'So sorry to hear about this. Can you talk now? X'. Moments later my landline rang and as I picked up I heard what seemed like a stifled sob.

"Di? Are you ok? Stupid question, of course you're not ok."

I heard a deep sigh and then Di's voice: "Well, I didn't see that one coming ..." She worked for a very large company, managing their many new recruits. I sat silently listening as she poured everything out - how after only three years she would get precious little in redundancy, how worried she was as she'd only recently moved house, how long it had taken her to find this job and how anxious she was that she wouldn't find another job.

When she finished I took a deep breath. "Di, you know that things will work out because they somehow always do. But that's not what you want to hear right now. Hey - where are you?"

"In London, but I've said that I'm coming back to the Midlands this evening. Don't suppose that you're around this evening are you?"

"Yes - you come straight over. I'll get us a bite to eat and we'll have a proper talk."

I sat on the sofa, holding my now cold mug of tea, absorbing Di's news. She'd been so thrilled when she'd found this job and put her heart and soul into it, it all seemed so unfair. I grimaced as I suddenly thought about how I coped, often only just, with the stresses of self-employment and I knew that Di wouldn't like living in the hand-to-mouth way that I had become used to. And Richard hates the way you just about make a living doesn't he the little voice in my head suddenly piped up. Now thoughts of Richard's disapproval and concerns about my financial state were firmly in my head and deep, deep down I knew that we really weren't fine.

Before I could think any more about what distressed me so much, I realised that I wanted to talk to Richard. I needed to hear his voice and be reassured that he cared. I rang his landline. There was no reply – there was still no reply twenty minutes later and twenty minutes after that. I slowly walked to the kitchen, feeling sad and deflated, a nagging sense of doubt clouding my mind.

Better start dinner I thought. As I slowly diced a piece of pork tenderloin, onions and mushrooms, thoughts of Di, Richard, Roger and Barbara swirled round in my head but when the food started to sizzle in the pan and the kitchen was filled with warm cooking scents, I felt calmer as the pleasure of cooking took over. After adding Dijon mustard and crème fraiche, I covered the simmering creamy stroganoff, opened a bottle of Merlot and lit the fire.

Before I knew it there was a knock on the door and I opened it to see Di holding a bunch of pink roses in one hand and a bottle in the other. She looked exhausted. Moments later we were sitting in front of the blazing fire I'd lit earlier, each holding a large glass of Merlot. "Now Di, tell me why they're being stupid enough to make you redundant." I tucked my feet under me.

She sighed. "It's a long story ..." and she explained what had been happening. "But at least I've got my three months' notice plus a tiny bit of redundancy so I can manage for a little while. I really thought this job was for keeps. I hate the thought of starting all over again."

"I know, I know." I felt for her. "It's a horrible feeling when you think you have something stable and then suddenly discover that you're on shifting sands."

"You're absolutely right, and that applies to lots of things, doesn't it?" Di gave me a sideways smile and raised her eyebrows.

"We're talking about you, not me. Don't you dare get me started." I wanted to change the subject. "Are you hungry?"

Di looked thoughtful. "You know, I'm starving. Yes please. Can I help?"

I stood up. "You can be in charge of the wine."

Di laughed. "I can certainly do that," and she followed me into the kitchen where she topped up our glasses as I quickly chopped fresh parsley and strewed it over the meltingly delicious stroganoff.

"We'll have this in bowls by the fire – let's slum it tonight, shall we?"

Di sniffed appreciatively and sipped her wine. "You really enjoy doing this, don't you?"

I nodded. "Love it, just love it." I looked up from serving up. "If I had my time again, I might have tried to make a career to involve some kind of cooking but it's a game for the young, not someone with cronky knees."

We both laughed and clinked our glasses before picking up our respective bowls. Moments later were relaxing in front of the fire and eating what proved to be an excellent stroganoff with a refreshing salad, after which we both leaned back and simultaneously sighed in contentment.

Later, we were still in front of the fire. We'd each eaten a large bowl of chocolate ice cream and then opened another bottle of wine and were both fairly tipsy.

She looked at her watch and sighed. "It's only ten thirty but I'll need to leave by seven, so I suppose I ought to get some sleep."

"Come on," I said briskly. "Time to hit the hay. Coffee?

As I made some coffee, I realised that Richard hadn't called that evening which was very unusual. Little prickles of unease swept over me. "You ok Lucie? You look a bit upset."

"It's just that I suddenly realised that Richard hasn't called me. It's so unusual. Something's happened or ..." my voice trailed away.

Di remained silent as I looked at her. "Aren't you going to tell me how stupid I am to stay with him?"

She shook her head. "No I'm not. I think you already know that deep down, but you love him – I don't see it myself. I think he's a rude, selfish, arrogant man."

I stared at her. "Don't look so surprised. You know how I feel and, very probably, how other people feel too. We only put up with him for your sake but would we want him around if he wasn't with you?"

I swallowed hard. Deep down I knew that she was right but it wasn't something I wanted to hear again. "He can be so kind ..." I started to say. Di looked at me and smiled sadly.

"It's getting late and you've got an early start. I'll get you a towel. Want a hot water bottle?" I stood up.

"You know I'm always here for you. And yes please, I think a hot water bottle would be wonderful."

The next morning was dull and cloudy but the rain had stopped. I made crispy bacon and creamy scrambled eggs while Di showered and got ready. "Yummy, really yummy - thank you." She wiped her plate clean with the last piece of toast. It was just after seven when I waved her off and started to get ready for my day. As I closed the front door I heard my landline ringing but ignored it. Instead, I got into the car and drove down the road. If it was Richard I didn't want to hear his excuses about not calling me last night.

The day passed quickly and enjoyably and before I knew it, it was lunchtime and I had to leave for a meeting at the university which went very well. I was pleased that it seemed that the initial two days a week for two weeks was very likely to be increased depending on student requirements. I drove home with a smile on my face; work going well always had that effect on me.

That evening, I debated whether to wait for Richard to call me but decided against it, so after I'd finished my meal and poured myself a glass of Dutch courage, I dialled his landline. "Hello?" His voice sounded guarded.

"Hello darling. It's me. Have you had a good day?"

"Oh, Lucie. Hello. Yes, I've been out and about today." He paused and I remained silent, waiting for him to say the next thing that I probably didn't want to hear.

"I missed talking to you last night," I said eventually.

He cleared his throat. "I was out and by the time I realised we hadn't spoken, it was a bit late."

I held my breath and waited. "So where were you?" I asked after what seemed like hours.

"I went over to see Julie." The words came out very slowly.

He must have heard my gasp of disbelief and pain. "Look, I'm really sorry I seem to keep causing you such upset. She's no threat to you." He hesitated. "You know full well what the issues are between us. I hate to talk to you like this but it's only fair I say how I feel. You have no real work stability which means you still have very little stability. The truth is that I see you as a financial liability and often a fairly miserable one at that. I want to enter old age with a decent amount of money at my disposal."

I sat clutching the handset, shaking with anger, disappointment and grief, unable to think of what to say in the face of this torrent of negativity.

"Lucie? Are you still there?"

"Yes. Yes, I'm still here."

"Look, despite all of this I stay with you. There's no question that I've got strong emotional links to you. I know that you want me to use words like 'love', 'darling' and so on, but that just isn't me."

"And is that why you still see Julie?" I said, more to myself than to him.

"I've told you, she's just a friend. I'm not interested in her. She's absolutely not my type at all. We have far bigger issues to deal with than bloody Julie Catchpole."

I took a deep breath. "So, what you're saying is that Julie can't cope without your help. Is that it? And that you always have to be at her beck and call?" I knew that my voice was shaking but I was a long, long way away from tears. I was furious with both of them. "I think that she's a mean, selfish ..."

"I certainly don't enjoy saying things to you that I know upset you but it's only fair that you know how I feel."

"I understand that, but don't you think saying all this over the phone is a bit cruel? Isn't it better if we talk face to face? Or do you have other plans for the weekend?"

"No, no," he sounded startled. "Of course I want to see you. Unless ..." his voice faded.

"That's settled then." And we agreed that he would come up for dinner at about seven as usual.

I was still shaking when I put the phone down but I was also proud of myself for challenging what I saw as his, and her, appallingly bad behaviour. I went to bed but tossed and turned, unable to sleep, so when the alarm went off at seven thirty felt, and looked, exhausted. Luckily, I didn't have to go into the school so took a leisurely shower and then spent some time considering a suitable menu for dinner. What was the old saying? That the way to a man's heart was through his stomach? And despite everything that he had said and done, I knew that I would still forgive him and look for a way forward.

I decided on a retro menu of prawn cocktail followed by steak diane and mini sherry trifles. As I shopped for ingredients plus, of course, Richard's obligatory bottle of Southern Comfort, I reflected on what kept me with him. Once I'd asked for us to have a weekend in London only to be told that he preferred his weekends in Stratford - they were an oasis of peace and tranquillity, he'd said and at the time I'd glowed at what I'd seen as a compliment, but now I could see that it was sheer laziness on his part. I shrugged impatiently at myself. The last five years had entwined our lives together and that investment seemed too much to throw away without a fight.

Richard arrived punctually as usual and, after a couple of large slugs of his favourite tipple, enjoyed dinner which made us reminisce about where we were and what we'd been doing in the 1960s and 70s. We laughed a lot which eased my tension and upset from the previous night's phone conversation. After dinner, as usual, Richard turned on the TV but at about ten instead of going to bed alone, I stood up. "Let's go to bed." I held out my hand.

Richard looked surprised. "It's a bit early for bed, isn't it?"

"I don't mean to sleep," I said archly.

He smiled. "I'll join you later. There's a film I quite fancy watching. Stay with me Lucie, you'll enjoy it."

"But ..." I started to say and then stopped. There was no point. He had said he wanted to watch a film and a film he would watch. I sat down again and watched a fairly bad thriller with him

It must have been nearly midnight when we went to bed and by that time I felt irritated and on edge. As usual, I was in bed before Richard and, as usual, I found myself on his side of the bed, acting as his bed warmer. He smiled as he came into the room and I obediently slid over to my side which was cold. I shivered.

I'd rarely felt as unsexy as I did that night but responded to Richard's touch automatically. It was as if I was watching myself. I saw a woman going through the motions of brief, perfunctory foreplay and being taken far too soon but obligingly faking in order to maximise her partner's satisfaction. I then watched him fall asleep while she lay still, tears oozing down her cheeks into her hair and I wept with her, feeling her resignation and pain.

Saturday morning saw yet more rain but it was clear that the clouds were breaking and by eleven, we were walking down into town. The day followed fairly predictably - we drifted round a few shops; we lunched at the One Elm and then strolled home. I cooked a prawn stir fry for dinner; we watched a couple of films and then went to bed. We had both been pretty guarded in what we said which made me feel tense. Much as I didn't relish confrontation, there was so much I wanted to say but didn't feel brave enough.

As Richard got into bed, he looked at me with a half-smile. "Well, Lucie, do you want to make out tonight?'"

I was amazed. Very rarely did he actually ask, love making was usually a given. I looked at him steadily. "I want us to be close Richard. I want you to hold me. I really don't care if we fuck or not."

He blinked at my candour and took a breath to say something but I stopped his mouth with a kiss. I yearned for and the harder I tried to feel erotic and amorous the more I didn't and after he came I was content to curl round him to sleep - having an orgasm was the last thing on my mind.

I was tumbling faster and faster into an abyss which became darker and scarier the deeper I fell. I awoke with a start in the pitch dark and reached for Richard, wanting the reassurance and warmth of his body only to find that I was alone in bed. Maybe he just couldn't sleep and didn't want to disturb you I thought. I realised that I wanted a pee so got out of bed and groped my way to the door, not wanting to put the light on as I wanted to stay as sleepy as possible. I opened the door and as I stepped onto the landing could see the light from the sitting room spilling into the hall and heard Richard's voice in conversation. I stood stock still and tried to make out what he was saying while my heart started pounding. After going to the bathroom I stood on the landing again and listened but heard nothing. Maybe I'd just imagined hearing him, I thought as I slowly walked back into the dark bedroom and pulled the duvet over my head. A few moments later I heard him making his way upstairs. "Lucie? Are you awake?"

"Yes Richard. I'm awake. Couldn't you sleep?"

He sat on the side of the bed. "No. I went downstairs to get a glass of water."

I felt his hand on my arm as he got into bed and we curled up together and fell asleep. When I awoke at about eight, we were more or less in the same positions. I gazed at Richard's sleeping face and a warm rush of love engulfed me. It seemed inconceivable that we wouldn't be together for many years to come. I closed my eyes and dozed staying as still as possible, not wanting to disturb him.

As it was a dry, reasonably fine day, we decided to take the train into Birmingham and spent a very pleasant few hours meandering round the shops and sitting with a coffee in the gardens surrounding the cathedral. Crocuses had pushed their way through the grass and the bright yellows and purples made the square look cheerful and welcoming. It was as if, by unspoken agreement, we avoided anything that might be upsetting and when we were sitting together on the return journey, I felt at ease.

It was nearly five when we arrived home. I prepared chicken with chorizo, tomatoes and olives for dinner and while it cooked, returned to the warmth of the fire Richard had lit with a glass of Southern Comfort for him and a glass of Merlot for me.

We were so comfortable in the sitting room that we agreed to eat dinner in front of the fire which wasn't something we made a habit of, but the warmth was just too hard to leave. Afterwards, we sat back contentedly. "That was very good Lucie, thank you."

"My pleasure." And it really was, as ever when we were at peace with each other, we enjoyed lovely days.

I didn't often bother, but occasionally bought weekend papers which I eked out for several days. I'd bought The Observer the day before and idly leafed through the supplements, before coming across the crossword. I picked up a pen as I scanned the clues and started to complete what I could. Richard looked across at me. "What are you doing?"

"Thought I'd have a go at the crossword - want to help?"

"Sure. I like crosswords." He smiled reflectively. "I do the Telegraph crossword most days."

"Really? I didn't realise you were a crossword devotee."

"Mmmmm. I do it over the phone with Julie. She really enjoys ..." His voice faded as he looked at my disbelieving face.

The calmness and tranquillity of the day evaporated in a heartbeat - I felt shaky and sick. "You do what?" My voice rose indignantly.

"Well, you know I talk with her and she misses doing the crossword with Patrick, so we do it together over the phone." He looked at me. "Now, don't start, Lucie. We've had a lovely day so don't spoil it." He started to look angry.

I knew what I wanted to say but his last few words had robbed me of the power of speech. We sat in silence for a few minutes while I struggled to make sense of what he'd said. I felt shocked, angry, frightened and powerless all at the same time.

I heard him take a breath. "I suppose you want me to leave?"

I looked at him stonily. "Do you realise how I feel about this? You've just said that you talk to that cow every day."

"Not every day."

"What does that matter? You do the crossword with her almost every day. That's pretty intimate stuff, don't you think?" He remained silent. I stood up. "This is all bollocks. Do you honestly think that behaving like this is ok?"

He rose to his feet and stepped towards me, holding out his hands.

"No, no, bed won't mend this. Do you think I'm that much of a fool?" I could feel tears threatening but blinked them back

He stopped. "Perhaps I ought to go now. I can see you're upset and if we talk now, we might say something we regret." He walked past me. I heard him go upstairs and slumped back into my chair, unable to think clearly, feeling sick with rage and fear.

A few moments later Richard came downstairs, bag in hand and stood in the doorway, looking down at me. "Do you want me to go?"

"You know perfectly well what I want," I replied, staring into the fire. "I want you never to see or talk to that awful woman again. I want us to be happy together but we can't while she's around and you continue to dignify her disgraceful behaviour." I looked up at him. "I don't know how you can treat me so badly Richard." He opened his mouth to say something and I looked back at the fire.

"Shut the door behind you please." I heard his sharp intake of breath and then the front door opened and softly closed. I continued to gaze into the fire and the flames blurred as hot tears ran down my face.

Sometime later the phone rang. It was Karen who wanted to come over but as I couldn't face anyone, I pretended to have a headache so we agreed that she would come for dinner the next day. Shortly afterwards, the phone rang again, this time it was Pennie who wanted a chat and again I used the excuse of a bad headache to avoid talking.

Several hours later I was still on the sofa, waiting to hear from Richard until, at about one in the morning, I came to terms with the fact that he wasn't going to get in touch, so I crept upstairs to bed where I tossed and turned, wondering just how much longer I would be able, or willing, to deal with this rollercoaster of emotions.

I actually enjoyed Monday at school, despite the events of the weekend still going round and round in my head. I left just after two thirty and on the drive home, reflected how nice Roger had been in our coffee break.

I was so relieved to get home and smiled as I opened the door to the welcoming cats. As I lit the fire, I suddenly heard ducks quacking and despite myself reached for my mobile eagerly but it wasn't Richard, it was now close to twenty four hours since we'd been in contact but this time I was dammed if I would make the first move. I smiled as I read the text. 'Hi. Hope all's good on Planet Lucie. Was wondering if you could mind the shop for me on Thursday? Albert's promised to be good. Kate x'

'Hi Kate. Love to but can't, so sorry, but really happy to do it another time. All ok with you? Let's catch up very soon. L x'

'No probs. Just thought I'd ask. All ok here but really busy which is great. Albert'll miss you! Kate x'

I sat back. I felt very pleased that Kate had thought of me and I smiled but the smile quickly disappeared as a darker thought hit me; the one person whose love, and approval, I craved not only withheld it but seemed hell-bent on destroying my happiness and self-confidence. Nevertheless, I stared at the phone, willing it to ring.

I gave up after a few minutes and slowly went into the kitchen where I poached some smoked haddock in milk with bay leaves and a couple of peppercorns for a few minutes after which I turned the heat off and left the pan to stand. Once I was sure that the fish had cooked though, I flaked it and poured the milk into a jug. The cats weaved round my legs so I gave them each a small piece of the fish. "That's enough," I told them sternly when they begged for more.

It was close to seven when Karen arrived, still in her smart work clothes. I had changed into old leggings and a comfy sweater and looked incredibly scruffy next to her chic dark grey suit, lime green shirt, shiny black handbag and shoes. Sitting in front of the fire, each holding a large glass of red, Karen kicked off her high heels and leaned back with a sigh. "That's better. God, what a day ..." and we chatted about our respective work while she unwound; I deliberately avoided talking about Richard. "Oh by the way," she suddenly said as she fished in her bag and pulled out the latest edition of 'Olive', "I forgot to drop this in to you. Enjoy." She gave me a mischievous grin which made me giggle as I took the magazine out of her hand.

We were still giggling over nonsense when we decided to eat but agreed that our next drink would be sparkling water. Karen made herself comfortable on the small stool that I kept in the kitchen while we chatted and shared our news. I softened leeks and garlic in sizzling butter and delicious scents filled the air.

"You're like me,' Karen smiled. "You find cooking really therapeutic." I nodded as I put the chowder together and served up with crusty bread that was keeping warm in the oven.

We decided to eat dessert in front of the fire so while Karen cleared the table, I crushed a couple of supermarket meringues, whipped up a little double cream with a low-fat vanilla yoghurt, stirred through some frozen summer berries and then added a few drops of Grand Marnier which was left over from Christmas, just to give it a little hit. It looked very pretty, piled up high in wide wine glasses and I carried them into the sitting room proudly. It tasted as good as it looked; we ended up by running our fingers round the inside of the almost-empty glasses to finish off every last bit.

I made some coffee which we sipped slowly as we continued talking about this and that when we were startled by the phone ringing. I looked at it and then at Karen. "Don't be silly, answer it," she said as she opened 'Olive' and started to flick through it.

"Are you sure? It's probably Richard. I might be a few minutes."

She nodded, her eyes on the magazine.

I picked up the handset - it was Richard. We exchanged the usual hellos and how are yous. "So, what have you been doing today?" he asked so I briefly told him about my students and how well they were progressing. "That's good, you must be very pleased."

"And what have you been doing?"

"Oh, this and that." There was a few seconds of silence. "Actually I went over to Julie's to help her with a couple of things she wanted to get done in her new flat."

I closed my eyes and took a deep breath. Was there any point in protesting yet again when he'd made it so abundantly clear that he wasn't going to change? "Tell, me Richard, why do you keep on doing this?" Karen looked up sharply.

"Keep on doing what?"

"Don't play games with me. I've said it so many times I've lost count about you seeing that woman - that it hurts me beyond measure and yet you continue to do so."

"Look here," he sounded wearily impatient. "I also keep telling you that there's nothing in it. These are not romantic liaisons, there're just a chance for me to add another dimension to my social life. I keep telling you that I'm not interested in her."

By this time Karen had moved to sit next to me and had her ear pressed against the other side of the handset. As he paused, she leaned back and stared at me with her mouth open and an incredulous look on her face.

"I don't want to talk about this now. You know how I feel." A sudden thought struck me and I looked down at the handset to see that he had called me from his mobile. "Tell me Richard, where are you?"

"What?" He sounded startled.

"It's an easy enough question. Where are you right now?"

"I ... I'm sitting at the side of the road. I've just left the motorway and realised that I'd be a bit too late home to ring you, so I thought I'd call now."

"So, you've just left her, haven't you?" My voice was very soft.

"Yes Lucie, I left her about half an hour ago and am on my way home."

I couldn't speak and as I lowered my head in pain, Karen put her arm round my shoulder and gave me a gentle, sympathetic hug.

"Lucie? Are you still there?" Maybe it was my imagination, but he sounded quite concerned.

"I'm still here Richard. I really don't know why, but I am."

"Yes, well ... Perhaps I ought to get home and we'll talk tomorrow. Is that alright?"

I nodded but still couldn't speak. Only after a few seconds did I manage "Yes. Drive safely. Bye ..."

"Drive safely?" Karen's voice rose. "I'd be telling the fucker to drive into a very deep ditch and stay there. Lucie, how can you stand this? He's just awful to you. I can't bear seeing you like this." Her voice was softer and gentler. "Honey - please, please stop this. It's destroying you - your well-being, your confidence, your faith in yourself. Can't you see it?"

By this time I was crying helplessly, leaning against her. "This isn't love. He knows he's hurting you. How can that be love?"

I blew my nose noisily and sat up. "You're right, you're absolutely right." I wiped my eyes. "I said to Felicity that I'd give it til the summer, the end of the summer, to try and make a real go of it." I looked pleadingly at her. "I've invested five years with this man. I simply can't imagine being without him ..."

"But can't you see that you're without him most of the time anyway?" Karen interrupted. "Right at the beginning he told you that he was perfectly happy with a weekends only relationship and that's exactly what he's got. I know it's not what you want but none of this is about what you want. It's all about him. He's mean-spirited and, quite frankly, I don't think he's capable of the kind of love that you want and that you deserve. Don't you see, Lucie, that you deserve so, so much better?"

I bowed my head again. Deep down, I knew that Karen was right but just couldn't admit it. I stood up. "I need a drink. Whisky?"

We returned to the sitting room where I refused to talk about Richard any more much to Karen's mild irritation. I knew she had my best interests at heart but found it too hard to listen to what was becoming more and more frighteningly apparent. Eventually, she took her leave. "Look after yourself Lucie." She embraced me gently. "Whatever you decide, whatever happens, I'll always be here. You know that, don't you?" It was those words that stayed with me and were in my head as I went to bed and tried to sleep.

Harps awoke me early the next morning and I took special care getting ready as it was my first day at the university. The day went very well with motivated and enthusiastic students and I was delighted that this continued for the following two days. On Thursday, as I was leaving the staffroom after lunch for my afternoon sessions, I received a message from the head of department asking to me to pop in for a chat when I had finished. At the end of the day, I gathered my papers together and walked down the corridor towards her office. As I opened the door, I saw a tall woman with elegantly bobbed grey hair and piercing blue eyes sitting at her desk. She stood up and extended her hand.

"Hello Lucie. I'm Beth Lawson, head of the business school."

We shook hands and as I sat in the comfortable chair, we regarded at each other. I broke the silence first. "Beth, haven't we met before?"

She smiled politely. "Have we?"

I searched my memory and couldn't bring a Beth Lawson, or indeed a Beth anyone, to mind, but I was so certain that we'd met.

I shook my head. "Sorry Beth, I must be wrong. It's just that you remind me of someone - never mind. You wanted to see me?"

"I did, yes. You've only been here for three days but I'm already hearing very positive things about you. I wonder if you'd consider coming back to us for the start of the year for two or three weeks to help freshmen and foreign students? You know - the basics of study skills, speed reading, referencing and the like."

I beamed back at her. "Well, it's always nice to have positive feedback and yes, I'd love to come back. Up to three weeks from late September suits me fine."

"Excellent. I'll get a contract out to you. So, what else do you do, Lucie?"

We then spent a very pleasant half hour discussing the variety of work I undertook as well as the university, the business school and students. I couldn't shake off the feeling that we had met before but then I'd met so many people over the years, of course I couldn't remember them all. At the end of the meeting, we again shook hands as we said goodbye and I walked out of her office feeling very good about myself.

When Richard called that evening I was still feeling very pleased with myself following what had happened at the university and couldn't wait to share it with him.

"That's good Lucie, but it is only two or three weeks, isn't it? And what will you do in the summer? I mean, what about a holiday? I quite fancy going to Cuba for a few weeks, is that something you could afford?"

He knew perfectly well that a month, or even a week, in Cuba was completely out of the question at the moment, so why, I asked myself, was he bothering to ask the question? I took a deep breath. "Well, Richard, I'd have to think about it. But if I can't manage Cuba, perhaps we could take a break in the UK?" The words sounded small and petty as I said them. I knew what his reaction would be and I was right.

"I want decent holidays before I'm too old to properly enjoy them. I really don't see why I have to wait until you manage your affairs better."

The argument continued for several minutes with him getting angrier and angrier and me getting more and more defensive until he finally said, "You know, I'd hate to see the back of you, but quite honestly it can't be far off if things don't improve. Maybe we'd both be better off starting again ..."

I dropped the phone and dashed to the bathroom, barely making it before being violently sick. I couldn't believe what he'd just said to me and the effect his words had had. It was several minutes later that I trusted myself to leave the bathroom and when I picked up the handset, he'd rung off. Whether he'd heard me or not, I didn't care. I crept into bed, fully dressed, and lay there shivering until I saw the lightness of dawn through the curtains.

Despite everything that had been said between us, I still went to the supermarket and bought Richard's usual bottle of Southern Comfort, a couple of halibut steaks, some salad, cheeses and the like. After unloading the car, I lit the fire and poured myself a large glass of Merlot and tried to relax. Richard arrived at six thirty and gave me a brief hug when I went outside to greet him. Once inside, I gave him a large glass of his tipple and topped mine up. He was sitting in front of the fire looking calm, the very opposite of what I'd expected and how I was feeling.

"Thank you Lucie, that's very welcome." He smiled. "I've been looking forward to seeing you. It's been a bit of a funny week, hasn't it?"

"You could say that, yes."

"Let's try and have a nice weekend, shall we? I'm tired of arguments. A lot's been said and perhaps we shouldn't talk too much at the moment. I just want to enjoy your company. What do you think?" He looked at me expectantly.

I didn't know what to say, so just nodded. Of course I didn't want yet another row but I was finding his hot-and-cold approach increasingly difficult to cope with.

"Why don't we go out for a curry this evening?" he suggested. It was clear that he was making an effort to be nice. So we went out for a curry which was pleasant enough.

As always, I got into bed before him and lay on his side of the bed, moving over when he came in. He joined me and put his arm round my shoulders. "I'm so glad we're together tonight." There was real affection in his voice as he leaned over and kissed me. I automatically returned his kiss yet felt weirdly detached from him. I desperately wanted the warmth, excitement and mindlessness that love-making brings but try as I might, I just couldn't get there. So, while Richard softly stroked my breasts and gently rubbed my nipples, nuzzled my neck, licked my ears and softly bit my shoulders, all of which had had me moaning in appreciation and desire in the past, that evening I had to force myself to respond. I kissed his neck and shoulders, then ran my fingertips over his chest and down his belly to find his cock, starting a rhythmic pressure but, after a few moments, I felt him move away from me slightly and push me onto my back. I knew I wasn't ready so quickly reached over for the tube of KY and smeared a generous dollop between my legs in readiness. He came after a few thrusts and lay back with a satisfied sigh.

"You ok?"

"Yes, I'm fine. And you?"

"Tired Lucie, very tired."

I nodded in the darkness. "Yes, I'm tired too." And even though the last few days had brought me so much distress and pain, I slept all the better with Richard's strong, warm body next to mine.

We got up late the following morning and after breakfast, strolled down the hill into town, spent a couple of hours drifting from shop to shop and, as usual, ended up at the One Elm where we ate a light lunch and chatted amiably by the fire. As we wandered back up the hill, I felt strangely calm. I hugged Richard's arm tightly and looked up at him. "I do love you," I said softly.

He looked down at me. "Where did that come from?"

I shrugged. "Don't know. But I do."

He smiled and patted my hand, and I wondered, for the umpteenth time, why he found it so difficult to say those words back to me.

There was a message waiting for us on the answerphone, we were invited to dinner at James and Felicity's that evening so I called them back, arranging to be with them at seven thirty.

So often we'd ended up in bed on Saturday afternoons and after the previous night's detached sex, I felt a need to reconnect. "Shall we go to bed?"

"You tired?"

"No. I'm not tired. I just thought that we could work up an appetite for Felicity's excellent dinner. What do you think?" I leaned against the mantelpiece in what I hoped was a seductive pose.

He sighed. "Let's just relax for a couple of hours, shall we?"

I dropped the pose. "Yes, of course."

The rest of the afternoon passed quietly. Richard continued to read the papers and I tried, unsuccessfully, to lose myself in a book. At about six I went upstairs to change and while I was freshening up my makeup I heard Richard's mobile ringing and then his voice in conversation. I sat on the edge of the bed in silent fury but unable to go downstairs and confront him. When I couldn't hear Richard's voice any more, I went downstairs. He looked at me warily as I walked into the sitting room. "I'm sorry

Lucie. I have asked her not to call me at the weekends but there was something she wanted to ask my opinion about."

I sat and regarded him coolly. "That's alright Richard. I quite understand. After all, she must find it terribly difficult to cope on her own." I paused while he sighed and looked pained. "No, really," I continued, "it must be so hard for her to muddle through with all her money and of course her many friends to rally round. I'm sure she must feel so alone. Thank goodness she's got you to lean on ..."

Richard stood up and stared down at me, pale blue eyes blazing. "Ok, enough. I don't know which is worse, you being upset and crying or this. You're keep on making a mountain out of a molehill. All I'm doing is helping a friend Lucie. She's sad and I'm trying to help her as best I can ..."

I put my hand on his arm. "I need to be sure that there's nothing between you. I couldn't bear it if ..." He stopped my mouth with a kiss and I gave myself up to the moment. I knew that, deep down, I almost certainly didn't believe him but also knew that I was still prepared to give him the benefit of the doubt, probably again and again.

Later that evening we were sitting in front of James and Felicity's fire, sipping ice-cold gin and tonics and catching up with each other's news, after which we sat at their elegant table eating large steaks with potatoes boulangeres spiked with rosemary and a salad of mixed leaves and olives. During the lengthy pause between the main course and pudding, I realised that I had the beginnings of a headache so excused myself to relax for a few minutes in their cool conservatory where I took a couple of painkillers washed down with a large glass of cold water.

On my return to the dining room, I was surprised to find no-one there. I went into the kitchen to find Felicity and Richard deep in a loud argument. James was nowhere to be seen. I backed out without either of them noticing me and went to find James who was in the living room. "What's happening?"

He shrugged. "Not a clue, well, maybe a bit of a clue. I think Felicity's having a go at him about this woman he keeps seeing and he's having a go at her about some holiday he wants to go on. Don't look so worried Lucie. They'll get bored with shouting at each other and then we can get on with dessert." He smiled at me in an effort to lighten the mood.

I felt mortified and embarrassed. "I hate rows. Can't bear them. James, I'm so sorry about this."

"Let's leave them to it and have pudding, shall we?" He ushered me to the table where Felicity's enticing crème caramels were waiting to be eaten. There was still no sign of Richard or Felicity. James left, only to return moments later. "Looks like they're running out of steam - they'll join us in a minute."

He was absolutely right. They both returned, Richard looking slightly shame-faced whereas Felicity still looked militantly angry. We ate dessert in stony silence. "Coffee?" Felicity asked. We all nodded.

"Let me help you." I picked up some dishes and followed Felicity into the kitchen. "What on earth was all that about?" I asked once the door was closed behind us.

"He was trying to justify seeing that woman. Said that you're too busy to do some of the things he wants to do, so why shouldn't he see her? And then he was telling me that he wants to book holidays and can't because you don't know when you're working or whether you're working at all. Sorry Lucie, I just lost it and once we'd started, I just couldn't stop. I quite like a bit of a spat - and he walked straight into that one."

She looked thoughtful as she picked up the tray and I followed her back to the table where James and Richard were making small talk.

The remainder of the evening passed without further incident but I was glad when we eventually said our goodbyes and drove back home. Richard was unusually subdued and as I switched the bright kitchen lights on to make our customary late night cup of tea, I realised that my head was throbbing worse than ever.

However, I warmed Richard's side of the bed before sliding over to my cold side. He reached for me and after a few moments of perfunctory foreplay, pushed me on my back and fucked me. I closed my eyes and clung to him, not in passion but in sadness and resignation. He fell asleep within seconds of coming and I lay next to him, listening to his deep, regular breathing, unable to sleep myself. My head throbbed, my heart ached - I felt alone and empty.

I must have slept because the next thing I remember was the weak morning light nudging through the crack in the curtains. I was alone in bed, so after I'd been to the bathroom, I padded downstairs to find Richard watching the news. He looked up and smiled at me.

"'Morning Lucie. You looked so peaceful; I didn't want to disturb you."

We ate our customary breakfast after which he sat back with a smile. "Let's go for a drive this morning, shall we? It looks like it's going to be a fine day - it'll be nice to go somewhere different. What do you think?"

"That sounds nice. I'll just clear away and then get ready. About half an hour?"

"No. I'll clear up. You go and get ready," and with that he gave me a gentle push out of the kitchen.

I went upstairs slowly, frowning in bewilderment. Clearing up the kitchen certainly wasn't one of Richard's favourite things to do. I took extra care as I dressed in dark grey trousers, a pale grey sweater and an ankle-length red cardigan topped with a black, grey and red scarf. Bright red lipstick along with masses of mascara and I was ready.

As usual, I drove and we made our way into the Cotswolds ending up, an hour later, in Chipping Norton. We wandered around, had a coffee and decided to move on. I drove along the quiet roads and we chatted about trivialities. If only it could be like this all the time I thought as I hugged the moment to myself.

We'd just crested a hill when Richard said, "Why don't you pull into that layby for a moment?" I did so and as I switched the engine off, turned towards him with a smile, imagining that he'd wanted me to stop so he could kiss me but I realised that he was looking at me rather strangely.

"Lucie, there's something I ought to tell you." My heart started to race but I sat silently still. He looked very uneasy as he cleared his throat.

"Well, last Wednesday Julie and I met to go to the Tate and I went back to her flat ... and ... well ..." He looked at me with an almost frightened look on his face.

I'd never known Richard lost for words but I was damned if I was going to help him out so I remained stony-faced, waiting for him to tell me what I'd been anticipating and fearing for so long.

"Lucie, I'm sorry. I stayed the night and we fooled around a bit ..."

I heard a small wail and realised the sound came from me. I stared into Richard's face, dreading what else he was going to say.

"Oh God, Lucie. I never meant to hurt you." He looked completely wretched.

I sat up very straight but remained silent, truth to tell I had no idea what to say.

I reflected on what Richard had just said. I now had no doubt that last Wednesday wasn't the first time they'd 'fooled around'. I also knew that Richard's idea of 'fooling around' was anything and everything short of penetrative sex. In the past he'd insisted that 'fooling around' wasn't really cheating which was how he had justified his past bad behaviour, so I was very clear about what had been happening.

"Say something. Please Lucie, say something." His voice was a mixture of disbelief and exasperation.

I blinked slowly and looked at him. "Just what am I supposed to say?" I paused. "So, how long have you been 'fooling around' with her?"

"It's not her fault. It was me ..."

"How dare you defend her? How fucking dare you?" My voice rose as anger started to kick in. "I know full well what you'd say if I behaved like that. You'd say that I was a slut, a selfish bitch, a tramp ..." I took a deep breath. "And you never meant to hurt me? Tell me Richard, how long have I been asking you, begging you, to stop seeing her? And for how long have you been saying that I'm silly, small minded, selfish? Me selfish?" My voice was now almost a scream and I could feel wetness on my cheeks. I closed my eyes as pain ripped through me.

I felt his arm go round my shoulders and dully accepted his embrace. He leaned his face against mine and kissed my cheek. "Lucie, I'm sorry. The last thing I ever wanted to do was to hurt you. I care for you very deeply ..."

I opened my eyes. "Really? And this is how you treat someone you care for deeply? Well Richard, I'd hate to see what you'd do to someone you didn't care for."

His arm remained around my shoulders but I could feel him tense as I spoke. We stayed like that for what seemed like hours but must have been only a matter of seconds. I felt him take a deep breath as if to say something. "No Richard. I can't bear any more. Not right now." I heard him groan softly and felt glad - glad that he too was in pain. I moved slightly and he took his arm from my shoulders. I looked at him and saw that he had tears in his eyes. I wondered who they were for, him, me or her, and suddenly realised that I was cold and shivered.

"Are you alright?" He sounded concerned, how odd I thought. After everything that's just been said, how odd that he seems bothered that I'm cold.

"Frankly no, I'm not. But I'm not surprised. I knew that she'd get you into her bed sooner or later. She wanted it and you made it very easy for her, didn't you?" I felt uncomfortable and shifted in my seat. "I need a breath of fresh air." I opened the door and got out. The view down into the valley was very lovely with trees hugging one side of the hill. There was the beginning of a soft haze of mist as the afternoon had started to darken which made everything look slightly out of focus. I looked down trying to concentrate on what lay before me to block out what Richard had told me.

I heard the car door open and close and then felt his hands on my shoulders as he stood behind me. Despite myself, I leaned back into his body as yet more tears prickled my eyes. He nuzzled his face into my hair and I felt him kiss the back of my neck. "It's getting really cold. Let's go home."

I twisted round and looked at him. "Home? You want to come home with me?"

He nodded. "Yes of course I do. I'm with you Lucie, not her."

I stared at him. There was so much more that needed to be said but I knew that now wasn't the right time. "Ok. Home it is."

It was dark when we arrived home so I switched on lots of lights and went to light the fire. "Let me do that." I hesitated. "Please," he added. I stood aside and watched as he cleaned out the grate and lit some kindling, piling logs on top. He looked up at me as I stared down at him, such a cosy domestic scene I thought, but such a lie.

I turned away, and sat on my usual chair. He took his normal seat on the sofa. We looked at each other in silence. I felt bone weary and could see that he was exhausted too. One of the cats wandered in and jumped on my lap. I was so glad of the warmth and comfort that stroking his soft fur and hearing him purr brought. I glanced across at Richard before leaning back and closing my eyes as the room became warmer and the cat stopped purring as he fell asleep under my gentle touch.

I opened my eyes and saw that an hour had passed. Richard was sprawled on the sofa, fast asleep, and as I looked at his relaxed face, I couldn't stop my feeling of love but this time it was overwhelmed with a deep, dark sadness. I shifted in the chair slightly but enough to disturb the cat who jumped down and resettled himself on the rug near the fire. It seemed ridiculous that we'd been able to relax after such a tumultuous conversation and also, I thought wryly, that he's still here at all.

I stood up stiffly, stretched and went into the kitchen. I was hungry and knew that he would be too. I chopped an onion and fried it in a deep pan with a little olive oil and then added a leek, a potato, some celeriac and a handful of peas. I stood, hypnotically stirring and watched the vegetables soften, finding, as always, the process of cooking soothing and comforting. I added some stock and turned the heat down to a gentle simmer. There was a loaf of olive bread in the freezer which I put in the oven on a low heat. I stayed in the kitchen, occasionally stirring the soup, mulling over what was going to happen next and why I wasn't throwing him out right now. I knew why - ridiculously, I still loved him.

I heard footsteps and looked up to see Richard standing in the kitchen doorway. He looked at me and raised his eyebrows. "You cooking?" There was a small pause as I nodded. "For me?"

"For us," I replied, still looking into the pan.

"Bloody hell. I thought you'd sling me out and here you are ..."

"I was hungry and presumed that you would be too. Don't read too much into this Richard. And don't think for one moment that I'm not terribly hurt and angry by all this. I just can't believe that you've betrayed me." I looked at him, his eyes were downcast and I could see a glint of moisture on his eyelashes.

I wanted to hug him and tell him that I still loved him but I didn't hug him or tell him I loved him. I was too deeply wounded and disappointed to do that, but equally I was unable to continue berating him when he was so clearly in pain.

The vegetables were cooked so, silently, I blitzed them and then added a small splosh of cream. The bread was very nearly ready so I picked up dishes and cutlery which Richard took out of my hands to lay the table. The silence felt tense and uncomfortable but I couldn't think of anything to say. I served up the creamy soup and brought the warm bread to the table which I cut into thick chunks. We sat in our usual places, opposite each other, and simultaneously picked up our soup spoons at which I smiled. He returned my smile with a look of relief.

The soup was tastily comforting and we both ate with relish. "More?"

"If there's any left, yes please." I refilled his bowl and returned to the table. He nodded his thanks and then looked across at my empty bowl. "Don't you want any more?" I shook my head. Actually I wouldn't have minded more, but as there was only enough for one, I'd given it to him. I sat and watched him eat. When he was on his last mouthful I rose to my feet and brought some cheese and a small piece of pâté to the table. As we ate, we tried to make small talk about our coming week's activities but the tension between us was palpable, we sounded like strangers.

After the meal, I cleared the table while Richard made us coffee and stoked the fire. I went to take my normal seat but he patted the sofa next to him invitingly so I joined him. We sat staring into the fire, holding the hot mugs of coffee in our cupped hands and this time the silence felt more comfortable.

"Lucie? What would you say if I told you that I'd slept with Julie? I mean, would that be the end as far as you were concerned?" Richard's voice came as if through a mist.

I stared at him unblinkingly. "Have you? Tell me the truth Richard. Have you fucked her?"

"No. No, I haven't. And I don't want to. I want you. I don't want her. She doesn't understand me the way you do. She doesn't make me feel the way you do. I'm ashamed of what I did, but no Lucie, I fooled around with her but nothing more. You do believe me, don't you?"

I took a deep breath. "Richard, I'm exhausted. I have a dreadful headache and need to rest. You can stay if you want to or you can go - your choice. But I'm going to bed right now." I stood up and swayed.

He stood up quickly and put his arms round me. "I'm so sorry Lucie. I don't mean to cause you all this upset ..."

"Stop, please stop – I'm going to bed now. Just go."

As I got into bed I heard the front door open and close, his car start and then the sound of the engine faded as he turned the corner. I was so emotionally drained, I was asleep in minutes.

Monday morning passed in a flurry of activity at school. I was operating on automatic pilot but no-one seemed to notice. The students were in high spirits and everyone in the staff room was cheerful and chatty. I noticed Roger talking to some colleagues but rather than join them, decided to keep out of the way. What I definitely didn't need was someone being kindly solicitous towards me which would have tipped me into the tears that I was constantly fighting.

I somehow coped with the rest of the week, but must have been putting out some strange vibes because lots of my friends unexpectedly rang over the coming days. Karen, Anita, Pennie, Di, Felicity - they all called saying much the same thing, that they had been thinking about me and felt concerned. Each time, I assured them that I was alright but I could tell that they didn't believe me. Roger called twice on flimsy work-based reasons and hard though it was, I made sure that I didn't give too much away but I could tell when I saw him at school, he hadn't believed me either. On Wednesday morning he asked me outright if everything was okay and when I smilingly said, "So-so," he looked at me intently and assured me that he would be there for me if and when I needed him. Clearly, I'm a rotten liar I thought to myself wryly.

True to our normal routine, Richard rang every evening. Our conversations seemed briefer than usual and somehow less connected as he seemed guarded - pleasant, friendly, affable, yes - but nonetheless reserved, cautious and circumspect. There was nothing I could put my finger on but my feelings of unease grew as I ricocheted from fury to fear and from disappointment to despair.

On Friday afternoon, I went shopping and found myself buying the foods he really liked along with a litre bottle of Southern Comfort. At home, I cleared out the grate and laid the fire ready for lighting and then prepared another of his favourite meals - king prawn and asparagus risotto. As I did so, I wondered what the hell I was doing, knowing that he was almost certainly still seeing Julie and, probably, still 'fooling around' with her. I shuddered with disgust and drove the thought out of my head.

At six o'clock I heard Richard's 4x4 pull onto the drive and moments later he was standing at the door, looking slightly embarrassed and holding, to my great surprise, a large bunch of red roses. I took them as he came inside. "Thank you so much - they're beautiful." I stood on tiptoe to kiss his cheek.

He shrugged. "I know how much you girlies like flowers and I wanted to give you something that would make you smile." He looked at me. "And it has." He looked smugly pleased with himself.

I filled a vase with water and put the roses outside the back door to keep cool while the bubbles in the water dissipated. Well, well, this is the third time he's bought me flowers in five years, I thought as I poured a generous measure of Southern Comfort in one of my favourite cut-glass whisky tumblers for him and a large glass of Merlot for me. "Shall I light the fire?" His voice came through from the sitting room.

We sat fire gazing and sipped our drinks. I told him about my week, focusing on the positives and omitting any negative thoughts and feelings. He then talked about some walks he'd been on, a couple of country pubs he'd found which had done good lunches and the latest news from Louisa; he, like me, missed his daughter and loved hearing about her adventures.

"Time to cook, I think. Refill?"

"Yes please." He held up his empty glass.

I took it, with mine, into the kitchen and refilled both. He joined me and as I started to sweat the onions and garlic, gave me a warm hug. "Lucie, I'm really weary. Would you mind if I had a doze for a few minutes?"

"Of course not," I said, thinking the opposite. I wanted reassurance and overt shows of love and commitment, not a man who thought that a bunch of flowers was enough to atone for what had happened. He disappeared into the sitting room with his refilled glass. I remained in the kitchen, staring into the shallow pan as I slowly stirred the rice, then wine followed by warm aromatic stock.

When the risotto was nearly ready, I returned to the sitting room to find Richard blinking at the fire. He looked up. "I needed that.

Feeling much better now." He stretched. "Something smells good. Dinner ready?"

"It is. Come on through." And with that I left to check the risotto, light candles in the dining room, lay the table and throw some leaves, cherry tomatoes and olives into a bowl over which I drizzled my garlicky dressing. As I squeezed lemon juice and sprinkled freshly chopped parsley onto the finished dish, Richard put a chunk of parmesan on the table with a grater.

"Looks as good as it smells. Thank you Lucie, this is excellent." He smiled as he scraped a large sprinkling of the cheese onto his plate.

I smiled back at him and started eating. I was delighted that this was one of my better risottos and, for a few moments, we ate in silence.

"Shall I get you a refill?" Richard asked suddenly.

"Yes please."

"What shall we drink to?" he asked as he raised his glass.

"To us?" I replied and we touched glasses and both said, "To us." Did he really mean it? I had no idea, but for just that moment felt cautiously optimistic.

We both had seconds of risotto and salad and more wine. By now I was feeling decidedly squiffy and suspected that Richard was the same. He swayed very slightly as he got to his feet and I giggled from the safety of my chair. "You go and sort the fire and I'll clear the table. And shall we have refills?"

"I think we've both drunk quite a lot, haven't we?"

I nodded. "Absolutely - but it feels rather nice to be very slightly smashed, don't you think?"

After quickly clearing up, I arranged the roses in a vase and placed it in the middle of the dining table. I poured a couple of refills and carried them through to the warmth of the sitting room where Richard had just heaped more logs onto the dwindling fire and, to my irritation, was mindlessly channel flicking. "Hey, Pretty Woman's on in a few minutes. Do you fancy watching it?"

Watching television wasn't what I particularly wanted to do but Pretty Woman was one of my favourites so I nodded my agreement. "Come over here then." He patted the space on the sofa.

"Well, this is nice." I settled myself next to him and, to my surprise, felt his arm round my shoulders. As I looked up at him he kissed me lightly. Normally, I would never have drunk so much but it seemed like a really good idea that evening. In fact after an hour or so, I went to refill our refills which I brought in together with some small oatmeal biscuits and cheese. He raised his eyebrows. "To soak up the booze," I explained as I handed him his plate.

We nibbled on the cheese and biscuits and polished off the refills. As I reached for Richard's glass, he held my hand. "No more Lucie, otherwise I won't make it up the stairs." We both laughed and snuggled back down on the sofa. As the credits rolled, he ran his fingertips up and down my arm and nuzzled into my neck. "Bed?" His voice was muffled through my hair.

We went upstairs together - as I lay on his side of the bed, it struck me as absurd that we were behaving as if nothing untoward had happened but I quickly pushed the thought out of my head. It was clear that we both were slightly on edge but equally that he was being conciliatory which, I hoped, augured well.

When he joined me, I slid over to my cold side of the bed. I shivered and jiggled my feet up and down to generate some warmth. He didn't seem to notice as he reached across for me. "Spoons," he whispered so I obediently lay on my side with my back to him. He fumbled for my breasts and rubbed my nipples a little harder than I would have liked while he kissed the back of my neck and shoulders. I tried to roll back so we could kiss and fondle but he pushed me firmly back onto my side. I stared into the darkness. Sex in this position tended to make me feel remote and uninvolved. I never knew what to do with my hands or my mouth and much as I liked it from behind, really preferred to be on all fours. I ground my bottom into his groin and tried to feel sensual and erotic, truth to tell, I felt pretty unsexy. He pushed his hand between my legs closely followed by his cock but was too soft to manage it. "Shit, shit, shit," I heard him growl as he continued to try and force himself into me. I squirmed in an effort to help him but it was very clear the drink had taken its toll on him.

With a muttered "Oh fuck it," he rolled over onto his back and I gratefully moved from my position to face him. I ran my hand over his chest, down his stomach and started a gentle rhythm but it was very obvious that semi-hard was the best he could manage. However, after a few strokes he came with a small moan and seconds later I heard his breathing deepen.

I must have slept very deeply because the next thing I remember was opening my eyes to see a mug on the bedside table. Richard was nowhere to be seen. I reached up to find that the tea was cold and as I peered at my watch, I saw that it was just after half past ten. I threw the duvet back and swung my feet to the floor. "Richard?" I called down the stairs. No reply. I called again but all I heard was a cat meowing. I pulled on the only pair of jeans that still fitted me and a cream sweater.

I ran downstairs to find the cats looking accusingly at their empty bowls but no sign of Richard except a brief note. 'Gone for a run sleepyhead xxx'. Relieved, I tumbled kitty biscuits into their dishes and put the kettle on before wandering outside to see what the day was like. It was warm and balmy considering the month, with a promise of spring in the air and I noticed, for the first time, more than a hint of pale green on the trees.

I had an old, slightly rickety bench under the sitting room window so I sat there, sipping my tea. I leaned back and closed my eyes. "Well, well, well," I heard Richard's slightly mocking voice. "Decided to get up did you?"

I smiled without opening my eyes. "I did indeed. Isn't it a lovely morning?" I looked up to see him standing in his running gear.

"You were completely zonked out. Wonderful day Lucie. You should have joined me."

I kept my mouth shut. He knew that I didn't do running; it was a conversation that really wasn't worth revisiting.

Later we walked into town where, as usual, we ambled round the shops, had a coffee by the river where we watched children throwing bread for the ducks and swans, and then drifted back to the One Elm where we savoured a late lunch. Unusually, Richard ordered a steak and kidney suet pudding and I virtuously asked for a small chicken fricassee. I decided to stick to sparkling water as I knew I would be driving over to Warwick to see Two Gentlemen of Verona later which allowed Richard to enjoy a couple of pints of Guinness. We then meandered home where we both relaxed on the sofa. It was all very peaceful and as I sat back with my head on Richard's shoulder, felt serene and calm. As we'd eaten a late lunch, we decided against dinner. "We can always pick up a take-away on the way home if we're peckish," Richard said and I'd agreed.

Two Gentlemen of Verona was wonderfully acted and presented, telling the story of friendship, love, normal Shakespearean crossdressing, betrayal and eventual reconciliation. "Well, Proteus was a bit of a shit, wasn't he?" Richard sounded very slightly amused.

"Absolutely was, but amazingly, Julia forgives him."

Richard looked sharply at me. "You think she shouldn't have done that?"

"Probably not but then she loves him and people in love tend to forgive, don't they?" I looked at him and he stared back at me impassively.

I started to drive home on the main road when Richard suggested that we should detour through villages. As we travelled along the dark narrow lanes, it seemed that we were the only people in the world. "Stop here," he said abruptly so I pulled into a small layby, wondering what he wanted, and suddenly was swept back to the heart-breaking events of the previous weekend. The minute I put the handbrake on, he leaned across, cupped my chin in his hand and kissed me softly and tenderly. "Ok, you can drive on now," he said after the kiss. I blinked at him, totally caught off-guard, and drove on with a smile on my face and his hand resting on my thigh.

Once home, he silently took me by the hand and led me upstairs. After lighting the candles on my dressing table, he turned towards me and kissed my cheek, my neck, my shoulder and then returned to my face which he cupped in his hands before kissing me deeply and tenderly. I responded to his kisses with longing and passion - then scattered butterfly kisses on his forehead, eyes, cheeks, chin and throat before working down to kiss and nibble his chest and nipples while my hand drifted down across his belly, skirted his crotch and caressed his thighs. I heard him sigh and softly moan and then felt him, very gently, pull me back towards his face.

"Hey, no hurry. No hurry at all," he breathed into my mouth as he kissed me and then moved his head down to softly bite my neck. "I want to watch you play." I gasped and then realised he was gazing at me with a gentleness and yet an intensity that took my breath away.

I leaned away from him and pushed an extra pillow under my shoulders so that I was reclining, raised my hands to my throat and putting them back to back, ran them between my breasts down to my thighs and back again, this time flat against my skin unable to stop my body pushing against them. Much as I was in the moment and wanted to be as abandoned as possible, I felt slightly self-conscious and closed my eyes as I softly scratched my way down to my breasts and encircled my nipples with my middle fingers, arching my back as I did so.

"Look at me," I heard him say and shook my head. He put his hand over one of mine, caressed me through my hand and then abruptly stopped. "Look at me Lucie." I obeyed and he smiled down at me. "Good girl. I want to watch you come before I fuck you." A small gasp escaped me - this was shades of our early days when going to bed was far more captivatingly exciting than our now normal, routinely predictable sex. I managed to continue looking into Richard's eyes as I licked my fingers before gliding my hands down my body to my inner thighs to start a slow, deliberate pressure and rhythm that rapidly became faster and faster as ripples of sensuality and desire overtook me. I tried to slow down but couldn't and as I closed my eyes and arched backwards, was hit by spasms of pleasure. I lightened my touch and squirmed my way to a second and then, under an even lighter touch, a third orgasm.

As my breathing started to return to normal, I opened my eyes to see Richard staring at me, holding his tumescent cock. He almost growled as fucked me hard and fast - I was still in a post-orgasmic haze of tingling sensitivity, but his excitement was infectious and as he reached his explosive climax, I revelled in a fourth, albeit gentler, orgasm. He collapsed over me for a few seconds and then rolled off, still panting.

"Wow," I said softly.

"Wow indeed."

And moments later we were asleep in each other's arms.

I was awake earlier than normal for a weekend. Richard was fast asleep next to me and I dropped a light kiss on his cheek before getting out of bed as quietly as I could. As I stood under the hot shower, memories of last night swirled round my head and I smiled. It seemed that, at long last, things were getting back on track. After dressing in black leggings and a red sweater and putting on some makeup, I went into the kitchen, fed the cats, cleared the grate and laid paper and kindling for our next cosy fire and then made tea which I took upstairs. Richard was still asleep so I left his mug and tip-toed back downstairs. I heard his footsteps about ten minutes later as he made his way to the bathroom.

He joined me a few minutes later, having dressed. I raised my eyebrows in surprise, he would normally have showered before dressing but I made no comment. He looked a bit uptight which I didn't understand. I stood up with a smile. "Fresh cup, darling?"

He handed me his empty mug. "Please, that would be nice."

As I made fresh tea, he wandered into the garden and spent a few minutes gathering up some fallen twigs and leaves. I smiled towards him thinking how kind he was to do this on a chilly March morning.

He joined me in the sitting room and sat down. He cleared his throat. "Lucie, I just can't do this."

As the words sank in I looked across at him, my heart pounding. "What? What are you talking about?"

He looked down at his clasped hands. "It's not good enough, it's just not good enough ..."

"What? What's not good enough? What are you talking about Richard?'

"Us. This ..." he swept his arm vaguely. "It's just not good enough. I want someone who can pay for some decent holidays. I want someone who isn't scratching around, trying to make some sort of a living. I want someone who doesn't still have a mortgage when that sort of thing should have been paid off long ago ..." I sat frozen. I had no idea why this was coming after two such lovely, loving days. The pain of what he was saying cut through me like a knife and I closed my eyes with a groan.

I felt him walk past me to the door and then heard him going upstairs. I followed him into the spare room to see him putting his things into his bag. He looked up. "It's no good any more. You know that, don't you?"

Of course I didn't know that. I'd believed him when he'd kissed me. I'd believed him when we'd made love the previous evening. I'd believed him when he'd said that he loved me. I'd believed him when he had told me he would stop seeing Julie. I'd believed him when he'd talked about us having a real and lasting future together.

"But ... but ..." I started to say, "don't you love me? Didn't the last couple of days mean anything to you?" He looked up into my stricken face. "So that's it, is it?" I said shakily. "After five years, you just walk away. It's that easy, is it?"

He stood up, bag in hand. "No. No, it's not that easy. But it's not working for me ..."

I screamed. I couldn't help it - all the frustrations and uncertainties of the past few months poured out as I screamed. And as I screamed, tears coursed down my face. He looked really alarmed and pushed past me. I followed him downstairs and stood in the doorway as he opened his car and put his bag on the passenger seat. "Richard, can we talk ..." I started.

"No. I don't want to talk. I want to go. I need to think. Look, I'll be in touch some time soon ..."

"Richard?" I said very softly.

He looked at me. "Come here." He hesitated. "Please come here."

He walked towards me. I was standing on the front door step and was taller than him as he remained on the driveway. As he came close to me I held his face in my hands and, very softly and very gently kissed his mouth. "I love you," I said, staring into his eyes. He broke away from me, walked back to his car and climbed in without looking at me. As I watched him drive away I could barely see, it felt as though my very future was disappearing as he turned the corner and the sound of his engine faded.

I don't know how long I stood at the door, but eventually I turned on my heel and went back into the house. I wandered around, not knowing what to do, but hoped that by moving I might be able to leave some of the pain behind me, and as I stumbled from room to room, I whimpered and cried in disbelief and grief.

The landline rang and I snatched it up eagerly, thinking that it might be Richard saying that he'd made a terrible mistake and could he come home. It wasn't. It was Felicity. "Hey Lucie, are you coming over for that walk?"

I remembered, we'd arranged to go for a country walk with Felicity and James that morning.

I opened my mouth but no words would come. "Lucie? What's wrong?"

Hearing her kind voice made me cry all the harder. "Lucie. What's wrong? Lucie, talk to me. Shall I come over?"

"Oh Felicity ..." I couldn't say anything else.

"I'm on my way," I heard her say and then the line went dead.

I was on my third whisky by the time Felicity arrived. She hugged me, made us coffee and then sat next to me, holding my hand. "Tell me," she said softly and between sobs I managed to pour out what had happened.

"But Lucie, I've been saying for ages that all this is damaging you and deep down I'm sure that you know that's true. So, why on earth did you hold on to something that kept hurting you?"

"Because I loved - love him." My tears and sobs were uncontrollable. "You know you can't just switch love off. I know he's behaved terribly badly, I know that he's been cheating on me for God knows how long, I know that he's unable to make any proper commitment - I know all this but I love him and just can't stop ..."

We talked some more. Felicity continued to try and convince me that I needed to move on and I continued to cry. Eventually, I couldn't talk any more and, amazingly, couldn't cry any more. She stood up. "You're exhausted. You try and get some sleep and I'll call you later." I was enfolded in a warm hug and could sense that she was willing me to be strong.

Later, when I went upstairs and sat on the edge of my crumpled bed, I buried my face into the pillow that still smelled of Richard and cried helplessly for the future that I now knew was almost certainly lost.

I awoke fully dressed and found I was still clutching the pillow I'd wept into. It was sodden with my tears and as I shakily got to my feet, the memory of the previous day hit me and I just made it to the bathroom in time before being violently sick. I felt cold and shivery, all I wanted to do was to creep into bed and stay there.

I stripped the bed unable to bear the thought of being able to detect Richard's scent that so often I'd breathed in lovingly as he slept, and shoved the linen into the washing machine. I knew that I couldn't face work - not today - so rang the school and left a message, saying that I had a migraine and wouldn't be able to come in. I crept back to the unmade bed and crawled under the duvet, dozing most of the day away, waking only when I needed the bathroom or when my crying woke me up. It was getting dark when I got out of bed and made my way to the kitchen where I made tea and drank a glass of water. I felt hungry so made myself a sandwich but after one bite threw it away. I sat in the dark sitting room and channel flicked but there was nothing that held more than a few seconds of my attention so I went back to bed and continued to doze and cry.

I woke in the dark and saw that it was just after five in the morning. My pillow was wet and when I looked in the mirror I saw a chalk-white face staring back at me with huge dark shadows under her eyes. I knew that I'd have to go to work so I stood under a steaming hot shower for twenty minutes and then washed my hair. I dressed and then put some makeup on. I looked a little better but not much.

I drove to the school very early in the morning, planning to prepare what needed to be done, see my students and then leave. I made myself a cup of coffee in the staffroom and then immersed myself in some past examination papers to find topics to give them some last minute revision. I found, to my surprise, that I was well able to do this and, for the first time in forty eight hours was in control. Just after eight, staff started to come in, all came over and solicitously asked if I was feeling better to which I said yes. The students worked hard and the morning passed quickly. I found that concentrating on them drove everything else out of my mind.

As I walked back towards the staffroom, I tried to hold onto the cheeriness but it seeped away and by the time my hand was on the door handle was back in aching misery. Luckily, everyone attributed yesterday's migraine to my looking so wretched and were gently sympathetic which almost made it worse for me. Roger took one look at me and got to his feet. I assured him I was alright but that the migraine was returning so I was going home. He looked sceptical but concerned so I left as soon as I decently could, and was crying yet again when I opened the front door.

I made myself some scrambled eggs on toast but after one mouthful retched so they went into the bin. Sugary tea was ok though and I drank a large mug greedily. I wandered aimlessly round the house. Everything reminded me of Richard - the towels he always used, his shaving tackle and toothbrush on the bathroom shelf, the grey shirt he'd left, the opened bottle of Southern Comfort, the blue mug that he preferred to use - the list went on and on. I took his stuff from the bathroom and chucked it in the bin. I threw the towels he always used into the washing machine and put them through the hottest wash, twice.

I'd just picked up the bottle of Southern Comfort when I heard the landline ring and picked up, hoping that it was Richard, not knowing what on earth I would say. It wasn't, it was Felicity. "Lucie, I just wanted to see how you are."

I opened my mouth, but all that came out was, "I love ..."

I heard a sigh of exasperation. "You keep saying that but it's not going to change anything. He's been distant and awkward for months. He's sidestepped any talk about what you want in terms of a future. He cheated on you. What more do you need to say enough is enough? Where's your pride? For God's sake Lucie, stop being such a fool."

We exchanged a few more words and as I put the phone down I considered what she'd just said. Was I being a complete and utter fool? I rang Anita and told her what had happened over the weekend; the advice she gave was softer but the same. I then rang Karen who didn't mince her words. "What a cruel arse. Don't you bloody dare even think about trying to get him back. Lucie, you can do so, so much better. You know that. Stop crying and stop being such a wimp."

I then rang Pennie who said much the same and whilst the words hurt, the truth started to sink in - that despite the fact that I loved him, the way Richard had behaved clearly demonstrated that he didn't love me. Well, I said to myself, maybe he did love me but not enough. And not the kind of love that I wanted or, from what my dear friends said, deserved.

I went to bed feeling very slightly calmer but slept fitfully and when the skies lightened, was tangled in the unmade bed, crying. I got ready for the day, feeling exhausted and still looking terrible. It took quite a lot of makeup to cover up the pallor and dark shadows but I managed the next day at work, and the next, although avoiding Roger became more and more difficult.

Karen phoned early on Thursday evening. "We're going to the movies this evening," she said briskly.

"But, but ..." I objected weakly.

"But me no buts. I'm coming to pick you up in an hour. You be ready, and make sure you put some lippie on."

True to her word, she picked me up at six and half an hour later we were settled in the dark warmth of the local cinema watching The Kitchen, a chaotic comedy set entirely in a kitchen, which made us both laugh a great deal. As we left to go to the One Elm to share a cheese board and a bottle of rosé, I realised that, for the first time in nearly a week, Richard hadn't been in my head for close to two hours. I still couldn't eat but watched Karen enjoying some excellent cheese. I managed the wine though but when, at about ten o'clock, she took me home, the misery of the past week, threatened to engulf me yet again.

She came in for a coffee and we settled down on the sofa. "It's going to be tough for a while. You know that, don't you?" I nodded weakly, tears in my eyes. "You're strong. You've been through much worse than this. I still don't know why you cared so much for someone who was such a bastard to you for so long, but I do know that love is love and if you're hooked, well, you're hooked."

I sniffed and wiped my nose. "I'm coping. I am - but only just. I mean, it's one thing to feel you want out of a relationship but it's quite another to see another woman for ages, pretend there's nothing in it, shag her, then leave saying it's just not good enough ..." I was warming to the subject and continued in this vein for another ten minutes with Karen nodding in agreement.

"I think the worst thing was the farewell fuck," she said as I drew breath. "I mean, if you'd known he was going to walk out, would you have gone to bed with him?"

"No. Almost certainly not."

"There you go then. And you're still shedding tears over lost love? I tell you Lucie, you're so much better off without that controlling shit ..." and it became her turn to wax lyrical on the subject which I found strangely cathartic.

I slept better that night than I had for a few nights and awoke feeling weepy yet somehow stronger. It was Friday and I wasn't working so I wore the brightest clothes and lipstick I could find, and drove into town to have a manicure. "Slapper red please," was my answer as to what colour I wanted and as I strode out into the weak March sunshine I heard a wolf whistle which made me smile despite myself.

Kate and Albert's shop was my next call and, as it was a quiet morning, I sat and told her my sad story. Albert laid his head on my lap and looked mournfully sympathetic while Kate looked aghast and then angry as I got to the events of the previous Sunday. "I don't know what to say," she said as I became silent. "I really don't know what to say."

I looked at her and shrugged my shoulders helplessly as yet more tears threatened. "I feel so wretched. I mean to be dumped like that after five years. Wasn't I worth any more than that?"

"How could you possibly love someone who treated you like that? What a fucking wanker."

I gasped. I'd never heard Kate swear let alone use the f-word so leaned down and put my hands over Albert's ears. "Not in front of the children," and we both then burst out laughing. It was the first time I'd laughed for nearly a week and it felt very good, strange but good. I stayed for another hour and then left, promising to keep in touch.

My mobile quacked and as I looked down, my heart raced but it wasn't Richard, it was Roger reminding me that it was Tracy's funeral the next day. I reflected on how Barbara must be feeling and felt ashamed of myself. All that had happened was that a lying cheat had left me, no-one had died.

Saturday morning was initially grey but the clouds dispersed leaving clear blue skies. I'd decided against black so wore grey with a fuchsia pink scarf and matching lipstick, it seemed entirely appropriate to wear something pink for a beautiful girl like Tracy.

The crematorium was crowded with as many people who could fit in, many standing at the back. I looked around and saw most of the staff and all Tracy's classmates as well as friends and family. Her coffin, adorned with a heart of white roses, was carried in by her closest friends to the music of Queen's 'We Are The Champions'. Tracy had shared a love of Queen with her mother and, after the service which was incredibly moving, as the curtains closed around her 'Don't Stop Me Now' blasted out. It reminded me of my own father's funeral when Alex had chosen 'Love Is The Greatest Thing' by Jack Hylton for us to go out by, so we'd almost danced out of the crematorium. As I walked out into the sunshine I felt a strange calmness and peace despite a deep, aching grief.

Barbara was surrounded by family but I managed to hug her with a promise of getting in touch very soon. She gave me a wan smile and squeezed my hand. As I slowly made my way towards my car, I felt a hand on my shoulder and a familiar voice said, "Hey, you ok?"

I stopped and turned with a smile. "Hello Roger. My God, that was quite a funeral, wasn't it?"

"It was." He looked sombre. "Makes one think about one's own kids, doesn't it?"

I shivered. "It does. And that doesn't bear thinking about."

He paused for a moment. "Look Lucie. I don't want to be pushy but I don't suppose that you'd come for a drink with me, would you?"

I was about to say no but heard myself say, "That's a really nice idea Roger, thank you."

He looked delighted. "I know a really good pub. Want to follow me?"

The White Hart was on the top of a hill with glorious views down into the valley. We found a small table in the window and sat sipping our drinks and talking about the funeral, Tracy and her family and how poignant the occasion had been. "Let's have a bite to eat," Roger suggested and I realised that, having not eaten for several days, I was starving. "Their fish and chips are wonderful," and indeed they were but I found I could only manage a few bites. As we talked and ate I felt relaxed until he said, "So, how are things with you?" which brought the memory of last weekend crashing back.

I blinked back the threatening tears. "Not that great, but I'm getting there."

"You talking about work or personal?"

"Both actually." I laughed at the realisation that that was true.

"Do you want to tell me about it?"

I shook my head. "It's all a bit raw at the moment. Do you mind if I don't?"

"Of course not," and he then started talking about his local pub quizzes which he enjoyed. "You might like to come along one evening. We could do with someone who's not just into sport."

"Sounds like fun. Perhaps I will. Not right now though." And I steered the conversation into safer waters.

A couple of hours and two coffees later we decided it was time to go. "It's been lovely Roger. Really lovely. Thank you so much." I kissed his cheek. He stared into my eyes with an intensity that was slightly disconcerting, and then moved a little closer to gently stroke my cheek before holding my chin and kissing my mouth very softly, very gently. It was a warm, affectionate, tender kiss and as he moved away very slightly, I could feel the wetness of tears on my cheeks.

"I'm here whenever you want to talk, you know that."

I looked at him gratefully. "I know, I know. And thank you."

He enfolded me in a hug - a kind, compassionate, companionable hug that meant so much more than a pushy, sexual embrace. I hugged him back and we then said our goodbyes.

"See you on Monday," was his final farewell and we waved to each other as we left the car park. I was so tired when I arrived home that I went straight upstairs, peeled off my clothes, crawled into the still-unmade bed and fell asleep.

I was woken on Sunday morning by the landline ringing but couldn't be bothered to get up to answer it and lay in bed til well after noon, it was only the need for a drink that drove me downstairs. I looked round the kitchen as the kettle was boiling and noticed the bottle of Southern Comfort. I made my tea first and then, very slowly, unscrewed the top and poured the contents down the sink. I knew it was wasteful but it felt so good. I smashed the bottle into the sink, listening to the sound of breaking glass. I then took Richard's favourite blue mug and banged it against a green mug I'd never liked so that too broke. I went into the dining room and ripped the red roses apart, not feeling the thorns spiking my hands and while I did all this, I cried in anger and bitterness, because I was seeing more and more clearly that I'd wasted my love and been taken for a fool.

Chapter 4 - April

Despite continued feelings of exhaustion and grief, I managed to get to work looking half decent. The positivity of working with my students buoyed me up amazingly and I found myself smiling and laughing with them. There was much talk about Tracy's funeral but, to my amazement, the students succeeded in staying focused on their work.

On Tuesday morning, Roger came over and asked me to go and see the Head who asked if I could continue until the end of May for one day a week so students could drop in for last minute tutorials. Could I? Certainly could, I said emphatically and walked out of the office with a spring in my step. I was smiling as I walked back into the staffroom and saw that Roger was waiting for me, holding up a celebratory cup of coffee. I took it with a smile of thanks and he looked at me sadly. "I'm really pleased that you'll be here for a while longer Lucie. But ..." his voice faded slightly as he continued, "you know that I like you. I really like you and I'd like us to be more than friends. I know that you're going through a hard time at the moment and just wanted to say that I'm here whenever you want." He looked slightly embarrassed.

I put my hand on his arm. "Roger, you're so kind. Thank you. You're right. I'm having a really shitty time at the moment, but I value your friendship more than I can say." I planted a soft kiss on his cheek and hugged his arm.

He kissed me back and then stood back quickly. "I know, I know. And I guess being friends with you is better than nothing, so friends it is," he paused again, "but perhaps when you're feeling better we can go out."

Much to my relief, other people coming into the room stopped him saying any more and we started chatting about school stuff. I knew it was far too early to even think about seeing someone else but had to admit that it was very flattering to know I was still fanciable and fancied.

That evening I cooked myself a prawn stir-fry which smelled delicious but after the first mouthful I felt nauseous and couldn't bring myself to eat more so after picking out the prawns for the cats, I reluctantly threw the rest away. Well, this is one way of losing weight I thought to myself as I drank yet another cup of hot, sweet tea.

Felicity called me later and after our how-are-yous she hesitated and cleared her throat. "Lucie, I'm not sure how to tell you ..."

"What?" I interrupted, my heart thumping.

"Well ... well, we had a call from Richard. He wanted to know how you were coping. I said that you were fine, sad but fine and he then said that he'll be in touch with you soon." She was silent for a moment. "Lucie, say something."

I was holding my breath while she spoke. "Why didn't he call me?" Tears were threatening again.

"He said that he didn't want to upset you."

"Upset me?" I laughed shakily. "What the fuck does he think he's done to me already?"

"I know, I know," Felicity sounded angry. "I said that I'd pass his message on but if he calls us again, I'm going to tell him to get in touch with you direct. That is, if you want to hear from him?"

"I kind of do and kind of don't - I certainly don't want more of the same that's for sure."

And we continued to talk - well, I continued to talk while Felicity patiently listened. After close to half an hour I'd talked myself out and said my grateful goodbye. Talking about Richard had brought back the rawness of the previous couple of weeks and I cried helplessly for the remainder of the evening before crawling into my still-unmade bed.

I awoke on Wednesday with my pillow wet with tears again, but the day passed in a flurry of work at the school which again made me feel useful and smiley. I spent the coffee break talking to Annie who took great delight in telling me about some of her latest dates. "But I have to say that it's Roger I really like." She sounded very sad. "I'm sure he doesn't even notice me. I hang around when he's here but apart from the usual colleague stuff, there's nothing else." She sighed.

"Why don't you tell him?"

She reddened. "Oh I couldn't, I just couldn't." She sighed again. "Maybe one day he'll notice me but til then, I'll just keep on hoping ..." What could I say to her when I'd made such a mess of my own love life I thought, so just made some sympathetic noises which seemed to do the trick.

A few minutes after I arrived home, a text came though from Karen, asking if I'd like to go out for a drink. 'Thank you darling but think I need an early night. So sorry ;-/ see you soon x'. I knew that I couldn't face being sociable, not quite yet. I'd planned to cook some fish for my supper but the mere thought of it made me feel sick so I didn't bother. I knew I ought to eat something so I dunked a couple of biscuits into a large mug of tea and managed to force them down, despite the continued feeling of nausea.

Thursday saw me starting work at the university, supporting first year students who were struggling with their assignments. I'd always relished this kind of work and was told that, provided I fulfilled an average of twelve hours a week, I could meet, text, phone, Skype or email with students. Wonderful to have that much flexibility I thought and sent a blanket email to my group, introducing myself to them and inviting them to get in touch as soon as possible.

Friday, Saturday and Sunday were spent at home, waiting for Richard's promised call. Of course he didn't ring and as the days passed I felt more and more wretched, hopeless, abandoned and worthless. Anita, Karen, Di, Pennie, Kate and Roger all called me to talk and ask if I wanted company which I didn't. I talked so much on the phone I started boring myself but just couldn't stop. The thought of eating made me feel even worse so I fed the cats with the fish languishing in the fridge which they much appreciated.

By Sunday, I felt that I was climbing the walls in despair and went to bed. Unable to sleep, I tossed and turned as I ran through the might-have-been scenarios that went round and round unendingly in my head.

What a dreadful week. The realisation that I was unlikely to hear from Richard was beginning to sink in which felt absolutely like unfinished business, so I was on tenterhooks all the time and whilst I managed to work, the times I wasn't working I cried more and more. The days were lonely and the nights lonelier still. I still couldn't eat but drank unending mugs of hot sweet tea which kept me going.

So many of my dear friends rang and called round, all saying the same thing - that I needed to get the grieving over as fast as possible and move on. John suggested that I went onto a dating website, but I knew I was in no state to even consider meeting someone new, so soon after five long years loving the same man. After what Richard had said to me on that final Sunday and his call to James and Felicity, I hadn't even been allowed proper closure which made me feel that I was being cruelly punished for a crime I hadn't committed.

I'd booked in for one of my regular hair appointments on the Thursday afternoon and as I sat in the chair, having colour combed through I talked to Rachel, my lovely stylist. She listened patiently to my sad story and stood with her mouth open as I told my story. "So he's not been in touch for a couple of weeks?"

I shook my head, blinking back the ever-present tears.

"Bastard." She wrapped a towel round my head and went to make me some tea. "You know, there're three things that you have to have in a relationship," she said as she returned holding a large cup with two biscuits on the saucer. "Eat those," she added firmly as I went to put them to the side, so I obediently dunked them in the hot liquid and as I took tiny mouthfuls, she sat down next to me. "There's basic compatibility, a real willingness to compromise and open, honest communication - that means listening loads more than talking."

I nodded my agreement. "You're right. I thought we had those, at least in part, but obviously not ..." my voice trailed off and I gazed into the mirror at the pale, sad face staring back at me.

When I was coloured, cut and primped I had to admit that I looked a whole lot better. "Put some lipstick on before you go out," she ordered so I obeyed. "Much, much better," was the verdict and I had to agree. "So," she said as we arranged for my next appointment, "lippie on every single time you go out from now on. You promise?"

"I promise," and I stayed true to my word. Despite the many more tears I shed over that and subsequent days, I made sure that I wore bright lipstick each and every time I left the house from then on.

It was the last week of term before the Easter break and the students were in high spirits so being at the school was fun and I found myself unexpectedly laughing which felt strange after so much misery and crying.

On Thursday evening, I was surprised to see an email from a small local agency run by Laurie and Lyn Henson who organised short spring and summer trips to Stratford for schoolchildren from Europe who were accompanied by their teachers. I'd hosted students several years ago while Susie was at school, she'd enjoyed meeting new people and it had been a useful income stream for me. Leigh said that she hoped I was well and, as they were expecting an unusually large number of visitors, was I interested in providing beds and food for some teachers. I certainly was I emailed back enthusiastically and as I pressed the send button I smiled, chances were I'd cook for some really nice people which I always enjoyed and generate more money which was always a plus. Lyn's reply came back almost immediately, visits were starting in May so could I host three teachers that first week? Absolutely yes I replied and as I sat back, calculating what income that would produce, I started to plan menus.

Of course, I didn't hear from Richard that week although every day I looked for texts from him and waited by the phone every evening. I refused invitations to go out from friends, feeling unable to be civilised company while I was so unhappy. I still awoke every morning on a pillow wet with my tears but they were beginning to be tears of disappointment and contempt at his cowardice as he continued not to get in touch to put a final full stop on our relationship.

On Friday evening I went to bed and, for the first time since he'd left, felt as if I wanted - no, needed - release. I reached into my bedside cabinet for my pale blue friend and slowly started to stroke and scratch down my throat, across my breasts, down my flanks and between my legs but, try as I might, I couldn't get to orgasm so after nearly half an hour, lay back, dissatisfied and exhausted. I'd always been able to make myself come and was angrily exasperated that I couldn't this time. I stumbled downstairs to pour myself a large glass of whisky and took it back upstairs to drink in bed, feeling unattractive and sexless which made me cry all the harder.

It was the first week of the Easter holidays and when I woke on Monday morning, I lay in bed, not knowing what to do and spent a couple of hours aimlessly wandering round the house. I walked into town and mooched around but found it hard when so many shops, cafes and bars reminded me of times spent with Richard. I ended up in the One Elm and sat by the fire that had just been lit, sipping a coffee and gazing into the flames, wondering what the future held.

"Well, hello stranger," a familiar voice said and I glanced up to see Kyle looking down at me smilingly. He pulled up a chair and joined me. "So, what's new?"

I started to tell him about the school and other bits of work. "That's not exactly what I meant," he very gently interrupted. "I've not seen you for ages. Are you feeling ok? Not ill, are you?" He looked at me more intently. "Come to think about it, you're looking quite pale."

"Well ..." I started and then stopped. "It's a bit of a long story Kyle. Sure you want to hear it?"

"Wait a minute." He went to the bar, returning a few moments later with a bottle of his favourite Cuvée Jean-Paul and two glasses. "Shoot," he said as he poured us both drinks and settled back comfortably. So I told him my sorry tale of love, betrayal, anger and disappointment. When I finished, he took a deep breath. "Well, well, well. I have to say that I never really warmed to him but I didn't expect him to behave like that." I blinked back tears as he leaned forward and held my hand. "Now, don't cry. You'll smudge your makeup and no man's worth that, is he?" I shook my head and stared into the flames trying to supress my tears. We sat together for what seemed like ages, the warmth of the fire on our faces and my hand in his.

The spell was broken by his mobile ringing and he stood up as he answered it. It was clearly a complicated business call and with a smile of apology he walked towards the back of the bar. I mentally shook myself as I poured myself a very small top-up and gulped the wine down. I picked up my bag and followed him. He was still talking so I waved him goodbye with a blown kiss which he returned.

On Tuesday afternoon I decided that enough was enough and cleaned the kitchen from top to bottom after which I stood back and surveyed the sparkling surfaces. That felt so good I did the same in the sitting room by which time it was dark so I lit some candles and sat gazing at the flickering lights with a yet another large cup of sweet tea and a small glass of whisky.

On Wednesday morning I awoke and looked round my bedroom critically. There were piles of clothes on the floor and the bed was still unmade, it all looked grubby and sordid. No more of that, I said to myself as I sorted through the clothes, hung up some and threw the rest into the washing machine. I dug out an old duvet cover covered in roses, not my usual style but I wanted something pretty, and made the bed, spraying a little perfume to make it feel more luxurious. I stood back - better I thought, much, much better.

I opened a drawer to put a sweater away to see a tangled mess so tipped the contents of the drawer onto the bed and threw away a couple of sweaters I'd been meaning to get rid of for ages, carefully folded up the rest and replaced the full drawer.

I then opened my underwear drawer to see an even bigger tangle and with a sigh emptied everything onto the bed. Loads of knickers and saggy bras went into the bin which left a few, reasonable pieces. Need to get more tomorrow, I said to myself, and pretty stuff too. As I was folding and putting things away neatly, I came across an expensive-looking business card. I read the name 'Philip Ellis' and frowned in puzzlement for a few minutes before remembering the conversation in the One Elm in January. Had it been a silly chat up line or was it a serious proposition I mused. I went to throw the card in the bin but something stopped me and I put it on the bedside table.

I went shopping for underwear the next day and made sure that I bought bright colours - anything different and anything to cheer myself up, even a little.

I spent the rest of the week continuing to clean the house until, on Friday the whole place gleamed, much to my satisfaction. I lost count of the number of times I picked up Phil's card, wondering what to do with it, but each time it was returned to the same place as I did nothing.

Karen called round on Friday afternoon to bring round the latest edition of 'Olive' and nodded in approval at what she saw. "Wow, this looks wonderful Lucie. Want to come and sort out my place?"

I shook my head. "I hate cleaning but just had to do it. It kind of felt symbolic. You know, throwing out the stuff I didn't want and just keeping things that I know are pretty or useful?"

Karen nodded. "Good girl. You're getting there."

Unexpectedly, I started to cry and Karen gently put her arm round my shoulder before suggesting that we go out for a curry, so a couple of hours later saw us sitting in a local Indian restaurant scanning the menu, sipping Cobra beer. Much to my surprise I felt that I could eat so we nibbled hot, spicy food, drank more beer and talked interminably about work, our kids, clothes, latest movies and my spring-cleaning which reminded me yet again about Phil's card so I told Karen about what had happened.

"Why haven't you been in touch with him?" Karen asked.

I frowned in concentration as I reached for my fourth Cobra. "Richard said ..."

"Oh for God's sake," Karen interrupted, "it's got fuck all to do with Richard. What do you want to do? And don't you dare mention that bastard's name again this evening."

"I don't know, I really don't know. I mean, was it just a chat up line or was ..."

"Does it matter?" Karen interrupted me again as she could tell I was almost certainly going to say what Richard had said. "Just call him. Or email him. Or don't. But don't even think about making the decision because of what some lying cheating ..."

"Stop. Please stop. I know what you feel about Richard but he was such an integral part of my life for nearly five years and it's really hard to stop thinking about him. Know what I mean?" I blinked through a mist of tears.

Karen held up her hands. "Ok, ok. I'll stop, but only for the moment. I don't want you ever to excuse his appalling behaviour. Anyway," she said quickly to stop me saying anything else about Richard, "what are you going to do about Phil?" She sat back with a kind yet exasperated look on her face.

"I ... I ... I'm going to contact him. I just don't know which way is best. What do you think?"

Karen sighed as we spent the next few minutes discussing how best to contact Phil. "I can't believe how indecisive you are. Just email him." She shook her head at me. "Where's the positive, determined, purposeful woman we all know and love gone? I don't like this Lucie half as much."

"I'm sorry," I said softly as the reality of what she'd just said hit me. "Truth to tell, I feel pretty lost at the moment and have to say I don't like me much right now. Maybe that's why he ..."

"Left?" Karen asked shrewdly. "No, he didn't leave because of that. He left because he was shagging someone else who happened to have more money than you. And then, to add insult to injury, he calls one of your friends to tell them to tell you he'll be in touch and then doesn't. And who behaves like that? A cowardly rat, that's who ..." I could tell she was warming to her theme and this time didn't stop her as she continued for the next few minutes. I could tell she was enjoying herself.

Another Cobra each later, followed by coffee and we were ready to leave. Karen had driven us into town but it was very clear that neither of us was in a fit state to drive and we earnestly debated whether to walk or get a taxi. The taxi won so after dropping Karen, I was home. The house smelled fresh and welcoming and as I fell into bed I revelled in the feeling of crisp, cool linen and, for the first time in many nights, slept the night away.

After my first cup of tea of the day on Saturday morning, I drafted an email to Phil but it didn't read quite right so I saved it in drafts to return to later. I called Karen who sounded dreadful. "I've got such a headache. Haven't you?"

"You know, I haven't. And I'm usually such a lightweight with booze. I feel fine."

"Well, I'm going back to bed for a while. Oh no, I can't. I need to get the car ..."

"No you don't. I'll come down, pick up your keys and bring it back."

Of course Karen argued for a few moments before agreeing that she'd let me collect her car but in less than half an hour, it was parked snugly on her drive. I refused a cup of tea, realising that she really did need to sleep her way through her hangover and headed towards the supermarket to buy some vegetables for soup - after the previous night I felt ready for food. The remainder of the day passed peacefully as I made roasted butternut squash soup while I ate a crispy bacon sandwich slathered with tomato ketchup, it seemed that my fasting days were over.

I was woken by the phone ringing on Sunday morning and, for a split second, thought that it might be Richard. Of course it wasn't and I shrugged away the pang of disappointment as I heard Pennie's voice inviting me to join her for a walk that afternoon. "Nearly everyone can make it," she added.

There were seven of us who'd been friends for well over twenty years; our children had brought us together through toddler groups and school. There was Anita who I'd met at a pre-natal class, Cate who's children had played with Susie as we lived in the same village when I was married, Helena with whom I'd worked before we'd had our babies, Catherine I'd met through Anita and was now semi-retired in Devon, Pennie who I'd met through Catherine and Celia, an American writer who'd married an Englishman. We'd all been married, divorced or widowed and seen each other through some very hard times, but despite not seeing each other that often, we still remained steadfast friends, always there for each other when needed.

"Anita says she'll pick you up just after two." I looked at my watch and saw, to my surprise, that it was nearly ten o'clock. I yawned, stretched and wriggled my toes, for the first time since Richard had left I'd had a good night's sleep, woken dry-eyed and felt relatively calm. It still felt very odd to wake up alone at the weekend which of course continued to hurt, but I was trying not to think about that too much.

There was some bacon left in the fridge so I crisped it up and made one of my favourite breakfasts, a bacon and egg sandwich on toasted thick white bread slathered with ketchup, washed down with a large mug of tea. Yummy, I thought to myself as I used the final piece of toast to mop up the last of the ketchup and sat back on the sofa with a contented sigh.

True to her word, Anita arrived just after two and I saw to my delight that Cate was in the car. We chatted non-stop on the way to some local woods where Pennie was already waiting with her beautiful coal-black Labrador, Saffy. We all hugged and, as we donned our walking shoes, Saffy bounded around impatiently, wagging her tail. We were about to set off up the hill when Helena arrived. "Isn't it great so many of us could make it?" Anita said and we all nodded in companionable agreement.

We set off. Saffy barked delightedly and ran around us in circles, looking at us expectantly. "She's desperate for stick throwing," Pennie explained as she picked up a small stick and threw it into the undergrowth. We watched as Saffy disappeared from view, heard lots of scrabbling around and then saw her appear triumphantly with the stick in her mouth. This was repeated many times as we talked nonstop and made our meandering way up the gentle slope which suddenly got much steeper.

I noticed a large stick, more of a staff really, and picked it up. Saffy bounded over. "No Saffy, this isn't for you. It's for me," I explained to her but she barked her disagreement. Pennie managed to distract her with other sticks but every so often she came over to me with a hopeful look in her eyes and each time I told her that I was using it as a walking stick on the increasingly steep, muddy path. She clearly wasn't impressed.

There were a couple of benches along our walk and as we sat to catch our breath, Saffy sat bolt upright in front of me, staring intently at the stick, whining pleadingly. "Stop it Saffy," Pennie said sternly, only to be ignored.

After another hour or so, we started the gentle descent towards the main path and I decided that it was Saffy's turn so I called her. She came bounding over and as I held the six-foot stick above my head she barked and circled round me. I threw it as far as I could and we watched as she dashed after it, returning to us with the huge stick held in her mouth at one end, so lopsided that she could barely carry it. There was quite a wide gateway we had to go through to get onto the gravelled main path, and as we walked through and realised that Saffy wasn't with us, we turned round to see her trying to carry the stick through the gap but unable to do so. I returned to her and tried to get her to hold the stick in the middle but try as I might, she just didn't get the idea. "I've tried to help you, it's up to you now," I told her and turned away only to feel a glancing blow on the back of my calves as Saffy tried to get past me with her mammoth stick but running so fast that she cannoned into the gate post next to me. She dropped the stick and looked up at me with such an air of injured bewilderment that I started to laugh and just couldn't stop. The laughter turned to tears but, for the first time in a very long while, they felt like healing tears and I knew, with absolute certainty, that I was on the road to recovery.

Chapter 6 - May

Monday dawned to grey skies and drizzly rain, a day to hunker down and do very little, I thought to myself. I then remembered that my first group of guests were due to arrive the following evening so I spent most of the day making up the spare room beds, cleaning the bathroom, finalising the menu, shopping for the week and preparing what I could in advance. Everything was done by late afternoon and I sat back, feeling happy that everything was well in hand.

I'd been hearing my phone make chirruping sounds which meant that emails were coming through, so I logged onto my laptop and saw that several of my university students had replied to my introductory email. I spent about an hour answering them and was about to log off when I suddenly remembered promising Karen that I'd email Phil. I must have written half a dozen drafts before I was satisfied and as I pressed the send button I held my breath and crossed my fingers. Would he think I was an idiot? Would he think I was coming on to him? Would he even remember me?

Well, he did remember me his emailed reply said an hour or so later, and was I free to meet him on Tuesday evening? That was tomorrow. I was about to say yes when I realised that my guests were due to arrive at the coach park at six thirty so I replied, saying I couldn't make the evening but was free at lunchtime and as I sent it, I held my breath at my temerity. There was another lengthy delay by which time I'd convinced myself that he wouldn't get in touch before his reply came back, saying yes, he now could make tomorrow lunchtime and would twelve thirty at the One Elm be ok? Before I could change my mind, I said yes and then sat back, my heart thumping.

I rang Karen and told her what had happened. "That's brilliant Lucie. I'm so pleased."

"But ... but ..." I started to say.

"Now, just you stop it." She sounded very firm. "You've emailed him; he's replied and wants to see you. Get yourself looking glam, go down there and see what happens. And then call me - I want to know everything. Deal?"

"Deal," I said weakly and we went on to talk about our respective weekends. Every time I tried to steer the conversation back to meeting Phil she refused to talk about it until she eventually said, "Look, I know this must feel really odd. You know, seeing someone relatively soon after coming out of a long-term relationship but it's all ok. I mean, you don't know why he gave you his card. It might be that he fancies the pants off you, or it might be that he just wants someone to work for him. You won't know until you go and see him so just go, look great and have a good time."

"But ... but ..."

"Stop it Lucie. Just get yourself down there and have a great time. Yes?"

The following morning I spent a long time showering, dressing, doing my hair and makeup and by the time I was ready to leave, my bed was littered with discarded clothes. For early May, it was a chilly day so I'd eventually settled on black leggings, black high-heels, and a belted long white shirt topped by an ankle-length red cardigan with a black and red scarf.

I parked in the One Elm's car park two minutes after twelve thirty and took a deep breath as I strode in with my head held high. Phil was at the table Richard and I used to sit at, and as I walked towards him I felt a sudden, albeit ridiculous, jolt of disloyalty. He stood up as I joined him and greeted me with a warm smile and firm handshake. "Lucie, I'm so glad to see you." We sat down and regarded each other. "Well, it's been a long time. What would you like to drink?"

"Sparkling water please. Ice, no slice."

He ordered the same and as we smiled at each other as we simultaneously picked up our glasses. "So Lucie, tell me, why's it taken you so long to get in touch with me?"

"I'm not sure where to start," I said slowly and paused while he continued to look at me expectantly.

I took a deep breath and told him a little about my teaching, about Tracy's untimely death and Barbara. "That's not why you didn't get in touch with me, is it?" he asked as I came to a stop.

"No. No, it's not …" I felt my cheeks redden.

"I do believe you're blushing. How sweet." He paused. "Well, tell me. Why couldn't you meet me this evening? Are you cooking for your man?" He looked very slightly mocking.

I took a deep breath. "Well, as someone who's self-employed, I find it really helpful to have several income streams. One thing I do is have foreign teachers stay with me. The kids stay with host families who tend to have children of their own but I prefer to have adults. They're out all day so they don't impact on my working life and I enjoy cooking for them. This week's group arrives at about six thirty which is why I couldn't …" my voice faded as I looked into Phil's twinkling eyes which were, I noticed, a soft hazel.

"And what about your man?" he asked very softly.

"Gone." I stopped while I collected my thoughts. "Long gone actually."

"Really?"

"Mmmm. Probably because he was shagging someone else. That's a bit of a give-away that things aren't quite as they should be, isn't it?" I could feel my eyes prickling and blinked away the threatening tears.

"It is, it is," he agreed. "Are you ok? I didn't mean to upset you Lucie. I'm sorry if I did."

"You didn't. It's still a bit raw but I'm getting there." I gave him a radiant smile. "So Phil, were you surprised to hear from me?"

"I was. But I was very pleased. In fact, I'd almost given up hope." He put his hand on mine for a moment. "Ok Lucie, I know that you like food, and you're probably a fair cook. But what makes it so special for you?"

I considered what he had just asked. "Well, I enjoy cooking for and eating with people. Food and pleasure kind of belong together in my mind. As a child I used to watch my mother cook. She was amazing - I mean she could create a great meal out of almost nothing and frequently did. Our door was always open and I remember people sitting round the table eating and drinking and having a great time. I suppose that's what makes me want to make food that makes people smile."

"Hmmm, I see. So cooking isn't just food for you, is it? It's much more complicated than that ..." And we went on to talk about the intricacies of cooking and eating. Phil explained that he used to be a chef, had run his own restaurant in which he now had an interest rather than being involved in the day to day operations and was in the lengthy process of launching a foodie magazine aimed at what he called 'the discerning diner'. "That's where I thought you might come in." I raised my eyebrows.

"Well, when I saw you in January, you were talking about menus and food with such enthusiasm it crossed my mind that you might just be the person to make some really good contributions." He paused to let me think for a moment.

"But I don't go out to eat now," I protested, "I used to when I was with Richard but eating out's really expensive ..."

"I think that we'd manage to pick up the tab," Phil said gravely. I looked at him and saw that he was grinning broadly. "Anyway, at the moment, you're going to be busy with your paying guests, aren't you?" I nodded. "Well, why don't you write me five hundred words on how you deliver good quality yet low-cost meals? I'm sure that you cook good food for your guests and manage to make a profit. I need to see how you write before sending you out and about. How does that sound?" I nodded again, unable to think what to say. "You ok? You look a bit stunned."

I took a deep breath. "I am. I didn't quite know why you wanted to see me ..."

He put his hand on mine again and this time left it there. "Lucie, I think you're a very attractive woman and I'd really like to get to know you better, maybe quite a lot better, but I can see you're in a pretty dark place at the moment, and I've never been one to make a grab at someone who'd probably be on the rebound. Anyway, I want to see whether you can write or not." I giggled at his very mild flirtation and he squeezed my hand gently.

We spent the next hour sharing an excellent board of fishy nibbles and warm pitta bread with some chips and salad on the side. I noticed that Phil remained on the sparkling water as did I. The time flew by - we didn't stop talking, listening and laughing. I realised, to my delighted surprise, that I was feeling relaxed and at ease. It was just after four when I said that I ought to go - what was it that my mother had advised me? 'Leave them wanting more.' With that in my head, I smiled as I rose to my feet. Phil stood, held my shoulders and kissed me softly on both cheeks and then stood back to look at me. "It was as nice spending time with you as I thought it would be. Thank you Lucie, I'm very pleased you contacted me."

"I am too. And I'll be in touch very soon with that article. Five hundred words you wanted? I'll do my best."

"I'm sure you will. I'm looking forward to reading your work." He sounded seriously sincere but his hazel eyes were dancing with merriment.

A few moments later I was outside and as I drove home I reflected on the past few hours spent with a charming, amusing, urbane man who'd been excellent company. I was still smiling as I did some last-minute tidying and preparation. "You're to be good with our visitors," I admonished the cats sternly as I grated cheese over the bolognaise pasta bake and checked the mango sorbet I'd made the night before with the over-ripe mangoes I'd found at the bottom of the fruit bowl. I sat down to consider what to write for Phil. How long had it taken me to plan the week's menu, then buy the ingredients, prep and cook the meals I mused - it was all so automatic for me, I'd never stopped to think about it. Thoughtfully, I started to make some notes. I needed to get my facts straight before drafting the article.

I heard ducks quacking and reached for my mobile. As always, my heart thumped because there was an ever-diminishing expectation that Richard would be in touch. Of course it wasn't him, just a confirming text that the coach was running late so would I meet my guests at seven thirty. My train of thought had been broken so I laid the table, made myself a drink and sat back to think about the day - how nice it had been to meet Phil and how exciting it was to have the possibility of something different in my life.

I met my three guests at seven thirty, drove them home and once they had freshened up, served up dinner. They were charming, talkative and appreciative, so the rest of the week sped by. We talked about families, students, our respective work, England, France, Stratford, Shakespeare, relationships, food, books, music - it was a very enjoyable week and when I waved them off on Friday morning I was genuinely sad to see them go.

"Well, they said they had a great time with you," Lyn said as we watched the coach disappear. "I've got lots more coaches coming this year. Are you up for more?"

"Absolutely am," I nodded enthusiastically. "I had a great time and have to say that that extra cash really helps."

I spent the weekend changing beds, cleaning the house, preparing for the next week's work at school, dealing with emails from my students and drafting, amending and redrafting again Phil's article. I found it incredibly hard to write about cheap food for 'discerning diners' but, by late afternoon on Sunday, I had something that I felt might be close to what he wanted. As I hit the send button I mentally crossed my fingers.

I checked my emails very early on Monday morning and was disappointed to see that there was nothing from Phil. Just a line, I said to myself, Richard had been right, and how stupid was I to fall for it?

I drove to the school on Monday morning, feeling melancholy, knowing that this contract would end in a couple of weeks. It seemed that sadness was now an integral part of my life. The students were very focused, clearly most of them had spent some of the Easter break in revising hard and it showed.

The staffroom was crowded at lunchtime. I saw Roger deep in conversation with a fellow mathematician and didn't want to disturb him so perched at the end of a table and started chatting to Les, one of the PE teachers. "Did you hear about Annie?" he suddenly asked.

"No. What about Annie?"

"Her dad had a stroke on Easter Sunday. He's very elderly, pretty fit for his age, but the real trouble is that he cares for her mum who's got MS so poor old Annie's having to sort things out. They live down in Devon so she's decided to stay down there for another couple of weeks."

"That's so sad. I must text her and see if there's anything I can do to help."

"I'm sure she'd love to hear from you. I think she's struggling to know what to do. We're all concerned about her."

It seemed that I wasn't the only one with sadness and trauma in my life but that didn't make me feel any better. I sipped my coffee and gazed out of the window, wondering what else the year was going to throw at me.

With a sigh, I returned to my students and when, at two thirty, I'd finished I slowly walked down the corridor towards the door to the car park. "Lucie?"

I turned round. "Roger. How are you?"

He stepped close to give me a peck on the cheek and as I sniffed, he laughed. "My boys decided that I shouldn't be eating chocolate so gave me some aftershave for Easter instead. It's not too bad is it?"

"I like it," I leaned in for another sniff. "I love it when men smell this good."

"I must remember that," he said solemnly putting his hand on my shoulder and looking deeply into my eyes. As I returned his gaze I heard giggles and, glancing up, saw a few of my students watching us. I sighed and moved away slightly. "Kids," he shrugged.

"Kids will be kids. Better go anyway, lots to do."

"I'll see you tomorrow then." His hand was still on my shoulder.

"Absolutely will." And I gently moved away.

On the drive home I reflected on Roger's attention. There was no doubt that he was a very good colleague and friend but did he mean any more to me? I felt slightly shocked that I was thinking thoughts like this so soon after Richard's departure but there was no doubt that his continued interest made me feel less bad about myself than being totally alone would have done.

That evening I texted Annie saying that I was thinking of her and then checked my emails that evening - still nothing from Phil. I'd felt so sure that he'd been genuine but clearly I was wrong. I blinked at the screen mistily, to my irritation it continued to take very little to tip me into tears.

There was however an email from Lyn offering me guests in June, July and August to which I said an immediate yes as I calculated a potential profit of well over two thousand pounds, being paid to have agreeable company seemed ideal. There were also more emails from my university students and I arranged to go onto campus on the Friday of the next three weeks so we could discuss their respective progresses personally.

After I'd finished on my laptop, I made myself some tea which seemed to be my staple at the moment and joined the cats in the sitting room. As I sipped I looked round critically in the bright sunshine and realised that things were looking decidedly shabby, it had been years since the place had been decorated and it was showing.

Anita rang me that evening and as we were chatting, I mentioned that I was thinking of doing some decorating, even though it wasn't my pastime of choice. "I love painting. You get the colour you want and I'll come over and help."

"Really?"

"Really." As we said our goodbyes, we agreed that the end of the month was her best time.

The phone rang again shortly afterwards, it was Karen who said that she wanted to make sure that I was alright. "Good days and bad days but I'm working hard on making every day better and better ..." and I went on to tell her about my soon-to-be-smartened sitting room.

"I'd be more than happy to lend a hand - I really enjoy painting. Why don't you get a few tester pots and try out some colours? And then maybe change cushions." Karen regularly transformed her house by moving furniture, pictures and changing soft furnishings which meant that she never got bored with her space, a talent I'd long admired.

I visited a couple of DIY stores at the weekend and bought a selection of tester pots, ranging from shades of blue and green to yellow, pinks and even a red and on Sunday morning decided to try some of the colours out on the walls. I opened five of the pots I'd bought and started to dab a little paint on the wall but then Richard came into my mind and I slowly and painstakingly painted the word 'cheat' in large green letters on the wall. 'Contemptible' in pale blue, 'fucker' in yellow and 'treacherous' in a darker shade of green followed. I felt breathless and stood back, staring at what I'd just done. I was about to paint out the words when I heard the front door bell. Karen stood in the sunshine with a carrier bag in her hand. "I fancied a bacon buttie, so here I am with bread and bacon."

"Karen - how lovely to see you. I can't think of anything nicer. Come on in."

We walked through to the kitchen where we fried bacon, toasted bread and made coffee. "So, you trying out some colours in the sitting room?" Karen asked through a mouthful of bacon.

I nodded. "I have indeed. Want to have a look?"

We stood in silence for a few minutes as Karen surveyed my handiwork. "Well," she said eventually and looked at me.

"Want to contribute?" I held out a pot of pink.

"I'd love to, but just the one. This is your story," she replied as she painted a large 'rude' above the yellow 'fucker'. "Hey, amazingly satisfying isn't it?" She giggled and I joined her until we were both helplessly laughing.

After Karen had left I took down all the pictures and stared at the empty walls in the sitting room, it looked sad and unloved. Not for long though, I said to myself as I thoughtfully opened more tester pots and painted 'liar', 'untrustworthy', 'sneaky', 'dickhead' and 'coward' in different colours, weeping as I did so. True and cathartic it might have been but it hurt so much to finally realise that I'd given my love to a selfish, traitorous and misogynistic man who had deceived me for a long time on so many different levels.

The following week was good as far as work was concerned. All my students were working hard and as always their continued successes was a source of great personal satisfaction. On Tuesday one of them came to see me in distress as she'd just discovered that her boyfriend of some four months had been seeing her best friend behind her back. I tried to comfort her and whilst I talked about how devastating it must have been for her, how bad I thought cheating was and how it was absolutely not ok in anything like a respectful and meaningful relationship, it brought sharp and painful memories back to me and I ended up crying with her. I drove home that afternoon in a sad and sombre mood that stayed with me for many hours.

Kate texted me on Wednesday, asking if I could commit to one day a week at her shop for the next few weeks to free her up for painting furniture so I agreed to every Thursday in June. That'll be fun I thought as I noted the dates in my diary.

Anita called that evening. "Still ok for decorating at the end of the month?"

"Certainly am - so looking forward to freshening the place up."

There was a pause. "Lucie, I hope you don't mind ..."

"Mind what?"

"Well, John and I are trying to declutter and have just realised that we have an easy chair that we really don't want. Don't suppose that you'd like it, would you? I mean, we're not trying to palm anything off on you but just thought you might like it."

Half an hour later I was standing in Anita and John's snug looking at a pale yellow chair that looked, and indeed was, extremely comfortable. "We'll bring it over after the painting's been done," John offered as I thanked them for their generosity.

Thursday morning saw me at school but at lunchtime, instead of my usual gossips in the staffroom, I spent half an hour online, looking for a sofa to go with Anita's, soon-to-be-mine, yellow chair. Much to my delight I found a terracotta three-seater sofa that looked ideal, so with some nervousness, I ordered it for delivery in four weeks' time and as I sat back I felt a glow of pleasure and achievement. "You're looking pretty smug." I heard Roger's voice.

I looked up. "I have to say that I'm very pleased with myself. Just ordered a sofa as I'm doing up the sitting room." I was beaming as I spoke.

Roger laughed. "Well, it's good to see you looking so happy even if it's because of soft furnishings ..."

"Nothing wrong with soft furnishings," I interrupted with a smile and we continued to banter about whether preoccupation with cushions, curtains and the like was exclusively a 'girlie thing' as Roger put it. "It's so not," I eventually concluded as Roger held up his hands in laughing mock surrender.

I enjoyed meeting with some of my university students on Friday, it felt good to be working with fresh, bright, challenging intellects and as the day drew to a close, I realised that there had been whole hours when Richard hadn't been in my head at all.

Di called me on Friday evening and we arranged to meet at a large garden centre near to her the following morning as she wanted a sounding board for selecting plants and garden furniture. We had a lovely day together but, for some reason, I found myself talking about how disappointed, angry and sad I still was about Richard. "It'll pass, it'll pass," Di said consolingly. "It takes time though. You were together for nearly five years, he'd painted a picture of a future and when that was cut away from you in the way that it was, you were, understandably, devastated. You weren't exactly given a right of reply that Sunday, were you?"

I shook my head through my tears as she put a comforting arm round my shoulders.

I'd been continuing to paint up different colours during the week so many more words had been added: 'prick', 'despicable', 'unfair', 'arse', 'dishonest' and 'traitorous' now adorned the walls, each one being accompanied by bitter tears. Sunday morning saw 'shallow', 'crass', 'arrogant', 'shabby' and 'mendacious' daubed up and as I sat in the oddly-decorated room with a scalding hot cup of coffee looking at the walls, the truth of what I was reading sank in - I was getting there.

It was my last week working at the school so last-minute points were raised and final answers analysed and assessed. "You'll all be fine," I assured my lovely students again as they confessed how apprehensive they were. My last day was Wednesday which I'd earmarked for final hand-holding and reassurances. I walked into the classroom after lunch to be surrounded by smiling students who presented me with a huge bunch of flowers, an equally enormous card that had been affectionately signed by everyone and a small box in which was a tiny Govinder cat. Bless them; they'd remembered our discussions on price elasticity when I'd given the example of a wonderful artist whose work I'd long admired. He'd died far too soon before his time when his work then rocketed in value in the face of no more ever becoming available. Warm hugs were exchanged as I wished them luck and said a reluctant goodbye.

I then went to the staffroom to say goodbye to whoever was there but the two people I most wanted to see, Roger and Annie, were sadly conspicuous by their absence. I'll drop them an email, I thought to myself, as I carefully placed the flowers onto the back seat of my car and left the carpark for the last time. Even though I had been self-employed for many years, I still found it hard to say goodbye to colleagues, many of whom became friends, at least for the duration of the contract. I drove home misty-eyed - I knew I'd really miss everyone.

As I sat with my inevitable cup of tea, I realised that I hadn't heard from Barbara so rang her that evening. She sounded pleased to hear from me but very low. "I feel that I'm in such a rut," she said in answer to my 'how are you?'. "Change really scares me but I feel I need something different in my life." We went on talking for a few minutes more, ending with a promise to keep in touch and as I put the handset down, I felt sad and wished I could say or do something to make things better for her.

On Thursday I arranged for a local charity to take away my old furniture to make room for the yellow armchair and my new sofa. A colour swatch for the new sofa had arrived so I went out to hunt for new cushions and managed to find four that seemed ideal - Roger was right, soft furnishings were exciting.

Even though I'd decided on a soft cream colour for the walls and had bought a large tin and some brushes ready for the weekend, I'd also bought more tester pots so that evening 'pathetic', 'tosser', 'egocentric', 'hurtful', 'wanker' and 'condescending' joined what I'd painted up. For the first time I didn't cry, but let a deep anger start to overcome my sorrow and desolation.

The sessions with my university students on Friday went very well which made me feel pleased and optimistic. That evening I prepared a fish pie, ready for cooking on the Saturday; that was the least I could do for my decorators.

Early the next morning I opened the last tester pot which, symbolically, was red and painted 'cunt' in large letters above the fireplace before eating some fruit for breakfast.

Karen arrived just after nine thirty, bearing yet another copy of 'Olive' which made both of us smile and as I made her some tea, she looked at the walls and nodded approvingly. "Excellent Lucie. Couldn't have put it better myself."

Ten minutes later Anita was reading the walls. "My God Lucie, you certainly said it loud and clear didn't you?"

I nodded. "At the beginning it hurt terribly, but the last few felt wonderful. This one especially ..." I pointed at the final red daub. Anita laughed and shook her head in disbelief.

We sat on the hard chairs I'd brought in from the dining room and finished off our tea. "Before we start though," Anita said, "you have to paint out all these words - that's your job. We're not doing that, are we?" She looked at Karen who nodded.

"Absolutely not. We're going to watch you obliterate each and every one." She opened the large tin of pale cream, poured some into a plastic tray and handed me a very small brush. "Off you go then."

And they both sat back and watched as I slowly and deliberately painted out every word I'd written up and as I did so I said it out loud as it disappeared. I left 'cunt' til last and as I watched the red paint vanish under the elegant cream I let out a sigh of relief - as far as it was possible, the last five years were gone.

Chapter 7 - June

It felt very strange not to be going to the school after so many weeks but I was kept busy with my three French guests who were great company, appreciative both of my cooking and the time we spent together, sitting at the table over dinner, discussing their days. It was with genuine regret that I waved them goodbye early on the Friday morning before setting off to the university to meet those students who wanted to see me face-to-face rather than correspond by email.

Thursday was my first day at Kate's shop and was great fun. Much to my delight I'd sold a couple of chairs as well as candlesticks and some other small bits and bobs. My French guests' schedule meant that they and their students were in Stratford on that day, so they'd visited the shop and bought some small items as more unusual souvenirs from the town.

Di came round on Saturday morning. She'd finished her job at the end of May and had spent the last few days scanning the internet for jobs with no real success. We strolled into town and sat by the river in soft sunshine talking about our respective situations. "I'm just so nervous about starting all over again," she said reflectively. "I really thought that this would last at least a bit longer. I mean, just how many times does one have to reinvent oneself?"

"Probably more often than we'd like. It just gets harder as one gets older, doesn't it?"

"It does, it certainly does - so how are you managing?"

"Fine. Well ok ..." and then for no apparent reason I started to cry as I felt a deep melancholy sweep over me. "I'm so sorry," I hiccupped through diminishing sobs. "It's just that sometimes I can't stop this terrible feeling of loss. I miss the good times."

"Quite honestly, the good times were getting fewer and fewer, weren't they?" Di asked astutely. "You weren't that happy for lots of the time anyway. At least now there's a real possibility of doing something else, working somewhere else, meeting someone else. You're no longer tied to someone who belittled you all the time."

"Ok, I get it, but please stop. It's terribly hard to hear that I was blinkered for so long."

Di laughed. "Not blinkered sweetie. Just misguided. Yes, he might have bought you things, but they came at a high price. Anyway, you're looking loads better which is great to see." She paused. "Hey, I don't suppose that you'd like a few days away, would you? I really want a break and I'm sure a change of scene would be really good for you too."

We ended up agreeing that a few days in July before the schools broke for their summer recess would be ideal. "That'll be great," Di said as we walked to the Dirty Duck for a drink before heading home. "Something to look forward to. And in the meantime, I'm going to take a long, hard look at where I am and what I want. It doesn't feel right to go straight into another job."

We continued discussing possibilities as we sat on the terrace at the front of the pub, gazing out at the busy river, enjoying a beer. Those discussions continued as we walked home and I prepared an early dinner of pancakes stuffed with onion with a hint of chilli and shredded ham smothered in a creamy cheese sauce, which I served with a salad of sun-dried tomatoes, mixed leaves and my standby garlicky dressing.

"This is so good." I beamed my thanks at the compliment. "I don't know why you don't do something with food as far as your work is concerned."

"Well, I wrote an article and sent it off to Phil but haven't heard anything back, so that was a waste of time, wasn't it?"

"Shame. It seemed such a great thing to do - just up your street. And I have to say that he sounded like quite a nice bloke. I mean, why spin a line like that?"

I shrugged. "Who knows. Looks like Richard was right about ..."

"No, no, no. Just stop that. Why think about what Richard said all those months ago? There may or may not be a perfectly good explanation for Phil's silence, but it's absolutely nothing to do with anything anyone else."

"You're right. I know you're right. It's just I miss ..." My voice faded as I heard Di's exasperated sigh. Looking at her I saw a glint of tears. "Oh God Di, I'm so sorry ..."

Di had lost Henry to another woman about twelve years ago. They'd been together for over twenty years, working and living together, sharing some wonderful and amazing times. Di had begun to suspect something was wrong when Henry used work as an excuse to come home later and later, go to conferences and exhibitions, and generally be away from home more and more.

After overhearing some gossip at the office she'd tackled him. At first he'd protested that Hannah was simply a friend but, after a few weeks, admitted that they'd been having an affair for nearly a year. Di was devastated but had been very strong and told him to leave. Of course they'd had to continue working together which had been very difficult and for some time Di hoped that the affair would blow itself out and they would be able to rebuild their lives. After all there had been a twenty-year investment with most of that time joyful and loving.

One day, Henry had gone into Di's office to talk things through and, much to Di's sorrow, said that he really didn't feel they could recreate the life that they'd once shared. As he stood to take his leave, he wrapped his arms around her, saying that he would always love her. At this, Di saw red and without thinking had taken a swing at him. Unfortunately, for him, she was wearing a large dress ring that caught his face, scratching his cheek badly and as he lurched forward, she raised her knee, connecting with his balls and as he doubled up his glasses fell onto the floor. Di stepped forward, crushed them under her heel, then ordered him out of her office and as she closed the door behind him, she heard ripples of applause that grew as he made his shambling way back to his office. That had been the dramatic end to a relationship that Di had assumed would last forever.

"It's ok Lucie. Really. It's just memories do pop back sometimes, don't they?"

"I'm so sorry Di. I've been so preoccupied with what's been happening to me that I ignore the fact that other people have stuff that they're dealing with."

"My 'stuff' was over a long time ago but you're right. The pain of betrayal, and disbelief that one woman can do this to another stays for a very long time."

"And we can't just turn love off, can we?"

"No. No, we can't."

We sat in silence for a few moments. "How come we still go on loving such treacherous shits?" I asked. "And when does the pain of being cheated on go away? I mean, the fallout from this is so wide-reaching. I've barely been able to work properly or function some days without this dreadful feeling of abandonment and worthlessness getting into my head. I can remember word for word what he said and that still has the power to hurt me, and influence how I behave with other people, which I hate, but just don't seem to be able to stop."

Di laughed. "God knows. My memories are over a decade away and very, very occasionally I reflect on how much Henry hurt me but we just have to recognise that it's a shitty thing to happen and the people who do this are real shits - never worth what we gave them. We deserve so much better than this and I have to say that I'd rather be on my own for the rest of my life than tolerate that level of bad behaviour. And Lucie, if you have any sense, you'll make sure you feel the same way." She raised her glass. "Here's to us. Here's to lots of laughs, a lovely holiday and loads of good things happening."

I raised my glass and we solemnly clinked after which we sat and talked about where we might go in July. "World's our kipper," I said eventually after about an hour.

Di chuckled. "Well, maybe not the world but we've certainly got a few options, haven't we?"

An hour later we were still talking but then Di had to leave. "Got an early start tomorrow." We hugged goodbye and as I slowly made my way to bed I reflected yet again on how very, very lucky I was to have such wonderfully caring, supportive friends and it was with those thoughts in my head, I fell asleep, smiling.

I was woken by the sun streaming in and as I yawned and stretched, I sensed the impending warmth of the day. Time to get the summer dresses out, I thought to myself as I opened the basket on top of the wardrobe in which I kept my maxi-dresses and hung them up at the side of the wardrobe as they were too long to fit inside. I chose my favourite, a low-cut black and white silky one with spaghetti straps over which I slipped a pale pink shrug and as I swished my way downstairs, I felt pretty and feminine for the first time in a long while.

I sat in the garden sipping my first cup of tea of the day while the cats lazily basked on the patch of grass I laughingly called a lawn and which would soon need yet another trim. I went inside to cook some bacon, scrambled a couple of eggs and then took the plate outside to eat in the sunshine. My peace was broken by the landline ringing. As always, whenever I heard the phone the possibility that Richard was getting in touch briefly flashed into my mind.

"Lucie?" a woman's voice said hesitantly. "It's Barbara. I wondered if you had a few minutes to talk."

After a few moments, it was very clear that she wanted much more than a few minutes. "Barbara, would you like to come over? It's a lovely day. We could sit in the garden, have a chat and I'll get us something to eat."

Half an hour later Barbara had arrived bringing with her two large slices of her sublime chocolate cake which we ate as we sat in the garden, sipping ice-cold weak gin and tonics. "Who'd have thought that gin and chocolate would go so well together," Barbara said with a note of surprise in her voice.

"I think that chocolate goes with most things," I replied and we went on to talk about recipes and the pleasure it gave us to cook for people. "You'll stay for lunch, won't you?" I asked after about an hour by which time we'd finished the cake and our second drink.

She nodded enthusiastically so I delved into the fridge where I found a small pack of asparagus. I always kept a roll of pastry in the freezer. "How about an asparagus quiche?" I asked over my shoulder as I picked up a small carton of cream.

"Sounds perfect. Can I do anything to help?" Barbara grated a piece of Cheddar while I rolled out and then pressed the pastry gently into a small flan tin after I'd greased it, pricked it all over with a fork and then baked it for twenty minutes while we sat in the garden.

"So, what did you really want to talk about?" I prompted gently. Her eyes filled with tears and for a few moments she was unable to speak, but then her grief over losing Tracy, her unhappiness with her current job and concerns about money all spilled out only to be interrupted by my mobile's timer buzzing. Assuring her that I'd be back, I dashed into the kitchen to paint the partially cooked pastry case with a slick of beaten egg and put it back into the oven for a further five minutes. I returned with another very weak gin and tonic. "Last one because you're driving," I said as I handed it to her.

She blew her nose and then took a large gulp. "I'm so sorry. I didn't mean to ..."

"Don't be silly. You've had a dreadful few months. I'm not surprised you're buckling - anyone would. Let's get this quiche sorted so we can soak up some of that gin. Ok?"

The pastry case was done so I set it aside while I prepared the filling of cheese, cream and egg and poured the mixture carefully over the asparagus I'd steamed and laid in the bottom of the pastry case. I'd found a fragment of Parmesan so grated that on top before putting it back into the oven.

Barbara had stayed in the garden to compose herself and looked up with a smile as I rejoined her. "So how are things with you?" she asked. "I've been so tied into my problems; I always forgot to ask people how they are. Not good ..."

I briefly told her about teaching, lodgers and supervising university students at which she widened her eyes. "So, you have lots of different bits and pieces of work?"

I nodded. "It's funny but I really prefer it. I mean, I know I'm missing out on a predictable, regular income but it gives me the freedom to pick and choose a bit which certainly stops me getting bored. But Richard didn't like..." my voice died away.

"Richard?" she prompted.

I sighed. "It's a long story …"

"So tell me." She leaned forward.

So I did until it was time to prepare the salad. Barbara joined me in the kitchen and as I threw some leaves, finely shredded raw fennel and a few radishes into a bowl and laid the table, I finished off my sad story. "So you've not heard from him since?" I shook my head, not trusting myself to say anything more.

After a moment or two I swallowed hard. "I'm getting there. It's just when I stop to think about the possibility of the future together that he dangled in front of me I get upset. Anyway, what's done is done. I try not to think about it too much now - it still hurts but I guess that will pass in time."

I checked the quiche and saw to my pleasure that it was slightly puffy and a glorious golden brown. The centre felt firm to my light touch and as I took it out of the oven it had a satisfyingly soft wobble. "Perfect. Let's eat." It was perfect too - we finished off the whole thing at the end of which we sat back with satisfied sighs. After clearing the table and loading my battered old dishwasher I made some coffee and we sat in the garden again, where we talked more about work.

"It's funny," I said reflectively, "but I've found that taking control of one bit of one's life kind of ripples out to other areas as well. However much it hurts, dealing with something is better than dealing with nothing - know what I mean?"

"Trouble is I just don't know where to start." Barbara sounded very sad.

I thought for a moment. "Barbara, you bake the most phenomenal cakes. Do you enjoy doing that?" She nodded. "Well then, why not make that the way you make your living? There's birthday cakes, wedding cakes, engagement cakes, children's party cakes. Goodness, there's even lets-have-a-party-for-the-hell-of-it cakes," I paused, "and then there's separation cakes, divorce cakes, changing job cakes, office party cakes, passing exam cakes …"

"Really?" Barbara sounded doubtful.

"Why not? You'd have to start off small but who knows where it could lead? Why not capitalise on something that gives you so much pleasure anyway?"

We spent another hour drinking coffee and talking about the pros and cons of cake making as a viable business with Barbara nervously exploring various options. "It's a good idea but it's all a bit scary isn't it?"

I nodded. "It is. But it could work. You've said you don't particularly like what you do and this could just be the answer. Just tuck it to the back of your mind and keep thinking about it. I'm very happy to talk about it whenever you want, provided you make me the odd cake or three of course." And that's how it was left. Barbara went home shortly afterwards, promising to give careful and serious consideration to my idea and as I waved her goodbye I felt a surge of satisfaction and happiness that there was someone else who had faith in me and my abilities.

More French teachers arrived late afternoon on Monday for the week with their students. They brought me a couple of bottles of wine and a beautiful box of hand-made chocolates and were hugely appreciative of my hospitality. We spent four very pleasant evenings sitting round the table, eating, drinking and talking and again, as I waved them goodbye very early on Friday morning, I was sad to see them go. "More next week," Lyn said as we watched the coach disappear.

"Suits me - I'm really enjoying this," I replied and she smiled her thanks for the care I was taking of her business.

I'd spent another very pleasant day at Kate's shop on Thursday but as it was a rainy day, fewer people came in and the day passed more slowly than the previous week. However, I kept myself busy with tidying, dusting and trying on some of the vintage clothes that Kate had for sale. Much to my irritation and distress, most of them didn't fit so I ended the day feeling fat and lumpy. Later, I found myself defiantly eating a large second helping of the lentil and vegetable curry with fragrant rice I'd cooked for my guests, and sighed in frustration at my clearly inadequate efforts to lose weight.

Saturday morning saw me changing beds, doing the washing and cleaning the house so that by lunchtime everything was clean and sparkling. I spent the afternoon shopping for the first time in ages and bought myself a pair of white linen trousers, a red and white stripy top and a large bottle of my favourite perfume. As I was trying out some eye pencils I heard a voice just behind me saying "Very glamorous." I turned to see Helena smiling warmly at me. "Finished your shopping?" she asked as she nodded approvingly at my purchases.

"I think so. I'd like to do some more but I should probably quit while I'm ahead otherwise I'm going to buy a load of stuff I'll only want to return."

So we made our way to the One Elm and sat outside on the small front terrace, enjoyed a coffee together and caught up with each other's news. Helena's daughter was getting married at the end of July at Helena's village church so she was being kept very busy with last-minute preparations. As we said our goodbyes an hour later I drove home feeling very relaxed and calm. It had been a very pleasant day.

I Skyped Susie on Sunday but she was offline so I left her a video message. Although we emailed each other reasonably regularly, we both missed more normal conversations so being able to see each other was an added bonus. I felt disappointed that she wasn't online but my rational side fully appreciated that she was taking full advantage of every wonderful opportunity. I'd be doing exactly the same thing I said to myself as I started to check my emails.

To my delight, I saw Susie's name. She'd sent me a brief email telling me that she'd just acquired her first tattoo. I wasn't that keen on them so my heart sank until I saw a photograph of it, several small elegant Chinese characters on the side of her left foot which she'd translated as 'If you are not a better person tomorrow than you are today, what need have you for tomorrow'. I emailed her congratulating her on such a stylish tatt - it was too, and I thoroughly approved of the sentiments.

I suddenly saw Phil's name in my inbox and petulantly thought to delete his email without reading it - but that would be really silly I said to myself. So I opened it and as I read his long email I sat very still with my mouth open. Phil's sister, Phoebe, was married to an American; they lived and worked in San Francisco. Last year, much to their surprise, they'd found that she was pregnant. She'd endured three miscarriages after which they'd assumed that they would never have children. It had been a difficult pregnancy but, incredibly, she'd gone to just two weeks short of full term when she'd gone into labour and had given birth to a perfect baby boy. Tragically, the umbilical cord was wrapped round his neck, not detected in time and so their beautiful baby had been born dead. They were devastated and after speaking to her, Phil had taken the first available flight out and was still with them as they struggled to come to terms with their loss. He went on to say that he'd read my article, really liked it and thought I had talent but as he was planning to stay with Phoebe and Hank for at least another two weeks he'd prefer to discuss future articles on his return when he promised that he'd get in touch with me.

By the time I had finished reading, I was in tears. I felt ashamed of presuming the worst about him, grief for the family and an overwhelming gratitude that at the age of forty I had given birth to my perfect Susie.

I re-read his email and then slowly typed a reply, saying how sad I was to hear his tragic news, to please pass my heartfelt condolences to his sister and that I'd be happy to hear from him when he returned home. I hit the send button and blew him an unseen gentle kiss.

My French guests this week were pleasant enough but slightly more reserved than those in the previous weeks and although they were appreciative of my efforts, I didn't have the usual tinge of sadness as I waved them goodbye on Friday morning.

I spent much of the week online, giving support to my university students, some of whom were panicking that their deadline of the end of June was all too fast approaching. I read so much online that by the end of the week my eyes ached. As several of them wanted to see me, I arranged to go to the university the following week on Tuesday and Wednesday for final feedback and advice.

Susie emailed me on Tuesday, bringing me up to date with her latest news and I smiled as I read about her work and trips to new and exciting places. She was thrilled that the day before, it had been confirmed that her contract was to be extended for another twelve months which meant that it would be the end of next year before she returned home. 'And Mum, a group of us were thinking of spending our three weeks' holiday touring Australia in the summer so would it be ok if you visited me next year instead?' started her penultimate paragraph. Naturally I was a little disappointed but had to admit that it was a financial relief so I replied saying of course that was fine, that she was to have a wonderful time and tell me all about it. I felt a little sad but an overwhelming contentment that Susie was well, happy and clearly having a great life.

As I had guests and was therefore cooking for four people, I spent more time at the supermarket than usual and, one morning, while I was carefully selecting some tomatoes, I heard a hesitant voice behind me speak my name. I turned round to see a pretty, blonde woman. "It is Lucie, isn't it?"

"It is," I answered, not recognising her.

"It's Naomi." I must have looked blank because she then went on to remind me that she had been one of my students from over twenty years ago. "I've never forgotten you. I was going through such a hard time - you were so kind, you gave me time and encouraged me to complete the course."

I smiled in thanks. "Now I remember you. I'm sorry Naomi, but it's been a long time. So, what are you doing now?"

She explained that she was married, had two teenage children and was the UK marketing manager for an international security company. Her widowed father was ill which was why she was spending a week in Stratford, looking after him. "I'm so lucky. And, looking back, things seemed to start getting better while I was at college. You made such a difference to my life." By this time we both had tears in our eyes and as I hugged her goodbye, I felt very privileged to have been in a position where I had touched someone's life so profoundly.

I had a wonderful day at Kate's shop on Thursday, busily selling a table, four chairs and some china. I always rang Kate at the end of my day and as I told her what I'd done I heard a small gasp. "You're doing so well. I might have to make you permanent." I laughed, it was very nice to be so overtly appreciated and I glowed at the compliment.

Barbara called on Friday evening after I'd had a long exhausting day in front of the laptop and was relaxing with a restorative glass of Merlot, so it was a real effort to rouse myself to pick up. I could tell she was very excited. "Lucie, I've made up my mind - I'm going to try to start up my own cake business."

I sat up. "What wonderful news Barbara. That's terrific."

"You know you said you'd be happy to talk things through?"

"I do, and I'm more than happy to help out as and when I can."

"I can make cakes," she said ruefully, "but I know diddly squat about running a business."

"No problem. I can help with some of that." We went on to arrange to meet in a couple of weeks to talk things through. "I'll come to you then, shall I?"

"That's wonderful. Thank you so much Lucie."

"Hey, no need to thank me. I think it'll be a great thing to do and I'm sure you'll do really well. The first thing you need to do is a bit of market research to make certain that there's a high enough demand, although I'm fairly sure that there is. Ask different people how often they buy special cakes, how much they're prepared to spend, where they go for the cakes, whether they'd buy more if they were readily available - you know the kind of thing. Once you've got some people giving you some information, it's easier to make a plan. That ok?"

There was a pause. "Yes, I've jotted down everything you've said." There was a real note of enthusiasm and optimism in her voice which gave me a feeling of tremendous satisfaction and, as I put the phone down, I was smiling.

My new sofa was delivered early on Saturday morning. Thankfully I took the hard chairs back to the dining room, put new cushions on the sofa, shooed the inquisitive cats off and spent a happy half hour rehanging all the pictures. I then stood back and surveyed the room. There was a gap for Anita and John's chair, but apart from that, the room looked and felt calm, peaceful and welcoming. I rang Anita and told her about the new look. "Shall we come and bring your chair over this afternoon?"

"That would be terrific, yes please." I sat back and felt my heart thumping with pleasure.

I then called Karen, Di, Pennie, Helena, Felicity and a few more girlfriends to ask them round for a 'room warming' party that afternoon. Most said yes so I prepared a pile of delicate sandwiches, plated some chocolate biscuits and made lemon drizzle muffins. Anita and John arrived just before three. They carried the yellow chair in and placed it at the end of the room. We all stood back and looked at it. "Fits in very well, doesn't it?" John said. Anita and I nodded.

"It's perfect. Thanks so much."

"More than a pleasure." John kissed Anita and then me goodbye. "I know when I'm outnumbered, I'll leave you to it," was his smiling parting shot.

By half past three my small sitting room was crammed with about ten of us. Everyone had kindly brought a gift: four pretty gold coasters, a book on gardening, another on interior design, a household plant, scented candles, flowers and bottles of wine and as I handed round cups of tea and nibbles, I felt a surge of affection for these women who I'd known for so long and who had always been there for me. The cups of tea changed into glasses of wine by five and we continued talking well into the evening.

Next morning I was woken by my mobile ringing and groped for it. "Hey, wake up sleepyhead." It was Karen sounding far too bright for my liking. I peered at my watch to see that it was just after ten. "Fancy meeting for brunch? About half past eleven?"

I thought about it for a moment. "Love to." We agreed where to meet and as I sank back onto the rumpled pillows, I looked at the time again and calculated that I had about an hour to get ready which, considering I had a slight headache, I'd probably need.

By eleven thirty Karen and I were sitting in Bensons, a little café in the middle of town that specialised in brunches with unlimited tea or coffee, and as we ordered a full English each we sat back and smiled at each other. We talked about our respective children and work. I told her about my French guests and Karen said that she had decided to let one of her spare rooms on a Monday to Friday basis, that she had already seen four people and opted for a senior manager in the car industry who was on a six-month secondment, was married and lived some hundred miles away from Stratford. "It's a way to make the house work for me," she said reflectively and I nodded in agreement. "I mean, it's not something I'd necessarily choose to do but it's not a bad way to supplement income, is it?"

"I think it's a great way," I replied. "My guests give me a framework to my day, especially when I'm not out working. I like meeting new people and I particularly like the extra dosh that allows me to have a few extra treats. What's not to like?"

She laughed, I sensed in relief. Both of us had struggled financially in recent years, me because Alex had tragically died so unexpectedly, and Karen because her serially philandering husband had emptied their considerable savings account before she had realised what had happened and kicked him out.

Brunch arrived and we fell silent as we munched our way through a delicious plateful of sausage, bacon, egg, baked beans, hash brown, mushrooms and tomato. We were on our second pot of tea when Karen asked me to join her on Thursday evenings for an hour of Zumba. "But I'm so unfit," I protested.

"That's ok. I'm not exactly the world's fittest and there'll be loads of people starting. Oh, do come Lucie, it'll be fun."

And I found myself agreeing to join Karen as often as I could. "It'll depend on my guests as well," I warned. "If they arrive late then I won't be able to come."

Karen smiled. "You'll come," she said and I knew that she would make quite sure that I'd be there.

I was firmly in the groove as far as meeting and greeting, welcoming and looking after my foreign guests were concerned and, much to my satisfaction, my repertoire of reasonably priced, tasty meals was fast growing.

Whilst clearing up the kitchen on Monday evening, I heard ducks quacking and saw, to my surprise, that it was a text from Roger. I still felt a tiny frisson of tension whenever I heard a text come through as the thought that it might be Richard flashed into my mind, but that expectation and the subsequent pain were gradually, very gradually, diminishing.

I read then re-read the text. Roger wanted to take me out and wondered if I was free one evening for dinner. How nice to be asked out I thought and texted back that I was free on Friday. Within seconds his enthusiastic agreement came through and we settled on meeting at six at Morgan's Bar in nearby Leamington.

Tuesday and Wednesday passed in a flurry of activity as I gave last minute advice and guidance to those students who hadn't finished their work. When I was a student I tended towards what I used to call 'last-minute-it is' so I was well able to empathise with them, and was delighted that by late on Wednesday all but one had completed and handed in their assignments.

Well, that's that til mid-September, I thought to myself as I walked down the corridor towards the lift. As I did so, I saw Beth Lawson's strangely familiar walk ahead of me and it suddenly struck me where I'd seen her before. It must have been over thirty years ago when I was at teacher training college as a mature student. Except Beth wasn't Beth then, she was Ben Lawson who I'd dated for a few months before meeting Alex. I gasped audibly and was about to call out when I saw him - her - open a door to her left and go into one of the meeting rooms. I walked past the closed door thoughtfully and by the time I was driving home was giggling helplessly.

It was a fairly quiet day at Kate's shop on Thursday which gave me time to relax and plan the next few weeks' menus. I met my guests at the coach park at six thirty and drove them home. I'd prepared an enormous salad which was laid out ready for them and was in the middle of explaining that I had planned to go to an exercise class that evening when Karen arrived to pick me up, bearing my monthly 'Olive'. I was ushered out amidst assurances that my guests were perfectly happy to eat without me and that I was to work hard. It was hard work as well; I ached all over and had to sit out some of the routines when I could barely catch my breath. "That was fun, wasn't it?" Karen said on the way home. I wasn't so sure but she insisted that we'd be there next week.

"Really?" I asked feebly as I opened the front door.

"Really," she said firmly as we collapsed on the sofa amid sympathetic laughter from my visitors who'd joined us.

After dropping my guests off at their coach bright and early on Friday morning, I drove to Rachel who put a few streaks through my hair before cutting my fringe so I looked less like a Shetland pony. I then had a wax and pedicure by the end of which I felt pampered, glamorous and ready for the evening.

The traffic was heavier than expected, so it was nearly ten past six when I walked into Morgan's Bar to see Roger waiting for me, looking very smart in stone-washed chinos and an open-neck-shirt. He stood up to greet me and as he kissed me on both cheeks, I could smell the same wonderful aftershave I'd commented on a couple of months ago. "I've ordered a bottle of champagne - hope that's ok."

"That sounds wonderful. Thank you Roger." We went on to talk about what we'd both been doing until, at about seven a waiter came over to tell us that our table was ready whenever we were. "Thought it would be nice to sit here," he commented as we made our way to a small table close to the window.

"I hope you didn't mind driving over but I had a meeting that I knew wouldn't be finished til well after five," he explained as we sat and looked through the menu before he decided on Cornish crab salad with curry oil, mango, avocado and brown crab croquettes followed by duck with the most delicious sounding accompaniments including pickled quince and a pancetta terrine.

I wavered for a few more minutes but then settled on pigeon with charred sweetcorn, walnuts, truffle and pancetta followed by sea bass with clams and gnocchi, caper sauce, celery and grapes.

"Everything reads so scrummy," I sighed. "It's just too hard to decide."

He laughed. "Still into your food then?"

I nodded. "Certainly am ..." and I went on to tell him about how much I was enjoying having my foreign visitors, spending time with them and cooking for them. "It's not that easy, you know. Cooking the best dishes possible on a tight budget is a real challenge."

The food tasted every bit as delicious as it read and we savoured every mouthful. Roger told me about his sons and I brought him up to date with Susie's adventures. I told him about some of my university students and he talked about the students at school. We finished off the bottle of champagne. It was a very relaxed and easy evening.

The waiter came over proffering the dessert menu. "We have to have puds." Roger had a knowing smile.

"You know me all too well." I pointed at the chocolate mousse with a pistachio macaroon and raspberries.

Roger laughed. "If I have the soufflé will you let me have a taste of your chocolate?"

I nodded. "Of course. I'm all for sharing."

The chocolate mousse was wonderful as was the apple and cinnamon crumble soufflé accompanied by a blackberry parfait with a tiny quenelle of apple sorbet, at the end of which we both sat back with contented smiles. "Let's have coffee in the bar," he suggested and as we made our way through I could see a table already set with a tray of coffee and chocolates between two large easy chairs, into which we sank with grateful sighs.

We were on our second cup of aromatically strong coffee when Roger fell silent for a few moments before clearing his throat. "Lucie?" He then stopped.

"Yes?" I prompted.

"There's something I want to say. Please listen to me."

"Of course Roger. What is it?"

Nothing prepared me for his response. "Well, you know I really like you, don't you?"

I nodded. "I like you too Roger ..."

"I more than like you." At my startled gasp he paused and then went on. "Please hear me out. I've missed you so much since you left us. I wake up thinking about you. I look for you in the staffroom even though I know you're not there. I miss our talks. I want you in my life more than I can say ..."

"Roger, I had no idea that you felt like this."

He sat back. "Frankly, neither did I. Not for some time. But missing you the way I do is driving me mad." He stopped and looked at me. "Well?"

"I don't know," I said slowly. "I didn't realise how you felt. I know it sounds really silly, but Roger, I need to take in what you've said and think about it. Is that ok?"

He shrugged slightly. "Well, at least you haven't told me to fuck off."

At this I pretend-gasped. "Do you know Roger, that's the first time I've ever heard you use the f-word?" Although some of the tension seemed to dissipate at that, as we finished off our coffee and nibbled on the last chocolate, my head was spinning. The evening was now anything but relaxed and easy.

We left the restaurant in soft darkness about half an hour later and Roger walked me to my car. I was still struggling to take in his declaration when he stopped me, held my face in both hands, bent and kissed each corner of my mouth before kissing my lips. It was a tender yet insistent kiss and as I opened my mouth, his tongue grazed over the inside of my lips before softly butterfly kissing my nose, eyes and forehead. Then, with a soft groan he enfolded me in a hug. I felt his hardness against me and as we continued to embrace, he kissed me again, this time more passionately. I put my hands against his chest. "Easy tiger," I whispered and he moved away very slightly.

"I'm sorry ..."

"Don't be. It's ok. But I think it's time to go, don't you?"

He nodded. "I'll call you. Is it ok for me to call you?"

"Of course it is." And I could see him watching me as I drove away.

Sleep eluded me that night. I tossed and turned, wondering what to make of the evening. I knew I liked him, that we had a lot in common - but love him? I really didn't know.

True to his word, Roger called me on Saturday evening and did most of the talking. He insisted that he loved me but said that the last thing he wanted to do was to scare me off, and I was to take as long as I wanted to think about it. He added that he would rather have me as a friend than nothing at all. Such emotional honesty and generosity took my breath away and we finished the conversation with a promise to talk again very soon. As I put the phone down I felt a flutter in the pit of my stomach that I hadn't felt for several months.

Chapter 8 - July

The next week's guests were charmingly excellent company which made cooking for, sharing meals and spending time with them a very pleasurable way of generating income.

My mobile rang late Monday morning and to my surprise it was Roger. "I've been thinking so much about you and wanted to talk to you anyway, but this is work. Remember you helped get some of the kids ready for work experience? Well, three of them went to a big engineering company who were really impressed with them - not just their ability but their attitude. Your name was mentioned as one of the teachers involved with tutoring them and they wondered if you did any training work. You know, personal effectiveness, that kind of thing."

I held my breath as he continued. "Well anyway, they'd like to talk to you to see if you could help them with their apprenticeship programme."

I couldn't restrain myself and let out a small squeak. "Yes of course I'd be interested in talking to them. Love to. And thank you for letting me know Roger, I really appreciate it."

"You send me your CV with the kind of training you've done and can do and I'll forward it to them. Of course I can't promise anything concrete Lucie, but they were really impressed and I'm pretty sure that they'll want to meet you."

"Thank you so much Roger. You're an absolute star. You very busy at the moment?" I knew he would be with the end of term fast approaching. We were on the phone for only a few more minutes until he said he had to go and that he would be in touch again very soon and not just about work, at which I put the phone down thoughtfully.

Di rang on Monday evening to talk about our proposed holiday. We plumped for the third week of July, just before the schools broke up for the summer holidays, and agreed to get together at the weekend to make a final decision on where to go. "And we'll make the bookings there and then," Di said, "otherwise we'll carry on faffing and end up not going anywhere." I emailed Lyn straightaway to advise her I wouldn't be able to accommodate any visitors that week and received a reply within a few minutes thanking me for giving reasonable notice and wishing me a great holiday.

To my surprise, I received an email on Tuesday morning from a college in nearby Birmingham for whom I'd done some training work a couple of years ago, asking if I was free to deliver some workshops for one of their clients and if I was, could I attend a meeting on Friday at eleven. Yes I was interested and yes I could be at the meeting I emailed back. It was strange, I thought, how work seemed to be popping up from so many unexpected places. A bit hand-to-mouth it might be, but boring it certainly was not.

Even though I wasn't working at the shop, I went in to see Kate and Albert on Thursday morning. "Thank you so much for everything." Kate handed me my wages for the previous four Thursdays.

"It was a real pleasure. Do let me know as and when you want me again, won't you?"

"Certainly will. You did really well and I can't tell you how helpful it was to have someone who I can trust looking after things. And you had a good time?"

I nodded enthusiastically. "Loved it. It was a real change from other stuff that I do which made it quite exciting."

Kate laughed and Albert gently waved his tail as we drank tea and continued to talk about Kate's promotional ideas for another hour or so, which I found fascinating. I'd always been interested in business, especially when Alex and I had set up his embryonic concern, and enjoyed being involved in different projects.

That evening, with my visitors' approval, I went to my second Zumba class with Karen. It might have been my imagination but it seemed that I was able to stay on my feet for very slightly longer than the previous week. After the hour I was running with sweat and could barely breathe, but had a sense of real achievement.

"Want to join us for a drink?" one of the class asked us.

"Thank you - but not this week. Maybe next time?" I was mindful of my visitors and Karen nodded her agreement as we left.

"You know, we ought to join them sometime," Karen said as she drove me home.

"That would be great, but I need to tell my guests that's what I'm doing. I'd love to next week - it'd be so nice to relax afterwards, have a drink and put on all the calories we've just sweated to get rid of." We were still giggling as I poured Karen a drink and explained the joke to my guests.

I made sure that I arrived at the college at quarter to eleven on Friday morning and was met by Marc, one of the project managers who explained that one of their clients wanted to run a two-week induction programme. He'd heard some positive comments about me by the Business Head of Department and wondered whether I'd be interested in delivering six days of the programme scheduled to run in August for them. I said an emphatic 'yes' whereupon Marc confirmed that he'd email me the materials and arrange for a purchase order to be raised. An hour later I was shaking his hand in farewell and grinned broadly as I made my way to my car.

In one week I had been considered for and offered a considerable amount of work. Unexpectedly Richard suddenly came into my mind as I wished that he could see how well I was faring and, to my irritation, that thought stayed with me for the whole journey home.

I arrived at Di's late Saturday morning and was greeted by a warm hug and the appetising aroma of her excellent chicken and ham pie which was as tasty as it smelled. Afterwards, we sat and discussed where we wanted to go on holiday. After two glasses of rosé and much debate, we decided on Brittany in northern France. Di had a soft-top car and said we should use that, so the first thing we did was to think about where we wanted to visit. I suddenly remembered one of Susie's school trips when her class visited Bayeux. "Di, could we stop off in Bayeux? I've always wanted to see the Bayeux tapestry and as we're so close ..."

"You know, I've never seen it either," Di said thoughtfully, so that was agreed, and we then spent some time poring over maps to decide which ferry to book and where we could stay.

We eventually decided to use the ferry crossing between Dover and Calais as it gave us the most flexibility in terms of time, not to mention being the cheapest by miles. It was a drive of over three hundred miles, so we agreed to share the driving and, as Di said, we'd be travelling through some marvellous countryside. "Let's try and get to Calais really early in the morning, then we'll get to St Malo for lunchtime," she suggested, so we booked the 0640 ferry which arrived at 0910. We booked one night in St Malo so we could explore the city and then found what looked like a charming little hotel in Aber Wrac'h very close to the coast and booked for two nights. "We can move on when we want to." I agreed. We spent the rest of the evening talking about our holiday. "It's just what I need," Di said and I nodded. It had been so long since I'd had a holiday, years in fact, and I was more than ready for a change of scene.

The first name I noticed in my inbox on Sunday morning was Phil's and I opened it eagerly, perhaps more eagerly than was seemly. He said that he'd just arrived back in the UK to a mountain of work that he needed to spend a couple of days on, but after that he wanted to see me. He, and his business partner, liked my style and wanted me to write a few articles for them and see how they, and the magazine, were received. He asked if I could see him the following week, perhaps on the Friday evening. I replied, saying that I was off to France for a week's holiday but could see him at lunchtime. His reply came back within minutes agreeing with a small PS 'Are you not allowed out after dark?' The man clearly had a sense of humour which made me smile.

The next week's guests came from Rouen, so much time was spent over the dinner table talking about good places for Di and me to visit. I sat at the table making copious notes. As neither of us had visited that part of France, it was a very happy coincidence that I had three people advising me which wonderful places to see. It felt quite strange not to have any days scheduled for teaching, coaching or meetings but it was wonderful to be able to take some time out and relax for a change.

Barbara called on Tuesday evening and we agreed that I'd go to hers on Wednesday afternoon. "I've done a bit of market research and it's looking quite encouraging. Scary, but encouraging."

I laughed. "Change can be scary but it's exciting too. What would life be like if we stayed safe all the time?"

She was saying much the same on Wednesday afternoon and it was clear that although she was very nervous of potentially changing the way she was working, the thought of being self-employed and in charge of her own destiny was increasingly tempting. We discussed carrying out more market research, premises, health and safety issues, what target market she was aiming for and what marketing and advertising was likely to cost. After much debate, we decided that working with other catering companies to provide them with cakes they couldn't make themselves might be a workable strategy, as well as operating on her own and, as Barbara said, that felt like a huge step forward. "Always helps to have a plan." I was very firm about that. "Then at least you can measure the level of success."

Barbara had tried out some different recipes in cupcake sizes so of course we had to sample and grade them. The problem was that they were all so delicious that they all ranked a five out of five. "Your product is perfect. You've just got to think about how to get it out to the right people at the right price." She nodded thoughtfully. It was a very good afternoon and when, at five, I left to meet my guests, I had a warm feeling of contentment and satisfaction.

Roger called on Wednesday evening. He said that he was very busy as the end of term was fast approaching but that he'd just heard from the engineering company who wanted to see me so asked if I could meet with them next week. I told him I was going away for a few days but he assured me that the following week would be fine and that he'd get in touch with them and explain. He was away on holiday himself for the first two weeks of August but wanted to see me. "I don't want to put you under pressure but I can't tell you how much I'm missing you." I held my breath. It was very beguiling to be wooed so overtly and I suddenly remembered our kiss when I'd felt his insistence and passion. "Anyway," he continued, "you go and have a great holiday and I'll look forward to seeing you when you get back." We said our goodbyes and I wondered how I'd feel when I next met him.

Zumba went quite well and Judith, the instructor, was very encouraging but I knew and she knew that I was struggling. "I'm sure you're getting better each week," she said with what I thought was a sympathetic smile. I had to agree but wondered if I would ever be a natural exerciser like Karen. I rather doubted it.

When I walked into the One Elm on Friday, I saw Phil sitting at the same table we'd occupied previously. He saw me and stood up and as he did, I could see that he'd lost weight and looked tense and pale. Clearly he'd been much affected by the last few weeks. He held my shoulders and kissed me on both cheeks. "Lucie, it's so good to see you." His hands stayed on my shoulders a second longer than was necessary. "What would you like to drink? Your usual?"

"Goodness, I didn't expect you to remember that."

"I remember more than people think." The smile lit up his face and, for a moment, he looked like the Phil I'd first met all those months ago.

He joined me in sparkling water with ice, no slice and we sipped while, on my prompting, he told me how Phoebe and Hank were coping. "It's been so very hard for them. They'd kind of come to terms with the fact they wouldn't have kids and then for this to happen ..." His voice faded and I saw his eyes filling up.

I put my hand over his. "Such a tragedy for everyone. I'm so, so sad for you all."

"Thank you. It's good talk about it to someone who isn't family." He cleared his throat and paused. "So, tell me Lucie, who are you going on holiday with next week?"

"With a very dear girlfriend. She's just been made redundant and wants to spend a few days away to clear her mind. I think she wants to change direction but isn't quite sure what to do and I really want a break, so combining the two seemed a really good idea."

"So it's not with your man then?"

I stared at him. "Absolutely and emphatically not. He's gone. Even if he crawled on his belly for a mile on broken glass, I wouldn't have him back. Some things are just not ok and doing what he did fell squarely into the 'not ok' category." I took a breath and could have continued but Phil held up his hands.

"I think I get the picture." He paused again and looked at me intently. "Anyone else on the scene then?"

"No. I'm taking some time out to get myself sorted. I don't think it's entirely healthy to skip from one relationship to another. I'm quite enjoying focusing on work, and spending time with friends. You know, being single isn't so bad."

He nodded. "I know." There was a long pause and I wondered what he would say next. "I really liked what you wrote Lucie. Interesting and, more to the point, very well written. I don't know whether we'd use it but it's very clear that you know a lot about food and how to cook well on a budget." He paused again. "Tell me, what's your favourite restaurant?"

I blinked and flicked into work mode. "Gosh, that's a hard question. There are so many good places to eat but for atmosphere and entertainment, it's hard to beat Sarastro's in Covent Garden for Sunday lunch."

"Interesting choice. Which day are you returning from France?"

"Sunday week. Why?"

"Well, why don't you take yourself and your friend to Sunday lunch at Sarastro's on the way home, make some notes and then write an eight hundred word article about it? Does that fit in with your travel plans?"

"I'll make sure that it does. And I'm sure Di will be delighted to come with me."

"Excellent. Now, let's eat …" After reading the menu, we decided to share the One Elm's huge surf and turf board which was, as always, delicious. The next couple of hours passed very enjoyably until I regretfully said that I needed to get home to pack and get some sleep as I was leaving at midnight. Phil stood to say goodbye and as he kissed my cheeks, I returned his light embrace with a feeling of real affection. As I walked out, I sensed him watching me which made me smile and wonder what the future might hold.

I spent some time packing, rang Anita who'd very kindly volunteered to check on and feed the cats while I was away, put my bags in the car and then went to bed. I fell asleep almost immediately to be woken by harps at eleven thirty and was on the road to Di's just after midnight. By one o'clock, Di and I had loaded everything into her car and were on our way. We arrived at Dover at about half past five on Sunday morning, having stopped for a motorway breakfast at four and, by seven, were watching the white cliffs of Dover fade away in the distance.

Di and I had a wonderful few days together as we walked, talked, shopped, ate, drank and enjoyed some great experiences, touring around Brittany and Normandy.

St Malo was, many centuries ago, a pirate city with forts built into the sea to protect it from invaders, which were accessible at low tide. So after a lunch of moules and fries, we walked the causeway to one of them, relishing the soft sea breezes. We'd found a very basic hotel in St Malo and left after an early breakfast on the Monday morning, travelling to the first chambre d'hôtes we'd found on the internet in Aber Warc'h. Pierre and Hélène Le Garrec made us very welcome and we spent a couple of restful days beach-combing, eating marvellous seafood and drinking the local cider and calvados. We walked the cliffs of Pointe de Raz, saw the ruins of a beautiful ancient church and took a boat to Ouessant and stood on the shore, staring out at the seascape surrounded by its indigenous shaggy, friendly sheep.

On Wednesday morning we said a regretful goodbye to our hosts and drove inland to Forêt de Paimport which Pierre and Hélène had assured us was well worth a visit. As I drove Di's speedy sports car along the N12, she read from a guidebook that said its other, older name was Brocéliande and was, according to legend, the forest of the wizard Merlin and that medieval Breton minstrels, just like their Welsh counterparts, had told tales of King Arthur and the Holy Grail. It took us just under three hours to get there, so the first thing we did was to look around for a hotel. Amazingly the first place we found, run by Mme Sylvie Le Bihon, had available rooms with views over the bustling marketplace. We spent a day wandering around the forest and visiting Viviane's tomb who, according to legend, was a powerful fairy and had bewitched Merlin, making him drink some enchanted water which had, unfortunately, petrified him for all time. Afterwards, we ate chicken that had been simmered with what were known locally as navy beans, which I realised were haricot beans, with baby beets and bacon in apple cider and a delicious flan with prunes washed down with local beer and, of course, as we were in Normandy, we ate innumerable crêpes. Crêpes with orange butter, crêpes with home-made lemon curd and savoury crêpes - all meltingly scrumptious, not to mention quite a few crusty baguettes with pungently soft Camembert.

There was a local town fête on Thursday with many stalls which included, of course, food, so we tried the local sablés which were very like shortbread biscuits but so flakily delicious that we felt we had to buy some to bring back. There was country dancing, pony and trap races, a dog show and many other attractions. We lingered in the drinks tent and sampled several different ciders, all of which had their individual charm. The vendors chatted to us about their products, one in particular who, after half an hour or so, asked me for my number and when I laughingly told him we'd be on our way the following day, he kissed my hand sorrowfully saying he regretted not meeting me sooner.

"Well,' Di said as we left, carrying several bottles each, "I think you pulled there."

"Yeah, right." But I was secretly delighted that a much younger man had flirted with me so openly.

Friday morning saw us on the A84 to Bayeux where we found a small pension run by Henri and Mathilde Flochard who were as welcoming as our other hosts. They also ran a small café so, over the next two days, we ate Mathilde's tripe slow cooked in cider and calvados which was surprisingly good, mussels cooked with white wine, garlic and cream, the most amazing Normandy apple tart and a sublime teurgoule which proved to be a baked rice dessert which tasted infinitely better than it sounded.

We sat in Bayeux cathedral, enjoying the splendour of its architecture. We visited a memorial dedicated to the 1,889 journalists who had lost their lives while reporting between 1944 and 2007, a sobering reminder of the price of free speech. I spent a couple of hours gazing at the Bayeux tapestry, marvelling at the intricate workmanship and fresh colours that had survived for over nine centuries. I was so glad to have had the opportunity of fully appreciating something I'd wanted to see for so long.

I'd told Di about lunching at Sarastro's and we had managed to change our ferry booking from mid-morning to an earlier crossing, so we decided to leave Bayeux on Saturday afternoon and book into a hotel near Calais so we wouldn't be driving through the night again. This time, Di drove the five hundred plus kilometres to Calais and we talked again about her possible future plans.

"I really don't want more of the same," she said as we waited while a herd of sheep were being slowly moved from one field to another. "I think it's time for a total change." She went on to say that she had almost decided to let her house for at least six months and go travelling. "I've got family in Australia, so I could start there."

"And then?" I prompted.

"I don't know," she paused. "But I'm sure I'd find somewhere to go."

"I'm really going to miss you ..." My eyes filled with tears and I blinked them away. "Just ignore me, I'm being silly. It's a great idea darling. You've talked about it before. You'd have a great time. You really should go for it."

She glanced across at me. "We'll keep in touch loads. And you can always come out and visit me wherever I am. I just need to take some time out. I'm tired of being on this treadmill of work and worry. It kind of depends on being able to let the house but I don't think that'll be too much of a problem." We continued to discuss Di's plans that evening as we enjoyed our last French dinner, choosing bœuf bourguignon which was served with crusty bread, ideal for mopping up all that delicious sauce, washed down with a bottle of excellent locally made red wine.

Sunday morning saw us on the 0825 ferry, sitting on deck with coffee and croissants, watching the beaches of Calais disappear and the white cliffs of Dover eventually appear. We were both a little sad that the holiday was over, but as we disembarked and headed towards London, we agreed that we'd shared a wonderfully relaxing and pleasurable time.

"I'm not sure I can manage any more food though." Whilst I agreed, I knew that she wouldn't be able resist Sarastro's menu.

We parked near the Oval cricket ground and took the tube to Leicester Square which was only a short walk to Drury Lane and as we strolled into the restaurant, I heard Di's gasp as she took in the opulent yet slightly shabby surroundings. "It's the ultimate shabby chic, isn't it?" I asked as we were shown to our seats.

"Fabulous. Just amazing."

"You just wait til you see the loos, they're very, very rude." So we headed upstairs and freshened up under the very explicit and very erotic art that adorned the walls.

Back at our table, Di chose salmon with potatoes, slow roasted tomatoes, grilled Turkish peppers, an onion confit and lemon butter sauce. "You will let me have a little taste, won't you?" I asked, mindful that I had to write eight hundred words on our experience.

"Of course, provided I can do the same," Di agreed as I selected the lamb Anatolian which was served with mixed vegetables and a potato gratin.

We started with their Mezze platter which consisted of cheese and mushroom filled puff pastries, hummus, yoghurt with chopped cucumber and garlic with a Turkish style cous cous salad, all served with thin slivers of flatbread accompanied by ice cold light beer.

"This is simply scrumptious," Di said as she picked up a third pastry.

"Isn't it? I've not been here very often but absolutely love it. I'm so glad you like it, but the best is yet to come, I promise."

We were halfway through our main courses which were equally excellent, when two musicians and three singers from London's Royal Opera House started to play and sing to us for over an hour while we finished the salmon and lamb, then grazed on mascarpone and coffee cake, accompanied by the strongest coffee I'd ever tasted. It was a magical experience, we were completely captivated as we ate, drank and listened to the divas perform from Madame Butterfly, Porgy and Bess, Carmen, La Traviata, Phantom of the Opera and a couple of Queen songs. It was with real regret that we left when the entertainment was over.

With very full tummies, we slowly meandered back to the Oval and Di drove us back to hers where I'd left my car. After an uneventful journey, we shared a farewell coffee before I drove home. The cats greeted me before remembering that I'd been away for a week and then spent the next hour ignoring me. It took a tin of tuna to persuade them to acknowledge my existence but eventually both joined me on the sofa after I'd unpacked, put a load into the washing machine and poured myself a glass of Merlot. With a purring cat on each side of me, I looked at the very brief notes I'd made at Sarastro's and added a few more thoughts until I was satisfied I had enough material to be able to write Phil's article. I sat back with a satisfied sigh; it had been a very, very good week.

Roger called me on Monday morning sounding brisk and business-like; I guessed he was in the staffroom. "I've fixed a meeting for Wednesday morning at eleven with that engineering company we talked about, is that ok for you?"

"That's perfect. Thank you so much for this Roger, I really appreciate it."

"It's a pleasure Lucie. I'll come with you if that's ok?"

"Of course it is." And we agreed that we would meet at the school as Roger had a meeting at nine, and that he would drive.

I spent the rest of the day cleaning the house and shopping for my guests who were due to arrive at six that evening. They were from Caen in Northern Brittany, twinned with Warwickshire's Coventry, which was the main reason they'd decided to stay in Stratford. As was the norm, they were very appreciative of my efforts and we spent several evenings sitting over dinner discussing their trips and my very recent experiences in their region. Most came with small gifts and this week was no exception, I was delighted with the wine and chocolates that were pressed into my hands.

After seeing my guests off on their daily trip early on Tuesday morning I settled down to write the article on the Sarastro's experience for Phil. It took much longer than I'd anticipated, but after a couple of hours I had the first draft ready and after another hour I had what I thought might be the finished article. I knew I needed to leave it for a while and then re-read for final proof-reading before submitting it. So, after enjoying a coffee in the garden, I went for a stroll up to the Welcombe Hills where Pennie and Simon lived in a barn conversion. As I passed their door I heard Saffy barking. I paused and saw Pennie open the door with a very excited coal-black dog straining at her leash.

"Lucie, how nice to see you."

"You too." I bent and stroked Saffy's glossy fur. "May I join you?"

We had a very pleasant amble to the top of one of the smaller hills while Saffy ran around us begging for stick throwing which interrupted us as we caught up with each other's news. An hour later we returned to Pennie's and sat in her spacious kitchen, drinking tea and nibbling on her excellent home-made biscuits after which I made my way home, re-read the article, made a couple of alterations and then sent it off to Phil with my fingers mentally crossed.

I arrived at the school just after ten on Wednesday; it felt very strange to be there after so long. I saw Roger striding towards me and as I got out of the car I was enveloped in a bear hug. "Lucie, it's so good to see you.' He stood back and looked at me critically. 'You're looking good - very good ..."

"Glad you like it." I was wearing a lime green and pale purple ankle-length dress I'd bought in France and teamed it with a darker purple shrug. That, combined with the slight tan I'd acquired had given my skin a glow. I knew I looked good and that boost of self-confidence had put a smile on my face.

"Yes, you look different somehow," he paused. "Anyway, we'd best go now. You ready?"

I reached into my car and pulled out my laptop bag. "Absolutely. Let's go, shall we?"

Half an hour later we were sitting in a smart office with a tall, good-looking, dark haired man dressed in a pale grey suit. "I'm Tony Singh, head of training and development for this group of companies. We offer work experience to school and college students and also a graduate scheme, so we're really dedicated to providing opportunities locally whenever possible. We provide all the technical training in-house but use external trainers for soft skills workshops. Roger was telling me that you prepared some of his kids for their work experience with us and I have to say that I was very impressed with them, especially with their general attitude and work ethic. We want to put a programme in place for people coming to us on work experience and wondered if you'd be interested in working with us." He paused and looked at me searchingly.

"I'd like to very much and can certainly help with that. I guess you're looking for areas like time management, personal effectiveness, communication skills, dealing with difficult people and situations, how to behave in a team - that kind of thing?"

Tony leaned back and smiled at me. "Yes, that's exactly the kind of thing I had in mind. I wonder if you'd put a proposal together for me?"

I took out my notepad and pen. "Of course ..." We went on to discuss timeframes, length of workshops and budgets while I made copious notes. "I think that's everything I need. I'll email you my thoughts and proposal by Monday at the latest, is that ok?"

I was still smiling as I got into Roger's car. "Roger, I can't tell you how grateful I am. Do you fancy lunch?"

"Love to, really love to, but I need to get back for another meeting. I'm trying to get everything sorted so that I can go away on holiday on Saturday morning with a clear conscience." He glanced at me. "But when I'm back I'll have lots of time for lunch, tea, dinner - whatever you'd like."

We continued chatting on the way back to the school and as I thanked him again for introducing me to Tony, we hugged goodbye on the promise that he would be in touch on his return from holiday. "You have a really lovely time, won't you?" I gently disentangled myself from his insistent embrace.

I worked busily on the outline of the programme for Tony for the rest of the day, and continued on Thursday after seeing my guests off after breakfast. I was deep in thought when I heard my landline ring and, as often happened, there was a momentary jolt as Richard flashed into my mind, but of course it wasn't him - and would I even want to talk to him now?

It was Barbara who sounded very upbeat. "Everything's going really well." There was a small silence. "Maybe too well because nothing's gone wrong yet."

I laughed. "Give it time, it probably will, but that'll just be a little glitch. Anything I can do to help?"

"Well yes, I think so. I need to get a business plan for the bank. I'm working on it but wondered if you'd help me?"

"Of course I'll help. When were you thinking of?"

She was away the following week in Wales seeing some friends so we agreed that we'd get together after that. "You have a great time." As I put the phone down, I smiled at her bravery and enthusiasm.

After dinner, Karen came round with my monthly gift and we went to Zumba where I just about managed to stay on my feet for most of the time.

"I'm away for the next three weeks," Judith announced as we collapsed at the end of the class. I felt a sense of relief but several people looked stricken. "Don't worry, I've arranged for another teacher to carry on with all my classes while I'm away. Her name's Jasmine - she's really good. I know you'll love her."

"Dammit," I muttered under my breath to Karen who shook her head in amused mild exasperation at me.

Half an hour later a few of us were sitting in the courtyard of the One Elm: Judith, Sara, Bev, Rose, Karen and I, all sipping ice-cold beers. It never ceased to amaze me how quickly and freely many women talk and this group was no exception. We talked about work, weight and fitness issues, our personal circumstances and, of course, men.

"Well, I've been divorced for three and a half years now," Sara said. "I know that there are loads of arses out there," we all nodded, "but I really don't like being on my own so I'm on a couple of dating websites ..."

"And?" we prompted, sensing some good stories.

"Well," she leaned forward, "there was this chap whose profile read like Brad Pitt but when I met him he was about five foot six and not the six-foot plus he'd said."

Bev looked slightly disapproving while the rest of us giggled. "I don't think I could go on a website," she said at which we asked an indignant why. "Well, I've not dated since I was seventeen ..."

"Well then," Sara said. "Some of us aren't lucky enough to be married and have to keep looking." She looked cross and upset at the same time.

"I was on a website before I met Paul," Judith said. "Had quite a laugh actually but I have to say that I didn't meet anyone I wanted to be with. In fact the only one who looked nice, reeked of BO and almost sat on my lap. I couldn't wait to get away."

By now we were happily on our second beers. "Well, I've used a dating site," I volunteered. "In fact that's how I met Richard ..." Karen snorted but I ignored her. "I remember arranging to meet one bloke on the steps of the theatre, thought it would be such a romantic place to meet. Anyway, I got there early and went up to the balcony for a coffee while I was waiting, looked down and saw him walking up the steps. I just bottled it and hid in the Ladies for ages until I thought he'd gone and crept out only to find him still standing on the steps. It was so embarrassing - he didn't look anything like his photo and I knew it was all wrong but we had a quick drink and then I made an excuse and left. I felt awful but just couldn't stop myself."

"I'd been dating this man for about three months," Sara said after our laughter had died down. "We got on pretty well. He'd been divorced for a couple of years and had said that he was ready to move on. Anyway, there we were driving through a really pretty town in the Cotswolds on our way to a pub for lunch when suddenly he pushed my head right down under the dashboard, held me down for a few moments and then let me up. I was livid! All he could say was that he was really sorry but he'd seen his ex-wife was walking by and didn't want her to know he was dating." By this time we were all sitting with our mouths open. "He kept on apologising but the next day he was terribly depressed and after another few days I knew it was over. I mean, he never said anything but – well, you know what I mean?" We all nodded.

"And then there was Bill," Sara was on a roll now. "I really liked him and we saw each other for a few weeks but I had to stop it - he just kept talking about his ex-wife all the bloody time. It did my head in. I mean if he was still that much in love with her, why didn't he try and get back with her? One day I lost my temper and said as much to him ..." She paused.

"And?" We said in chorus.

"Well, he burst into tears. Said he'd always loved her but kept dating to try and get over her. It felt awful but I knew that much as I liked him, we'd never amount to anything, so there was no point in us continuing." She blinked as a tear rolled down her cheek.

We sat in silence for a few minutes until Bev told us how she'd met her husband when they were at school, married at seventeen, had her daughter at eighteen and then miscarried three times before they decided to stop trying for more children. "But I have two adorable grandchildren who I look after a couple of days a week for Katie which fits in perfectly with my business." She went on to tell us that her husband had progressive multiple sclerosis and caring for him took up much of her time, which was why she'd decided to qualify as a book-keeper and work on a self-employed basis for a couple of firms of accountants, helping their clients get their accounts in order before annual audit. Her daughter came to sit with her dad on Thursday evenings so Bev could go out to Zumba. "He's so brave, never complains and never minds me going out. He's so strong and selfless."

Karen and I talked about Bev on the way home. "I think she's pretty amazing, never mind her husband," Karen said and I agreed.

"But just imagine being in your thirties and knowing that you'll only ever get worse, that there's no way out of your suffering and how much that impacts on your family. It kind of puts things into perspective, doesn't it?" As we said our goodbyes, we were both slightly reflective and sombre.

After I'd waved goodbye to my guests on Friday morning, I changed beds, cleaned the house and, after a couple of hours sat in the garden with a large mug of hot, strong coffee and a toasted bacon sandwich. The cats joined me and the three of us relaxed in the hot sunshine. I'd taken my laptop into the garden to complete the proposed programme for Tony and by midday it was done.

"What should I charge for this?" I asked the cats who yawned lazily at me from the shelter of the honeysuckle that clung shaggily to the fence. I knew that I needed to spend some time not thinking about it, then re-read it to make sure everything made sense, so after a large glass of ice-cold water, went for a stroll down to the river where I sat for a while, people watching.

I was roused from my reverie by ducks quacking and saw that it was a text from Helena who was in town and wondered if I fancied meeting for a coffee. Indeed I did I texted back and, as I was close to the theatre, we met on the balcony, drank coffee, caught up with each other's news and did more people watching. Helena's daughter, Kesia, was getting married to her lovely Max at the local village church with the reception being held in Helena's large, rambling garden.

"I think that everything's all sorted for tomorrow. Would you like to come over sometime in the evening? We'll have finished eating by seven when there'll be some of their friends playing loud music and probably drinking far too much beer."

I laughed. "Sounds a typically good wedding. Yes please, I'd love to come."

"Anita and John are popping over. Why don't you come with them?"

After another half hour we parted and as I ambled home in the sunshine I called John who said that they'd be delighted to pick me up at about half past seven.

I logged onto my laptop as soon as I arrived home and saw Phil's name in my inbox. Nervously, I opened his email and read, to my delight, that he'd enjoyed reading my article, and it would be in September's first edition. I hugged myself with excitement and glee. I couldn't believe it and emailed him back saying as much.

I walked round my tiny garden a couple of times to try and calm down but couldn't. I knew that I wasn't in a fit state to read Tony's proposal sensibly and decided to do so later. I called Karen and told her my news at which I heard a squeak of joy down the phone. "We need to celebrate, don't we? I'm cooking a Thai curry this evening. Would you like to come over?"

"Love to. I'll bring the beer." We had a lovely evening, eating Karen's excellent curry, drinking a couple of beers and talking endlessly about my news, her news, our kids, work and holidays - we were never lost for anything to say to each other.

John was nothing if not punctual and at seven thirty precisely they arrived to give me a lift to Helena's. Kesia was in her wedding dress which was a white, 60s-style dress teamed with almost fluorescent red high heels and Max was in a cream suit with a tie that matched Kesia's shoes.

"Such style," I said to Anita who was in complete agreement. It was a lovely party but, sadly for me, it reinforced that I was on my own, despite Helena's warm welcome. There were several singletons around but it still felt strange and I was in a pensive mood when I was dropped home at about midnight.

The following day I emailed the proposal across to Tony and then sent another email to Phil, saying how pleased and gratified I was that he was using my article. I added that I'd love to continue contributing and looked forward to September's edition which would, I hope, be the first of many.

Chapter 9 - August

One of the souvenirs I'd brought back from Brittany was a French cookbook which I used extensively over the next few weeks for my guests. That week I served French bean salad to accompany English sausages, sole Véronique and a twice-baked goats cheese soufflé. The latter was an unmitigated disaster, so I had to dash out to buy fish and chips that were much appreciated as they gently laughed at my culinary attempt. It was much more daunting than I thought to cook French food for French people.

It was an unusually hectic week as I'd delivered four days training for the college's client and had a daily round trip of some ninety miles in the rush hour. By Thursday evening, I was really tired. Karen came round to pick me up for Zumba and wouldn't brook any arguments from me about why I was too weary to go, so I grudgingly dragged myself upstairs to pull on leggings, a tee-shirt and sneakers.

Jasmine was very young, very pretty and very energetic. She worked us very hard and by the end of the hour I was completely wiped out - never had a restorative drink felt so welcome. Sara suggested that we should go to a different pub, but Karen and I insisted on our usual haunt. So, happily ensconced under the dappled shade in the courtyard at the One Elm, the usual brief discussions on how hard this session had been ensued, and then talk moved on to work, kids and, inevitably, men.

Sara had been busy last weekend and told us about her experiences. "The one on Saturday was a real lulu," she sounded pensive. "On his profile, he said that he'd been divorced for three years but all he could do was talk about his ex-wife ALL the time. Everything I said, he managed to bring back to her. After about an hour I'd had enough, but when I tried to leave he got quite nasty."

We gasped in disbelief. "Really? So what happened?"

"Said I'd wasted his time, that he didn't fancy me and that his ex was worth ten of me." She paused for a moment. "You know, that really hurt - I mean I knew in my head that he was an arse but it made me feel really bad about myself."

We sat in silence for a moment. "And I met someone else on Sunday."

"You're nothing if not persistent," Judy grinned.

"I don't smoke and I'd much rather have someone who doesn't smoke," we all nodded, "and his profile said he was a non-smoker but when I met him he reeked of stale smoke. I mean, why lie about it when it's so obvious the minute you meet? And when I said I was going he got really offended - called me narrow minded. Why would I want to be with someone like that?" We nodded again.

"Well, I was at this conference," Judy said, "and I met this man. He wasn't that good-looking but he seemed really nice. We sat and talked for over an hour about this and that. Anyway, I needed the loo and as I stood up, he made a grab for my tits and when I told him to stop he got all huffy and stormed off. Some men are so odd, aren't they?"

I suddenly recalled a date I'd had a year or so before I'd met Richard. "I remember this man I met ages ago. He seemed really nice, was looking for a long-term relationship and we seemed to have lots in commons so loads of boxes were ticked. I met him and we really got on. We had a lovely dinner, good wine, it was all going so well until ..." I stopped and looked at the ring of expectant faces round me. "Until he said he was married ..." There was a collective gasp but I continued. "He was married and would I sleep with him and his wife."

"And?"

"I said no - he looked really hurt and surprised so I just stood up and walked out. I didn't think there was anything else I could do."

"It sounds that at least there was a level of honesty between him and his wife," Karen sounded sadly reflective. "My ex serially cheated on me from the word go and always with much younger women. It took twenty years and six affairs to make me realise that I was worth so much more than that - eventually I booted him out but I can't see myself ever trusting anyone again. It's a shame because I like men but I'll never let anyone in to be able to hurt me that much." We nodded in sympathy and understanding. "I seem to attract younger men now," she added with a smile. "I don't know why but that suits me just fine. No game-playing and some great sex - what's not to like about that?"

"Makes sense," Judy said.

"But don't you want ..." Sara looked anxious.

"No I don't. I really don't. I have a great job, great friends," she grinned at me, "and great kids. Why would I want to mess that up?"

There was a few moments silence as we digested that.

"I hated being on the dating scene," Debbie said. "Sifting through all those men was just like being on a treadmill. I know how lucky I am to have Iain in my life." She paused. "Mind you, we're awash with kids at the moment but that's ok."

I stifled a sigh. "I thought I'd be getting married this or next year but ..." I stopped as I felt a soft kick on my ankle and saw Karen looking sternly at me.

"Go on," two or three voices chorused.

"No, not today," I was conscious of Karen's eyes on me. "It's a bit of a long story so I'll save it for another day."

"I had a fling with Lee recently," Judy volunteered. "He was much, much younger than me and it was mainly about sex of course ..." She looked at Karen knowingly. "Well, he came in one afternoon with a bag of vegetables and I said, great, I'll cook us a ratatouille." She stopped for a dramatic moment. "He said that he hadn't bought them for that." She paused again while Bev looked puzzled and Karen and I giggled.

"Courgettes. Aubergines. Cucumbers." Judy said and Bev's eyes widened in understanding.

"Anyway, I cooked a ratatouille that time but then the next weekend when he brought in some more vegetables we did what he'd originally intended." She sat back with a smirk as we chuckled, and it was on this culinary note that we parted company.

As Karen drove me home we agreed how much we'd enjoyed the evening. I said goodnight to her and then spent ten minutes preparing my guests' packed lunches for their final day in England. I was still smiling at the stories we'd shared, certain that there would be many more.

It was a hot, dry weekend so after changing beds, cleaning the house and buying in food for the next week, I spent time in the garden with the cats before looking through the training materials that Marc had emailed me in preparation for the final two days' training for the college the following week. In the evening I sipped a glass of chilled white wine under the fading sun and realised that I was feeling content and, to my surprise, almost happy.

More French recipes from my new cookbook appeared on the menu for my guests as well as a couple of typical English dishes. I cooked a wonderful Poulet à la Provençale which went down a storm whereas the seared scallops in ginger and lime sauce was less well received, but my sausage and mash with mustard gravy was definitely the winner of the week. I was realising more and more how important cooking and entertaining was to me and how much I enjoyed it.

My last two days' training in Birmingham went very smoothly and after dinner on Wednesday I emailed my invoice across to Marc, hitting the send button with a satisfied sigh. I'd enjoyed this contract and felt fairly confident that there'd be more in the coming months.

I still hadn't heard from Tony but decided to wait until the next week to email him. I didn't want to appear pushy but, at the same time, realised that I needed to look keen. Such a hard balance, I thought to myself and sighed.

The second Zumba week with Jasmine was just as hard as I'd remembered from the previous week. By the end of the hour my legs were trembling and I could barely walk across to the One Elm where I sank into a wicker chair in the courtyard with a thankful sigh. We'd persuaded Jasmine to come with us and while Karen went to the bar to order drinks, she sat next to me. "You ok?"

I returned her smile. "Sort of. I hate that it's such hard work and everyone else seems to be so much better than me."

"Everyone starts at their beginning," Jasmine replied. "Believe me, you're doing fine. And you keep coming which is great."

Karen rejoined us and the five us of settled down. "Bev called to say that she couldn't make it this evening," Jasmine told us. "Seems like her husband had a really bad day today and she felt she just couldn't leave him."

We fell silent for a few moments. "Kind of puts things into perspective doesn't it?" I said eventually to which the others nodded.

"I can't imagine what it must be like," Judy said. "Caring for someone when they're old is one thing but to face that in your thirties, knowing that he's only going to get worse. Well, it doesn't bear thinking about."

"We all have different realities," Karen added and we fell silent again.

As the drinks arrived and broke our contemplative moods, I started telling the group about my lodgers and some of my culinary disasters and very soon we were laughing.

"So you do this a lot?" Judy asked.

"I certainly do. It's a great way to make my house work for me and being paid weekly, really helps cash flow. Luckily, I enjoy it and have to say that I've met some great people. Made a few friends along the way too."

Judy looked thoughtful. "I'm not sure that I'd like having other people living in my house. I'm in the process of buying a flat and want that space for me."

"I have a lodger," Karen added. "He's married and lives in London but he's on a six month rolling contract in Coventry so he stays with me Monday to Friday, goes home straight from work on Friday and doesn't appear again til Monday evening. He's very agreeable company and we have a laugh but I have the weekends to myself which is nice and I have some extra money for treats which is even nicer."

"I used to rent my driveway," Debbie volunteered. "Before Iain and I got together, trying to make ends meet was really difficult, so I contacted a business that was just down the road and said I'd let some of their staff park on my drive. I could squeeze five cars on, six if I was really careful. I was paid per car per hour. It was a real life saver."

"Resourceful," Jasmine sounded impressed. "Really resourceful."

"You kind of do what you have to do," I said softly, almost to myself. It felt very good to hear the others agree.

Talk became lighter as we started sharing dating experiences.

"I met this man," Sara started. "First date, so of course I made an effort and all he did was criticise my dress sense, my makeup, my hair, the way I spoke, it was awful. I wouldn't have minded quite so much but he was in old jeans, his shirt could have done with an iron and I noticed his shoes were all scuffed. I was about to leave when he said he didn't think we had anything in common and stood up. I was just upset that I didn't get in first."

"I've only been on a website once, and that was for a couple of weeks," Judy said. "It was a really good site too ..."

"Naturally," Debbie whispered. We all quickly shushed her.

"Anyway, this man contacted me and asked to meet. We exchanged a few messages and he seemed really nice, so I agreed to see him in the bar of a local hotel. The bastard didn't even turn up." She sounded so indignant we couldn't stop laughing. "I came off the site immediately. Told them I'd assumed that their subscribers would be half-decent and I wasn't prepared to be treated like that ..." By now we were laughing hard and she ruefully joined us.

"I used to sleep with men much too fast," Jasmine said sadly. "So, when I met Pete and really liked him, I decided to take things slow. We had a great first date. He was a real gentleman, kissed my hand as we said goodbye. It was so lovely. We met a few more times. I was so attracted to him and when he took me home after our seventh date, I just couldn't resist, so I invited him in. He was fantastic in bed and I remember lying next to him afterwards thinking that I'd really struck gold. Anyway, he left in the morning ..." Her voice faded.

"And?" we all urged.

She looked at us sorrowfully. "Never heard from him again. I texted him and emailed him but it was like he'd never existed. I felt such a fool." There were tears in her eyes.

Dallas, one of the waiters, paused at our table and asked if we wanted more drinks and as he returned with a full tray, we were still discussing Jasmine's date.

"You know something? Ships in harbour are safe, but that's not what ships are built for," he said as he placed our drinks on the table. We all stopped and stared at him.

"That's pretty profound." I was impressed by what he'd just said.

"So you have to decide whether to stay safe or risk stormy waters," he threw over his shoulder as he went to another table.

We mulled over whether still or stormy waters were best and, as Karen drove me home, were still considering what Dallas had said. As I thanked her for the lift and said an affectionate goodnight, I sensed she would be spending more time thinking about it.

On Saturday morning I received a postcard from Roger which showed an expanse of beach under a blazing sun. He wrote that he and his son were having a very good time but that he was missing me and was looking forward to seeing me on his return – how nice to hear from him I thought.

I'd arranged to meet Karen that morning for coffee. We sat outside Carluccios at one of their pavement tables watching the world go by and I showed her the postcard.

"That's really nice, isn't it?" Karen had a slightly mischievous smile.

I tapped her hand in reproof. "I suppose it is. And he's a very agreeable man ..."

"But?"

"I like him. I like him a lot." I stopped to I gather my thoughts. "But I don't love him and he's made it clear how he feels about me. And Karen, that's very flattering. It would be all too easy to fall into a relationship where someone thinks I'm wonderful and adores me ..."

"Sounds good to me."

"Well yes, yes it is. But I know he's younger than me."

"Hey, you're talking to a confirmed cougar here."

I laughed with her for a moment before saying, "it just doesn't feel fair ..." and going on to tell her about Annie. "You see, she's liked him, loved him I suppose, for a long time. And I come swanning in and snatch him up - she'd be so hurt and angry."

We talked some more but with no resolution. As we parted I still felt uneasy about the 'R-question' as Karen had put it while talking about Roger.

I ambled round aimlessly and then saw in a shop window a two-foot high woman's torso which was covered in tiny mirrors. Wouldn't that look beautiful on that chest of drawers in the bedroom my inner voice whispered. I had to agree so bought it then and there. It fitted in wonderfully and, over the coming months, continued to give me much pleasure.

Barbara came round on Sunday afternoon, bearing more cake samples, so we drank tea in the garden, nibbled cakes and discussed her business plan. As always, I found talking about business invigorating and fascinating, and after suggesting a few amendments to her plan, felt a surge of pleasure and satisfaction. We both glowed in anticipation of her business making good.

Much as I was enjoying having guests, I was looking forward to having more time to myself. However, this weeks' were more fun than usual so spending time with them was no effort at all. I continued to use my French cookbook and tried out sweetbreads sautéed with mushrooms and garlic and ham in a sherry sauce which I served with a disc of puff pastry and braised carrots which, to my delighted surprise, was easier than I thought. Flushed with success, another evening I sautéed chicken breasts with a sauce of button mushrooms, white port and a little cream which also turned out very well and, amazingly, came within my self-imposed budget which made me feel smugly pleased with myself.

I was doing a little gardening on Tuesday morning when I heard ducks quacking, it took very little to distract me from one my least favourite chores. The text was from Roger who'd had a great holiday and wanted us to get together very soon. We arranged to meet for lunch on Thursday, but that evening he got in touch again, asking if we could make it the following week as something had cropped up. I explained that weekdays that week were slightly tricky, so we agreed to meet for lunch on the Friday which was the day my visitors would leave. He was profuse in his apologies and much as I reassured him that it was perfectly alright, he continued to text me during the day.

One of my guests, Jean-Michel who taught English, was especially good company and when the other two decided to go down to a local pub, he asked me to accompany them. I wasn't sure that I wanted to spend the evening with a dozen or so people most of whom I didn't know so I politely declined. About half an hour after they had left, Jean-Michel returned carrying a bottle of sparkling rosé so we sat in the garden, talking as we polished off the bottle between us. He told me he'd recently divorced because his wife had been having an affair for over two years. I could only empathise and sympathise with him. Most of the evening was spent talking about the devastating impacts of being cheated on, with both of us shedding a few tears.

Phil emailed me on Wednesday morning and said he wanted to see me to discuss further work and was I free on Wednesday evening. Unfortunately I wasn't because of my guests I emailed back, but I was free on Friday evening. He emailed back saying that Friday evening would be fine but would I mind meeting him in Oxford? We agreed to meet at the Trout in Wolvercote, a popular riverside pub just outside Oxford, at about six. I felt a small flutter of pleasure but didn't know whether it was the prospect of work or just seeing him - either way it was a very pleasant feeling.

Karen came over to pick me up for Zumba. "This is getting to be a habit," I said as I got into her car.

She grinned at me. "That's the idea, or hadn't you worked that out?"

"Smart-arse," was all I could think of saying. It was a hot evening and keeping up with the fast music and Jasmine's urgings was very hard work, so at the end of the hour most of us were gasping for breath.

"And this is good for us?" I panted to Karen who breathlessly nodded.

As always, we congregated in the One Elm's sunny courtyard. "This is getting to be a habit," Judy smiled as she settled herself down comfortably.

"That's just what I was saying to Karen." I pulled over a couple more chairs.

"It's good to see you," Karen said as Bev joined us who smiled her thanks.

"Nathan's much better this week. Last week was very bad for him but it's good days and bad days, know what I mean?" We all made sympathetic noises. I couldn't imagine what it would be like to love someone who was only ever going to deteriorate and I was sure that the others felt the same way.

Dallas brought our drinks order over which we gulped gratefully - the first one rarely touched the sides. It was the second one that was savoured so he dutifully returned a few minutes later to check what we wanted for the second round.

After the usual how-are-yous, Sara told us about her latest date. "I met this man last weekend for lunch. He was really good-looking, very well dressed, spoke beautifully and our profiles showed that we had loads in common." We leaned forward anticipating that this might be a story with a happy ending. "Trouble was that every other word was 'fuck' which completely put me off." She looked at us and we all nodded.

"Not nice," Bev said.

"Not acceptable," was Jasmine's contribution.

Sara sighed. "I don't think I'm ever going to find someone ..." Her eyes filled with tears.

"I remember this man I met," I said to lighten the mood. "Like yours, his profile looked very good and we got on very well but instead of saying fuck all the time, he just kept farting. No, honestly ..." Everyone was laughing but I kept going. "He didn't apologise or even acknowledge what he was doing. After about an hour I couldn't stand any more so left."

"And then there was Cy," Sara said. "He was really nice for the first couple of dates but then he talked about his bi-polar ex-girlfriend continuously and I realised that he still cared a lot for her. I kind of counselled him and after a few weeks he got back with her. I felt a bit sad but quite proud that I'd helped him. Anyway, we met for a final drink to say goodbye and he then said that, as a thank you, would I let him re-style me as I was a bit of a mess. I couldn't believe my ears and felt completely taken for granted." By this time we all were sitting with our mouths open. In fact there were many more jaw-dropping revelations on the Thursday evenings to come.

"I met Frank from a dating site," Jasmine said. "His profile was interesting but when we met he told me that he was married ..."

We gasped. "Said his wife was ill, that he needed company and some release ..."

"And we all know what that means." Judy curled her lip while the rest of us nodded.

Rose had joined us this evening and had been listening to our stories. "Ages ago I met someone who really put me off dating sites," she said. "It was our first date. He'd already had a drink before we'd met which put me off a bit and he then had several more drinks, getting more and more pissed and unpleasant. I got scared so I pretended I was going to the loo but left. I texted him once I was out of sight of the pub saying that I'd paid for my drinks at the bar and not to call me again. He did text me a couple of times with grovelling apologies and then the third time was really abusive. A friend of mine had suggested I should have a separate mobile for dating which is what I did, so it wasn't as scary as if he'd had my main mobile number."

"What a good idea," Sara said. "Never thought of that. So, you're not on the dating scene now?"

"No. No, I'm not. I'm with Al. He's lovely, but very depressed at the moment." We sat waiting for more. "Well, he's eleven years older than me, not in the best of health and finding it very difficult to find more work. He'd only worked in his last job for four years so there was hardly any redundancy. I wasn't working at the time so had to find a job fast. The only one I could find was in a call centre which is ok, but it doesn't pay much so things are a bit of a struggle at the moment." There was silence as we contemplated what Rose had told us.

Sara turned to Judy. "And what about you?"

"I'm waiting for Ross to leave his wife," Judy said softly. There was another, smaller, collective gasp.

She looked slightly rueful. "I guess I know what you think. But it's not always as easy or clear cut as people think. He married her because she was pregnant. He's been unhappy for a long time, but now they've got three kids so it's difficult."

"Three kids," Bev repeated softly.

"You have no idea how hard it is, loving someone who's trapped in a loveless marriage. He's been talking about leaving her for the past year or so but there's so much to consider ..." Her voice faded and we sat quietly. I knew that Karen would be struggling with what Judy had just said; after all she had endured her then-husband's numerous affairs before deciding that enough was enough.

Judy's revelation had made us all thoughtful and the last twenty minutes of the evening were spent in talking about it, for some of us trying to be as non-judgemental as possible. Karen drove me home as usual and although it was quite late, I asked if she wanted a coffee. We sat in the cool, dark garden with the cats at our feet, cupping mugs of hot coffee, talking about Judy and how Karen had felt year after year as affair after affair had been borne and forgiven only for the next one to be discovered. An hour later, when we'd both wept, we said our goodbyes and as I hugged her, we both said how much we valued our friendship that seemed to transcend so many other relationships.

It was early on Friday morning when I sat at the table for the last time with my latest guests. As they finished off their packing and brought their bags down to the car, Jean-Michel asked me for my email address, saying that he'd really like to keep in touch. What harm I thought, so gave him one of my business cards that I'd recently had printed. He thanked me with a sweet smile and when, at the coach park, I kissed everyone goodbye and wished them bon voyage, he gave me a very English hug.

"Well, well," Lyn said as we watched the coach disappear, "you certainly made an impression on that one."

The rest of the day was spent changing beds and cleaning the house. In the afternoon, I showered, did my hair and makeup and decided to wear the French green and purple dress and, as I did a small twirl in front of the mirror, I had to admit that I looked good - overweight but good.

The traffic was heavy so it was nearly ten past six when I parked at the Trout and as I walked through the old building onto the riverside terrace I saw Phil stand up and wave. "What a great table," I exclaimed as we kissed hello. It was right next to the wall so we had an uninterrupted view of the River Thames with boats lazily chugging along.

"I thought you'd rather be outside."

"Absolutely. It's far too nice an evening to be inside." I made myself comfortable.

"And I thought you might like a glass of bubbly." He raised his hand and a waiter came over with a bucket in which was a bottle of very expensive champagne.

We watched as the bottle was skilfully opened and then raised our glasses to each other. "To success for the magazine."

"And to a great future," was his enigmatic reply.

We sat for nearly an hour, sipping the ice-cold champagne, nibbling on a dish of delicious Nocellara olives and talking about all sorts of things - from his sister to the magazine and from my guests to Susie's adventures.

"Before we relax and order, let's talk business."

I sat up and concentrated as he told me that the next article he wanted from me was a critique of some thousand words about the Pudding Club which was run by the Three Ways Hotel in Mickleton. "I know it very well and it'll be wonderful to go there again." I noticed that he didn't ask me when or with whom I'd been there.

"It'll be for November's edition so we'll need your copy by the third week of September," I was told, to which I said there was no problem. "Feel free to take a friend," he added and then paused.

"I'm sure I can find someone to come with me," I said and when he raised his eyebrows, "I think that my friend Karen would love it.'" Was it my imagination or did he look pleased as I said that, I wondered.

We then spent a few minutes reading the Trout's extensive menu before he decided on chicken liver parfait and I plumped for the salt and Szechuan pepper squid both of which proved to be sublime as we ate from each other's plates as much as our own. Phil had suggested that we share a Chateaubriand with peppercorn sauce. "Plus a lobster tail?" he suggested. Who was I to refuse such a culinary delight I thought and as we ate and talked, I felt an unexpected deep relaxation and calm.

The dessert menu was as comprehensive as the mains and after dithering for several minutes, what they called the House-Sharer seemed the obvious choice. When it arrived we knew we'd made the right decision as we enjoyed crème brûlée with cherries under a crackling sugar crust, a salted caramel chocolate pot that made my toes curl, a slice of meltingly scrumptious pear tarte tatin and an American-style ice-cream cookie sandwich. As we ate and talked, I was very glad that my dress had a high waistband and a wide skirt.

It was getting chilly as we ordered coffee so I took my pale green shawl and put it round my shoulders. Phil stood to help me and rested his hands on my shoulders for a few seconds before resuming his seat. It must have been close to midnight when we made our ways to our respective cars and said goodbye. Phil kissed me on both cheeks and then held me close for a few moments - it was a heart-felt embrace.

I drove home slowly along dark lanes, playing a CD of Donna Summers' greatest hits very loudly and an hour later arrived home to my usual feline welcomes. Even though it was one in the morning, I didn't feel tired so made myself a large mug of tea and sat in the garden, snuggled in a warm coat, staring up at the stars, wondering what the rest of the year would bring.

The final week of hosting teachers dawned hot and bright and when I went to the coach park at seven on Monday evening, I was met with three very hot and tired people who were delighted to sit in my garden with restorative coffees, while I served up chicken cacciatoria, which had been gently cooking all day in the slow cooker, with crusty baguettes and a crisp salad. We ate in the garden and sat talking until the sun sank and they then retired to bed. The following evenings we dined on sautéed trout topped with brown butter and almonds, a recipe taken from my French cookbook which they enjoyed and a basic pasta dish with anchovies, olives and tomatoes topped with parmesan cheese. On the final evening they decided to eat out and, very sweetly, invited me. We had a lovely evening in Il Morro eating delicious Sardinian food and when they left on Friday morning I was sad to see them go.

Lyn looked exhausted. "It's been a hectic season, hasn't it?"

"It's been busy, that's for sure," I replied. "I think most people had a great time, don't you?"

She nodded. "Yes, the feedback's been mostly very good. I'm looking forward to my holiday now though, before we start planning for next year's season. You up for that?"

"Certainly am, count me in." With that we said our goodbyes. I knew that they were planning a very well-earned holiday in the Caribbean in September before getting back to work.

I saw an unfamiliar name in my inbox on Wednesday morning and when, slightly suspiciously, I opened it, saw that it was from Jean-Michel. He said how much he'd enjoyed last week, told me about the journey and ended by sending me best wishes from his colleagues. It would have been rude not to reply so I did, telling him about this week's guests, what I'd been cooking and some general silly bits of news from Stratford. It was the start of a regular correspondence that I very much enjoyed over the ensuing weeks.

I bravely emailed Tony that day and he replied, apologising for the delay in getting back to me, saying that he needed to look more closely at budgets so would get back to me in the next few days. Well, I thought, that's better than a downright no, so I continued to keep my fingers crossed for a few more days.

Judith was back from her holiday in Greece looking incredibly tanned, relaxed and happy. Although the class was tiring, we all agreed she wasn't pushing us as hard as Jasmine had and we were panting very slightly less as we made our inevitable way to the One Elm. As we settled down at our usual table, Dallas brought our drinks over. "The usual I presumed?" he said as he handed the drinks out.

"You know us all too well," we smilingly replied.

"Well, this is nice," Judith said as she raised her glass. She waved her left hand up and down for a few moments until we realised there was a twinkle that kept catching the light. It was a beautiful ring and as we exclaimed over it, she sat back smiling. "He proposed on our last night on the beach with a bottle of champagne and a single red rose. He'd organised a few people to play our favourite tune on the balcony of the restaurant we'd gone to. It was all so romantic." She was bubbling with delight which was lovely to see, but I could see that there was a tinge of sadness in Sara's eyes.

Inevitably, our conversation turned to the usual subject. Rose told us about someone she'd dated several years ago. "It was the second or third date. He was quite nice, not amazing, but we seemed to get on well. We were out at a restaurant and he suddenly said 'won't it be nice to be to a couple again, you can cook us dinners. My family will love that'. I've told them all about you. In fact I thought you could do us Sunday lunch. Be one big happy family."

"Cheeky sod!" was our combined opinion.

"Well, on one level, it was quite sweet," Rose said, "but on the other hand it felt like a huge assumption. Anyway, that kind of soured things for me and I finished it pretty much then and there."

Judy leaned forward. "I met this guy at the gym. He was hyper-fit and incredibly good-looking. He wasn't overly bright but one can't have everything." Bev looked slightly disapproving. "Anyway, muscly he might have been, but not where it counts." She held up her little finger. We looked at her with raised eyebrows and she shook her head. "Useless. Too little, too fast ..." our laughter interrupted her, "and, much more to the point, no imagination," she added with a wry smile.

"Imagination wasn't the problem with the last guy I went out with before Paul and I got together," Judith said, looking lovingly at her ring. "He got off on taking photos of me. He'd have me dress up in kinky little outfits and after taking his snaps, we'd have really good sex. Anyway, one time he set up his camera and filmed us making out and then the little shit posted it on YouTube ..." We gasped. "I didn't know he'd done it and was livid when I found out. Luckily, it wasn't our faces he'd focused on but even so ..."

"Not ok," Rose exclaimed and we all agreed.

Samantha had joined us after a few weeks away from Zumba. She seemed to have an inner sadness but the last couple of stories had made her smile. "I was on a site ages ago and started messaging this man who lived in Spain. He was really insistent that we should Skype so eventually I set it up on my laptop and one day we talked." She looked at us. "You know when you just know someone's jerking off?" We grinned and nodded. "Well, there we were talking and I could see his arm moving. It was funny in one way and really gross in another, so once I'd realised what he was doing I said something like 'I can see you've got your hands full' and logged off." By this time we were laughing helplessly as we envisioned the picture. "He called me a few times afterwards but I never replied. I just couldn't."

"I contacted this man on a site," I said. "He called himself talktalktalk. His profile looked very interesting and we exchanged some really funny emails before I gave him my number. He had the most wonderful voice – just made you want to melt. But there was a drawback - of course there had to be." I paused for effect. "He wanted phone sex. Wouldn't Skype, wouldn't meet. He was ok with phone sex, or even text sex but that was it. It's not that I mind phone sex ..." There was a gasp from Bev, "but I think it has to be with someone you're in a relationship with. Don't you?"

They all agreed with me even though Bev and Sam weren't at all sure about the concept of phone sex. "Don't knock it till you've tried it," Judy added to which I chuckled.

Debbie smirked. "I think outdoor sex beats phone sex. One time Iain and I were making out in a field. Well, it was the school playing field actually. In the holidays," she added quickly as Bev took a breath to say something. "Anyway, there we were and we thought we could hear a lawn mower in the distance that was getting louder and louder." She giggled. "The groundsman was on his sit-on mower and was just going round and round us in circles as he took in the view ..." She dissolved in laughter at the memory as we joined her.

We were all chuckling and shaking our heads through Debbie's story until Judy said that she had to go. "The penalties of being a working girl." We had to agree. "Same time, same place next week?"

"Absolutely," we chorused.

It was on this note that we said our goodbyes and made our way home. "I really like our Thursday evenings," Karen said as I made us coffee and we caught up with each other's news as we sat in the garden, watching the moths dance over the flickering candles on the table.

Tony emailed me early on Friday morning saying that he'd been given the all clear as far as concept and budget were concerned, so would I go ahead and design a three-day programme that could be delivered in half-days on a need-to-know basis. I emailed back enthusiastically and when he asked if the materials could be prepared in the next couple of weeks, I did a quick calculation of work that was already in my diary and replied that yes, absolutely I could. He then, very generously and unusually, told me that they were happy to pay for the preparation of the programme as a stand-alone cost plus a fee for every day I actually delivered the workshops, so after agreeing costs we signed off. I felt breathless with success, so to celebrate I put an old CD of the Kinks on very loud and danced round the house, much to the astonishment of the cats who watched me warily from the safety of the windowsill.

I met Roger on the balcony of the theatre on Thursday lunchtime as we'd agreed. He looked tanned and fit yet tense, and as we hugged hello I could feel him trembling slightly. Neither of us was hungry so we left the theatre and wandered down the river bank to Holy Trinity Church, and made ourselves comfortable on one of the weather-beaten wooden benches, gazing across at the ducks and swans busily avoiding the rowboats as they foraged.

He looked at me and cleared his throat. "I can't tell you how good it is to see you Lucie. I've missed you so much."

I smiled at him gently and held his hand at which he looked stricken until I started talking. I told him that I cared for him a great deal and valued his friendship more than I could say before going on to tell him about Annie.

"I had no idea," he said as I explained how much and for how long she'd liked - probably loved, him.

"Well, she's felt that way for a couple of years. How do you feel about her?"

He looked thoughtful. "Well, I like her. She's good fun, great company, very good at her job ..."

I put my hand on his arm. "Roger, why don't you let her in and see what happens?"

"You're giving me the brush-off?" He was beginning to sound irritated.

"No, I'm not giving you the brush-off, but I am pointing out that there's someone who's had the hots for you for a very long time. And as I've said, you're a wonderful friend, but I'm don't think we're going to be more than that."

There was a strained silence for a few moments until I felt him relax. "I certainly don't want to lose you Lucie and if we're just to be friends, well, that's better than nothing. You know I love you but I don't want to be some puppy at your feet."

We sat quietly for a few more moments. "Perhaps I should go now," he said, almost to himself.

"I'm always here for you as a good friend," I said softly. He turned to look at me and we smiled at each other as we stood and slowly made our way back towards the theatre, holding hands as we went.

As we said goodbye, I kissed him on both cheeks. He then hugged me tightly, burying his face in my shoulder before breaking away from me. I heard a muttered "Goodbye," and he then walked, almost ran from me, and as I watched him go I felt a deep melancholy even though I knew I'd done the right thing.

Karen said as much when I picked her up on Saturday evening to drive us to the Pudding Club, but it didn't stop me feeling distressed that I'd hurt someone who didn't deserve it.

The evening was a huge success. It began at seven thirty when the Pudding Master started things off by offering us a glass of elderflower pressé before showing us to large tables, enabling us to share the experience with other diners. Knowing that puddings were going to figure large, we both chose the lightest starters and mains available before the seven puddings were paraded in. We sampled a frothy gooseberry fool, a silky lemon syllabub, a tongue-tingling wild berry summer pudding with clotted cream and a richly sumptuous Eton mess as well as a thick syrup sponge served with hot custard, the stickiest ever sticky toffee pudding and a molten chocolate fondant that was toe-curlingly good. I knew I had to try everything so persuaded Karen to take different ones to mine so that I could make notes on the entire menu. We ate, drank and talked to our fellow diners and finally voted for our favourite pudding. I'd opted for the gooseberry fool that had vividly reminded me of my mother's which she'd cooked with fruit from our garden whilst Karen had favoured the summer pudding. However the chocolate fondant took the winner's rosette. It was a very, very enjoyable evening and when, at about ten thirty, we made our way to the car park clutching our Pudding Club Certificates and swearing not to eat for at least week, we agreed that this absolutely was an experience to be repeated.

I spent Sunday drafting Phil's article while everything was fresh in my mind. I drank lots of sparkling water and ate fruit, so by the evening I felt much cleaner and fresher than I had that morning. "Mummy's got to be good," I told the cats as I shook kitty biscuits into their bowl - they purred their agreement.

Chapter 10 - September

It felt very strange not to be preparing for guests but I had to admit that it was a welcome change. Much as I'd enjoyed the last few weeks, not to mention the income, having the house back to myself, at least for a while, was lovely.

The first thing I did on Monday morning was to re-read the article I'd drafted for Phil. It was, as I'd expected, not quite right, but after another hour of work it flowed much better. Not quite right yet though - I decided to leave it for a few hours so I could return to it fresh to make any final amendments. I spent the rest of Monday working on the programme for Tony. That work cascaded into Tuesday and Wednesday but, by the evening, everything was ready in draft so I emailed him, assuring him that this was the first draft and I was very happy to take on board any comments he wanted to make.

I managed to finish Phil's article by the end of Tuesday and sent it off, as always with fingers crossed and a little prayer. I saw his reply on Wednesday morning, saying that he liked it and was happy to have it in November's edition. I couldn't resist sending back a little smiley face which, as I hit the send button, suddenly felt childish and silly but it was too late now. I sat back and wondered what he would think, can't change it now I said to myself and shrugged.

I went shopping in town for a few bits and bobs on Wednesday morning and decided to have coffee in the One Elm where I'd cheekily left my car. As I walked in I was greeted by Kyle who, when I ordered coffee told me not to be so ridiculous and join him in a glass of champagne. "I'm on my second, had a great day out yesterday ..." and he went on to tell me about his day. He'd started off with a couple of business meetings in the morning, had lunch with a couple of friends and then the serious drinking had started. "I woke up this morning in this woman's red silk dressing gown ..."

"Anything else?" I prompted.

He rubbed his forehead. "No. But there was a large tabby cat lying next to me - I don't even like cats that much."

My laughter stopped him and he ruefully joined me. "You'd have thought I'd have learned not to do things like that by my age, wouldn't you?"

"Never too old to be a bit disgraceful." I kept my face as straight as I could. "Was she nice?"

He lowered his head and groaned. "Can't remember."

We went on to enjoy another glass of champagne and more banter. After about half an hour I said my goodbye to him and we hugged affectionately. I could tell he wanted another hair of the dog and really didn't want to drink any more, but was still smiling as I made my way home.

Di called me on Thursday morning asking if I fancied catching up over a coffee so we met that afternoon in a small hotel that was about halfway between us. It was a lovely warm afternoon and we sat in the hotel's sprawling grounds sipping a slightly guilty Pimms. She told me that her packing up was going well. She'd placed the house in the hands of a letting agent and was looking forward to her new adventures. "It feels a wee bit scary but I think I'm right to do this. I need to get out of my rut and this is certainly going to do that."

"I think it's a wonderful thing to do but I'm going to miss you so much ..." My eyes filled with tears as I thought of Di not being within a few miles and impatiently blinked them away. "Ignore me, I'm just being silly. Tell me, where are you starting off?"

"Melbourne. I've got some family there and they're happy for me to stay with them for a couple of weeks, so I'm going to use that as a base while I plan the next leg. In fact, I'm going to stop off in Singapore for a few days on my way, so that'll be fun." She paused. "Have I told you about Zara?"

Zara was Di's younger daughter who was married, had two small children and had held down a demandingly powerful and well paid job for the past ten years or so but had been aware of a growing sense of dissatisfaction with her worklife balance. She'd recently seen a local shop becoming vacant and decided then and there to open a fruit and vegetable shop combined with a few tables so she could serve teas, coffees, soft drinks, soups, smoothies and the like. "I'm sad I won't be here to see the opening but I'm sure that it's going to be a great success."

"It sounds wonderful," I replied. "A real change and a tremendous challenge - I'm sure she'll do really well." We spent the next hour or so talking about Di's impending adventure, Zara's business venture and my work. Eventually, after another Pimms, we said our goodbyes and as I drove home, I contemplated what life without Di being around would be like. It didn't feel very comfortable but I knew that our friendship wouldn't be compromised by distance which was a great consolation.

During the week, I received a couple of emails from Jean-Michel. He wrote about his students, his fond memories of his visit to the UK and he said again how much he had enjoyed my company, especially that evening when we'd sat alone in the garden, sharing a bottle of wine. Reading and replying to them gave me a little lift and made me smile.

I said as much after Zumba as we sprawled in the comfortable wicker chairs in the One Elm's courtyard, sipping our beers.

"Well, well," Judy said with a mischievous smile, "so, when are you going out to see him?"

I reddened. "I'm not. He's lots younger than me and anyway we're just friends ..."

"Yeah, right," was the consensus which I decided to ignore.

"You're all being silly. We just got on really well and we shared a bottle of wine and a few chats. Stop it you lot." I had to raise my voice to be heard over the giggles.

The group from Zumba had increased so, for the first few minutes, conversation was a little restrained but after talking about Jean-Michel it was clear that everyone was up for our usual chats, especially about men and dating sites.

"Oh, I couldn't use one of those," Gillian said seriously. Some of the group smiled, it was clear that Gillian was well into her seventies.

"Why not?" asked Judy slightly teasingly. I frowned at her.

"Well, I don't own a computer." She looked at us and broke into a smile. We all giggled - there was clearly more to Gillian than met the eye. "Anyway, I'm seeing someone." She raised her eyebrow as Judy looked slightly surprised. "Jim's a lovely man," she continued. "We have great times but he keeps talking about us moving in together and I really don't want that. I hate to hurt him but I couldn't share my home on a full-time basis. We see each other about four times a week and he stays over, but that's enough for me."

"So affairs of the heart never stop, do they?" I asked.

"Not if you don't want them to, no," was Gillian's reply. I grinned at her and she winked back, I'd really warmed to her.

We were still mulling over Gillian's story when Debbie told us about a friend of hers. "Well, she walked out on her cheating husband and left him to it with his girlfriend. Anyway, one day she went back to the house while they were away in Barbados for two weeks and, very carefully, she planted some spring bulbs in the lawn." We all looked puzzled. "Six months later the bulbs sprouted to spell 'slut' and wanker' in the middle of the garden." We were all laughing. "But she also sprinkled the shag pile carpets with fast growing grass seed, watered it and turned the heating up. It's amazing how fast grass can grow in a fortnight." By this time we were all crying with laughter.

"You couldn't make it up, could you?" I hiccupped through tears of laughter.

"Darren and I were taking a week out in Barbados," Sunita said as our laughter subsided, "and one evening, we were having drinks on the rooftop balcony. It was so beautiful up there, it was very, very late, no-one else was there, we were feeling romantic and started making out. Well, one thing led to another and I ended up bent over a table ..."

"And?" we demanded as she stopped.

She smiled sweetly. "It was amazing. But, the next morning we went to the dining room and as we finishing breakfast, the manager came over to us and asked if we realised that there were CCTV cameras all over the hotel, including the rooftop balcony. I was mortified, especially, as he turned to leave, he looked at Darren, winked and said 'good show sir'. I think Darren was so pleased at the 'good show' that he forgot to be embarrassed."

"Let me tell you about a friend of mine," Gillian said. "A few years ago her husband had a heart attack and when he died she found out that he was on the verge of bankruptcy. She'd not worked for years but managed to find a part-time job which enabled her to hold onto the house by her fingertips. Anyway, she met this very nice man who, after a while, admitted that he liked to be dominated - you know? Being handcuffed, spanked, ordered about, that kind of thing. She was very nervous about it but gradually did as he asked ..." We sat in spellbound silence. "They were very happy but, for all sorts of reasons, decided not to live together so, of course, she still needed to earn money. One day, after he'd told her how good she was at being his mistress, she decided to change her job," she paused, "so, she's now a dominatrix. Makes a very good living I understand - she's just had a lovely big conservatory put on the back of the house"

That was, we agreed, one of the better jaw-dropping stories until Judy looked at us. "Well girls, I think I can top that." We fell silent in eager anticipation. "I dated this man for a while and found out pretty quickly that he was like your friend's guy, liked to be dominated. I'd never done it before but thought oh well, in for a penny, in for a spanking." She was interrupted by laughter. "It gets better. He liked to be handcuffed, gagged and smacked – you know the kind of thing. But then he asked me to dress up as a schoolgirl."

"Oh no!" Bev's hand flew to her mouth.

"And pee on him. Well, for me that was a step too far so I said no. He said if I didn't, we were over and he'd find someone who would."

"So what did you do?" Gillian asked.

"I put my knickers back on and left him to it. Never saw him again. For all I know he's still handcuffed to that bed ..." We were all laughing so much that other guests at the bar stopped talking and looked round at us, but we couldn't stop and it was on that show-stopping note that we said our goodbyes.

I was pleased to see two names appear in my inbox on Friday morning. One was from Tony suggesting a couple of minor amendments to the programme which I made on Sunday afternoon while sitting in the garden. The other was from Phil who had sent me two smiley faces and one with a slightly quizzical look along with the message that he was in Scotland for a couple of weeks and would be in touch on his return. I wonder why he's in Scotland my little inner voice muttered in my ear. Nothing to do with us, I retorted and the little voice fell silent.

Early Monday morning I sent the modified workshops to Tony and smiled. It felt very good that my working life was moving in a slightly different direction. I was in the garden later, deadheading the roses, when I heard my mobile ring. It was Tony who said that he was delighted with what I'd done, he was happy to sign it off and would I like to send him my invoice. I'd be delighted to send him my invoice I said seriously at which he chuckled; he did have the most attractive voice.

"We ought to meet up to discuss what other programmes you can work on with us."

"That would be very good," I replied going in for my diary. "When's good for you?"

We agreed to meet the following week on Tuesday and as I put the phone down I was tingling with anticipation but wasn't sure whether it was the prospect of more work or just seeing him that was the cause of my pleasure.

Annie called me on Monday evening on the pretext of talking about some of her students but I could tell that wasn't really the reason and after about five minutes as she was running out of steam on the subject, I gently interrupted her. "So, how's everything else for you?"

There was a pause. "Annie?" I heard a stifled sob. "Annie, what's wrong?"

There was a deep sigh and then she told me how remote Roger had been for the past couple of weeks, how sad he was looking and how concerned she was about him. "It's so not like him and I'm worried about him. Every time I ask if he's ok, he brushes me off which is really hurtful. I just don't know what to do ..." Her voice faded and I sat in silence for a few moments, collecting my thoughts.

"Why don't we meet up for a drink so we can have a proper chat?" I suggested eventually.

"That would be great." Annie sounded relieved. If only you knew I thought to myself guiltily even though I knew perfectly well that I had nothing to feel guilty about. We agreed to meet for a drink at Loxleys on Friday evening

The 'R-question' continued to haunt me over the next few days, so much so that I rang Karen to ask her for advice. She came round after work on Wednesday and as I cooked us salmon with a couscous salad spiked with a finely sliced raw courgette, quartered baby tomatoes, a few shredded mange tout and half a chilli, we talked things through.

"I feel really bad about this," I said. "I know that this isn't my fault but that's not how I feel. I mean, I like him, I like him a lot but I'm not in love with him and the last time we saw each other I said as much."

"Well, he obviously hasn't taken it on board, has he?" Karen poured us each a cold beer. We continued to discuss what could be done as we ate the succulent fish and then enjoyed a second beer in the garden. "So, what are you going to do?" she asked eventually after we'd talked and talked but come to no real conclusion.

I sat back and thought for a moment. "I'm going to tell Annie that we dated a couple of times, that he likes me a lot and that I've told him that I value him as a really good friend but nothing more."

I paused while Karen looked at me quizzically. "And?" she prompted.

"And that she should ask him out. At least she'd know if he was interested. Waiting for him to make a move hasn't worked. I told him she liked him but clearly that hasn't clicked."

"Or he's not interested."

"True. But surely it's better to know one way or the other than to carry on like this?" Karen nodded and we spent the remainder of the evening talking about how tricky affairs of the heart were, at the end of which Karen reiterated her opinion that, for her, singledom was preferable to risking heartbreak. Grudgingly, I found myself agreeing with her but wished I wasn't.

As I came downstairs the following morning there, on the doormat, was Phil's first edition magazine and when I read it saw, to my delight, my name on the list of contributors. I eagerly turned to my page and there it was - my article about the Pudding Club. I showed the cats who were singularly unimpressed but I was so pleased I danced round the kitchen before breathlessly making my tea.

Later I saw Phil's name in my inbox. He was still in Scotland and was wondering if I'd go to an Indian restaurant called Lasan's in Birmingham for him for December's issue and of course I was welcome to take a friend along with me. I replied saying that I'd be delighted to go and as I pressed the send button, again wondered what was keeping him in Scotland. Stop that, just stop it, I thought to myself - it's got nothing to do with you.

I called Di for a chat on Thursday and while she was telling me about Zara's new venture, Barbara popped into my mind. "Di, I know someone who makes the best cakes ever. I wonder if Zara might be interested in selling them."

"Zara was going to come over to mine on Saturday evening to talk about my upcoming adventure." I could hear amusement in Di's voice. "Why don't you join us? Zara would love to see you and you could bring your cake lady along."

"Her name's Barbara ..." and I went on to tell her all about her.

"She sounds lovely and I'm sure that Zara would like to meet her." We went to chat a little more before agreeing that Barbara and I would get to Di's at about eight. I rang Barbara straightaway who sounded thrilled and said that she'd be very happy to join me, so we agreed that I'd pick her up at about seven thirty.

Thursday evening saw me at Zumba. Karen wasn't able to come as she had a works do. I had been very tempted not to go but the thought of our after-class chats made it just too beguiling to miss. As usual, the class saw me gasping for breath but perhaps very slightly less than in previous weeks. It was a warm evening so we were able to sit in the courtyard. "Not for much longer though," I said as we settled down at our usual table.

"We'll have to bring blankets in the winter if we want to stay outside," Debbie said at which we chuckled.

As we settled down with our first drinks, I became aware that Bev was looking very upset. I was sitting next to her so put my arm round her shoulders and asked her what was wrong. She shook her head and was obviously fighting tears. "Nathan and I had a terrible row and I said some awful things. It's just that I've been so stressed since he's come home from hospital. He's trying so hard not to ask for help but that feels so forced and unnatural. I just want to us get back to the way it was but perhaps that's not possible. I know he's angry about having to be so dependent but that doesn't help me." She leaned into my shoulder and wept.

We all clustered round her, making consoling noises until she was more composed and then went on to talk about how hard it was to love and care for someone who was disabled with a condition that was only ever going to worsen.

"It's ok to get angry sometimes," Gillian said.

"And it's absolutely ok to talk about how you feel," Rose added.

We were still discussing Bev's situation an hour later. "Thank you all so much," she said as we parted. "It's really helped. Just to vent a bit - know what I mean?" We did and as we said goodbye, I was aware that the group were becoming good friends.

I received an email from Marc on Friday morning asking if I was free to work on another contract in early October, to which I replied an emphatic 'yes' with thanks for thinking of me. I felt ridiculously peaceful and contented.

I met Annie on Friday evening and after rather stilted greetings, we sipped our drinks, exchanging pleasantries until I sat back. "Ok Annie, you wanted to talk about Roger didn't you?" Her eyes filled with tears and she blew her nose noisily. She told me how distant and unapproachable Roger had been over the past couple of weeks and how unusually snappy he was with students. "And he just looks so sad so much of the time. The other day, I'm not sure why, but your name was mentioned when we were discussing exam results and he just walked out of the room. I hate seeing him like this."

I took a deep breath. "Did you know that we went out a couple of times?" She blinked. "Annie, I really like him as a good friend but that's all. I know he cares for me but believe me I've made my position very clear." I watched as fat tears rolled down her cheeks.

"I think I fell for him the moment I met him and that's three years now. But it's as if he doesn't really see me, like I'm part of the furniture. I was so cross when you came along and I could see that he liked you from the word go."

"I know, I know. And I'm sorry." I felt awkward but continued. "May I tell you something?"

She looked angrily upset but nodded and so I told her the story about how I had been with Richard for some five years, how I'd loved him, how he'd deceived, cheated and left and how, gradually, I was getting over him. "So when Roger showed me some interest I was very flattered and yes, I went out with him, but I promise you Annie, I thought we were friends. I knew he liked me but had no idea that he cared for me and when I did, I told him that much as I valued his friendship, I didn't love him."

"That's no reason for going out with him." She was starting to sound very angry.

I knew there was no use in labouring the point. "Why don't you make a move on him yourself?"

"I suppose I could invite him out for a drink." She looked surprised at my suggestion.

I grinned at her. "I think you should do something more dramatic than that. Oh Annie, don't look so shocked. I'm not suggesting that you snog the face off him in class but surely a gentle little kiss wouldn't go amiss? Just go for it." To my relief she stopped looking angry and we continued to talk about what she could do as we share another drink.

The way Annie was wondering what to do vividly reminded me of how I must have sounded to Karen when dithering about whether to contact Phil or not, so I told her about that and how glad I was that I had. "The very worst that Phil could have done was blank me but he didn't and we've had had a couple of really nice evenings together."

"Do you like him?"

"Yes, yes I like him. We seem to have things in common and when we're together it feels really nice."

"Made a move on him, have you?"

"No I haven't. Annie, I'm working for him but we do get on very well. Anyway, we're talking about you, not me, so just shush." I was painfully aware that my words rang hollow but she took the hint.

After coffee and further deliberations, we hugged an affectionate goodbye and I hoped with all my heart that things might work out between them. "You will let me know what happens, won't you?" I asked and her parting shot was that she certainly would. I drove home in a reflective mood.

That reflective mood was still with me on Saturday morning and I debated whether to call Roger or not. More than once I found my hand hovering over my phone but decided against it. You've done all you can, my little inner voice whispered and I had to agree.

As arranged I picked up Barbara at seven thirty and by eight we were happily ensconced in Di's elegantly comfortable sitting room. Zara arrived shortly after us, looking a bit distracted and harassed but, as I said to Barbara, didn't we all look that way when our kids were small. She laughed and nodded her agreement.

Zara was full of enthusiastic plans for her new venture. "Lucie tells me you make amazing cakes," she said, turning to Barbara.

"Perhaps you should be the judge of that." Barbara opened a box of beautifully decorated cupcakes in different flavours. We sampled triple vanilla, white chocolate, pina colada, liquorice, green tea, rocky road and banana, honey and cinnamon cake and ooh-ed and ahh-ed our way through them. "There's more." She then opened another box of chocolate orange, pear and salted caramel, lemon drizzle, tiramisu, gooseberry fool, and, amazingly, Guinness. "Just thought I'd bring along a baker's dozen," she said with a delighted grin as each one was greeted with rapturous applause.

Zara and Barbara decided to go into the kitchen to talk business while Di and I remained in the sitting room discussing Di's last minute plans and arrangements. Much as I didn't want her to go, it was heart-warming to see her excitement and enthusiasm. We agreed that I would take her down to Heathrow. "I promise I won't cry," I said to which Di laughed.

"I'll be crying so for sure you will too." I nodded and blinked as the reality of Di's departure started to sink in.

Before we became too morose, Barbara and Zara rejoined us. Both looked smugly pleased. "Meet Turnips' cake maker extraordinaire," Zara said and we all clapped while Barbara beamed. "We've decided we'll have themed months," Zara explained. "Chocolate, summer fruits, tea and coffee, boozy as well as Christmas, Easter and so on - we thought that that would keep customers interested and wanting more. We're also going to have tastings and Barbara thought that we could have small groups learning about cake decoration. What do you think?"

"Great ideas," I said and Di nodded her agreement as we went on to talk about the finer details of how things would work and it was only when I glanced up at Di's clock that I realised that it was just after midnight.

The conversation continued on the drive back to Barbara's. "I can't thank you enough for this evening," she said as she gathered up the empty cake boxes.

"More than a pleasure. I'm very excited for you both. I think this is a great start for your business," I said as we hugged our goodbyes.

On Sunday, I met Karen for brunch in Bensons after which we strolled down by the river and watched the swans drift past while we caught up with each other's' news. It was a leisurely day that I relished and as I made my way home in the slightly chilly afternoon I felt very calm and tranquil.

I awoke on Monday morning with a thumping headache and the beginnings of a sore throat. I knew I wouldn't cope with a business meeting so emailed Tony, apologising for the late notice and asking whether we could meet later in the week as I was ill. His reply came back within a few minutes saying that he quite understood and was I free Thursday week instead. I was indeed I replied gratefully and then returned to bed.

I took painkillers and snuggled under the duvet and was just dozing off when the phone rang. It was David's daughter - I realised to my shock and embarrassment that I'd not been in touch with him for months but it was too late now. "Dad died yesterday morning. His funeral's next week. I know you were really good friends when you were working together and thought you'd want to know." Her voice started to crack. I wept as I tried to say how sorry I was and how much he would be missed, and as I put the phone down I mourned the wasted months of not keeping in touch when I was so self-absorbed with my own problems. I lay back in bed and fell into troubled sleep.

Phil sent me a text on Wednesday morning, asking if I was free to meet him for lunch that day and when I replied saying that I'd love to but was too ill there was an immediate reply asking if I'd like him to call round with some chicken soup. Oh, how kind I thought but replied with a thank you but no thank you. I looked and felt like shit and didn't need an attractive man to see me like that. I also mentioned that I didn't think I'd be able to go to

Lasan's at the weekend as I'd promised to which he sent a little sad face and assured me that the following week would be fine.

I continued to feel dreadful for the rest of the week. I rang Anita and asked her to bring me some milk which, bless her, she did. Both she and Karen called every day to check up on me and bring in the occasional treat. Karen went to Zumba and said that the evening just wasn't the same without me which I thought was an exaggeration but very sweet. By Friday I was feeling a little better but very weak as I'd hardly eaten anything for several days. I stood on the bathroom scales and saw, to my great disappointment, that I'd only lost a couple of pounds so made my way downstairs and ate three slices of toast with butter which tasted amazingly good.

As I hadn't checked my emails since Tuesday, my inbox was full and as I deleted unwanted advertising email after unwanted advertising email I noticed Jean-Michel's name. He said that he was taking a few days leave as his students were on work experience placements and would I care to visit him in the second week of October. I felt slightly breathless and when Karen called round with some fruit and the latest edition of 'Olive' after work, asked her for her opinion.

"You liked him, didn't you?" she asked. I nodded. "Well then, why on earth not? You go and have a nice time. I'm sure he's not an axe murderer. Just make sure you've got enough money for a hotel if need be, and tell me all about it when you get back."

I grinned at her. "You and the Zumba group?" She laughed and then brought me up to speed with the stories that had been shared on Thursday evening which kept me vastly entertained for the next hour or so.

I emailed Jean-Michel on Saturday morning, saying that if I could move a couple of working commitments around, I'd be delighted to accept his kind invitation and as I hit the send button could feel my heart beating faster.

I spent some of Monday preparing for Tuesday and Wednesday at the university as well as the meeting with Tony on Thursday. I still had the vestige of a headache so took it easy as far as was possible which delighted the cats and as I curled up on the sofa in the afternoon to watch an old movie with a large cup of tea, the three of us dozed a few hours away.

Thankfully I felt much better on Tuesday and the personal effectiveness workshops that I'd been asked to deliver at the university went smoothly. By the end of Wednesday I'd worked with over two hundred students and felt tired but happily satisfied. It was nearly six and I was packing up when a familiar figure opened the door.

"Hello Beth," I said warmly. "Good to see you."

She hesitated for a moment and then closed the door behind her. "Lucie, sorry I didn't realise that you were still here." She looked slightly uncomfortable.

"I think the last couple of days have gone pretty well." I put my laptop away. "Have you had any feedback yet?"

She nodded. "Yes, and all very positive. The students are delighted but of course we'll have to see how well they act on your pearls of wisdom to see the real effect of your work." I shot her a glance but could see that she was smiling.

"Absolutely. Proof of the pudding and all that." I picked up my bags. Ridiculously I was beginning to feel a little uncomfortable and I could see that as I slowly made my way to the door, she was starting to look relieved. I held out my hand. "Thank you for this contract."

She took my hand and held onto it for a fraction longer than was necessary for a handshake. "Thank you for all your hard work Lucie." And with that I took my leave.

I drove home thoughtfully. I was now certain that Beth remembered me and, very possibly, realised that I had remembered her in the days when she was he and we'd dated. I wished that I had been able to talk to her but, very clearly, she had found our encounter awkward and I had no wish to cause any embarrassment.

I found a lovely long email from Jean-Michel awaiting me that evening. He said that he hoped that I'd been able to rearrange my diary and was looking forward to seeing me again. As I read and then reread it I was smiling, a few days of relaxation in beautiful St Omer would be wonderful I said to myself.

Eleven thirty on Thursday saw me suited and booted in Tony's office, discussing his various training plans and how he saw me contributing over the ensuing months. We were still talking when, at twelve thirty, he glanced at his watch. "Coming up to lunchtime. Shall we continue our discussions over lunch?" So we did, in a small local pub a mere ten minute walk from his office and we still there at two thirty having talked about work, his last relationship, my last relationship, cars, music and lastly, keeping fit.

"I try and cycle at least fifty miles a week," he said at which I drew my breath. "I know it sounds a bit obsessive but I think it beats going to the gym."

"To each their own. I go to a Zumba class once a week. Trouble is that some of us go to a local wine bar afterwards which kind of undoes the good we've done."

He laughed as I giggled. "So which evening do you dance?"

"Actually, tonight. I have to say that it's the post-Zumba chats and drinks at the One Elm that I enjoy more than the actual classes." We both laughed and he shook his head in mock disapproval. We enjoyed a coffee and then parted just before three thirty when we shook hands warmly and he wished me luck for that evening's Zumba. It had been a very fruitful and enjoyable meeting.

Judith drove us quite hard with some new routines that evening which, after my indulgences at lunchtime, felt unusually demanding so I found myself sitting out a couple of times. "It's because you didn't come last week. That and you're probably still not completely recovered from being poorly," Judith explained as I sat watching the others glumly. "Don't worry, you'll be back up to speed really soon."

She said as much again as we settled at our usual table in the courtyard. "I hope you're right," I said. "It's a bit depressing though."

She laughed. "Keeping fit is always work in progress but as long as you don't give up, that's the main thing."

Why, oh why, was it that those who were really fit offered platitudes to us unfit souls who always struggled, I thought to myself, but smiled sweetly at her.

It was getting chilly but, thankfully, there were now heaters in the courtyard so we stayed toasty warm as we made ourselves comfortable. After the usual brief how-are-yous, conversation turned to the inevitable.

"I met Chas a while back," Judy said. "He was quite a sexy man but his idea of foreplay was to endlessly send me pictures of his cock. I remember I was standing in the checkout queue in Tescos and opened a text from him not realising that I'd be looking at a close-up. The woman next to me saw it and nearly had heart failure." We laughed. "I have to say that it didn't do much for me and I told him so but he kept on doing it. He hated it when I ignored them so that's what I did. We lasted for all of six weeks and when I told him we were over, he was stunned. Said that he thought we had something special." She snorted as we shook our heads in amused disbelief.

"A lot of them do that," Sunita said. "I'm sure that they think we go weak at the knees at the sight of their dicks and they never take the hint that that's so not the case." She stopped for a moment. "A friend of mine was telling me about this man she was with. They were making out one night, she said the foreplay was wonderful but when she felt both his hands on her waist, without thinking, she said 'is it in yet?'. Trouble was that it was. He was mortified and she was so embarrassed. That was the last time they were together."

"I'm not surprised." Debbie was crying with laughter.

Harps played very early on Friday morning and as I pressed the snooze button to allow myself another ten minutes in bed, it hit me that this would be the last time I would see Di for several months. Heaving a huge sigh, I got up when the harps played for the second time, showered, dressed and then made my way downstairs to be greeted by the ever-present cats. After giving them breakfast, I ate a small bowl of muesli with a banana and a little honey and set off. I was at Di's at six thirty and by seven, the car was packed and we were on our way. We'd allowed ourselves three hours to make the eighty five mile journey that, given open roads, would take about an hour and a half. The M1 was free-flowing but, as we'd anticipated, the M25 was very busy so it was nearly eleven o'clock when we arrived. "Come and have a coffee with me," Di urged as we unloaded the car and piled her luggage onto a nearly trolley.

There was hardly any queue at check-in, so by eleven thirty we were sitting by a huge window watching planes come and go with amazing frequency.

"I'm going to miss you so much." I just managed to keep my voice from cracking.

"Me too, me too." Di's voice was less steady.

We spent the next hour drinking coffee and talking non-stop but at twelve thirty Di said that she really ought to join the queue for security, and reluctantly we rose to our feet.

"I promise I'll keep in touch." We hugged our goodbyes and I then watched her walk away.

I thought I might have time to wait and watch her flight depart but needed to be back in time for David's funeral. I knew I'd miss her dreadfully but equally I knew that with technology's help we'd stay in touch with each other.

I arrived home just before three - plenty of time to freshen up my makeup and change into a dark grey dress and black high heels. I made sure that I wore the bright fuchsia scarf that David had once said he liked and set off for the crematorium. The funeral was dignified and sad but the party afterwards - there was no other word for it - was bright, fun and enormously enjoyable, a true celebration of David's life and achievements. There were over a hundred people at the small local pub where the wake was held, representing many different aspects of David's life. It went on for hours, ending only when the staff at the pub very reasonably wanted to go home as it was well after midnight. I drove home slowly, reflecting on what a privilege it had been to know David and to share in his final goodbyes.

On Saturday morning I saw an email from the university that said in the light of the very positive feedback from my work on Tuesday and Wednesday, a further contract to give similar training for foreign students for six days over the last two weeks of October would be offered, should I be available. I glowed as I sent a reply confirming that I was indeed available and sat back with a self-satisfied grin.

Helena and I had arranged to go to Birmingham by train together and enjoyed the fifty minute journey in a compartment full of excited girls who were obviously out on a hen night. "Reminds me of Kesia's hen night," Helena said with a nostalgic smile. "She had a weekend away with a few very close friends and then an evening to include both Mums which was very sweet."

"If it was anything like the wedding party it would have been a great evening. I had a blast." We continued to talk about our respective girls for the remainder of the journey and the short walk to Lasan's, which proved to be an immaculately presented place with stunning pictures adorning the walls. The inviting tables were laid with snowy white cloths and gleaming glasses that were not too close so diners had plenty of room.

"Wow! This is impressive," we agreed.

The menu was even more impressive so we had a beer and took our time to read it through and talk about what we wanted to order. "Now remember, this is work for me," I said taking a notepad out of my bag, "so you will let me have a taste of yours, won't you?"

"Of course I will, provided I can taste yours." I smiled.

I was very tempted by the Mahi machli, salmon that had been marinated in a tomato and roasted red pepper puree - it sounded wonderful, but as it was heavily seasoned with coriander, I discounted it. "I can cope with a little dried coriander," I explained, "but I really don't like it fresh. Strange, isn't it?"

We continued to scan the menu but with such huge choices, it was too hard to decide, so I suggested that we have three starters. "It's our job to taste as much as we can," I assured her so we settled on a pakora of crispy cabbage and onion fritter which had been dredged in a light gram flour, fenugreek and cumin batter and was served with spiced mango and lentil chutney, a cake of crab, green pea and potato that had been cooked in chilli batter and served with a cucumber raitha and sour raw mango chutney and finally a breast of chicken marinated in creamed garlic and fennel infused yoghurt accompanied with honey beetroot and green chutney.

When we placed our order the waiter raised his eyebrows but made no comment which, to me, was a huge plus. We had asked to order our main courses after eating the starters and had been assured that this was no problem, another plus.

"We can't have three main courses," Helena protested after we had munched our way through all three starters, all of which proved to be as tasty as they'd read. "We'll go pop." Reluctantly I had to agree. Making a selection from the fourteen options was even harder but eventually we managed to decide on Kunju xacutti which was a chicken curry with potatoes in a poppy seed, roasted coconut and Kashmiri chilli masala with whole cloves of garlic and whole Keralan peppercorns, and Dum ki biryani; a goat and basmati rice dish cooked in yoghurt, mint, cardamom, mace and dum masala.

Both dishes lived up to their promise and were aromatically appetising so despite being very well fed from the starters, we managed to eat at least half of each. The waiter returned to clear the table and we apologised for leaving some. "Eyes bigger than tummies," I said and he smiled understandingly. We ordered coffees and sat back in the comfortable chairs.

"Well, I think I ought to come on more tastings. It's been a wonderful evening," Helena said with a satisfied sigh.

"And it's so warm and welcoming too. So often restaurants that serve this quality of food are a bit up themselves but they've got the balance just right here. I love it." And I leaned back to allow my stomach to relax a little more. We stayed for another half hour, enjoying the excellent coffee and ambiance as the room started to get busier and busier. "Great buzz too," I said as I asked for the bill which, I felt, gave very good value for money.

We meandered back to the station to catch the last train back to Stratford and as we said affectionate goodbyes and Helena thanked me for asking her to accompany me, she smiled. "You're going to enjoy writing this article, aren't you?" She was right. I wrote the article on Sunday and enjoyed every minute and, after carefully proofreading it twice, sent it off to Phil with a smiley face and fingers crossed.

I then emailed Jean-Michel thanking him for his invitation and saying that I'd love to visit him. As I hit the send button I could feel butterflies which continued when I booked my place on the Eurotunnel. I then sat back, wondering what on earth I'd just done.

Chapter 11 - October

I worked for Marc's client from Tuesday to Friday which was very enjoyable but exhausting so by Friday evening all I could do was slump on the sofa and stare mindlessly at the TV. As I did so, I reflected on the last six months which had certainly been one hell of a rollercoaster. I felt proud that I'd managed as well as I had.

Jean-Michael had sent a couple of emails and we'd agreed that I should arrive in St Omer between three and four on Thursday week when he assured me he'd be waiting for me. He offered to meet me from Calais to guide me but, having looked at maps and driven in that area a couple of times before, I was confident that I wouldn't get lost too often.

Despite feeling weary on Thursday evening, I managed to drag myself to Zumba on Karen's insistence and surprised myself by almost keeping up with most of the others, and was quietly smug as we made our way to the One Elm. It was definitely autumnal and too cold to sit outside, even with a heater, so we found a large table near the fire and as we settled down I looked round "Ladies, I need your wisdom and advice ..." and I went on to tell them about Jean-Michel and my impending trip.

"Well, well," Judy said, "you old dark horse you."

I ignored her. "I don't know quite what to do. I'm going as a friend ..." I was interrupted by laughter. "What?"

Judy leaned forward and put her arm round my shoulder. "I'm pretty sure that he's thinking of you as just a friend and that a shag or three's absolutely not on the cards," she teased.

I reddened slightly. "Well, he is very nice ..."

"There you are then."

We spent the next hour or so discussing what clothes I should take, whether shags were likely to be on the menu or not and finally, safety. "You've got to be safe." Everyone nodded. "And you can't depend on him having any so you should get some," Karen said sternly. That advice was agreed by everyone so I promised to add a trip to Boots for my 'something for the weekend' list.

"And you've got to tell us all about it," was the final consensus as we left the bar.

"Of course, how could I not?" I promised as we waved our goodbyes.

"Bloody hell, this going away for a weekend is more complicated than I thought," I said to Karen on the way home.

"Absolutely," Karen agreed as she dropped me off. "Shall we have a coffee on Sunday?" she added.

"Great idea." And we agreed to meet at the RST café overlooking the river so we could sit outside if the weather was warm enough.

I was still feeling tired on Saturday morning so had a lazily self-indulgent day. Much to the delight of the cats I lit the first fire of the autumn in the afternoon and cosied down on the sofa with a good book. I'd eaten a late breakfast and by three was beginning to be hungry so cooked a batch of butternut squash and feta cheese muffins while a large tray of red onions, tomatoes, sweet potatoes and peppers roasted. When the muffins cooled, I added chunks of leftover feta to the vegetables and turned off the oven so the dish continued to cook in the residual heat. The smell of the sharp cheese gently cooking filled the kitchen and I smiled in anticipation. The muffins were surprisingly good, and I made a mental note to tell Barbara about them. I piled the roasted vegetables into a large bowl, sprinkled a little balsamic vinegar over them and settled back on the sofa to graze on them as I continued with my book.

As I ate and read, I was thinking about my trip the following week when, for some unknown reason, Annie popped into my mind and I idly wondered what was happening on that front. At seven, I was still musing about her and feeling slightly cross that I couldn't get her out of my mind, so I decided to call her. However, I found myself tapping out Roger's number instead. He sounded very surprised to hear from me and initially guarded.

"Roger, I was thinking of you and wondered how you are." I tried to sound as warm yet non-committal as possible.

"I'm fine Lucie," and he went on to talk about what was happening at the school.

"That's not why I called," I interrupted gently after a few minutes. "Tell me, how's Annie?"

"Annie?" He sounded startled.

"Yes, Annie. Roger, you know that she likes you. Really likes you. Would you please ask her out and just see how it goes. I don't know why, but I've got a really good feeling about this."

"And why are you so bothered about my love life?" He sounded puzzled.

"Roger, you're a dear friend and I want to see you happy. Annie's been wanting you to show some interest in her for years. I think you should give it a try; you might be very pleasantly surprised. And if you're not, then at least she'll know and have some closure."

There was a pause. "You mentioned this before and I thought it was just a line to get rid of me so I didn't do anything. Anyway, I was still hoping that there might be something between us but I guess that's not the case. Is it?"

I shook my head even though he couldn't see me. "I honestly don't think so. You deserve someone who thinks you're the most special person in the world but I'm afraid that's not me." I held my breath.

I heard a sigh. "Roger, I care for you as a dear friend, you know that."

There was another sigh. "Ok Lucie, you really have made yourself very clear. At least you've been honest and I appreciate that."

"And Annie?"

"I'll think about it." He paused. "Really, she's liked me for years?"

"For years," I repeated and couldn't resist a tiny giggle. As we then said our goodbyes, I felt a tingle of self-satisfaction. At least I'd done my best.

True to my word, I'd added 'condoms' to my shopping list so when I was in town on Sunday on my way to meet Karen, I went into Boots where the array of condoms was bewildering.

"I want to buy some but don't have a clue which to get." I deliberately asked an older sales assistant who was stocking up the family planning shelves.

"What size?" she asked.

I blushed slightly. "I really don't know."

"I meant how many do you need?" She blinked, trying to remain serious.

I blushed again and after I'd told her I was going away for the weekend, she suggested a pack of ten average-size might be suitable to which I hastily agreed. As I paid, she winked at me and wished me a very good weekend. I told Karen about it as we sat over coffee in the autumnal sunshine and we both laughed at my ineptitude in such matters.

"So, what are we going to do for our birthdays?" she asked. Both our birthdays were in October and rather than exchange gifts, it had become our custom to share an experience. In the past we'd gone to the theatre, seen a movie, spent a day at the coast and had dinner somewhere swish. She held out an A5 leaflet which was advertising a male strip show at a local nightclub, all proceeds being donated to our local hospice. "I thought this might be fun." She had a very mischievous smile.

I looked at it again. "I guess we could go - have you been to one of these things before?"

"No. Have you?"

"No. So we should probably go before it's too late." We sat back and chuckled. "We'll almost certainly be the oldest strip show virgins in the place, but it'll be a giggle."

"It's on Friday the fifth of November, so it's bound to go with a bang."

"And it's for such a good cause - it would be rude not to go."

And so it was agreed that for our collective birthdays we would, for the first time in our lives, go to a male strip show. The thought of this kept us giggling for the rest of the afternoon.

I had no work the following week which felt rather strange. I invoiced Marc and then spent the rest of the day sorting and then re-sorting my wardrobe. I noticed a small, crumpled, pale lilac heap at the back of the wardrobe and suddenly realised that it was the dress and jacket that Richard had bought me on the spur of the moment in Broadway, all those months ago. When he'd left, I'd ripped it from its hanger and slung away it out of sight. I looked at it again. It was a lovely dress, so I washed, ironed and then packed it thinking that it would be ideal for an evening out. By Tuesday, I'd made my final decisions about what to wear and take away with me and in the afternoon sat down with a sense of satisfaction tinged with apprehensive anticipation. I realised that I hadn't been in touch with Susie so sent her a long email, telling her about my impending adventure and also to Di in the hope that she would pick up my email some time.

On Wednesday I visited Purity, a local brewery, and bought a bottle of their light Saddleback and darker Storm King Stout. I then went on to buy a further ten bottles of assorted English beers ranging from pale Worthington White Shield to velvety Fuller's London Porter. I even managed to find a bottle of Double Chocolate Stout along with Bishop's Finger, Old Peculiar and Speckled Hen which I chose simply because I thought the names would amuse him. I remembered that he had enjoyed English tea for breakfast so bought him a very large box of Yorkshire tea as well as the biggest jar of Marmite which he'd cautiously tried one breakfast and found it as tasty as I did.

I finalised packing, deliberately - and perhaps rather childishly - placing the pack of condoms on top of the lilac dress. I wondered why I was being so forward when I was almost certain that he didn't think of me in that way, he was easily ten to fifteen years younger than me. Presumptive but perhaps hopeful, my little inner voice whispered to me. I loaded up the car, double checking that I hadn't forgotten anything. The cats knew that something was different and wandered around suspiciously. Anita had promised to feed them for me and called round to collect my spare key, reassuring them that she would be back the following days to make sure they were alright.

I managed to sleep but woke very early, so after making myself look and feel as bright as possible, I set off. I wasn't due at Folkestone until eleven but certainly didn't want to be late and was happy to have a leisurely drive. I decided to stay in the car as the train whizzed through the tunnel and some forty minutes later was waiting for the gates to be opened. This seemed to take ages but eventually I was driving onto the streets of Calais in bright autumnal sunshine.

I found my way to the A16 easily which swept away from Calais and then onto the D300 that meandered through flat fields towards St Omer. The roads were long and straight, many tree-lined, the leaves beginning to turn red and gold. In the distance I could see people working in the fields and tractors collecting boxes of harvested produce. As the kilometres passed, I could feel the butterflies in my tummy flutter more and more. We'd got on so well when he stayed with me but I wondered how it would be when I was on his territory, and why on earth I was about to stay with a virtual stranger. In just under an hour I had arrived at the small town and found his apartment block without any difficulty. I looked up at the big rambling house that was next to the Jardin Public. I texted him and within a minute, saw him walking towards me, indicating where I should park and as I got out of the car was enveloped in a bear hug and warm kisses on both cheeks.

"Lucie, I am so, so glad to see you," he said as he released me and picked up my bags.

"There's more." I opened the boot and he gasped in appreciation as he saw the boxes of beer.

His flat was beautifully appointed with high ceilings, big windows with shutters and a balcony from the spacious sitting room that overlooked the park. It boasted a modern kitchen where there was just room for a small table and two chairs, a large master bedroom and a smaller bedroom that clearly doubled as an office, and a generous bathroom with an old-fashioned bath. I exclaimed as I was shown each room and as the spare room door was opened, I asked if I should put my bags there. He smiled. "Whatever you wish Lucie."

He was delighted with the beers, teabags and marmite and hugged his thanks. "You are very generous, thank you. Would you like a glass of wine?" We sat on the balcony, sipped ice-cold white wine and exchanged some of our news. He was as easy to get on with as I'd remembered and I started to properly relax.

"There's a very good seafood café in town. I wonder if you'd like to eat there this evening?" he asked after about an hour and I'd asked for a cup of tea rather than a second glass of wine.

"That sounds wonderful, but I'd like to freshen up before we go."

I had a quick, hot, refreshing shower, redid my makeup and stepped into the lilac jersey dress that Richard had bought. It floated over me, skimming my figure, falling almost to my ankles. Very flattering I thought, as I swished the skirt, but as it was short sleeved, I teamed it with a three-quarters length, dark purple cardigan and black suede ankle boots. A chunky black necklace completed the outfit. When I reappeared, Jean-Michel's approving smile greeted me. "Magnifique." I smiled my thanks for the compliment.

Arm in arm, we strolled through the Jardin Public to the town square that I clearly remembered from a previous visit several years ago, which took all of ten minutes. We arrived at a little café in a side alley which was furnished with rustic tables and chairs that were surprisingly comfortable. The waiter was smilingly efficient. I could understand some of what he and Jean-Michel were discussing but was certainly left behind on the intricacies of the conversation. I did, however, understand the menu and was more than happy to be guided to the foie gras which was served with very thin slices of brioche followed by the most wonderful bouillabaisse, served with crusty French bread to mop up the fishy sauce. We drank more white wine. I insisted on having a couple of glasses of water as well, which made the waiter smile and shrug.

It was close to eleven when we'd finished our espresso coffees and ambled back to Jean-Michel's apartment. We walked through the streets and I gazed at the typically French architecture in the pale moonlight. He had taken my hand this time and we walked hand in hand which I found companionable and comforting.

As he opened the front door, he turned and smiled at me. "You must be very tired after your journey."

"I am, I really am." The adrenalin had kept me going but I realised that I was, in fact, exhausted. I put my hand on the door handle of the spare room and he smiled gently.

"You sleep well Lucie. I too am tired. See you in the morning."

I leaned forward and kissed him on both cheeks. "Thank you for such a lovely evening Jean-Michel, I've so enjoyed it."

"That's all that matters. Bon nuit Lucie."

I was woken on the Friday morning by ducks quacking and saw, to my delighted surprise, texts from Anita, Helena, Pennie, Karen, Di and Susie. All had remembered that it was my birthday. In the excitement of my trip, I had completely forgotten so I texted everyone my thanks. I lay back in bed and wriggled my toes in anticipation of my first full day in France in all of three months.

I must have dozed off again because the next thing I remember was hearing Jean-Michel moving around and the tempting smell of fresh coffee brewing. I pulled on the long, silky, dark pink dressing gown I'd brought with me and went into the kitchen. We kissed cheeks good morning and decided to breakfast on the balcony. It was another glorious October morning but slightly chilly so he brought me the dark chocolate-coloured throw that was draped on the sofa so I could keep warm. I noticed that he was wearing slouchy pale blue pyjamas that showed a flash of hip with a dark blue sweatshirt over the top, he looked effortlessly stylish and, it had to be admitted, very sexy. "I'd love to show you the side of Calais that French people go to," he suggested as we were debating where to go that day. "The tourists tend to go shopping in the modern stores but the old part of Calais is so beautiful ..."

"I'd love to," I interrupted with a smile as I tucked into a buttery warm croissant and sipped the hot coffee.

I dressed in dark grey leggings, red flat shoes, a lightweight black sweater and my long red cardigan with my favourite red and black scarf. "C'est bon," was the verdict. I could have said the same; he was dressed in black jeans, cream sweatshirt and dark brown brogues.

He drove slowly to Calais through several charming little villages and smiled as I exclaimed my pleasure at each one. We arrived in old Calais at about twelve thirty and drifted round the narrow streets, looking at the shops, cafés and the marvellous architecture while Jean-Michel, at my request, told me some of the history of the place. "The old part of Calais is actually called Calais-Nord, but when the Romans used it as a launchpad to get to England, it was called Caletum. Did you know that it was the property of England from 1347 when King Edward III took it from us after winning the Battle of Crécy? Francis, the Duke of Guise won it back but that took over two hundred years. And Napoleon used Calais when he was planning to invade England." He paused and looked at me. "You're really interested in this?"

"It's fascinating, do please go on." I really meant it.

"What's less well known is that Calais was captured by the Spanish in 1596 but we managed to get it back in 1598."

I shook my head. "What an eventful history."

"Oui. And it's still eventful today. The refugee camps and people risking their lives to walk the tunnel ..." As we continued to walk round, we reflected on how people's desperation to find a safe sanctuary made them take terrible chances. Suddenly he took my hand and kissed it gently. "And now, we're going somewhere else." He tightened his hold on my hand very slightly as we slowly returned to the car.

Within minutes we arrived at the beach and he parked on the road directly in front of large rolling sand dunes. I saw that we were very close to the Hotel de la Plage whose restaurant overlooked the dunes and out to sea. We were lucky enough to find a table with a great view and as I gazed out Jean-Michel read the menu. "Do you like mussels?"

I dragged my eyes from the vista of sand and sea. "Love them." The huge platter of moules marinière was served in a thick broth of cream, garlic and parsley along with warm crusty bread and an equally large bowl for the discarded shells. I had rarely eaten such good mussels and the Chablis that accompanied them was excellent. "That was simply delicious." I mopped up the last of the sauce and licked my fingers.

"I love seeing you eat with such enjoyment." I blushed.

"Well, the sauce is far too good to waste." I felt slightly defensive.

He put his hand on mine. "I like watching a woman eat." His hand stayed on mine as he slowly sipped his Chablis.

We started talking about his students while we finished off lunch with coffee. I attempted to pay but he said he wouldn't hear of it so, wishing he'd accept my offer, I thanked him. "So Lucie, what would you like to do now?"

I thought for a moment and looked across the road at the tall dunes shining under the autumn sun. "I can think of nothing nicer than walking along the beach and feeling the sand between my toes."

"I'm very happy to grant you that wish," was his smiling reply as he got to his feet, holding out his hand.

We crossed the road and both bent to take off our shoes and socks. We started to climb the dunes but the sand was dry and very slippery and we slid all over the place, giggling so much that we fell over. He leaned over me, stroked my cheek and kissed my lips very softly and then, as he felt me respond, more ardently. I felt slightly stunned but, to my surprise, delighted. We stayed in each other's arms for a few moments until I sat up. "Come on, you promised me a walk on the beach."

"Certainly, if that's what you wish." He rose to his feet pulling me up so that we stood very close. "Come, the views are wonderful." And he turned towards the sea, still holding my hand. I couldn't believe the sight that lay before me as we reached the top of the dunes - there was a line of brightly coloured beach huts below us, between them and the Channel that was sparkling in the low autumn sun was an expanse of smooth white sand. We slithered down the dunes, cut through the beach huts and onto the firm beach where walking was much easier and wandered barefoot, holding hands, exchanging the odd kiss and watching the ferries going in and out of the port in the distance.

It was only as I felt the chill of the breeze from the sea that I realised how long we'd been walking and shivered. He looked a little anxious. "I think you're getting cold - perhaps we should return to the car." So we retraced our steps back to the beach huts, over the dunes and back to the car. I ran across the road in bare feet and he followed, laughing.

I sat in the car as he slid his shoes back on, not bothering with socks while I remained barefoot. "It's been the most wonderful day Jean-Michel. Thank you so much."

He looked at me. "It's not over yet Lucie," and with that he started the car.

We talked about the morning on the journey back to St Omer and I felt tingly but slightly apprehensive with fear of the unknown. It now seemed almost certain that we'd end up in bed together, and I was acutely aware that I had not slept with anyone since Richard who'd been well used to my body. Feelings of self-consciousness swept over me as I again reflected on how much older than him I was and how he was certainly much more used to younger, firmer bodies than mine. I sighed.

Back at the apartment I felt slightly awkward. "Shall I make us a cup of tea?"

"You English," he smiled. "When in doubt, make tea. Yes?"

"Absolutely." I busied myself with the tea. As I took the two mugs through to the balcony where he was standing, gazing out at the park, I heard ducks quacking. I put the mugs onto the small table and looked at the text - to my shock and disbelief I saw it was from Richard. 'Hope you're having a good one. R x'. My gasp of disbelief must have been audible because Jean-Michel looked up.

"Lucie, ma chérie, what's wrong?"

Wordlessly I handed him the phone. "Is this the man?" I nodded and to my horror felt tears running down my cheeks.

He stepped towards me and held me close, kissing the tears away and then, holding my face in both hands, kissed my mouth with a passion that was impossible to resist. We stood close together, kissing for what seemed like hours and then he leaned away from me with a gently quizzical smile on his face. I nodded and, hand in hand, we walked into his bedroom. He pushed the long red cardigan off my shoulders and then gently pulled the black sweater over my head, kissing my shoulders and neck as he did so before tugging his sweatshirt off. Shoes kicked off, we tumbled onto his bed, kissing more and more passionately as we pressed our bodies together and clumsily pulled off our remaining clothes. Somehow my scarf had stayed on and as I reached up to untie it, he stopped me. "Please leave it on," he breathed and with that he held it, pulling me towards him so closely I could hardly breathe and our kisses became so deep I felt I was drowning. His tongue skimmed my lips and traced down to my breasts, tugging and nibbling at my nipples softly with his teeth and then moved down my stomach which I vainly tried to keep as flat as possible. His mouth grazed my hips and I moaned in appreciation and desire. I ran the backs of my fingers down his sides and over his belly which made him squirm.

He reached into his bedside cabinet and, after fumbling for a moment, brought out a small silver packet. I took it from him. My eyes never left his as I tore the foil carefully with my teeth. I'd never realised how erotic undoing a condom could be but the blaze in his eyes told me it was so. Holding him in one hand, I began to kiss and lick his chest, nipples and stomach before sitting back and slowly rolling it over his more-than-ready cock. As he penetrated me I let out a long sigh of satisfaction. He was a very gentle and considerate lover but I struggled to reach the heights. I felt his jerking orgasm and could feel his heart beating next to mine as his breathing slowed. I snuggled into his shoulder. He turned towards me and kissed my cheeks, my eyes, my chin my lips whilst one hand drifted down to explore and stroke me until I'd come too. He looked at me and as I gazed into his green eyes, saw nothing but care and affection.

We lay back, side by side. "So tell me Lucie, what does 'have a good one' mean?"

"Well …" I hesitated.

"Yes?" he prompted. I could tell he wasn't about to give up.

"It's my birthday today and it's wishing me a good time."

He sat up. "Merde! Why didn't you tell me? I wish I'd known." He sounded genuinely cross.

I put my hand against his chest that was still damp with sweat. "Jean-Michel, it doesn't matter. Anyway, I've decided that I'm counting backwards from now."

He laughed and the tension was instantly dissipated. "We should go out and celebrate your birthday."

"That's a lovely idea darling, but quite honestly I'd rather stay in and have an evening with just the two of us."

He hugged me. "That's a lovely thing to say Lucie. Shall we see if the fridge will give us enough to eat?"

He pulled on a burgundy towelling bathrobe and went to bring me my dressing gown. "Come." He held out his hand, pulled me to my feet and helped me into my robe. Such a sweetheart, I thought to myself and smiled up at him.

As we went into the kitchen hand in hand he looked at me. "Are you going to tell me what number this birthday is?"

I stopped, heart pounding. I was sure if I told him that he'd be appalled that he'd slept with me. "Older than you …" I paused as he continued to look expectantly at me. I cleared my throat. "Can I just say that I'm now firmly in my sixties?"

He didn't look appalled, instead he hugged me. "Forgive me Lucie, of course I know you're older than me but I thought, for you, it was important to acknowledge that." He kissed me and smiled. "I'm a very lucky man that you allow me to share your birthday."

I couldn't help it, tears came into my eyes. He shrugged - a typical Gaelic shrug. "A beautiful woman is a beautiful woman. And Lucie, a number is just a number."

And a shag's just a shag I thought to myself but despite that, I stood straighter and smiled before hugging him tightly; it seemed that another ghost had been laid.

The fridge was very kind to us. We found a couple of cheeses, some duck pâté, ham, tomatoes, olives, cornichons and a bottle of white wine. There was bread that just needed a quick re-crisp in the oven to be edible and lots of fruit. "I'd like to eat on the balcony please." He shook his head as if to say mad dogs and Englishmen but compliantly opened the doors and we laid out the food on the small table.

"We need to be warm." He disappeared, reappearing moments later with two soft, blue blankets we wrapped round ourselves and sat as dusk fell with the light of the sitting room behind us, barely illuminating the balcony. We picked at the food and sipped the chilled white wine, talking nonsense. "You still look a little sad which is not good on your birthday" he said after a while. "Some champagne to celebrate will cheer you up." And with that he disappeared for a few moments, reappearing with a chilled bottle of Champagne Jean Saint-Omer, one of the best local champagnes of the region.

I stood up to hug him. "You're such a sweetie. Thank you."

He hugged me back. "It's getting very cold out here. Perhaps we should go inside?"

The 'inside' he meant was, of course, his bedroom and as I dropped the blanket and slid under the fluffy duvet, he deftly opened the champagne and filled the two cut glass goblets he'd also brought through before joining me. He piled up the pillows and some cushions he'd brought through from the sitting room so we reclined against a soft wall of feathers and down. "A happy, happy birthday Lucie," he said and we gently touched the rims together before drinking. It was excellent champagne and that, combined with the wine I'd been drinking, made me feel mellow and very relaxed.

"Thank you so much. It's been a wonderful day." I leant towards him and kissed his cheek.

He turned towards me, green eyes soft and loving. I held my glass to my lips and sipped more champagne, he did the same. We kissed, letting the champagne we both were holding in our mouths run together. He stopped for a moment and reached over for my goblet which he put on the bedside table before returning to graze his lips over my neck, my shoulders and arms. I ran my fingertips down his sides to his waist and then across his stomach and up his chest as he leaned back and watched me. I did it again, this time letting my hands drift down to his hips, gently scratching the soft skin over his hip bone and then very lightly up and down the length of him. His breathing quickened and he arched towards me very slightly so I laid the flat of one hand against his chest while the other set up a very slow but firm rhythm which made him squirm and moan.

I leaned over him and kissed him, still keeping up the inexorable rhythm then leaned away from him and held him ready. As soon as he was sheathed, I straddled him and felt him push into me. He came very quickly and started to apologise as soon as he caught his breath at which I took his face in both hands and kissed him deeply.

We snuggled down under the covers and Jean-Michel put his arm round my shoulders as I cuddled into him. "Lucie?" I heard his voice as if from a distance as I was starting to drift into sleep.

I nodded against his chest. "Hmmm?"

"Tell me Lucie, why did he text you?"

"Who?"

"You know. That man."

I was suddenly awake and sat up to look into his face. "I have absolutely no idea Jean-Michel. I certainly didn't expect to hear from him."

He paused and looked thoughtful. "You cried when you saw his text. Do you want him back?"

I looked down at him and saw warmth tinged with painful concern. "No Jean-Michel. He lied to me, he betrayed me." I paused. "Would you take your wife back?"

A spasm of pain crossed his face. "No. No, I couldn't. Like you, I was betrayed and know I can never forgive her."

"That's just how I feel. That text was a jolt from the past Jean-Michel. I cared for him very deeply. He'd promised a future and when that was snatched away from me I was devastated. But he probably did me a favour ..." I paused. "You know, often he'd say 'all's fair in love and war'. Is that true?"

"Of course it's not true Lucie. If you love someone, you do the best for them and treat them honestly and fairly. How can anything else be acceptable?"

I lay down again and pressed myself against his warm body as closely as I could, wanting to absorb his kindness, affection and honesty. "You're a good, kind man Jean-Michel. Never ever forget that." And we fell asleep in each other's arms.

The next morning we were still tangled together and as I drowsily moved against him I could feel his arousal, morning glory Karen would have said. He softly kissed me and I felt instant excitement. He must have realised as his kisses became more insistent. "Yes, Jean-Michel, please love me now," I whispered and he thrust into me. I hit orgasm within moments, triggering his, which in turn sparked a second for me. A quickie it might have been, but it was very, very good and as we fell apart, panting, we looked at each other and laughed in delight.

After we'd showered, I dressed in an ankle length brown skirt, brown sweater, chunky cream cardigan, fluffy cream scarf and red flats to match my red handbag and went through into the kitchen where he was brewing coffee and unwrapping croissants. He looked up and smiled. "You look lovely this morning."

I kissed his cheek. "So do you my dear." He did too - faded jeans, pale tan sweatshirt over a checked shirt and brown brogues. We breakfasted on the balcony as he knew that I preferred to and, although it was overcast, it seemed that the clouds were beginning to thin.

"Today is market day," he remarked as we started discussing what to do that day.

"I love markets. Can we go?" I clasped my hand in mock supplication.

"Of course," he laughed. "Are you sure that's all you want to do?"

"For the moment." I rested my hand on his and he leaned across to kiss me.

We strolled hand in hand to the large market square that was bustling with shoppers and wandered through stalls selling fruit, vegetables, clothes, plants and kitchen wares. I bought some garlic, a beautiful blue pottery dish that I fell in love with and large bunch of flowers which I solemnly presented to him - he then bought me an enormous cream silk scarf that was covered in a print of pale pink and red roses nestling in their foliage. "Thank you very much Jean-Michel, it's really gorgeous." I took off my scarf and draped my present round my shoulders.

"It suits you. I knew it would. And thank you for my gift. It's not often that a beautiful woman gives me flowers." I blushed.

It was nearly one o'clock and I could see that most of the traders had started to pack up so we made our way to a small café that was next to the Town Hall. Even though the clouds had thinned there was still an autumnal nip in the air but despite that we decided to sit outside at one of the small tables on the pavement. We ordered ham and cheese omelettes with chips washed down with beer. The omelettes were meltingly moist and the perfect skinny frites were crisp on the outside and fluffy on the inside. We were on our second beers when I suddenly jumped as I heard a series of louds bangs to my left. Jean-Michel laughed and explained that it was customary for fire crackers to be thrown at the ground when a bride and groom came out of the Town Hall after their wedding ceremony. Moments later we saw a tall, dark-haired groom with his slender blonde bride walk through the ornate doors into the square. A large wedding party followed and, for the next hour or so, lots of photographs both formal and informal were taken as people stood around chatting. A pony and trap adorned with ribbons and flowers then appeared and, amidst much laughter and waving, the newly-weds climbed aboard. We were able to hear the clip-clop of the pony's hooves for a few minutes, after which the wedding guests went to their cars and followed the pony.

We looked at each other and smiled. "Well, let's hope that they have better luck than we've had." I had to agree.

"I know that it's the day after your birthday but I didn't know it then, so I want to take you to the best restaurant in St Omer."

I protested but could tell that I was fighting a losing battle so I gave in graciously and said a heartfelt thank you for his generosity.

We gathered up our packages and meandered back through the narrow streets to his flat. He made coffee while I put his flowers in water and set the overflowing vase onto a side table, he nodded approvingly. "Very pretty Lucie, thank you."

It was clouding over again and, to my disappointment, too cold to sit outside so we curled up on the sofa to drink the hot, strong coffee while we listened to Christophe Maé's most recent CD. Jean-Michel put his arm round me and I nestled down as he kissed me, at first very gently and then more demandingly as I moved against him. After a few minutes he stood up, held out his hand to pull me to my feet and we made our way to his bedroom where he gently undressed me, kissing my skin as he did so. It seemed that we were more at ease with each other so that as we stroked, kissed, licked and caressed each other I sensed what he liked and it was clear that he understood that I love kissing and petting, and that my throat and the little dimple between my collar bones were preferred spots. We took our time in teasing, tantalising and giggling until we couldn't wait any longer. Seconds later he was inside me and minutes later we both came explosively.

It was dark when I awoke and as I stretched, I realised that I was alone in bed. "Jean-Michel?"

He appeared almost instantly. "You were so asleep; I couldn't bear to wake you. It's fine though. There's plenty of time. It's only six thirty." And with that he disappeared.

I stretched again. Truth to tell, I'd have been very happy to stay in bed but I made myself get up and had a quick shower, after which I dressed in a long black skirt with black ankle boots, cream sweater and my new scarf. Make up done, I joined him to see he was wearing black chinos with a dark red shirt and a matching red sweater slung over his shoulders, and as we pulled on our coats he smiled down at me with a tenderness and affection that was incredibly beguiling.

We walked by the side of the Jardin Public, through the market square and into a smaller square where I saw an old building in front of us. Inside were small tables, immaculately laid out with gleaming silverware and twinkling crystal glasses. The Restaurant le Cygne was everything he'd promised, a pleasantly convivial atmosphere with understated service and some of the most amazing food I'd ever tasted.

It was so hard to make a choice as everything looked wonderful but we eventually managed to make our final selection. I'd decided on a chicken liver and pineau pâté, it was explained to me that pineau was a sherry-like aperitif which made the pate unusually moist, followed by roasted duck breast with a sun-dried cherry red port wine demi-glace sauce served with some artfully presented autumn vegetables. Jean-Michel had chosen a softly poached egg on a puff pastry shell in a light lemon hollandaise sauce with baby broccoli. The waiter assured us that this was almost better than spring asparagus, followed by a seared sea bass with crabmeat in a sherry butter sauce. Both dishes were sublime and we ate each course slowly, savouring every mouthful along with a bottle of chilled Pouilly Fume, talking and laughing as if we'd known each other for ages.

We were coming to the end of the main course when Jean-Michel leaned across and held my hand. "This is a wonderful weekend Lucie and I really don't want it to end." He paused. "Do you have to leave tomorrow?"

I squeezed his hand. "I'd much rather not. Perhaps I could leave on Monday morning? I guess you have to go back to work then?"

He nodded sadly. "I wish I didn't have to but I do. It would be great if you could stay an extra day."

"I'll check it out later." I reached up and touched his cheek. "Now, smile for me." He did so and I kissed each corner of his mouth.

I was about to look at the sweet menu when Jean-Michel suggested that we should share the restaurant's renowned cheese board. I was a little sad to abandon the incredible desserts but agreed and was very glad I did. We ate Comté Vieux which was a hard salty cheese not unlike raclette, Epoisses which was a little like Camembert but much stronger and slightly more crumbly, Fourme d'Ambert, a mild blue cheese with a slightly nutty flavour, a slightly acidic ewe's milk cheese with a name I couldn't start to pronounce, much to his amusement, from the Basque country, Neufchâtel which was a pungently soft creamy cheese and Morbier, a hard cheese that was by far the smelliest on the board but with a flavour that was unexpectedly silky and smooth - all accompanied by plump fresh grapes and wafer thin slices of fruit bread which, amazingly, enhanced all the cheeses. "And as it's your birthday celebration, we must have champagne." So, another bottle of chilled Champagne Jean Saint-Omer was brought to the table to complement the cheese board.

It was close to midnight when we left the restaurant and made our slow way back to the market square where there was a gentle hum of people leaving the cafés and restaurants. There was no doubt - I felt slightly squiffy and said as much to Jean-Michel who needed to have the word 'squiffy' explained to him which made us giggle. We weaved our way back to his flat and as he made some tea, I'd insisted that tea was the right drink at this time of night, I lay back on the plush leather sofa, feeling very relaxed and peaceful, albeit very full.

"Remember to check your travel times," he called so I roused myself and went online where I saw that I was able to change my crossing to eleven thirty on Monday morning.

"Is that ok?" I looked up as he brought the tea through.

"That's perfect Lucie. It would be even nicer if you were here on my return from work ..." He paused and raised an interrogative eyebrow.

I turned my head and kissed the hand that was resting on my shoulder. "I don't think that's possible Jean-Michel. We're both busy people, aren't we?" I looked up at him and saw him nod.

I changed my booking as I sipped my tea while he watched me. "Now we have all day tomorrow," I said as I logged off and finished my tea. "You know what? For a Frenchman, you make pretty good tea."

I was rewarded by a pillow thrown at me from the bedroom so I picked it up and hurled it back at him. The pillow fight continued in the bedroom until I held up my hands in laughing surrender. "I can't do this any more. I'm too full to fight." So we cuddled down under the duvet, gently embracing each other and, being tired and very replete, fell asleep in each other's arms.

I woke to find Jean-Michel curled round me spoon-fashion and became aware of his early morning erection pressing against my hip. I gently ground myself against him and felt kisses and tiny bites on the back of my neck and shoulders as one hand gently fondled between my legs. "Yes?" I heard him whisper at which I half turned my head to kiss him and arched my back even more. He took the hint and seconds later I was firmly pushed onto my front. His thrusts were fast and furious and he came with an explosive cry before collapsing over my back. Although I hadn't come, I revelled in his excitement and lay still, feeling him slowly slip away from me. "I don't want to leave you," he whispered into my hair before slowly moving off me.

I turned over and hugged him wordlessly before we got up, showered, breakfasted on the balcony and planned our day. "Have you been to Boulogne?" he asked. As I had a mouthful of croissant all I could do was shake my head. "Well, I'd love to show you somewhere you haven't seen, so let's go there."

I swallowed. "That sounds lovely Jean-Michel, thank you."

We set off in his small pale blue Deux Chevaux, driving through open countryside towards the coast and in less than an hour had arrived and parked in a central underground car park. We wandered to the Notre Dame de Boulogne, a beautiful pale stone building which boasted the longest crypt in France and the tiny Chateau Musee which had an eclectic collection of items that had been donated by Belgian collectors, gathered from all over the world.

We then drifted down to a beachside café where we gazed at an extensive menu, but decided that all we could manage was a large bowl of steaming French onion soup topped with a pile of finely grated Gruyère cheese that melted into the soup, accompanied by crusty French bread. A bowl of soup it might have been, but it was satisfyingly filling and as I mopped the last shreds of caramelised onion from the bottom of the bowl with a piece of bread, I sat back and sighed. "That was absolutely delicious." I leaned forward. "And Jean-Michel, I absolutely insist that I pay for today." He started to protest so I said, "Well, you can always pay me back in kind later."

He looked slightly baffled. "But you are very kind Lucie."

I smiled. "Don't you worry sweetie, you'll soon understand."

Hand-in-hand we strolled to the fish market that was closed as it was Sunday, but the residual smell of fish combined with the sea breeze was clean and fresh. I watched the muscular fishermen preparing their boats for the next day. "Down to the beach?" Jean-Michel asked.

I looked up at him. "That would be lovely."

He smiled. "I remember you like walking on the sand." We spent an hour walking slowly along the soft smooth sand, holding our shoes in our free hands and pausing occasionally to kiss each other lightly. I felt more relaxed and at peace than I'd felt for a very long time.

As we wandered back to the car, we passed the beautiful pale grey St Nicholas Church which was just off the main street in Place Dalton, where I could hear the purity of boys' voices singing Berlioz's L'Adieu des bergers from L'enfance du Christ. It brought tears to my eyes and I stood still as the music washed over me. Jean-Michel stood next to me silently and as the last notes died away, put his arm round my shoulders and dropped a light kiss on my cheek.

We drove past the Boulogne Eastern Cemetery which was created during the Great War and stopped to look at the white headstones with the names and ages of the pitifully young men who had fallen, and then drove on in comfortable silence back to St Omer. It was getting dark as he opened the door to his flat. "Would you like some tea?"

"Love some, please." I sank gratefully into the plump cushions on the sofa.

He brought the tea through with a plate of small biscuits which were perfect to dunk. I had to explain the intricacies of dunking to him as time after time he let the biscuits become too tea-logged so they fell into the hot liquid. Eventually, I could bear it no longer, so made some fresh tea and held his hand as he dunked, pulling the biscuit out a micro-second before it became too wet. "Too complicated," was his initial opinion, but eventually he had to agree with me that a dunked biscuit was the perfect accompaniment to English tea.

By seven, we realised that we were hungry so we made our way back into the town where I had noticed that a large pub called the Queen Victoria that overlooked the market square. We looked at the menu and couldn't resist their special - fish and chips, which we ate, washed down with French beer. It had been, we agreed as we strolled back to his flat a couple of hours later, a really lovely day.

As he closed the front door behind us, he took me in his arms and kissed me with a warmth and passion that was impossible to resist and, locked together, we stumbled towards his bedroom. We were naked and under the duvet in seconds. After our initial passionate kisses and caresses, we slowed down both wanting to treasure every last moment. He leaned over me and kissed and nibbled my throat, my shoulders, my arms, my belly and my hips and as I moved under his mouth I moaned softly as my excitement and desire grew. As his hand brushed my sides and then down between my legs, I squirmed in delight. I reached down for him only for him to gently, but firmly, move my hand away. "I wait for you," he breathed at which I flung my arms above my head and abandoned myself to his tongue until, with a cry of pure pleasure, I came.

My breathing slowed and I opened my eyes to see him looking down at me. "I am very happy that you are happy."

I took a deep breath. "Well, that was a wonderful payment in kind."

He looked bewildered so, between kisses, I explained what the phrase meant which made him laugh. "My turn now," I ordered. He obediently did so and lay still as I caressed his neck, shoulders and back, following my hands with my mouth. I worked my way down to the backs of his thighs before returning to his buttocks which I tenderly bit. "Turn over." He rolled over and, as I'd expected, he was more than ready. I giggled softly and straddled him, rocking us to blissful release.

I fell asleep with my hand stroking his tangled thick dark blond hair as his head rested on my breast, feeling sad that the last few days had passed so quickly, yet tranquilly happy that we had had such a wonderfully companionable, comfortable and, I had to smilingly admit, passionate time together.

I became aware of the smell of coffee brewing and realised that Jean-Michel was up. Pulling my dressing gown on, I padded into the kitchen to see him dressed in a dark grey suit and an open-neck snowy white shirt, he looked amazingly hot. Clearly he hadn't heard me so I stood behind him and gently patted his bottom. He spun round with a smile. "Lucie? That's very cheeky."

I looked down in mock-shame. "I apologise Jean-Michel, I shouldn't have been so forward but," I ran my hands over his chest, "I just couldn't resist the temptation."

He caught my hands in his and bent to kiss me and I could feel his desire as I leaned my hips towards him. "You're very bad Lucie. You know I have to go to work."

I took his face in my hands and kissed his mouth very gently. "Then you must go Jean-Michel." I paused and looked deep into his eyes. "The last few days have been wonderful. I can't thank you enough." He looked puzzled and I laughed to lighten the mood. "Thank you for your fantastic hospitality. I've had such a lovely time." I reluctantly stepped away from him. "Now you must leave. I'll make sure that everything is safely locked up when I go."

He caught me up in a bear hug and kissed my hair. "Thank you for being here Lucie. I've loved every minute with you."

He broke away and picked up a battered brown leather briefcase and a smart black laptop case, the two looked incongruous and yet surprisingly right together. "I must go. I really don't want to but ..."

"You go right now before you're late. Go. Shoo." I walked with him to the front door and almost pushed him out. The front door closed and I ran to the balcony to watch his pale blue Citroen disappear from sight and, as I stood and waved him goodbye, tears filled my eyes. I gazed across to the Jardin Public, not knowing why I felt so bereft.

I returned to the gleaming kitchen, drank the coffee he'd brewed for me, ate the buttery croissant he'd left for me and cleared up. After showering and dressing, I went through the flat, tidying and dusting with care. I made the bed and as I plumped the pillows, I hugged the one that smelled of his aftershave before writing a short note, again thanking him for a wonderful weekend, which I left on his bedside table.

It was exactly nine o'clock when I pulled his door firmly shut behind me and made my way down to my car. The roads into Calais wound through farmland and I could see freshly ploughed fields. The train left on time so I disembarked in Folkestone at twelve noon English time. The journey home took me close to four hours but I'd stopped twice, once on the M20 and again on the more familiar M40. I played lots of hard rock very loudly, reflecting on the past few days which had, in truth, been the best in many years.

The house was cold so I lit the fire and sat, watching the flickering flames, holding a large mug of tea in my cupped hands. I knew that whatever happened, I now felt so much more confident, positive and self-assured. My faith in men had, at least partially, been restored.

Jean-Michel emailed me on Tuesday morning saying how much he had enjoyed our time together, that he missed me and had slept breathing in my perfume that lingered on the bedlinen. As I read it, I felt an unexpected surge of tenderness that made me smile. There was no doubt that I too missed him, but equally knew that I needed to be realistic about what the weekend had been, a lovely loving interlude that was almost certainly just that and no more.

I worked at the university for the remaining four days that week and by Friday evening was shattered. I certainly couldn't face going to the Zumba class so gave my apologies to everyone via Karen who tutted at me sympathetically when I explained that I was exhausted and needed to sleep.

I was woken all too early on Saturday morning by the phone ringing. To my surprise it was Annie, sounding very upbeat. "I thought I'd do some shopping in Stratford today, would you like to meet for a coffee, or perhaps lunch?"

I yawned. "Sounds good Annie. Let's make it lunch, shall we? It's been a really hectic week and I need a leisurely morning."

I snuggled back down under the duvet and dozed the next couple of hours away so was ready to get up shortly after ten. We'd arranged to meet at the One Elm at twelve before the lunchtime rush and by the time I'd had a leisurely shower, dressed and sipped my first cup of tea of the day, it was about eleven thirty so, pulling my boots on, I strolled down the hill.

Annie was comfortably reading a paper at a table by the fire and as I joined her, looked up with a warm smile. "Lucie, great to see you. How are you?"

"I'm very well thanks Annie. You're looking very upbeat. Tell me your news."

Before we started to talk properly, we decided to share a cheese board and a bottle of Merlot. After we placed our order, she sat back and grinned at me.

"Well?" I prompted.

She giggled. "Oh come on Annie, stop teasing and tell me what's been happening."

She leaned forward and went on to tell me that last Tuesday Roger had asked her out, they'd gone out for a drink that evening and again on Thursday and last night he'd taken her out to a wonderful restaurant in Leamington.

"Was it Morgan's Bar?"

"Yes, yes it was. How did you know?" She suddenly looked anxious.

"It's one of the best places in Leamington. I've been there a couple of times and thought it was excellent. So, a good meal? A good evening?"

"It was lovely, really lovely. We seemed to get on really well. I don't know where it's heading of course …"

"Just enjoy it for what it is at the moment," I interrupted. "Don't rush him and see where it leads, you never know."

And we went on to talk more about what was happening at school and how delighted she was that, after so many years, Roger was showing some interest in her and how she hoped they would end up together.

We slowly ate our way through the cheese board and then decided to indulge ourselves in the dessert that was on the specials board, a white chocolate brûlée that was every bit as delicious as it looked.

"So, what are you doing?" Annie asked.

I brought her up to speed with my work and what Susie was doing.

"Anything else?"

"Well, now you come to mention …" and I told her about my weekend in France. "It was all lovely Annie. But he's miles younger than me, he lives and works in France and he's got an ex-wife who, despite what he told me, I actually think there might still be some kind of connection with. I'm sure there's no future," I paused and smiled, "but it was a wonderful four days that I'll never forget." I smiled nostalgically and stifled a small sigh.

Work took over the whole week. I was at the university on Monday and Tuesday where I saw Beth again. I was tempted to suggest we have a coffee together but thought better of it. I certainly didn't want either of us to be embarrassed or uncomfortable and, if I was being honest, certainly didn't want to jeopardise any future employment prospects.

On Wednesday I made the final preparations for Tony's test induction programme and on Thursday went in to meet the eight delegates to discuss their expectations, lay some ground rules and start to get to know them. We started the programme proper on Friday and it continued for three days a week for the first two weeks of November.

Tony came into the training room on Friday afternoon as we were drawing to the end of the day to see how things were progressing. "I think it's going well," I said and he smilingly nodded.

"That's what I've been hearing. They're very happy with what's being covered and like your style so we're good to go for the rest of the programme." I smiled my delight. "You still go to that wine bar after your dance class?" he asked suddenly as I was packing up.

I glanced over my shoulder at him. "I do indeed. Mind you, I've not been for the last couple of weeks, must get back to it."

"Keeping fit is a serious business. You really should keep going otherwise you'll find it's much harder work when you do go back."

"True, true." I stifled an inner sigh. This all sounded so familiar. All too often Richard had talked about fitness and how bad I was at it, and the memory irritated me.

Unexpectedly, and to my surprise, Phil called on Friday evening. "I'm in London, trying to finalise some contracts. We're lunching at Heston Blumenthal's place in Knightsbridge tomorrow and I wondered if you were free. It would be great to see you again and, quite honestly, I could do with your incisive mind."

"Well, how can I refuse such a gracious invitation? Me and my incisive mind would be delighted to join you."

We bantered a little more and then agreed that I would join them at the restaurant at about twelve thirty. As I rang off, I considered what I should wear and smiled at my continued preoccupation about how I looked.

I had an early night as I had to be up bright and early to catch the nine fifteen train from Stratford that got into London's Marylebone at about quarter to twelve, giving me plenty of time to catch a tube to Knightsbridge. As I made my way towards the restaurant I checked myself out in a couple of windows. I saw a tall, albeit very curvy, woman dressed in black trousers, black boots, a cream sweater and black jacket with a beautiful silk scarf adorned with roses and soft green foliage fluttering round her neck and carrying a large red bag. She looked self-possessed, confident, poised and happy.

I couldn't restrain myself from gasping as I opened the door to see a restaurant which was decorated in shades of grey with sleek, modern lines. A smart young maître d' guided me to a table where I saw Phil with two men and a very glamorous woman. I mentally rechecked my appearance out and nodded to myself, I would do. The men stood up as I came to the table and Phil lightly embraced me and kissed my cheek. "Lucie, how lovely to see you. Let me introduce everyone ..." There was Angus his business partner, Claudia his wife and Jacob the general manager of the prestigious Ham Yard Hotel. Handshakes over, I took my place next to Phil.

"So, you're this blossoming food critic," Claudia said. I glanced at her but there was no sarcasm in her face, she looked genuinely interested.

"I'm enjoying it so much. I get to eat in great places and then have the opportunity of telling other people about it. What's not to love about that?"

Phil put his hand on my shoulder. "She's written some great reviews for us. I can see a real future for her in this field."

I turned towards him and gave him my sweetest smile. "Should I be making notes today?"

They all laughed. "No Lucie. You can relax and enjoy. I just wanted you to meet Angus and share lunch with us."

We looked at the menu which made me blink at its range and complexity. Most of the dishes had been taken and adapted from very old recipes which I found fascinating. We discussed the dishes in depth before making our final selections. I finally decided on the starter of a 1730 dish of Earl Grey tea cured salmon served with lemon salad, gentleman's relish, wood sorrel and smoked roe which proved to be aromatically succulent followed by a rib of prime Hereford beef with mushroom ketchup and triple cooked chips - this was a recipe from 1830 and a dish for two, so Phil and I shared it, only fighting over the last chip that was perfectly crisp on the outside and softly fluffy inside. Conversation between the five of us flowed and time sped by all too fast.

"No wonder you two get on so well," Claudia said as we came to the end of the main courses. "You both appreciate the same kind of food."

I looked up from the dessert menu. "Good job I appreciate food, otherwise I'd make a rotten food writer, wouldn't I?"

She laughed her agreement.

After a great deal of debate, I ordered Sambocade, a dish from 1390, which was a goats cheese cake with elderflower and apple, roast figs and a couple of smoked candied walnuts. It was scrumptious but as Phil's brown bread ice cream with salted butter caramel, a pear and malted yeast syrup looked equally good. I managed to trade spoonfuls with him which was well worth the time spent in arguing my case for sharing.

We all sat back, enjoying strong aromatic coffee accompanied by tiny shards of dark chocolate, discussing the magazine. All too soon, it started to get dark and I realised that I needed to make a move in order to be able to catch my seven o'clock train. "I'm catching a train out of Kings Cross, so why don't we share a taxi?" Phil asked. Ten minutes later we were sitting in a cab, speeding through the busy London streets. He turned to me and smiled. "I'm very glad you could join us."

"It was an incredible lunch and it was very good meeting Angus and Claudia, and Jacob of course. He's very interesting, isn't he?" I paused. "So where are you heading now?"

"Musselburgh. It's a small town just out of Edinburgh. I'm not intending to stay long this time." He fell silent and although I was intrigued and wanted to ask him more about his frequent trips to Scotland, there was something about his reticence that kept me quiet.

After a few moments, he seemed to rouse himself out of his reverie and we started to discuss the lunch menu. As always, when we talked about food, he was animated and we spent the next twenty minutes or so, arguing the finer points of the dishes we'd been enjoying. All too soon, the taxi pulled into Marylebone and as we said our goodbyes, he put his arm round my shoulders, gently stroked my face and kissed each corner of my mouth before pressing his lips to mine with an intensity that took my breath away. "We really must spend more time together," he murmured as he let me go.

I spent the journey home reflecting on the day which had been entertaining, astonishing, delicious and very unexpected in equal measure. I was still musing, especially about the kiss, as I went to bed and fell into a dreamless sleep.

Before meeting Karen for Sunday brunch, I sent Phil an email thanking him for his invitation and saying how much I enjoyed meeting everyone, not to mention the amazing lunch. I hit the send button and again wondered quite what we meant to each other.

Karen and I had decided to use brunch as part of our mutual birthday celebrations and after our usual catch-up, I told her about my day. She, like me, was slightly mystified by Phil's behaviour. "Just go with the flow," was her advice which made me remember what I'd said to Annie.

I shrugged. "I'm not going to worry about it. He's a nice man and he's probably the gatekeeper of some interesting and worthwhile work, but I'm not into game-playing or second-guessing. It might be that he's got someone in Scotland but I was sure that he's single. Oh God, Karen, I couldn't cope with another cheat." I turned to her. "You don't think …"

"I don't know Lucie, I just don't know. Don't condemn him until you've talked to him. There's probably a really simple explanation to all this but you certainly can't assume the worst."

"Or the best."

"Or the best. Best to assume nothing. You know you'll see him again about work if nothing else, and then you should talk to him and find out what's what."

That agreed, we changed the subject and talked about work and our kids. As we finished our brunch, she gave me my monthly 'Olive' and we then went for a mosey round the shops. As always, it was very good spending time together and when we parted in the gathering gloom we hugged goodbye with heartfelt affection.

Chapter 12 - November

I spent Monday double-checking that everything was ready for Tony's six-day programme which started on Tuesday. He'd decided to spend some time with the group on the first morning and again on Wednesday afternoon but, that apart, I was left on my own which suited me just fine. The delegates were keen and worked hard so, by the end of Thursday, I felt that we had succeeded in our objectives and were well set up for the following week. Fortunately everyone agreed with me.

Karen came over on Thursday evening to pick me for Zumba which I found almost as challenging as the very first time. "Well, that's to be expected, you haven't been for a couple of weeks," was all Judith said in response to my complaints as we settled ourselves in front of the blazing fire at the One Elm.

"And that's just not fair," was all I could think of saying in the face of her irrefutable logic.

The first beer saw us generally catching up but by the second one, attention was turned to me. "So, did you have a lovely time in France?" Sara asked.

I nodded. "It was wonderful. I had such a great time ..." and I went on to tell them about the excursions Jean-Michel and I had taken, the great meals we'd enjoyed together and the wonderful walks along the beaches at Calais and Boulogne.

"And what about this Jean-Michel?" Judy asked as I drew breath.

"He's lovely. Gentle, kind, thoughtful. We had a great time together and got on really well."

"And?" asked Sara and Judy simultaneously. Karen smirked which didn't go unnoticed.

"It was very, very good," I said at which they all clapped.

"Details please," was the unanimous demand which made me go pink.

"What can I say? He must be at least fifteen years younger than me, very good looking, has great dress sense and is ..." I paused for dramatic effect, "a wonderful lover." An unexpected little

367

flutter in my stomach made me fidget slightly and I sighed nostalgically as the others stared at me.

"Sounds like you've fallen for him," Judy said, Bev nodded.

"Don't be silly. He's a lovely man. We get on really well, shared lots of laughs and some amazing sex, but he lives in France and I live in England, I'm much older than him and I can't see us being more than good friends even though the weekend felt magical." Ridiculously I felt tears prickling as I realised the truth of what I was saying.

As Karen pulled onto my drive, she turned to face me. "Have you fallen for him?" she asked gently.

I shrugged. "I miss him, that's for sure." I stopped to think for a moment. "You know Karen, those four days really restored my faith in men and quite a bit in me too. I feel so much better about myself now and no, it's not just because we slept together, although I have to say it was terrific. He kind of put me first a lot of the time and when we talked he really got what I was saying. And that doesn't make him some kind of wimp. He's just emotionally adept which, as we know, is all too rare. Know what I mean?"

She knew what I meant and as we hugged goodbye, were both in reflective moods.

Our moods had lightened by the next evening when we met at the Cazbar, which was crammed with woman of all ages, all obviously keen to see the strippers start their act. I'd never been to a male strip show and was expecting to see a small stage. That certainly wasn't the case as I soon found out when the first stripper, who was dressed as a cowboy, pushed his way through the tightly packed crowd of women. As he made his way to the bar, we left a small space for him and watched as he slowly unbuttoned his very tight checked shirt to cheers and screams that got louder and louder the more he took off. After a few minutes, he was left wearing cowboy boots, his hat and a minute red thong which barely contained his very obvious bulge. As he continued to gyrate, several women reached forward to stroke his smooth oiled chest. He reached inside his thong with one hand, while holding an aerosol of shaving cream with the other, pulled it away to reveal his very large cock and immediately sprayed foam all over his shaved pubic area. I didn't know whether to be shocked or titillated but the sight of an almost naked man with shaving foam dripping from his swinging dick made me laugh so much I almost cried. As he made his way back through the crowd, he pushed past Karen who reached down and patted his pert bottom, much to my astonished amusement - gentility and sophistication were her norms.

There was a pause for us to buy more drinks and then the second stripper appeared, dressed as a fireman. "Bit obvious isn't it?" I whispered to Karen who shushed me. Clearly she was having a great time. This man was much older but had the most amazing body that he was very happy to teasingly show us as he slowly stripped. He was much more into interaction with the audience and wandered around in his black leather thong, fireman's helmet and boots, lap dancing to some of his audience who'd been lucky enough to find a ringside seat. I thanked my lucky stars that I was standing as I didn't think I'd have coped with an all but naked male bottom, albeit very well waxed and oiled, in such close proximity. Eventually he made his way back to the bar and amidst encouraging shouts and whistles, pulled away his thong. I glanced at Karen who looked at me wide-eyed. Neither of us had ever seen such an enormous cock.

"Makes your eyes water, doesn't it?" Karen had to shout to be heard and a few of the women standing next to us grinned.

This man also used shaving foam and as he swung himself from side to side some of the foam spattered onto some of the onlookers. As I watched I thought how very unsexy it all was.

There was an interval where nibbles were served and more drinks were bought. "Enjoying yourself?" I asked Karen tentatively. She'd just decided not to drive home, so was on her third glass of wine.

"It's such fun. I've not laughed so much for ages," was her response. I stifled a sigh. I'd have been more than happy to leave, but the last thing I wanted to do was be a party pooper, so I plastered a big smile on my face and tried to get into the groove.

The younger stripper reappeared twenty minutes later, this time dressed as a gladiator and the same routine followed. However, this time he invited a tall blonde to stand behind him and massage his chest as he swung from side to side. I took a step back to make sure that if he wanted a second volunteer it wouldn't be me. His thong was tan leather with bright studs that caught the light as he moved. More shaving foam was used as he bared himself. I found it so ridiculous I couldn't stop laughing and the thought that if men laughed at women as we were laughing at men that evening, there'd be an outcry, flashed through my mind.

The final act of the night was the older man who came out dressed in white just like Richard Gere in An Officer and a Gentleman. I leaned forward. Now that, I thought to myself, was a very sexy outfit and for the first time that evening I felt myself get caught up in the moment. When he passed close to me having removed his jacket, I reached out and brushed my fingertips over his smooth glistening shoulder. His thong was white which turned blue under the ultra-violet spotlight, making his tanned skin look even darker and when he eventually stripped it away, there was a collective gasp. He looked even bigger than before and this time when he used the foam, there was less laughter.

As he left the bar, we all applauded loudly. The last act was well worth being there for and I said as much to Karen as we stood at the bar to get another drink. She grinned at me. "So it wasn't all a waste of time then?"

I shook my head. "They were both very well endowed, weren't they?"

"Elastic bands," she said succinctly. I raised my eyebrows.

"Oh don't be silly Lucie. They use elastic bands to make sure they remain - impressive."

"Well, the last act was certainly - impressive," I said and we laughed.

I was woken from a deep sleep on Saturday morning and as I groped for my ringing mobile saw that it was just after nine thirty. "Hello?" I really wasn't in the mood for conversation.

"Lucie? Are you alright? Is it a bad time to talk?"

"Phil? No, I'm fine. You woke me up. Just give me a moment to get my brain in gear."

"I'm so sorry Lucie. Shall I call you back?"

I blinked the sleep out of my eyes. "No, no Phil. I'm awake now." And I sat up to make myself concentrate.

"It's silly really. I woke up myself only about an hour ago, thinking of you. Weird feeling that. I just thought it would be good to talk with you. Is that ok?"

The next time I looked, I saw that it was nearly eleven. We'd been talking for well over an hour - about work, his dreams for the magazine, my dreams to get more eatery review work because I enjoyed it so much, Susie, Angus and Claudia, his sister and her recent traumas, so many things. All the time it had felt like an easy and relaxed conversation between two people who had an understanding and empathy with and for each other.

"I suppose I'd better let you get up" he said eventually.

"Well, I guess I ought to get dressed and face the day."

And with that we said our goodbyes. In the shower, as the hot water cascaded down my back, I reflected on the past hour or so. I'd always felt comfortable with Phil but after this morning's chat felt much more - a real connection. It now felt that our friendship, relationship, whatever it was, had reached a deeper level and that thought kept a smile on my face all day.

I'd planned a quiet day for Sunday so after enjoying a lie-in, I walked to the nearest shop to buy the Sunday papers which I read in front of the fire. The cats were clearly delighted with my plans and made themselves comfortable on their respective chairs. In the afternoon I checked my emails and saw one from Jean-Michel who told me that he'd been cleaning the flat and found one of my earrings under the bed. 'I think I should keep it safe to make sure you come and visit again. Perhaps in the New Year?' he'd written. I replied that of course I'd be back, if only to pick up my earring and smiled as the email left my laptop.

The programme for Tony ran on Tuesday, Wednesday and Thursday so I had only Monday to make sure that everything was ready for the ensuing three days. The sessions ran very smoothly and it was clear that the delegates found what was being discussed useful and beneficial. Tony came in on the Wednesday afternoon and started off just sitting in, but I soon involved him with the activities which he said he thoroughly enjoyed.

At the end of Thursday, I glanced at my mobile which had been on silent for the day. I saw a text from Phil, asking if I was free on Saturday to join him for a chocolate demonstration and lunch at the home of the redoubtable Pudding Club in Mickleton. It was chocolate so how could I refuse? As I sent my reply I smiled. An afternoon with chocolate and Phil seemed like a wonderful combination.

Despite being very tired on Thursday evening, Karen wouldn't take no for an answer, so we went to Zumba which was, as always, enjoyable, albeit challenging. Of course we went to the One Elm for our usual beers and catch-ups. I told them about Phil's invitation for a chocolatey lunch on Saturday, the wonderful lunch in London where I'd met his business partners, the kiss in the taxi and our long conversation the previous Saturday. "I think he really likes me," I said and everyone nodded vigorously, "but I think it's just that. I write for him occasionally, we have things in common and get on really well. He's been kind of hinting that he wants to see more of me but that's it - just hints."

Just go along, have a great time and see what happens on Saturday was everyone's opinion. "And we want to know all about it," Sara added.

I sighed. I knew that we would have a good time together and wondered for the umpteenth time whether I wanted more or not. And as I did so, Jean-Michel came into my mind.

Judy told us that she and Ross had managed a couple of days away on the pretext of attending a conference. She was so delightedly happy that it was impossible to be disapproving but as she talked about the wonderful times they'd shared, Karen and I exchanged glances. "I tend to sleep very badly but there we were, sleeping on the first night having made the most wonderful love ever. Anyway, he moved which woke me up, rolled over, kissed me, said 'I love you', then rolled back and was asleep in seconds. I spent the next hour or so watching him sleep. It was so romantic." She stopped and gazed into the middle distance, obviously reliving the moment.

"I found out that my husband had been deceiving me for almost a year with the same woman," Gillian said pensively as Judy finished. "I was in my late forties and our children were only teenagers. I could have kicked him out, wanted to in fact, but felt I'd invested too much to give up without a fight. It took over a year but we ended up stronger than before in a place of calm and, funnily enough, trust. He never cheated again." She turned to Judy. "Do be careful my dear. If this man hasn't left his wife in the year or so you've been together, he probably won't. Why would he?" She paused. "And the truth is that even if he does leave her and you end up together, you'll always be wondering if he's doing to you what he did to her. Leopards rarely change their spots, you know."

Judy stared at Gillian wordlessly and then got to her feet and walked out. "I'm sorry that I upset her." Gillian didn't look sorry. "But I felt I had to say it the way it is."

And much as we felt for Judy, we all agreed with Gillian.

I was still thinking about Judy on Friday morning and reflected on my own situation. I'd recently spent four wonderful days with a charming, sexy man and was about to spend the next day with someone else. Was I any different to Judy? I met Anita for a drink on her way home from work and asked for her opinion. "Don't be silly. Of course you're different," was Anita's unambiguous judgement. "You're not in a committed relationship with Jean-Michel, or Phil for that matter. Cheating is when you're with someone and deliberately deceive them and you're not doing that. You're," she stopped to think for a moment, "playing the field a bit. And you're single. That's very different to having a relationship with someone who's married." I rang Karen later that evening and asked for her view and when she echoed what Anita had said, I felt validated and comforted.

Phil and I had agreed to meet at the Three Ways at eleven. I pulled onto the car park and saw him standing at the door waving at me.

"Lucie, lovely to see you," he said, kissing me lightly on the lips. We went straight into the dining room where there was a demonstration of how to work chocolate, followed by a few sample dishes all featuring chocolate as one of the ingredients, which we tasted. They were all delicious albeit, in some cases, slightly odd. After an hour, we strolled into the cocktail bar and enjoyed a glass of champagne before returning to the dining room for lunch. Although there were dishes with chocolate, we both decided to have a more traditional prawn cocktail followed by a light chicken and pineapple casserole. Neither of us wanted a dessert so we returned to the lounge to drink coffee.

"Let's go for a walk," he suggested so we strolled round the village arm in arm in the gathering gloom, returning to the hotel in the dark. We agreed to have some tea and once ordered he disappeared for a few minutes. "This evening is usually for weekend guests only but I've managed to book us in for dinner. It looks as if it'll be fun. Care to join me?"

"I'd love to."

At about seven, other chocolate aficionados came down to the lounge and we were then invited to enjoy cocktails, made with chocolate of course. I chose a white chocolatini that was made with vanilla vodka which I didn't know existed, white chocolate liqueur and cream which was stickily delicious. Phil chose chilli-spiked hot chocolate which had a large slug of spiced rum. When tasting each other's drinks, I gasped at the heat of the chillies in his cocktail which made him laugh.

As with the Pudding Club, we were encouraged to sit with other diners so we joined four other people. There was a married couple from Manchester who were celebrating their twenty-seventh wedding anniversary, and another couple who came from London and had been together for just over six months, having met through an online dating website. All four of them were very interested to hear about Phil's venture so we spent some time talking about that as well as discussing the pros and cons of the menu.

Phil and I had agreed to at least taste each other's dishes. I'd chosen scallops which were served on a bed of buttery leeks with a dark chocolate sauce and were sublime. Phil had chosen a risotto which was unctuously mellow with a grating of dark chocolate and coarsely ground black pepper which blended surprisingly well with the mushrooms, parsley and rocket.

We moved on to rabbit in chocolate and brandy sauce, an unlikely sounding combination but one that I failed to defend against Phil's invasive fork so I moved across to his salmon with white chocolate and pink peppercorn sauce which was, I thought, unexpectedly good. The others at our table had ordered chilli with dark chocolate, pork with cocoa balsamic and chilli, venison with white chocolate and a chocolatey lamb stew. It all looked scrumptious, so Phil and I negotiated hard and persuaded them to share. By the end of the second course, we were all very relaxed and giggly with each other.

"So, you two work together, do you?" I was asked.

I nodded. "We met at the beginning of the year and started working together in the summer. I love it. I get to eat wonderful food and then share what I think about it with lots of other foodies ..."

"She's very good," Phil broke in. "Has real insight into what makes food engaging and is able to explain dishes without sounding patronising - know what I mean?"

The others nodded and I noticed the older man wink at me which made me feel a little uncomfortable.

We were interrupted by the waiter coming over with the dessert menu where the men were amused by our feminine oohs and ahs over the offerings. After much debate, it was decided that we would order all seven sweets and sample all of them and as we did so our waiter's smiling amusement was obvious. All the puddings were placed in the middle of the table and we seriously and painstakingly sampled all of them: the creamy white chocolate crème brûlée, the fluffy chocolate soufflé, the succulent chocolate ricotta figs, the wonderfully soft chocolate, pistachio and nougat semi-freddo, the chilly chocolate sorbet, the spicily double chocolate cardamom pot and finally the silky dark chocolate tart drizzled with white chocolate. All were exceptional and we were very hard pushed to decide which was our favourite, but happily spent nearly half an hour tasting and debating the finer points of each one.

Hot chocolate or mocha coffee was on offer so we sat chatting at our table for another hour or so. Eventually, the couple from London said goodnight and the other couple followed shortly afterwards. "I suppose I should make a move too." I rose to my feet reluctantly.

I'd been aware that I was driving and so, after the lunchtime champagne, chocolate cocktail and one small glass of red with dinner, I'd moved onto sparkling water. Unusually Phil had not done the same, and swayed very slightly as he got to his feet. He fumbled in his pocket and pulled out his car keys. I looked at him. "Look, I don't want to nag, but do you think you should be driving?"

He looked thoughtful for a moment and then nodded. "You're right Lucie. I'll book in." He grinned. "Want to join me?"

I stared at him. "Really?" I hoped he could tell that I wasn't being serious.

He laughed. "Just kidding."

It seemed that the chocolate weekends were extremely popular so the hotel was fully booked. "I can sleep in the car," was his answer to his dilemma.

"You can't do that, it's freezing cold. Look, why not come home with me and I'll bring you back tomorrow morning." He raised a quizzical eyebrow. "The spare bed's made up," I added firmly as I opened the car and started up.

The journey back to Stratford took about fifteen minutes during which time Phil apologised at least eight times. Each time I told him not to be silly and that I didn't mind at all. As always, the cats were waiting outside and rushed through the door as I opened it. They then circled round Phil. "They're checking you out."

"I like cats." He bent to make friends with them.

"Tea or coffee?" I asked.

He followed me into the kitchen and looked round approvingly. "Nice, very nice. Much as I'd expected." He wandered round, looking at my favourite pans high up on the stainless steel rack, the array of utensils and knives and then the three shelves crammed with cookery books in the dining room.

"Tea or coffee?" I repeated patiently.

"Coffee please. I don't suppose you've got a little nightcap to go with it, have you?"

I was about to say that I thought he'd probably had enough to drink but thought better of it so looked in the cupboard where I knew there was a bottle of Boulard Calvados Pays d'Auge that I'd brought back from my trip to France with Di and held it up. "This ok?"

He took the unopened bottle from me and looked at the label that boasted three apples. "This is excellent, Lucie. You sure you don't mind us cracking into it?"

We went into the sitting room and I quickly lit the fire that, unusually, was already laid so just needed a match to start the flames spitting round the kindling. As soon as he sat, one of the cats jumped up and settled himself on his lap which made me smile. We talked our way through two coffees, several glasses of the aromatic apple brandy and half a packet of chocolate biscuits until, at about two thirty, we agreed that it was time to retire. I showed him into the small spare room, gave him a towel and a new toothbrush I'd found in the bathroom and wished him goodnight, but felt a distinct flutter when he thanked me with a kiss.

It felt very strange to know that there was just a wall separating us and I found it hard to settle but soon tiredness overtook me and I fell asleep. It was dark when I awoke and as I peered at my mobile, could see that it was just after six thirty. I wriggled in bed, trying to get comfortable but the more I did the more awake I felt. I slid out of bed to go to the bathroom and as I padded across the landing, heard nothing. I had a pee and washed my hands and face, rubbing the smudged makeup from my eyes, hoping that after this small fresh-up I'd be able to get more sleep.

As I stepped onto the small landing and took the first step towards my bedroom, the spare room door opened and Phil faced me. I took another step and he moved forward so we were only a matter of inches away from each other. With an almost inaudible sigh he reached up with one hand and ran his fingertips down my left cheek. Then, with his hand now curved round the back of my neck, he pulled me to him and lightly kissed my cheek, chin and lips. My left hand was now resting on his waist and our bodies were less than an inch apart. I could feel his warmth and was sure that he could hear my heart beating. Gazing into his eyes I reached down for his hand and took a small step towards my bedroom. His eyes widened and I smiled. "Oh, I think so, don't you?" My voice was soft and husky. He looked slightly stunned and I half turned away from him, pushed the door wider open and stepped through, still holding his hand.

We stood at the side of my bed where, for the first time, I saw him look a little unsure. I took his face in both hands and tilted his head down a little so I could kiss his forehead, his temples, his eyes, his cheeks and finally his lips. We slowly explored each other's mouths, still standing with a fraction of an inch between us, but feeling rising heat.

He pushed the spaghetti straps of my nightdress off my shoulders, bent and ran his lips over my throat and shoulder. I leaned against him with my head thrown back and, for the first time, could feel the beginning of his arousal. I shivered, partly from cold and partly from anticipation and heard a very soft groan.

I pulled away from him and sat on the bed, gathering the duvet round me. Of course he joined me, and as we touched, stroked, fondled and caressed each other, our excitement built until I could hardly bear to wait any longer. When eventually the moment came, I held my breath as slowly, very slowly; he pushed himself into me and, holding my face, kissed me deeply as we rocked our bodies together. I couldn't believe it. It seemed that we were the perfect fit - the way he read my movements and responded to me. It felt as though we'd made love many times before and when at last his thrusts got faster and faster I was tipped into glorious spasms that triggered his which in turn made me tumble into more shudders of mindless pleasure.

We stayed locked together for a few more moments until the beginnings of cramp made me move and he reluctantly opened his arms. I could feel him staring at me as I rubbed the cramp away and when I looked over my shoulder at him, thought I saw a glint of moisture in his eyes.

"So often wondered what going to bed with you would be like," he murmured as he reached up to pull me down to him again. I nestled next to him and closed my eyes.

"Are you going to let me use your kitchen?"

"What? Why?" I must have moved because I felt his arm tighten round me.

"I want to make you breakfast. May I?"

"I'm not sure what's in the fridge ..." I started to sit up, automatically running through the contents in my mind's eye.

"No, no. You've missed the point. I make breakfast while you stay in bed. I bring breakfast up to you while you're all warm and sleepy, we eat and then I make love to you for the rest of the morning." My toes curled.

So, despite my very mild protestations about helping him in the kitchen, I stayed luxuriating in bed while he left me, reappearing about ten minutes later with the Sunday papers tucked under one arm and a mug of coffee. "Just to keep you going for a little longer," he said as he disappeared. I sipped the coffee and dipped into the papers until he reappeared with a large tray of orange juice, coffee and softly poached eggs on toast topped with a scattering of crumbled black pudding sitting in a pool of pale yellow, freshly made hollandaise sauce. It was as delectable as it looked and I ate slowly, wanting to savour every last mouthful.

We finished breakfast and I lay back, stretching as I did so. He loaded the tray with our debris and put it on the floor. "So, papers bought, papers read a bit, breakfast made, breakfast eaten ..." he ticked the list off on his fingers. "I'm sure there was something else I was going to do." He looked at me questioningly and I gazed back at him, trying to look as inscrutable as possible. He frowned. "I just can't think what it was ..." I remained silent while we locked eyes and started to feel a little tingle in the pit of my stomach. "Hmmm, now what on earth could it be?" Almost absent-mindedly he ran his fingertips from the inside of my right wrist up my arm and as he was just past my elbow, "Raise your arm please," and continued up to my shoulder. I left my arm raised as he continued up my neck, then bent my head, caught his forefinger in my mouth and softly bit it. When I released him, he leaned back slightly and looked into my eyes. "Tell me what you want me to do."

I stared at him for a moment in disbelief. The memory of Richard saying the same words to me, but never really meaning it, flashed into my mind and I wondered if Phil would be the same. Unbelievably and gloriously he wasn't. I gently touched his mouth with my forefinger and then held it up. "See this?" He nodded. "Everywhere this finger goes, your mouth should follow." Very slowly I traced my finger down my throat, between and then round each breast, down to my hips and then, raising one leg up high, down the outside of my thigh to my knee and back up the inside of my thigh. I skirted my crotch and returned up my side back to my right breast and circled the nipple. He followed obediently, kissing, licking and nibbling his way round my body while I squirmed in delight.

"And now my back. Please," I murmured, and without lifting his lips from my skin, he slowly and gently helped me to roll onto my front. He straddled me while gaving the nape of my neck, my shoulders and my upper back the same treatment of kisses and soft bites. I could feel the heaviness of his cock resting on me and involuntarily arched my back. I wanted him so much but equally didn't want these wonderful tingling sensations to stop - the tension made me whimper. He lifted his head. "And now?" His voice was low and when I didn't reply, "I'm only going to do what you tell me to."

I tucked my hands under my shoulders and lifted myself up, pushing him away, so that I was on my hands and knees and as I did so suddenly felt ridiculously self-conscious and shy. He ran his hand down my back, over my bottom and the backs of my thighs. "Say it Lucie, just say what you want."

I felt tears threatening and swallowed the sob that was hovering at the back of my throat. Turning my head I saw him gazing at me, he didn't look repulsed at my body or even amused. I saw nothing but desire and lust. "You've been such a very good boy," he smiled and licked his lips, "that I think you should fuck me right now." And he did with a strength and passion that literally knocked me flat into the bed but didn't stop until we'd cried and yelped into release.

We stayed in bed for the rest of the morning and made softer, gentler love once more before reluctantly agreeing that it was time to leave the sanctuary of the bedroom and face the rest of the day. As I stood under the hot shower, he watched me wash my hair and wrapped me in a towel when I stepped out, tenderly patting me dry before showering himself. I looked at myself when I'd dressed and done my hair and makeup and smiled in satisfaction. I looked as good as I felt.

The short drive back to the hotel felt slightly surreal as we talked business; he told me about more places he wanted me to review and where he saw the magazine in future. I was more than happy to join in these discussions but felt slightly bewildered after so many hours of intimacy. "Let me buy you lunch," he invited as I drew alongside his car.

"Well, that would be very nice, thank you."

There was a well-known pub just down the road so we strolled down and enjoyed a typical Sunday roast which was excellent. Talk remained business focused but on the short return walk back to our cars, he held my hand tightly and as we said goodbye I thought he would never let me go from his clinging embrace. "It's been the most wonderful weekend Lucie. Thank you so much." And with that he let me go, got into his car and drove away, leaving me wondering what had happened and, indeed, what the future held.

I was woken by someone ringing the front door bell and, blinking sleepily, stumbled out of bed. Bright sunshine flooded the room as I pulled the curtains open and I realised it was nearly nine o'clock. As I opened the front door, I saw a huge bouquet of flowers with a pair of denim-clad legs below. I thanked the smiling deliveryman and disbelievingly put the flowers on the dining table, filled every vase I could find with water and then re-read the card. 'I want you to smile every time you look at these because you'll be thinking of me and because I smile every time I think of you. Phil xx'. I read the card several more times before what he had written sank in. Minutes later almost every room in the house boasted an overflowing vase of beautiful flowers and the house smelled wonderful. I sat back with a cup of tea and gazed at the card again as the memory of the last two days washed over me.

I was still smiling as I showered, dressed and even though I wasn't planning to go out, put my makeup on with care. The first thing I did after booting up my laptop was to email Tony all the evaluations from the previous couple of weeks along with my invoice which, I'd calculated, would easily fund me through to the New Year. More emails to past and present clients were sent after which I sat back. There really wasn't much more I could do but I was confident that there'd be more work coming through in January if not before. Plus, of course, Phil would want more reviews from me. Just reviews? My little voice asked. You shush, I replied, it's far too early to say where we're heading, but I had an amazingly good feeling, especially after the weekend.

It was late Wednesday afternoon. I was half-dozing and half-watching daytime TV with the cats and jumped when the phone rang. It was Phil. "The last couple of days have been absolutely manic," was his explanation when I said that he sounded a bit frazzled. "Anyway, I was wondering if you're free, might you fancy a few days in Bath? We could see the sights, eat, drink and perhaps even ..." he paused and I giggled. "Sounds as if you agree with me." Suddenly he sounded more relaxed.

"That's a great idea Phil. I'd love to."

"Ok. I'll call you later," and with that he was gone.

I put the phone down, not quite knowing what to think or feel. I was delighted that he'd asked me, but confused about not knowing when or where. I needn't have worried. Half an hour later he called back and told me he'd booked us into a small boutique hotel from Friday to Monday this coming weekend. "Why not train it rather than drive?" he asked and I agreed that might be nice. "I'll call you back in a few minutes," and the phone went dead. True to his word, he rang again about ten minutes later. "Your tickets are booked. Be at Stratford station at about one to pick them up. You'll go into Birmingham, then onto Bristol where you'll have to change for Bath. You should arrive about half past four. Is that ok?"

"Lovely," was all I could think of saying and as I put the phone down I felt overwhelmed that he had taken charge of everything and, sinking back down on the sofa, started to think about what to pack.

By Thursday afternoon I'd managed to pack everything into one case but it had been a struggle. Karen came over to pick me up for our Zumba class with which I just about coped, but was relieved when we were settled at our usual table in the One Elm. Everyone seemed in a very upbeat mood and we giggled our way through more stories.

"I met this man," Sara started. "We'd seen each other a couple of times but with huge gaps inbetween dates so I wasn't taking him seriously. He was quite good company though, so I was happy to go on seeing him. Anyway, the last time we met, he drank a lot and the more he drank, the more suggestive he became. Eventually he said that there was nothing more he liked than looking down at a woman's well chiselled back as he fucked her and then ..." she stopped and looked at us. "He looked me straight in the eye and asked if I was good at it."

"What a cheek," Bev said through giggles. "What did you say?"

"I asked if he usually took up references ..."

She was interrupted by hoots of laughter and claps.

Debbie had joined us. We gathered that she had recently married for the second time and had met her Iain one stormy winter's afternoon while they were out walking their respective dogs. There had been an instant attraction and he'd come on very strong. Although she liked him a great deal she felt things were moving too fast. "So I said to him that I thought he ought to date other people. We still saw each other but only very occasionally. After about a year he came back to me and said 'Well, I've dated about sixty women in the last year but they just weren't you. So, what do you want me to do now?' " She smiled nostalgically. "What else could I do but love him? We moved in together in the next couple of months and married a year later. I thought that it was so romantic, him doing what I asked. A bit like the labours of Hercules, you know?"

"Makes you realise there's always hope, doesn't it?" was the consensus of opinion and we sighed collectively.

It was Sunita who brought us down and dirty as she told us about one of her boyfriends who happened to have a dog. "We were making out at his place. We played around a bit using a rabbit, stopped using it but didn't turn the thing off. It kind of vibrated itself off the bed and the next thing we heard was a loud cracking noise. It was the dog who thought it would be fun to try and kill the vibrator. By the time we rescued it, one of its ears had been chewed off ..." The mental picture was just too good - none of us could stop laughing as we imagined the scene.

"There was this man who insisted that I use a vibrator in front of him," Judith said. "I didn't mind sometimes but very quickly he'd get quite angry if I didn't and that felt really bad. He was really nice in all other respects but I just couldn't cope with him in bed so I finished it and left him and his vibrating friend to it." She sighed with a rueful smile.

Gillian leaned over and lightly touched her shoulder. "Never mind dear, there's no point in having a dick in your life just because it's got a dick. Is there?" She looked around as we applauded her sentiments and agreed with Judith that she'd been absolutely right to ditch vibrator-man.

Debbie smiled. "A friend of mine used to have a really big house, so decided to employ a cleaner for a few hours a week. She found a lovely girl who had just set up her own cleaning business which was great for both of them. She was a wonderful cleaner but there was one problem which was that she had terrible BO. My friend tried leaving all the windows open but that didn't work. Anyway, eventually she had to tackle her about it. The girl was terribly apologetic about it and explained that her husband wouldn't let her wash or use deodorant. He said that he loved her natural smell and it turned him on so much that whenever she washed, he'd get terribly depressed and couldn't get it up. She confessed that she didn't like it herself but that it was easier to keep her husband happy than confront him." We all agreed that as far as we were concerned, it would certainly be too high a price to pay to keep a bloke happy.

As our second beers arrived, I heard a familiar voice call my name and saw, to my surprise, that it was Tony who smilingly asked if he could join us. As he did, both Sunita and Sara looked intrigued. I introduced him to the group and asked Dallas to bring us another beer. I explained that Tony was the client I'd mentioned some time ago. "I was in Stratford and thought that I'd pop in to see you," he said. I noticed some exchanged glances. We talked about this and that until he excused himself and left.

"So tell," they chorused as he disappeared.

"Nothing to tell. I was amazed to see him." Everyone looked sceptical.

"He's rather nice," Sunita said slightly wistfully, Sara nodded her agreement.

I was about to say something when Tony reappeared, stood next to Karen, gave her his card with a smiling, "Do please drop me a text sometime," and disappeared again, leaving all of us open-mouthed.

"Not fair," Sunita said as we all laughed and looked at Karen enquiringly. She looked back at us, shrugged and refused to be drawn on what she was thinking.

She remained as tight lipped on the subject as she drove me home, but asked me lots of questions about him. "He's a wonderful client, very supportive and always appreciative of what I've been doing. I like him. He seems a really nice man but honestly Karen, I can't say more than that." She nodded and looked thoughtful but when I asked her what she was going to do, she simply smiled a sphinx-like smile.

An email from Jean-Michel arrived early on Friday morning. He said that he was sorry that he'd not been in touch but not only was he very busy but his aunt had collapsed and was in hospital so he'd been running all over the place. However, he was still thinking of me and could we please keep in touch. I emailed back saying that I hoped his aunt would soon be much better and of course we'd keep in touch. I felt slightly confused. We'd enjoyed a wonderful interlude together but weren't in anything like a committed relationship so any future, romantic or not, seemed extremely unlikely.

I felt slightly distracted as I checked my case to ensure that I had everything but, as Phil had asked, I was at Stratford station just after one where I picked up my tickets. I was at Birmingham Snow Hill station shortly before two and found, to my astonished delight, that the rest of the journey had been booked first class, so sat in splendid comfort for the next two hours. The change at Bristol was smooth and I arrived at Bath Spa to find Phil waiting for me with a large flat box tucked under one arm. "This is for you, but you can't open it yet." He had a slightly smug grin as we kissed hello.

"It's not that far but we'll take a taxi to save us carrying luggage." The journey took very few minutes as the hotel he'd chosen was less than a mile from the station. We alighted in a tree-lined street with large elegant houses. I looked up at Grays Boutique Hotel which I soon discovered was beautifully appointed and couldn't contain my gasp of appreciation as he opened the door to a large room which was decorated in shades of charcoal and white dominated by a king-sized sleigh bed covered in huge silk cushions.

"Glad you like it," was all he said as I exclaimed how lovely I thought the room was. "And now you can open this." He gave me the box he'd been carrying. Inside, carefully folded in white tissue paper, was a scarlet silk floor-length nightdress with a plunging lace neckline, underneath was a matching dressing gown. "I remember you wore red the first time I saw you and thought how stunning you looked." His voice was soft.

I smiled at the compliment. "Phil, they're beautiful, just beautiful. Thank you so much." I held both up against me and turned to him to kiss my thanks.

"I can't wait to see you in them but now I just want you naked." He paused. "Is that alright with you?"

I pretended to think while my heart started to beat faster and faster. "That seems like a very reasonable suggestion, Mr Ellis."

He laughed and lay back on the bed. "I'd quite like to watch if that's ok with you."

Thanking my lucky stars that I'd had the foresight to wear pretty underwear, I slowly shrugged off my jacket and sweater, and then sat on the bed to take off my boots. He reached towards me and I gently pushed his hand away. "No touching - yet." Obediently he moved his hand and watched as I unzipped my black trousers and, with my back towards him, peeled them down before turning to face him in my bra, panties and long scarf with roses which I'd left on. I ran my fingers through my hair and stood, legs slightly akimbo, with one hand on my hip. "And now?"

"Why don't you join me?" He patted the space next to him.

I slowly walked towards him, keeping my stomach as flat as possible and sat near him, pulling a couple of the large cushions close to hide myself a little. He gazed up at me and raised one hand, grazing his fingertips down my back so lightly it was almost as though I wasn't being touched. His hand returned to rest at his side. "Your turn." His voice was so low I barely heard it.

It was very clear that he wanted me to take charge so I turned towards him, leaned over and kissed him softly, then with a harder insistence while one hand unbuttoned his shirt and gently pulled it from the waistband of his trousers. Without taking my mouth from his, I managed to unbuckle his belt, open it and unzip him. I could tell that he wasn't going to help so I moved to the bottom of the bed, pulled off his shoes, socks, trousers and boxers before running my hands up the insides of his calves and thighs.

He moved to discard his jacket and shirt. "No, no, leave them on," I breathed as I let my mouth trace the route my hands had just taken. I could feel him staring down at me and as I took him into my mouth, heard a sigh. I love the feeling of power when giving a blow job and Phil's enthusiastic gasps and moans told me that he was very appreciative of my efforts. As he reached orgasm I could feel his hands in my hair but he needn't have worried, I wasn't about to move away.

As his breathing slowed, I crawled up the bed, kissing my way up his stomach, chest and throat to his mouth after which I sat up and looked down at him. I realised that I must have looked smug because he burst out laughing. "What do you want? Marks out of ten?"

I reached down and cupped his penis and balls very firmly. "You might want to be careful what you say next."

"Hint taken. Thirteen out of ten do you?"

I clapped my hands together gleefully and giggled. "That'll do fine. Thank you." He held up his arms and we cuddled down under the downy duvet talking nonsense softly but after about an hour agreed that dinner was probably a good idea. We showered and as I dressed in a long black skirt teamed with a fuchsia pink sweater, he nodded his smiling approval.

"I know where you'd like," he said as we left the secluded street and strolled down the hill. About fifteen minutes later we were standing in Milsom Place that boasted many fine Georgian buildings, one of them being Jamie Oliver's Italian restaurant. We agreed that eating on the balcony probably wasn't the best idea given that it had started to spit with rain, so were shown to a table where we made ourselves comfortable.

The menu was scarily comprehensive so we spent ages going through it discussing the different dishes. Eventually we managed to agree that we would share a starter that was billed as 'Jamie's Ultimate Sharing Plank' which included fennel salami, mortadella, prosciutto, spiced chicken liver pâté, pork scratchings with grissini and rustic bread to which we added cauliflower fritti, mozzarella and aged pecorino, crispy shallot rings, olives, pickles and crunchy kale slaw. We spent nearly an hour nibbling our way through the delicious morsels which were washed down with most of a bottle of Barbera.

Phil had decided on calves liver and bacon Italian style but as the emptied plank was taken away, I asked if my baked king scallops could be starter size. Both dishes were delicious as I discovered when we dipped into each other's plates and when we finished, we both sat back and sighed simultaneously.

"We have to at least look at the dessert menu," Phil said.

I nodded. "It would be rude not to, wouldn't it?" We giggled our agreement.

Again there was a very wide choice, but I couldn't resist the chocolate, pear and honeycomb pavlova and Phil felt the same about the sour cherry and almond tart after which we sipped rich dark coffee accompanied by semi-sweet Marsala.

I realised that we had spent about three hours at the table which had flown by. The rain had stopped as we stepped outside so, hand in hand, we meandered around the centre of Bath for a while before slowly making our way back to Grays.

As the streets become less crowded the further from the centre we went, we stopped to kiss several times so by the time we were back in our room, we just couldn't wait and, pulling each other's clothes off, dived into the softness of the bed where we tempestuously made love.

"Ought to take my makeup off," I murmured against his damp chest.

His arm tightened round me. "You're not going anywhere." So I stayed pressed against him until we awoke many hours later to pale daylight, in almost the same positions.

Tempting though it was to stay in bed, and that possibility was discussed, we concluded that we ought to spend some time exploring the city. So, after getting ready, we went down to the dining room where we saw an array of cereals and fruits on the breakfast bar. The menu offered a seductive selection of cooked breakfasts but I managed to restrain myself to a small plate of eggs royale and watched as Phil munched his way through a full English accompanied by toast and marmalade washed down with lots of coffee.

We wandered outside and made our way into the centre of the city, gazing into shop windows as we went. "There's where I found your nightdress," he said suddenly, "and you've not worn it yet, have you?" He pretended to look hurt.

"You've hardly given me a chance," I retorted and we mock argued about when and where I'd be wearing it

American-style, we bought take-away coffees and continued to wander the streets, sipping as we went, eventually ending up at the Roman Baths where we spent over an hour gazing at the Roman Temple, Roman Bath House and finally the Museum. As it was my first visit, I found everything fascinating, but Phil had been several times before so made an excellent guide and explained much of the history to me as we made our way through the various parts of the buildings. I laughed when he told me about the ancient curse tablets, most of which related to theft of clothes while people were bathing for the benefits of the spa, about King Bladud and his herds of pigs, allegedly suffering from leprosy, that had been cured by wallowing in the mud of the then Baths and how, although the Grand Pump Room had been instigated by Thomas Baldwin in 1789, it was the Victorians who had fully embraced the advantages of the spa in earnest.

As we made our way into the dining room of the Pump Rooms, I saw, to my delight, a trio who played a selection of music for the diners. Phil insisted that we should have champagne while we looked through the menu which offered an excellent selection of dishes. We spent quite a long time poring over the menu and talking about what was on offer but eventually I decided on pork and pistachio terrine with apple and plum chutney and a warmed beetroot loaf followed by roasted sea bream with wilted spinach, gnocchi and mussel butter sauce. Phil chose grilled red mullet with warmed tomato and an olive tapenade followed by a pot roast ham hock with a potato rostie, cabbage and parsley sauce. We again shared our dishes as usual which now felt perfectly natural as did laughing at the same things and appreciating the music together.

Careful, the little voice in my head warned me, you'll be falling in love with him, won't you?

I think I already had - I really had.

Even though neither of us was hungry, we couldn't resist the dessert menu and once seen, it had to be ordered from. The caramelized banana and coconut ice cream with peanut brittle and steamed lemon and ginger sponge served with crème anglaise won the day and delectable they were too. Excellent coffee followed. Phil absent-mindedly caressed my fingers in time to the music as we relaxed after what had been an exceptional meal.

It was after three when we left the Pump Rooms and wandered back towards the main streets where we found a large Waterstones bookshop. We stayed for a short while before wandering on to find, to our joy, an independent bookshop called Good Buy Books. Too good to resist we thought, so spent a very happy hour in there. We wanted another coffee so reluctantly left, only to find another bookshop to entrance us - Mr B's Emporium of Reading Delights, where we stayed until we were politely thrown out just after six. Phil had bought foodie books in all the shops and I found a battered first edition entitled 'Women Writing about Money' from 1820. For Susie, I bought 'Costume Jewellery in Vogue', knowing how much she enjoyed her ongoing subscription to that magazine. We both were beaming by the end of the afternoon, albeit weighed down by three heavy carrier bags.

Rather than lug our books around, we returned to Grays and, by unspoken agreement, simply left the books in our rooms before going downstairs to relax in the spacious cream lounge and glance through the papers and magazines on offer. Phil had mentioned a wonderful Moroccan restaurant called the Tagine Zhor so we made our way there for about eight o'clock.

It was just like walking into North Africa. The walls were dark terracotta, there were dusky shades on the lights which gave an atmospheric ambiance, lots of flickering candles which gave each table a warm glow, many Moroccan pictures and mirrors festooned the walls and plush cushions were piled on the chairs. The staff were warmly welcoming. We were shown to a small secluded table and left to scan the huge menu. "I'm in your hands with this," I told him. "I know so little about Moroccan food."

"I like the idea that you're in my hands."

I tingled.

He returned to look at the menu in earnest while I reflected on the way he pushed his reading glasses down his nose so when he looked at me he was peering over the top of the frames. I smiled. "Shall we have a sharing starter?" he suddenly asked.

"Your choice. I'll go along with whatever you suggest."

"I might well hold you to that."

I tingled some more.

The starter was sublime - a selection of meats ranging from a Moroccan lamb sausage to spicy chicken wings and accompanying falafel, hummus, mushrooms, aubergines, other vegetables and lots of spicy dips. It was all beautifully presented and absolutely delicious. In our enthusiasm to share, we ended up feeding each other which was erotic beyond belief and when, as we were finishing the last of the platter, I held his hand and licked baba ganoush from his fingers, I could tell the effect my actions were having on him.

He'd ordered a lamb tagine with caramelised prunes which had been slow cooked in saffron, ginger and cinnamon and served with eggs poached in the sauce, sprinkled with roasted almonds and sesame, and a traditional Moroccan chicken and couscous dish incorporating many different vegetables with chickpeas and raisins, harissa, and a pungently delicate sauce which was served separately. We ate very slowly and drank slower still, talking all the time while the waiters smiled indulgently at us. It was as if we were kids in the first flush of love, unable to keep our hands off each other. We intertwined our fingers as we talked and occasionally dropped our hands to touch each other lightly under the table. We ate from each other's forks which was unbelievably intimate and I never wanted it to end.

Sticky baklava and thick, black, nutty Turkish coffee followed and yet more red wine as we held hands and continued to talk. "You are the most amazing woman," he said softly, kissing my fingertips. "I never thought I'd be able to feel this way again." I held my breath as he reached up and touched my cheek. "You must know that I'm in love you." I leaned towards him and we kissed with a depth of emotion that almost brought me to tears.

We didn't leave until about one in the morning and unhurriedly made our way back to Grays in cool, soft drizzle hand in hand, exchanging kisses every few moments. The minute we entered our room, he held me very, very close and then, teasingly slowly, undressed me as if I was a precious parcel, caressing the bits of me that he exposed. Once naked, he pushed me onto the bed and quickly stripped. "Time to return the favour I think," he murmured and kissed my mouth, flicked his tongue into my ears which made me quiver, softly bit down my throat, my breasts, my stomach and then, gently pushing my legs apart, nuzzled and licked me from one shuddering orgasm to another until I pleaded with him to stop.

I awoke with Phil's arm lying heavily across me and managed to wriggle away from him as he slept, to go to the bathroom. I stared at myself under the bright light and tried to make sense of last night, which had been one of the most intense of my life. As I was showering, Phil came in, blearily rubbing the sleep from his eyes. "May I join you?" We stood under the hot water and soaped each other. It was comfortable and companionable which, in some ways, was so much more intimate than love making.

"What about somewhere different for breakfast?" he suggested as we dressed.

I looked up from drying my hair. "Absolutely. You lead, I'll follow."

He kissed the top of my damp head. "That's good to know."

Getting ready took slightly longer than usual but eventually we stood in the tree-lined street and set off towards the centre of Bath, ending up on North Parade from where he led me down a narrow passageway to a small frontage that boasted 'Sally Lunn's House' over the door. It was packed but we managed to find a small table by the window that had just become vacant. As we looked at the menu, Phil told me the history of the place. There had been a young Huguenot refugee called Solange Luyon who had fled to England in 1680 in an effort to escape persecution in France. She'd somehow ended up in Bath and managed to find work in this very bakery, although, in those days, the street was known as Lilliput Alley. Sally Lunn, as she was soon known, began baking what she knew best, a rich, generous brioche bun, which astonishingly accompanied both sweet and savoury. Very quickly, this bun became a very popular delicacy in Georgian England, and soon customers were flocking to the Lilliput Alley bakery, specifically requesting the Sally Lunn bun.

I sat listening to him, my chin cupped in both hands, menu forgotten, until he realised I was gazing at him as he talked. He stopped suddenly, looking slightly self-conscious. "I don't mean to bore you ..." he started.

I put my hand on his. "You know I adore talking about food and hearing about the history of a place like this is fascinating. Do go on."

He laughed. "Let's order," and we went on to discuss what we fancied for brunch. The waitress told us that most dishes were half a bun which, she assured us, was plenty for the average appetite.

"We usually use the tops for sweet toppings and the bottoms for savoury," she added.

With that in mind, I ordered the scrambled breakfast which consisted of three eggs on a toasted half bun with a refillable pot of tea for one and Phil chose the top of a bun topped with cinnamon butter with a refillable pot of coffee. We certainly weren't disappointed when our brunches arrived. They were very large and as first the savoury and then the sweet were shared, we agreed that the part bread/part cake was a match made in heaven. It was clear that everyone in the place was of similar mind, all looking very content and satisfied. We spent a happy hour or so there but eventually we wanted to move on and, having settled on visiting the Royal Terrace, strolled towards Victoria Park.

I wasn't prepared for the sheer scale of the thirty Georgian terraced houses that lay before me; the almost white stone gleamed in the weak sunshine. It looked strangely familiar as many dramas including The Duchess and Jane Austen's Persuasion had been filmed there in recent years. We made our way to Number One which housed a museum, decorated and furnished in the style of the late seventeen hundreds. I found it enthralling, much as I'd been captivated by the Wallace Collection near Marylebone the previous year, and was more than happy to spend a couple of hours there. After such an enormous brunch we certainly didn't want lunch but when, just after three, Phil suggested we have afternoon tea in the Royal Crescent Hotel, I was quick to agree. An hour or so later, we stood outside and I could see that there were twinkling lights in nearly every window so the whole crescent glittered in the gathering gloom.

We started to make our way towards the city centre again. "I know we don't want to eat just yet ..." Phil started.

"We absolutely don't," I said firmly.

"But we will later," he continued. "What do you fancy?"

I stopped to think for a moment. "What do I fancy? Well ..." I stood still and looked at him. "Why don't we have a picnic?"

He looked puzzled. "It's a bit cold for that isn't it?"

"I wasn't thinking of picnicking in the park." I looked into his eyes and ran my fingers down his arm. "More of a picnic in slightly more ..." I hesitated for a moment, "horizontal comfort."

So, that idea having been painstakingly explored and established, we returned to Jamie's Italian where we bought boxes of salads, olives, bread and bread sticks, dips, pâté and some cheeses along with champagne, Merlot, orange juice sparkling water and a couple of sweets that would cope with not being in the fridge for a while - a lemon meringue cheesecake and what was billed as an 'epic' brownie. Laden with all our goodies, we made our slow way back to Grays. We passed a traditional-looking pub, the Old Green Tree, and at Phil's suggestion, stopped for a quick drink. He talked about the pleasure of waiting for treats. "I rather like deferred gratification," he explained over his beer. "Don't you think the waiting makes whatever you're waiting for even better?" I had to agree.

The immaculate bedroom that was now becoming so familiar opened before us. Phil had asked reception if someone would bring in a small folding table, two dining chairs, linen, glasses and cutlery. "Think I'll change for dinner," I murmured and went into the bathroom where I had a very quick shower, freshened my makeup, spritzed more perfume into my hair and dressed in Phil's gift which, to my delighted surprise, fitted perfectly. The scarlet silk and lace felt soft on my skin and as I twirled round, the long skirt flared out, reminiscent of fifties glamour. It all felt slightly breath-taking and, as I looked at myself in the mirror, had to admit that I looked pretty good.

I opened the door to see Phil standing at the window, gazing out. He heard me and turned. His reaction was everything I could have wished for and as I swished my way towards him, could see his eyes widen. I put my hands very lightly on his shoulders and kissed his cheek. I felt his hands on my waist and as he pulled me into him, took a small step back. "'Deferred gratification' I think you said," and he laughed.

I looked at the table. "Dinner not ready yet?" I tried to sound stern. "Tsk, tsk - what a bad boy."

He bowed his head. "I'm so sorry." He held a chair out for me. "Would you care to sit?"

I did so and watched as he busied himself, putting the food out and making sure our places were laid correctly. "Champagne please," I ordered after a few moments.

He dropped a fork. "Certainly," and throwing a towel over his arm to play waiter, deftly opened the chilled bottle and handed me a brimming glass.

"You may pour one for yourself." I was really getting into my role and thoroughly enjoying myself.

He poured another glass and went to sit down. "Really?" I raised an eyebrow.

He stood close to me as I held up my glass and we solemnly clinked. We sipped and I put down my glass. As I did so, he bent and caught my hand, turning it to kiss the palm. I tingled but pretended to be unmoved and picked up my glass again.

Holding his gaze, I took another sip and put my glass down again. "Closer please." I remained seated and, holding onto the front of his pink shirt, pulled him down to me. As his face drew close to mine, I stroked his cheek and then kissed him, skirting my tongue over his teeth and gently sucking his bottom lip. The moment I felt him respond, I drew back.

His crotch was almost at my eye level. I could see his burgeoning bulge and gently patted it. "Down boy, down." I wanted him to throw me on the bed but knew he wouldn't, not this time, so contented myself by turning the pat into a soft, rubbing caress. His hands balled into fists and I heard a soft groan.

I dropped my hand and slowly picked up my glass again, looking up at him enquiringly. "I wonder ..." I waited for all of ten seconds, "I wonder whether we should fuck before dinner. What do you think?" I leaned back in my chair and looked up at him.

He blinked and as he opened his mouth to reply, I stood up. "Now, I think. Follow me." And hooking my forefinger into the waistband of his trousers, led him towards the easy chair beside the bed where he raised his hand to touch my face.

I caught and held it firmly. "Mind my makeup. And my hair." And with that I half-turned away from him, leaning slightly over the back of the chair, glancing over my shoulder as I did so.

No-one could say that he couldn't take a hint. He scooped the wide skirt up to my waist, very tenderly bent me further over the back of the chair and, seconds after I heard him unzipping himself, penetrated me. I had to brace my hands on the seat of the chair as he fucked me. His excitement was infectious - I almost managed to keep up with him before his convulsive orgasm. Seconds later he withdrew and as I started to stand up, was pushed back down again as his hand stroked, rubbed and teased me into my own paroxysms of release. I remained bent over the chair, panting, and heard a very soft chuckle as he gently helped me straighten up.

"Will there be anything else?" He looked absolutely serious but his eyes were dancing.

"I shall expect dinner in exactly ten minutes," and with that I swept back into the bathroom where I freshened up again and reapplied my lipstick. I waited for a few minutes before returning to the table where as many dishes as the small space would allow had been laid out. He was sprawled in the easy chair, legs stretched out but as he saw me he rose to his feet, went over to the table and pulled a chair out for me.

I took my seat, glancing at him. "Thank you."

He remained standing silently next to me, towel draped over his arm until I looked up after all of a full minute. "Care to join me?" Those words seemed to be becoming a stock phrase for us. He nodded gravely and took the chair opposite me. I held up my empty glass and before I could say anything, it had been refilled.

I managed to keep up my alter ego for a little while longer but after a few minutes gave in so we sat side by side and, as in the Tagine Zhor, shared delicious morsels, talking nonstop, touching and kissing at every opportunity. Two hours sped past; we were now dipping into the sharp lemon meringue cheesecake and gooey brownie. Staring into each other's eyes, he held my hand and licked my fingers. I did the same to him. The tension between us intensified until I could barely breathe.

Unexpectedly he excused himself to go to the bathroom. A few seconds later I heard old fashioned dance music playing and as I turned my head saw him returning to me. "May I have this dance?"

I stood up. He took me in his arms and we danced. We held each other close - dancing, caressing, exchanging light kisses and as we twirled, my skirt flared out and curled round our legs. It was a different intensity and I loved it. I felt warm, feminine, desirable and beautiful.

"I want to make love to you," he murmured, "but I don't want this to end."

He held my chin, looked deep into my eyes and, for the first time that evening we kissed slowly and passionately. I melted against him. We slowly swayed past the window and I glanced outside - it had stopped raining and was now a bright, cloudless night, the moon shone down on the shiny streets. "Can we dance down there?"

He stopped and stared at me. "Where?"

I pointed towards the window. "Just for a few minutes. I want to dance under the moonlight. Shall we? Please?"

He stood still, looking incredulous for a moment and then realised that I was serious. Donning our coats, we ran downstairs into the cool of the night where he took me in his arms again and as we danced the length of the street and back again, he hummed 'You do something to me'. A passing taxi hooted at us and a couple walking on the other side of the street laughed and waved, but that apart we were on our own which was magical. It couldn't last though. I shivered as the cold crept under my coat to the thin silk and so, when we whirled to the front door and he suggested we should go back in, I had to agree.

We ran upstairs giggling like schoolchildren. As I took my coat off I shivered. "You need warming up." He disappeared into the bathroom leaving me standing alone and slightly bewildered. The sound of running water and a lovely hot soapy smell wafted into the room. A few moments later he reappeared, took my hand and gently pulled me towards him.

I lifted my face. "Not yet." He led me into the bathroom where he peeled the damp silk off my body and helped me into a foaming bath of bubbles. "You stay here while I get us a little drink." Moments later he returned with another bottle of champagne. He sat on the edge of the bath and filled two glasses.

I looked up at him and gave a cheeky smile. "I think there's just about room for two here. Want to join me?"

He didn't need asking twice. In a few seconds he'd joined me with such enthusiasm that water spilled over onto the gleaming floor. "We need to be careful; we don't want to cause a flood downstairs do we?"

He looked thoughtful. "So, slowly does it then?"

It was the first time I'd made love in a bath - it was mind-blowing. We sat facing each other and as he slowly lowered me onto his straining cock, we kissed and slid our hands over each other's warm, soapy bodies. I could barely contain the incredible sensations that washed over me and as we rocked, kissed, caressed and softly scratched, our excitement mounted until, despite our best endeavours, water splashed over the side which made us laugh as we cascaded into blissful ripples of release.

Afterwards we sat in bed, wrapped in fluffy white towels, sipping the rest of the champagne - touching, kissing and talking. Neither of us wanted the night to end but eventually tiredness overtook us so we exchanged towels for the duvet and cuddled each other into sleep.

We sat gazing at each other over Grays breakfast table. We'd arrived downstairs as late as we dared and lingered for as long as possible. "Perhaps you'd like to take coffee in the lounge," our smiling server suggested so we moved and sat for a while longer, finishing off our coffee and scanning the papers. I couldn't believe that the last four days had flown by so quickly. The thought of leaving what had become our grey and white sanctuary made me sad.

However, reality kicked in, so we rose to our feet and, holding hands, made our way back to our beautiful room. We packed silently and then hugged. "It's been the most wonderful weekend. Thank you so much," I murmured into his neck.

"I wish it could go on ..." he started and then, holding each other's faces, we kissed gently before picking up our cases and, without a backward glance, left.

He'd ordered a taxi to take us to the station for twelve thirty as my train left at one, his was half an hour later, "I want to wave you off, a bit like Brief Encounters," he said as we stood on the platform.

"They never meet again," I whispered as tears threatened.

"No, they didn't. But we will. I promise." He rained kisses on my cheeks, my eyes, my chin, my lips - I wanted it to last forever but all too soon my train was about to leave and, as I waved goodbye and saw him become smaller and smaller, still waving, the tears came.

A few minutes later, as I was composing myself, I heard ducks. 'We're a great team workwise and besides that you fuck like an angel. How can I let that go? I love you. Phil xx'

We pinged silly, flirty texts between us until, ten minutes later the train drew into Bristol's Temple Meads station and I had to change for Birmingham. As I settled myself into my first class seat I looked at my mobile and saw that I had a voicemail from him. Hearing his voice made me tingle. "Travel very safely Lucie. I need to focus on work now but can't wait to see you again. I'll call you later. I love you." I played and replayed that message several times throughout the journey and by the time I arrived home had a deep feeling of peace and hope.

True to his word, Phil called me that evening. Conversation was as easy on the phone as it was face to face and when eventually we said goodbye it felt that the future was bright.

I spent the next couple of days going through my training and teaching materials, updating bits and pieces. I rang Barbara to catch up with her news, all was going very well she said and although she was now incredibly busy, it would be good to meet up so we said we'd have tea on Saturday afternoon. I rang Annie but as she didn't pick up, left her a message suggesting that we catch up soon. I rang Anita, Pennie and Karen and whilst I didn't tell them any details, they could tell from my voice that I was buoyant and happy and were glad for me.

Karen came for me with the latest edition of 'Olive' and we went to Zumba which, for the first time, I felt I managed without falling in a heap. Of course we ended the session by going to the One Elm. As our first beers were brought over, Bev and Sara looked at Karen. "Well?" Karen looked bewildered. "You know, that man last week who gave you his card. When are you seeing him?"

Karen shrugged. "I've not been in touch with him."

We all looked cross in varying degrees and after a brief debate managed to persuade her to text him. "I'll text him tomorrow."

"You won't. Do it now." We hadn't expected Gillian to be quite so firm. Karen sighed and, with our help, drafted and then sent a brief text.

"There. You lot satisfied now?" She sounded slightly annoyed.

We sipped our drinks. I felt a little guilty that we'd put her under pressure but then her mobile chimed which showed her that a text had come through. It was Tony. We all looked a bit smug as she replied and a couple of texts later she sat back. "Ok, we're meeting for a lunchtime drink on Saturday." She was grinning as we clapped and cheered.

"And did you have a good weekend?" Sara asked me.

"Glorious. Just amazing." And I went on to tell them some of the highlights of the four days I'd spent with Phil. They sat in spellbound silence and when I told them how we'd danced on the last night there was a collective sigh. "I don't know where it's going but I've got a really good feeling," I concluded. There was a reflective silence and Sara sighed again.

Gillian could see that I didn't want to talk any more so she told us about her friend who'd become the dominatrix. "This was before she started her - business." We giggled. "Anyway, she'd met this man, really like him and he seemed to like her. They met several times. He'd been a perfect gentleman so she asked him over to her place for lunch one Sunday. They were enjoying the pudding when he smiled at her and then slid under the table. She thought he was ill but before she could move, felt him pulling her shoes off and sucking her toes. She heard him ask her to go on eating so she did and then he started rubbing her foot over his crotch. He came all over her foot, used his napkin to wipe her and then reappeared, asking for coffee. She was flabbergasted and demanded that he explain. He told her that he adored feet and preferred to have sex with them rather than anything else." We sat with our mouths open. "It didn't last," was Gillian's final remark which made us laugh.

Sunita looked sad as she told her story. "My oldest and dearest friend was engaged to Jas. He was lovely but did what he was told by his family who sent him off to India to get married ..." We gasped. "An arranged marriage," she explained, "so he went out there but didn't tell my friend about it - just said he was going out on family business. The first she knew about it was a couple of months later when he messaged her telling her he was married but really unhappy and if he came back to the UK would she have him back." She stopped for a moment, looking very upset. "She'd never stopped loving him but couldn't cope with the deceit so told him to stay with his wife. Hasn't heard from him for months now but it's made her very wary of trusting anyone again."

"Talking about deceit, let me tell you about a friend of mine," Sara said after we'd briefly talked about Sunita's friend and how right she had been. "She'd been seeing this man for a couple of years. A few months into their relationship he'd passed genital herpes on to her ..."

"What!" we chorused in disbelief.

"She told me it was an accident, he didn't mean to. I gather he apologised and she accepted his apology. Well, a year or so later she discovered that he was seeing someone else who he said was very keen on him. Apparently he told this other woman he was a carrier for herpes and she said it didn't matter. My friend said that was the thing that hurt her the most - he was protecting this other woman by telling her, yet he hadn't protected her. He got quite angry when she tackled him about it, telling her to get over it, loads of people had it and she shouldn't make such a fuss." We sat silently for a few moments, unable to think what to say.

"It's all very well having a go at deceitful men, but you have to remember that at the end of every lying, treacherous man's dick is a lying treacherous woman." Everyone stopped and looked at me. "Well, it's true," I said vehemently. "Takes two, doesn't it?" Of course they agreed and when, a little later, we said our goodbyes, we all were in reflective mood.

Friday passed in a haze of sociability. I guiltily realised that I hadn't seen Felicity for ages so we met in the theatre restaurant for a light lunch to catch up with each other's news. "I'm so pleased for you," was her comment after I'd told her about Phil. I glowed. The next two hours sped by as we gossiped about mutual friends, books we'd read and the pros and cons of some boots she was thinking of buying - the pros being that they looked superb - the cons being that they could be a lot more comfortable. We laughed as we agreed that even though we were of a 'certain age' the pull of glamour over sensible almost always won. And quite right too, was our final thought on the matter.

Barbara and I met at the One Elm late afternoon and cosied down by the fire. "It's all going so well. I'm working with Turnips a lot but also doing lots of wedding and birthday cakes too. It's nonstop which is exhausting but very good." I was delighted for her and said so. We then chatted about more personal things. She listened to me about Susie, Jean-Michel and Phil and I listened to her talk about her family, how she was continuing to cope with losing Tracy so tragically and how she had just met someone who seemed to be kind, caring and understanding. "I never thought I'd ever meet a man who would make me feel this way again," she said and blushed.

I hugged her. "I'm so pleased for you. You deserve this more than anyone I know."

It was just after seven when she left and I remained in the oversized leather chair finishing off my drink, gazing into the fire. "So this is where you are when I'm not around." I glanced up to see Phil looking down at me with an amused smile. He bent to kiss me and I felt what was becoming an all too familiar tingle. Before I could ask what he was doing in Stratford, he slid next to me so we were pressed close together and kissed me again.

"What are you doing here? How are you? Have you had a good week?" The questions tumbled out of my mouth and as I heard myself, I wished I didn't sound quite so gushing.

He laughed. "I have to be in Manchester tomorrow morning and was on my way when I wondered if you might be around." He ran his fingertips over the back of my hand. "Have you eaten? Do you fancy dinner?"

I wasn't particularly hungry but I certainly fancied dinner with him. "Would you like to have dinner at mine?"

His eyes widened. "Sample your cooking? I certainly would. Thank you Lucie." He looked like a small boy who'd been given a bicycle for Christmas.

Half an hour later I was delving into the fridge, hoping that something wonderful would present itself. I found a couple of pork fillets and minutes later had placed them in a shallow dish, to marinate in a silky mixture of olive oil, an egg and some salt. "Pork alla Milanese do you?" I asked. He nodded as he watched me and then, while the meat marinated, we sat in front of the fire, drank red wine and talked. Half an hour later, I dredged the marinated fillets in breadcrumbs and fried them, at the same time cooking some pasta which I ran through with butter and capers and then served both with a rocket salad dressed with my usual garlicky vinaigrette.

"So - you can write, you can cook, you're amazing in bed - is there no end to your talents?" he asked as he finished. I blushed and sipped more Merlot.

After dinner, we sat on each end of the sofa with a space between us for the cats, my feet up on his lap, while we drank coffee and Calvados. We talked, laughed and flirted while he gently stroked my feet. We'd established that he needed to be in Manchester by eleven the following morning. "So Mr Ellis, where were you thinking of laying your weary head?" I asked him.

"Guess I need to find a hotel." He paused. "What are your rates?"

We laughingly play-negotiated for a while and then, as the fire died down, slowly made our way upstairs, kissing on every step. We helped each other undress and snuggled under the warmth of the duvet, and slowly, very slowly and very gently fondled and caressed each other until neither of us could wait any longer. The piercing sweetness as he entered me almost brought me to tears and we tenderly rocked, kissed and held each other close. The connection was so strong; it felt as though we were melting into each other. Afterwards, we lay and murmured nonsense until the effort of talking was too much and we drifted to sleep.

This wonderfully tender love-making was in sharp contrast to an hour or so later when, after dozing together, I needed to go to the bathroom. I slid back into bed as quietly as I could, thinking he was still asleep but he wasn't. He ran his hands from my shoulders to my hips, griping me so tightly that a startled cry escaped me. He growled softly, biting the back of my neck. I arched and ground my hips, turning to kiss him but abruptly my head was pushed down into the pillow as another pillow was shoved under my stomach, raising my hips slightly. "Ready?" His voice was hoarse and low and as he pushed himself into me, I felt a couple of stinging slaps on my bottom. This wasn't gentle love-making, it was fast and furious fucking and when, with an explosive cry he came, I followed seconds later. He collapsed over my back, panting and remained still for a few moments before rolling off. He gently rubbed my back. "You ok?"

I giggled into the pillow and then turned to face him. "That was - unexpected." I paused. "I like the unexpected." And, leaning towards him I kissed and then softly bit his cheek.

Lying facing each other, we continued to touch and fondle, whispering what we wanted to do and have done. On his instructions, I reached down to grasp his semi-hardness and began a firm, slow rhythm that had him arching his back and closing his eyes. I watched him for a few moments and then breathed my instructions. He opened his eyes, obediently sliding his hand down my body. We stared at each other as we mutually masturbated - it was incredibly sexy as we brought each other almost to the point of orgasm twice before I begged him not to stop and we pantingly squirmed into blissful release.

He kissed me lightly. "What an amazing night. Goodnight Lucie. I love you."

"I love you Phil. Goodnight sweetheart."

It was a stormy morning with lashing rain that looked as if it was set for the day. "Do you really have to go to Manchester?" I asked as we ate bacon sandwiches in front of the fire I'd just lit.

"'Fraid so. It's a meeting that's taken forever to get sorted and I can't risk rescheduling." I nodded. "Why don't we have lunch on Sunday? I'll be coming back from Manchester in the morning. Let's go to your favourite place. Will you book us a table?"

He left an hour later with me promising to book us a table at the One Elm for Sunday lunch and him promising to drive safely.

After he'd left, I piled more logs onto the fire, made myself another cup of tea and settled down with a couple of magazines I'd bought earlier in the week. I was so tired, I fell asleep on the sofa, being woken up by Phil calling to tell me he'd arrived safely and was about to go into the meeting. "Wish me luck."

"You don't need luck. You'll knock their socks off. Go get 'em tiger."

That afternoon I emailed Di and Susie, missing them both. I watched a very old movie and nibbled on some popcorn I'd managed to make without it pinging all over the kitchen. I finished a crossword I'd been wrestling with all week. I wrote out my Christmas card list. It was a productive afternoon and I felt virtuously self-satisfied.

Karen called me just after eight, she sounded bubbly. "I met Tony for lunch. We got on so well, it was incredible. He's just left because he has to see his cousin but we're having lunch tomorrow."

"That's wonderful Karen. I thought you'd like him." We talked about the great time she'd had, how much they'd laughed, and how much she was looking forward to tomorrow.

We were on the phone for about half an hour but a few minutes after we'd said goodbye, the phone rang again. I picked up thinking that it was Karen again, but it was Annie who wanted to tell me that she was still seeing Roger but was feeling unsettled. "It's a bit hot and cold. Know what I mean?" I did indeed. "I think his head's somewhere else, his heart too if I'm being honest." There were a few seconds silence. "Has he been in touch with you?"

"He hasn't, no. And Annie, if he had I'd have been happy to talk to him but that would be all I promise you." I told her about Phil and my own cautious hopes. "I'm almost sure that we'll continue working together which is terrific of course, and it really seems that we'll continue seeing each other. We share so many things: food, writing, books, music and the sex is pretty amazing ..." I

407

heard Annie sigh. "Annie, you got what you wanted which was that he would show you some interest, take you out and maybe more. Has there been more?"

"Do you mean, have we slept together? Well, yes." There was another silence.

"Shall we have a coffee next week and have a proper talk? I'm sorry that things are tricky at the moment Annie. Wish I could wave a magic wand for you." We arranged to meet on Tuesday evening. As I put the phone down I felt a deep sadness for her that her hopes and dreams seemed to be crumbling away.

Phil and I met in the One Elm at twelve thirty. We were so pleased to see each other and couldn't stop smiling and exchanging light touches under the table. We both chose white onion soup with cheddar and crispy sage leaves followed by roast beef for Phil and roast lamb for me. As always, it was excellent. We were coming to the end of the course and vaguely thinking about the possibility of a dessert when his mobile rang. He glanced at it and suddenly his smile vanished. "Do excuse me Lucie, it's Marianne, I must take it." He was gone for over ten minutes.

On his return, he looked despondent and sat down heavily.

I reached over and held his hand. "Darling, what's wrong?"

He just looked at me and I suddenly had a cold feeling of foreboding. "Phil, who's Marianne?"

He looked at me. I could have sworn there were tears in his eyes. "Marianne's my wife."

I sat frozen and slowly drew my hand back. His eyes were downcast. "Phil, look at me." He didn't so I repeated it - I had to see what he was thinking. I took a deep breath. "Those days we had in Bath. The hotel, our picnic on the last night, the beautiful nightdress you bought me, all those days and nights we've had together ..." My voice was beginning to crack. "What other secrets do you have Phil?"

He looked up. "No other secrets Lucie, I promise you. I didn't tell you because I didn't think you'd understand or even want to listen to me ..." He paused for a moment and leaned over to take my hand. "I didn't bank on falling in love with you. Lucie, I love you. Please listen to me. Let me explain."

I sat silently as he told me that he'd been married to Marianne for fifteen years. They'd had their problems like most other couples, but the fact that they couldn't have children became a real issue between them. Just over three years ago, she'd told him she'd been having an affair with his best friend for the past year and that she was leaving. He was married as well and left his wife with their two small children to move up to Scotland with her. That was that as far as Phil was concerned and although he was devastated, buried himself in work. I nodded, that I well understood.

"It took me over two years to come to terms with what had happened but gradually I got over it and earlier this year, felt ready to move on, perhaps even find someone new." My mind flashed back to January when he'd given me his business card.

"About four months ago, she was diagnosed with early onset Alzheimer's," his voice was softer now. "Of course she was terribly shocked and felt completely overwhelmed. The man she left me for walked out on her saying that he couldn't and didn't want to cope with that. So now she's on her own up in Scotland where she doesn't know many people. She called me and I felt I had no option but to help her so I go and do what I can to support her." He looked at me pleadingly. "Lucie, she's desperate. I don't love her but I do care about her. I don't feel I can turn my back on her in her hour of need." He held my hand very tightly. "Do you understand?"

I took a deep breath. "I understand what you've said Phil. I understand that she's ill with a progressive disease that will gradually rob her of her independence. I understand that you feel you have to help her." He looked relieved and took a breath. "What I don't understand," I interrupted him, "was that you didn't tell me. That you felt it was alright to let me think you're single. That you've said that you love me. That I love you ..." I could feel tears on my cheeks but continued staring at him, "and that now you, the man who's said he loves me, has just told me that he's still married and feels he needs to care for his wife, a woman he chose not to divorce." My head bowed as more tears came.

"I can't lose you," I heard him say. "Please Lucie, can't we work this out?"

I raised my head. "I don't know Phil. I just don't know. I do know that I need some time to think."

"Is that saying we're over?"

"Phil, I don't know. I need to get my head round this. You've had months to come to terms with it."

He nodded, raised my hand to his mouth and kissed it. "You have to know that I love you. I'm not a player. I always thought you were attractive and interesting but now - well, I just can't imagine my life without you."

Of course I couldn't stay at the One Elm a minute longer. I wanted, needed, to get home where I felt safe, so I rose to my feet and despite his protestations, left him sitting at the table, scattered with our debris.

I was shaking when I opened the front door, feeling a myriad of mixed emotions: anger, uncertainty, disillusionment, sorrow, disappointment. The over-riding thought in my head was that it just seemed like more of the same and Richard's words 'it's just not good enough' came into my head as I gave in to bitter tears of fury and frustration.

Chapter 13 – December

Of course I didn't sleep so on Monday morning felt, and looked, terrible. I'd spent the whole night pacing the floor, drinking endless cups of tea and flipping from angry disbelief to heartaching sorrow, so by the time daylight broke I was exhausted. Not even a hot shower revived me. I slumped on the sofa with the cats looking up at me. They knew I was upset and tried to comfort me by pushing their heads against me, looking into my face and purring. "Fucking, fucking, fucking men," I whispered into their fur as I cuddled them. "I really thought I might have got it right this time." More tears spilled.

An hour later, having looked in the fridge and found precious little, I decided to go to the supermarket so pulled on a hat, applied bright red lipstick and went out. I filled my basket with some sensible food but spoiled it by adding a large box of chocolates and three bottles of wine. Sod it, I thought to myself as I searched in my handbag for my purse. My mobile was at the bottom of the bag and when I pressed the button it was dead - I'd forgotten to put it on charge.

I went home to cook a large bacon sandwich with lashings of ketchup which I devoured in record time. Why was it that when I was unhappy I ate, I asked myself. The answer came back - because food comfortingly dulled the pain at least for a few minutes - that was why. A scalding hot cup of coffee followed and I felt a little better.

I suddenly heard a succession of quacks from my mobile that I'd put on charge in the sitting room. There were over a dozen texts waiting to be read, all from Phil. In each one he apologised for not telling me his situation sooner, insisted that all he was doing was trying to support someone who was in a very dark place, reaffirmed that he loved me and begged me to at least talk to him about it, although he wanted and hoped that we would work something out so that we could be together. I read and reread each one through more tears. I then spent over half an hour wondering what to reply. I couldn't say that all would be ok - I doubted that it would. I couldn't tell him to fuck off - I cared too much. Eventually I sent: 'Thank you for your texts Phil. You have to realise what a shock your revelation was and how sad I am that you didn't feel you could tell me but I guess I kind of understand why you didn't. I have to ask myself if/when you'd have told me?

But nothing can take away the magic of the times we've spent together - there's no doubt we have a real connection - it's hard to break that. You have to understand how I feel - give me some time to come to terms with what's happening and if/how I can deal with it. L x'. I didn't know why I sent him a kiss but couldn't switch off my emotions nor, I told myself, should I.

He replied within a few moments saying that he was so sorry; he'd never meant to hurt me and again asking if we could talk. 'Please let's not keep texting - it's pointless. I need time to think - you probably do too. Leave me alone for a while. Lx'. I cried as I sent the second text. I didn't know whether I would ever see him again.

I felt a little better on Tuesday. Phil had obeyed me and my mobile remained text-free. I bought some Christmas cards and spent the afternoon writing them. I watched old movies on TV. I drank a bottle of wine and ate lots of chocolates. That night I slept.

Early on Wednesday morning I emailed Di. I didn't know when she would read it but it made me feel better to be in touch with her, even if it was one-sided. I told her what had happened and asked her advice and when I hit the send button, kept my fingers crossed that she would be in touch sooner than later. I then emailed Susie but didn't tell her about Phil, I knew what she would say.

I went into town to post the cards. Luckily, I was in time to get them to my overseas recipients for Christmas provided they went by airmail. I'd parked at the One Elm, knowing that I'd want to go in for, at the very least, a coffee. The chairs by the fire had been taken so I stood at the bar for a moment until I heard a male voice. "Lucie, haven't seen you for ages. How are you?" A warm hug engulfed me. It was Kyle who was, as always, warm and breezy. "Join us, do," he urged. I saw that two of his daughters were with him and happily joined them. The girls stayed for lunch and then left.

Kyle looked at me. "Now tell your Uncle Kyle all about it."

"What?"

He sighed. "Don't be silly Lucie. I can tell there's something up. What is it?" So I told him.

He took a deep breath. "Well, well ..." He looked thoughtful. "Lucie, I know that you had a rough time with the last one," I tried to look affronted but he ignored me, "but there's no need to visit the sins of that dickhead on this one. He may or may not be a player but from what you've said he's not. Frankly, it sounds like he's in a tough position. He's probably right. If he'd told you in the early days you'd have walked away." I nodded, he was quite right. He smiled. "Not all men are cheating wankers you know."

We stayed at the table, chatting about this and that until I realised that it was dark outside. "Thank you so much Kyle. You're a great listener - it's been so good having time with you." The hug he gave me was warm and comforting.

I drove home in a thoughtful mood. It had been very good to get a different perspective on things and certainly having some space was helping. I didn't hit the wine - or chocolate - that evening.

After Zumba we congregated in the One Elm as always. After some encouragement, Karen shared the fact that she'd seen Tony twice and that they were getting on very well. "No we haven't," was her firm answer to the inevitable question at which we all laughed.

"And what about you?" Sara asked.

I took a deep breath and told them. There was a stunned silence. "I can't believe it - are you sure?" Bev asked.

Gillian was very firm in her opinion. "He's married. There must be a reason why they're not divorced." She looked at me searchingly. "Effectively you've been having an affair with a married man. Is that what you want to do?"

I shook my head. "It's against everything I believe is right. I'm so upset - I know he loves me and I think I love him too, but if he'd told me in the beginning, I wouldn't have gone on seeing him."

Sara, Judy and, surprisingly, Bev weren't so sure. "You have to look at it from his point of view. What started off as one thing is now something quite different. You could say that he's a decent man who's trying to care for someone who's terrified with what's happening to her."

I sat with my head in my hands, in a state of total confusion. I knew that it wasn't as clear cut as it seemed and no matter what anyone said, I still had incredibly strong feelings for him. By the time we said our goodbyes, my head was still spinning.

Annie rang me on Friday evening to tell me that things with Roger weren't great. "He's blowing hot and cold Lucie. One minute he's really keen and the next he's practically ignoring me."

"That's not ok. You deserve better than that, we all do." And I meant it. We talked some more and as we said goodbye we agreed that affairs of the heart really shouldn't hurt as much as they seemed to.

Saturday was cold and wet, a day to hunker down in front of the fire so I did just that. It was early afternoon when I heard ducks. 'May I come and see you? Please? Phil xx'

I debated with myself before replying. 'Ok. When? Lx'

Two minutes after I'd sent the text there was a knock on the door and, to my amazement, Phil was standing on the doorstep holding a large bunch of flowers. He looked pale and nervous. I stood still for a moment before remembering my manners and asking him in.

"Tea or coffee?"

"Coffee please."

He followed me into the kitchen where I silently made some fresh coffee and put a few biscuits on a plate. It was horrible to be behaving as if we were virtual strangers after sharing so much intimacy.

We went into the sitting room and sat with him at one end of the sofa and me at the other, but this time there was no physical contact between us. We sat in silence for a few minutes. "Talk to me Lucie, please talk to me."

"I don't know what to say." And it was true; I had no idea what to say to him.

The awkward silence continued for another few moments. "I'm so, so sorry Lucie. I've been such a fool. I wanted to tell you but was terrified that you'd leave." That was true. Had I known, our relationship would have stayed firmly work based. "I promise you that everything I've told you is absolutely true. There's nothing else to say except," he hesitated, "that I love you. I don't think I've ever felt about anyone the way I feel about you. I can't bear the thought of not having you in my life ..."

He sank to his knees and I could see tears in his eyes. "I don't know what I can do to make up for what I've done, but I'll do anything you want."

I reached out and touched his shoulder at which he leaned into my lap and cried, body racking sobs that shook him. I bent over him and held him tight, trying to stop the dreadful noise that a man makes when he weeps.

Eventually his sobs abated and he sat back on his heels, smiling shamefacedly. "I'm sorry Lucie. It's been a hell of a week."

I stared at him. All I wanted to do was hug his hurt away but couldn't bring myself to do that - not now, maybe never. He sat back down and we started to talk properly: about the magazine, about future work, about his business partner. Once he tried to talk about personal stuff but I quickly blocked him - I couldn't cope with that.

More coffee was drunk and the remainder of the packet of chocolate biscuits eaten. It was dark; we'd talked for nearly four hours. "Are you hungry?"

I nodded.

"Would you like to go out for dinner?"

I shook my head. The last thing I wanted to do was sit in a restaurant with him after so many wonderfully intimate occasions doing just that.

"What then?"

I hesitated. "Why don't we get a takeaway?"

Ten minutes later I was driving into town with him at my side. We bought a couple of bottles at a local supermarket, he insisted on getting a pot of Ben and Jerrys Karamel Sutra ice cream which made me laugh for the first time that day. Then on to a Chinese restaurant that did takeaways where we spent ages poring over the menu before deciding on one portion of egg-drop noodle soup to share, cashew and pineapple chicken, steamed pork with prawn wontons and bok choi with chilli and oyster sauce.

We hurried home, put the ice cream in the freezer, opened a bottle and, at my suggestion, served up on trays so we could sit in front of the fire. Actually we ended up sitting on the floor, defending the loaded trays from inquisitive cats, sharing dishes, drinking and watching rubbish on TV while we continued to talk. I ached to touch him but restrained myself, feeling the same tension from him.

Chinese food finished, I took the debris into the kitchen while he refilled our glasses. We sat for another hour in front of the fire and finished off the bottle - still talking, not touching. The chocolate and caramel spiked with chocolate chunks ice cream followed. We ate from the carton so our spoons occasionally clashed, it was impossible to stop the habit of eating so closely together.

It was nearly eleven o'clock when he looked at his watch. "I suppose I should go ..." He half-heartedly started to get up but certainly didn't look as if he wanted to leave.

I reached up and touched his arm. "You know you shouldn't drive. We've both had a lot to drink haven't we?"

He looked down at me. "I suppose I shouldn't. Is it ok if I stay?" He hesitated for a moment. "In the spare room of course." There was a slight question in his voice.

I struggled to get to my feet and when he reached down to help me up it was like being touched by electricity. Subconsciously I leaned towards him for a second before standing up straight.

"Yes, spare room's best don't you think?" I tried to sound as matter-of-fact as possible.

We cleared up together, said goodnight to the cats and made our way upstairs. I gave him the toothbrush he'd used before and a towel. "Sleep well Phil." He reached out and held me close, kissed my cheek and said goodnight.

I stood on the landing for a few seconds, staring at the closed spare room door. Lying in my bed, knowing that he was in the next room felt awful but I knew that it was the right thing to do. I tingled with the wanting of him but knew that despite buzzing with longing, pleasuring myself wouldn't work, not that night, so turned onto my stomach, buried my face in the pillows and tried to sleep.

Sleep did come and when I awoke the next morning, it took me a few moments to remember what had happened the previous day and who was in the house. Tears came as I reflected on what we'd had together and the likelihood that it was gone made me close my eyes in pain.

I knew I had to be dressed when I saw him so went into the bathroom, had a quick shower and then pulled on black leggings and an old sloppy sweater, hardly seductive wear. The sitting room was cold so I quickly lit a fire, then fed the cats and started cooking breakfast of sausages, bacon, tomatoes and scrambled egg.

I was just thinking of waking him when I heard his footsteps and looked up to see him standing in the doorway. He had huge dark shadows under his eyes. "God, you look awful." The words were out of my mouth before I'd engaged my brain.

He smiled wanly. "I don't think I've ever had such a bad night. Knowing that you were so close was torture ..."

"Stop. Please stop."

It was no good, I couldn't help myself. I stepped close to him, took his face in my hands and kissed him. For a moment he stood still and then I felt his arms around me as he returned my kiss. It was like coming home, feelings of peace and safety swept over me.

It would have been all too easy to stay in his arms but I gently disengaged myself and returned to cooking. He laid the table, poured out fruit juice and made coffee as I served up. We sat over breakfast for nearly two hours. It seemed that we were completely incapable of spending less than that over a meal and it was nearly midday when we agreed that it was time for him to go.

"When will I see you again?" He sounded almost fearful.

"I don't know Phil. Much as I ..."

He reached for me but I gently put my hands on his chest to stop him. "Phil, you're married. And no matter what we think and feel about each other - won't, can't, change that. How can we possibly even consider being together? I think we both need to think about what we want and whether that's possible."

He put his hands on my shoulders. "I love you. Just remember that. I believe that we can work this out but I do understand that you need some space right now."

And with the promise that he wouldn't crowd me, he left. I watched him drive round the corner and then slowly went back into the house where, with the cats for company, I tried to rest. It had been a tumultuous week.

He crowded me. On Monday morning I found umpteen texts and voicemails. On Monday afternoon he emailed me talking about work, asking if I would go on writing reviews and articles for him. On Monday evening he called. It was a jolt hearing his voice.

"Lucie, can we have dinner this week?" I closed my eyes in exasperation, tinged with longing.

"Lucie? We need to talk - I can't bear it." He asked if we could meet at the Potting Shed in Broadway on Tuesday evening. "Bring your notepad. I'd like you to write a review please."

I snorted in disbelief but then my work head kicked in. Work was work after all.

I'd decided to declutter my room and found, to my delight, a dress that I'd forgotten all about so on Tuesday night wore the bright turquoise scoop-neck, three-quarters-sleeve, just-below-the-knee-length jersey dress teamed with brown boots and a brown and cream scarf. I felt a flutter in my stomach as I parked and checked my makeup in the car mirror. And does one ever stop worrying about hair and makeup I asked myself, and smiled as I realised that the answer for me was probably never.

Phil was waiting for me and stood up as I walked towards him. "You look phenomenal Lucie." I smiled modestly and accepted the compliment graciously as we kissed cheeks.

"Champagne?"

"I'm driving Phil. And working for you. Think I'll stick to sparkling water please, ice, no slice."

We sat and looked through the menu, discussing the various dishes. I made notes which made him smile. "You take this really seriously, don't you?"

"I always take work seriously Phil. You should know that."

"Point taken. Ok, what shall we order?"

I decided on chicken liver mousse with bacon jam and sourdough bread followed by an irresistible eighteen-hour slow cooked pork belly with mash, vegetables and gravy. He'd chosen a scotch egg with Gentleman's Relish and an oxtail ragout with pappardelle and garlic bread to follow.

"I've always struggled to cook pork belly well," I remarked as we placed our orders and I succumbed to a small glass of champagne.

"I could always show you." I shook my head in smiling reproof.

The dishes were excellent as we'd expected and as I continued to make brief notes, I knew that I'd be able to write a good article which made me smile with satisfaction. Phil noticed and when I told him what had made me smile, he nodded his approval. "I knew from the beginning we'd end up working together. I never dreamed ..." He stopped as I looked at him sternly and held up his hands in mock surrender.

For dessert I'd chosen chocolate swiss roll with vanilla mascarpone. He'd gone for the cheese board which featured mature cheddar, Cotswold blue and Ticklemore goat's cheese. We shared everything as usual and talked about the food, the presentation, the value-for-money factor, the ambiance of the place, the service and as we did, I continued to make notes.

"We'll take coffee in the lounge please," he said as he ordered coffee and brandy.

I followed him through and we settled down on one of the huge sofas near the fire. The coffee and brandies arrived. I sipped the coffee and ignored the brandy.

"I've done a lot of thinking," he started and then told me why he and Marianne hadn't divorced. He explained that for the first few months, he'd half expected that she'd want to come back although after the first three months or so wasn't sure that was what he wanted.

"As time went on I became ever more certain that things wouldn't work out even if she'd wanted to come back. I put all my energy into this new venture and making sure that the restaurant was ok. It didn't seem important or even necessary to go through all that legal stuff." He stopped and gazed deep into my eyes. "Until I met you ..." I sat, listening in silence. "So there's only one thing I can do," he continued, "and that's to divorce."

I held my breath.

"I have to talk to Marianne first. She's finding it really hard to cope at the moment," he stopped and looked at me, "but I respect your views, your integrity really, and I can see that there's no future with you the way things are ..."

I still didn't breathe.

"So, I'm going to see her at the weekend and tell her what has to happen." He leaned forward and held my hand. "You have to understand that that doesn't mean I'll stop caring about her or wanting to help her." His voice was resolute. "And I need you to be ok with that. I can't turn my back on her. But if divorcing her means that we have a chance of being together, that's what I'll do."

I stared at him unblinking, not knowing what to say. He'd just made a huge declaration but there was also a huge sting in the tail. "Well, say something Lucie ..."

I took a deep breath. "Well, that's one of the biggest elephants in the room I've come across for a very long time." I stopped for a few moments to marshal my thoughts. "Look Phil, I don't want you to do anything that you don't want to. I certainly don't want you to divorce her unless you're absolutely sure that's what you really want to do, whether we're together or not. And as far as her being an important part of your life? Well, that's more food for thought - it's a big ask ..." I hesitated as I saw him frown. "It IS a big ask - you know that, but I guess that's something we'd need to come to terms with ..." I was interrupted by him leaning towards me and stopping my mouth with a kiss which I found impossible not to return.

We remained on the sofa for another hour, drinking more coffee and talking. "And there are no other secrets? You're not sleeping with her, are you? You really don't want to get back with her? You swear?" I asked more than once and each time he reassured me that there was nothing else to disclose. "To me, a relationship without trust is worth nothing. So, if there is anything else, now's the time to tell." I was almost in tears. He remained silent but held my hand tightly. I knew I had two options: to walk away from him or trust that he was telling the truth and stay. I wanted to believe him which was why I stayed, but the elephant was there - he knew it and I knew it.

It was after midnight when I stretched and said that I should go. He'd booked a room but didn't ask me to stay. I was so glad that he didn't as I would have found it hard to refuse even though it would have been the right thing to do, but the kisses we exchanged as he held my car door open for me were passionate and heartfelt.

What we'd talked about swirled round and round in my head. I found it hard to concentrate but somehow managed to write the article about the Potting Shed and sent it to him on Thursday afternoon. He replied that evening, saying that it was good and would I send him my invoice. It was a brisk, business-like email until I scrolled down to his PS 'Dinner at the Fuzzy Duck. Friday at 8. I've booked a room so bring a toothbrush. Please xxx'

I didn't know what to reply for ages but eventually typed 'Dinner at the Fuzzy Duck sounds wonderful, thank you. Toothbrush? Wait and see... x' and as I hit the send button hoped that it didn't sound like game-playing. No reply had come by the time Karen arrived to collect me for Zumba.

The Thursday Christmas market had started. Christmas lights were twinkling in all the main streets, so instead of going to the One Elm after a typically exhausting Zumba session, we decided to wander down to the pig roast where, of course, we each bought a huge roll slathered with apple sauce and stuffing to accompany the pork and crackling that over spilled the bread. Judy was on a pre-Christmas diet but even she couldn't resist. "Why is it that food like this is so delicious but so bad for you?" she asked ruefully. We laughed as we continued to market-stall mooch while we finished off the massive rolls.

As we made our way homewards, I again talked to Karen about my dilemma. "That's a hard one Lucie." We talked further. "It all depends whether you trust him or not," was her final opinion as she finished her second cup of tea and I had to agree. It all depended on whether I trusted him or not.

I did take my toothbrush with me on Friday evening. Phil engulfed me in a warm embrace and as I hugged him back, I felt butterflies in my stomach and my heart started to beat a little faster all the more so when we kissed. "I so want to make love with you," he murmured into my hair. My knees buckled but I put my hands against his chest and took a small step back.

"Deferred gratification?" and ran my hands down to his waist.

He stared into my eyes and then laughed. "Touché my dear."

We went into the dining room and started to discuss the menu which felt like our normality and I caught my breath as, almost absent-mindedly, he stroked my fingers as I held my glass. I closed my eyes for a moment. There was no doubt; the chemistry was still alive and kicking - hard.

Luckily the menu was wide-ranging and interesting, providing a much needed distraction. My twice baked Cotswold goat cheese soufflé with pickled walnuts was scrumptious as was his duck liver parfait with brioche and marmalade. I'd opted for the lamb with nicoise potato, winter vegetables and red wine jus which went beautifully with his duck breast served with a bacon and potato terrine. Of course we shared food which only heightened the tension between us. As he held his fork for me to taste the terrine, his hand shook very slightly.

My room temperature dark chocolate fondant with icy white chocolate ice cream clung stickily to our teeth and his hot espresso over vanilla ice cream, spiked with dark rum cleansed our palates. We stayed at the table for coffee, holding hands which felt wonderful. I never wanted it to end.

I cleared my throat. "Phil?" He gazed at me, raising my hand to his lips to kiss my fingertips. "Phil, it's been such a lovely evening but ..." He frowned slightly. "But I can't stay with you. I want to. I still feel the same about you but I can't stay, not tonight. It just doesn't feel right." I looked at him, willing him to understand.

"I wondered why you'd stuck with water this evening." He paused. "What had you planned?" He didn't look cross, just puzzled.

"I brought my toothbrush. I wanted to stay, I want to stay, I really do, but it feels wrong. I don't know why ..." Tears were threatening and I closed my eyes.

"Lucie? It's alright darling. I can't pretend to really understand but if it doesn't feel right for you, it doesn't feel right for you and that's just the way it is. Lucie, don't cry. It'll all be ok. Trust me."

I took his hand, held it to my face and rested my cheek in his palm. "Thank you. Thank you so much." He raised his eyebrows. "Just for being you." I kissed his hand and held it tight.

We sat for another hour with more coffee, talking, holding hands, relishing being together. When eventually we realised that we were the last people in the dining room, we reluctantly left. He walked me into the dark, deserted carpark, held me tight and kissed me.

"Suppose a quick shag over the bonnet's out of the question then?"

I stepped back, unsure whether I'd heard properly. "What?"

He smiled cherubically. "Just thought I'd ask."

"Another time sweetheart, another time."

"I'll hold you to that."

Dam' right you'll hold me to that I thought but merely smiled sweetly, kissed his cheek and left.

The weather was dreadful over the weekend so apart from going over to see Anita and John for tea on Saturday, I did very little, finding it relaxing to crash out and read, watch TV, have a few telephone conversations and check emails. Another email had arrived from Jean-Michel; he said that his aunt was still very ill, that work was very hectic, that he was looking forward to the Christmas holidays and hoped to see me in the New Year. Susie had also emailed me - a long, chatty, news-filled email which made me feel more a part of her life. Both made me smile.

Phil called on Sunday evening to tell me he'd talked with Marianne who was upset to think that they were finally going to officially end their marriage, but had agreed not to block the process. "She's accepted that we're never going to get back together and really wants me to be happy. However," I held my breath, "she wants, needs, to know that I'm there for her. As a friend Lucie, as a friend. You know that I can't turn my back on her." We talked some more and he kept trying to reassure me. So why, I asked myself as I put the phone down after a further half-hour or so, did I have this sinking feeling of déjà-vu which stayed with me for the rest of the evening.

For several years I'd piled unwanted clothes into the spare room wardrobe until eventually the doors wouldn't close properly. It was lashing with rain when I awoke on Monday morning so decided to go through everything once and for all. It took over an hour to put the clothes into piles on the bed: trousers, sweaters, jackets, skirts and so on. Then came the difficult part - actually deciding what to keep and what to discard. Lunchtime came and went, cups of tea came and went and still I was trying to make decisions. I'd got as far as three piles: one to throw, one to keep and, hardest of all, one to dither over. I'd put the keep pile back into the wardrobe and determinedly stuffed the throw pile into black bags and then laid out the can't-decide pile so I could have a proper think.

I jumped when I heard the landline ring, it was Phil. After our how-are-yous when he laughed as I described my day he told me the main reason for his call. "I've just come out of a meeting with my solicitor who's going to draw up the divorce papers this week. Apparently, getting everything finalised can take up to about six months." There was a pause.

"That must feel very odd." I'd heard the pain in his voice and my heart went out to him.

He cleared his throat. "It does Lucie. It does. But Marianne understands why I'm doing this and I have to say that it feels like a huge step forward. Kind of clearing the decks - know what I mean?"

I did indeed. "So, where are you?"

"In Manchester. I'll be here for another day or two getting a few things sorted out." There was another pause. "What are you doing for the weekend?"

I giggled softly. "I might be seeing this man." We bantered for a few moments until we agreed that 'this man' was in fact him and he would come to mine on Thursday and as I put the phone down, I felt that all too familiar tingle.

I managed to complete my decision making by the end of Tuesday and spent Wednesday thinking about the weekend, tidying the house, buying in some food essentials and generally getting organised. I relaxed in the evening and the thought of whether I was falling into the same routine as I had with Richard came into my head; after due consideration, I decided that wasn't the case at all - Phil was very different.

He called me late Thursday morning, sounding rushed and harassed. "I'm so sorry Lucie. I know I said I'd be with you today but things are taking longer than I thought so I wouldn't be with you til very late. I don't want to disturb you so it's probably best if I get to you on Friday. Is that ok?"

"Of course that's ok." I soothed. We didn't talk for long, but that's ok I said to myself as I put the phone down. He's busy and you know that work is work.

Karen and I went to Zumba as usual. Judith told us that this would be the last class for three weeks, but as Christmas was fast approaching, no-one wanted to go to the One Elm or the market so the two of us decided to walk round to look at the lights, which always made us smile, and then go back to mine for coffee. We talked about Christmas. Neither of us had made firm plans as yet. "Perhaps we should get together?" she suggested. I thought it was a very good idea.

Phil texted me very early. 'Sorry about yesterday but things were manic. Got a meeting at 10 then I'll hit the road. That ok? Phil xxx'

I sleepily replied 'Perfect. Travel safely darling. L xx' and then snuggled down to doze for another hour or so.

Another text arrived just after twelve. 'Fucking M6 is a fucking carpark. No idea what's happening. And I was so looking forward to having lunch with you xx'

'Traffic's just traffic. Chill. See you when I see you. Kettle will be on ;-) bottle will be open ;-)) xx'

After a few more tetchy texts from him and trying-to-be-calming texts from me, he eventually arrived in the pitch dark, looking exhausted. "You sit here," I directed putting a mug of tea in his hand and pointing at the sofa before going upstairs to run a bath. "Upstairs. Now Phil." I called a few minutes later.

Obediently he came upstairs looking slightly puzzled. "Strip off, then into the bath."

He grinned at me. "Isn't that my line?"

I pretended to look shocked. "What a bad boy. Now do as I say." I pushed him into the spare room and threw a dark blue bath towel in after him. He joined me in the bathroom with the towel slung over his hips. I gazed at him. It would have been all too easy to kiss him and pull him into my body. I closed my eyes for a second, mentally shaking myself. "In you get." I tried to sound brisk.

With a sigh of relief, he shed the towel, sank into the hot foamy water and leaned back. I'd brought up a couple of glasses of Merlot, handed him one and then perched on the side of the bath with mine. "Now, tell me what's been happening on planet Phil." He told me about the visit to his solicitor and how strange it had felt at the time but how much a sense of relief he'd felt when he walked out of the office, about his meetings with various restaurants and potential advertisers and what had been happening at the restaurant.

"It's really hard. All this boxing and coxing, trying to coordinate everything and keeping everyone sweet. Angus is great but most of his time is devoted to the restaurant." He took another sip. "It's knackering Lucie, really knackering. Great when it's going well but sometimes, I do wonder ..." His voice faded and he closed his eyes.

I looked down at him, leaned down and kissed his forehead. "Phil. Time to get out of the bath sweetheart. Out you come." He opened his eyes but I could tell he was almost asleep. I helped him out of the bath and guided him into the spare room, rubbing and patting him dry as we went. He fell onto the bed and curled up as I tucked the duvet round him. He was deeply asleep the minute his head touched the pillow. I tiptoed out, returning half an hour later to see that he hadn't moved. An hour later he was in the same position, so I made a sandwich and a thermos of coffee and placed them on the bedside table with a note. 'Just in case you get the midnight munchies. I'll be in bed myself by eleven. Sleep tight. X'

I slept very well that night and awoke feeling refreshed and happy. It was just after seven and when I peeped into the spare room, could see that Phil had moved but was still asleep. The sandwich had disappeared and the thermos was open.

After a quick shower, I dressed and put makeup on, picked up the debris from the spare room and went downstairs. I was on my second cup of coffee when I heard footsteps and looked up to see him looking at me. He looked refreshed. "Gosh, what a difference a night's sleep makes,'" I said and held up my arms for his embrace. Breakfast took over two hours. We cooked and ate together, talking all the time. It had stopped raining so we decided to walk into town.

"We'll get a taxi back if it starts to rain," he said firmly as we donned coats and hats.

As it was so close to Christmas, there were market stalls in one of the streets which gave the town an even more Christmassy feel. I had already sent Susie her main Christmas present and a few silly little things, but when I saw some dangly amethyst ear-rings and a little amethyst butterfly pendant, I couldn't resist them. I saw a wooden pen and pencil set that I thought Phil would like so bought them and looked up to see him buying some silver hoop ear-rings at an adjacent stall. We drank coffee from a street vendor and sampled a bowl of curry from another stall. He went into the Pandora shop and told me to keep out. I did the same to him at a bookshop. We met minutes later, each looking smug, and were making our very slow way back towards the One Elm when I saw Karen.

After introductions and a few minutes of polite chit-chat he smiled at her. "We were thinking of a drink at the One Elm. Don't suppose you'd care to join us, would you?"

"Thank you Phil. That would be lovely." She glanced at me and raised an eyebrow.

"Oh yes, Karen, please come."

The three of us made ourselves comfortable at a recently vacated table near the fire and peeled off coats and hats. Phil went to the bar and came back with a bottle of Prosecco and three glasses. "Great to meet you Karen. Cheers."

The next hour sped past as we talked. Phil was a born raconteur and made us laugh with stories about his restaurant and magazine, he listened to Karen when she talked about her work and family and was quiet as we quickly caught up with each other's news. "I like him, I really like him," was her opinion when he excused himself to go to the men's room. "He listens. He asks questions. He's fun. And Lucie, he clearly thinks you're wonderful. I love the way he looks at you ..." She broke off as she saw him returning with another bottle of Prosecco and a couple of menus tucked under his arm.

"I think we need something to eat, don't you?"

We decided that sharing boards was the best idea so decided on one fish, one meat and one cheese plus a bowl of olives. "Just to start off," he said as he placed our order, "and don't you dare," he added as he saw Karen reach into her handbag.

We ate, drank and talked for another couple of hours. It felt warm, relaxing and very comfortable, as if we'd all known each other for years and when, eventually, we stood outside saying our goodbyes, Karen hugged me. "I approve. I really do," she whispered in my ear.

"You sure you don't want walking home?" Phil had asked to which she'd laughingly shaken her head.

"It's not that late Phil. But thank you for offering."

"I really like Karen," he said as we walked home. "Are all your friends as nice as her?"

"I think so, but then I guess I'm biased."

"Well, they say that people are often judged by the friends they have, don't they?" I had to agree and thought of how much I'd liked Angus, Claudia and Jacob when I'd met them in London.

When we arrived home I fed the indignant cats who looked accusingly at their almost-empty bowls and although we'd shared some boards earlier, thought we'd like something more to eat. "Savoury or sweet?" I asked as I tried to remember what I had in the larder.

"Sweet I think."

I knew I had some shop-bought meringues and found a carton of summer berries in the freezer. I didn't have any cream so took a half-tub of vanilla ice cream out of the freezer, added a few drops of Cointreau and, as it started to soften, whipped the two together, crumbling in meringue and stirring in the icy berries as I did so. I piled the mixture into big bowls and took them through to the sitting room where Phil had just lit the fire

"Wow, this is good," he said after the first mouthful.

I smiled modestly but must have shown a tinge of smugness. "You come over here for a moment," and he put his bowl down. I did so and was rewarded by a gentle slap on my rear, his touch made me shiver.

That evening, we played scrabble which I managed to win by a small margin followed by a game of dirty scrabble which he won. We then started a game of two-handed monopoly which, of course, wasn't anywhere near finished by midnight so that cascaded into the next day. As we played, we talked nonstop. We talked about our pasts and presents, our hopes, fears and dreams. I was very aware that I was holding some stuff back and presumed that he was too, but it still felt pretty good to be sharing more and more with every conversation we had.

"It's Christmas in a few days," he announced as we tidied away the scrabble board.

"So it is."

"I think we should be together for Christmas, don't you?" I pretended to think until his arms went round me and I melted into his kiss.

We decided to have a small nightcap of calvados and then put the guard in front of the dying embers, shooed the cats into the kitchen and went upstairs. He stood with his hand on the spare room door handle. "I know how you feel Lucie, so I'll say goodnight." He paused, I nodded and we then chastely kissed cheeks.

I lay in bed, tossing and turning, unable to get to sleep. Every nerve tingled and more than once I thought I'd have to get up and go to him. But I didn't. Instead, I reached for my pale blue friend, turned it on and slowly stroked it down my throat, over my breasts, down my stomach, the inside of my thighs and then, as I reached the point of needing release and imagining that it was him thrusting into me, pushed it in and, a few moments later, came. As the last spasms died away, my cheeks were wet with tears.

Sunday dawned dank and wet so we returned to the monopoly board after breakfast. Later we logged onto Aubrey Allen's website and ordered a goose for Christmas. "Let's make Christmas Day a party," he suggested so I called Karen who said that she'd love to come.

"And do bring Tony along if you'd like to," I added at which she giggled and said that she would.

I then rang Barbara and, after catching up with her news, invited her with her new man. "That'll be lovely Lucie, thank you so much." She sounded very happy not to be cooking for a change.

James and Felicity were, unfortunately, away for Christmas. "We decided that we wanted some sunshine, so we're taking a villa in Greece for a couple of weeks. Lots of good food, ouzo and seeing the sights. Shame though, we'd have loved to have come. Let's get together soon." With assurances that we'd see each other on their return, we said goodbye.

We continued with monopoly until I realised that, as banker, he was cheating, so we had a monopoly-fuelled argument which culminated in my chasing him round the kitchen, brandishing a wooden spoon. He fled upstairs. I was about to follow him when I heard ducks. 'I'll cook us lunch as penance. Is it safe to come back? Xx'

I stood at the bottom of the stairs, hands on hips, spoon in hand. "You're a very bad boy. Come here." My alter ego was kicking in.

He came downstairs slowly looking mock-apprehensive. "It'd better be an outstandingly good lunch - otherwise I'll be very, very cross." I did my best to sound irate and tapped his bottom lightly with the spoon as he went past me, trying to stifle my giggles.

So, I lounged on the sofa with the cats, reading the Sunday papers he'd brought in for me, until he produced a truly excellent lunch of spice-rubbed chicken that had been roasted impaled on a half-full can of beer which made it succulent beyond belief, accompanied by potatoes boulangère and cabbage that had been cooked with bacon, garlic and a little cream topped with a dusting of parmesan cheese. We sat opposite each other and, as was our custom ate slowly and talked endlessly until when, under the table our knees touched, we both fell silent for a few moments.

He reached for my hand and twined his fingers round mine. "Did you sleep well last night?"

"Eventually."

"Me too - eventually ..."

The atmosphere between us positively crackled. We both stood at the same time, leaned across the table towards each other and kissed slowly and gently, tongues skimming over teeth, lips softly bitten. I felt his hand briefly touch my face and then he was by my side, holding me tightly. I returned his embrace as we stood toe to toe, hip to hip, breast to chest, still kissing.

"Dessert?" he whispered as we came up for air. I didn't know what dessert he was suggesting but was more than happy to say yes. He reached down, grasped my bottom and lifted me slightly so that I was perched on the edge of the table. Standing between my legs he unzipped my trousers, stood back and pulled them off before standing close, running his hands up my body under my sweater, pushing my bra up over my breasts. I leaned back as he nuzzled, licked and softly bit my nipples. It was like little bolts of electricity were sparking all over my body and I moaned softly as I felt myself want him more and more. I tried to sit up to reach him but was pushed firmly onto my back, dirty glasses and dishes all round me. I held my arms up to him pleadingly as he looked down at me, hazel eyes smoky with lust. "You have to ask Lucie. I have to know that this is what you really want."

"Now Phil - please - I want you to fuck me right now ..."

He pulled my hips into his, sliding into me easily and, staring into my eyes, thrust hard and fast. I threw my arms over my head in abandon and heard tinkling as a glass I'd hit fell on the floor. I didn't care - all I cared about was feeling his hands holding my legs, his cock buried deep inside me and the look in his eyes as we climbed higher and higher with excitement until, with a cry he came. I followed within seconds. He stood, panting and trembling slightly, holding my legs as my final spasms abated and then slumped onto a chair. I stayed as I was for a moment before sitting up and crossing my legs in a vain attempt to be ladylike. A bit late for that my little inner voice said and I giggled.

He knelt to help me back into my trousers. As he did so, I pushed my fingers through his thick brown-with-a-tinge-of-grey-at-the-temples hair, and gently pulled. As he stood up, he smiled at me. "Dessert?" This time, dessert was an apple and pear crumble which he served with vanilla ice cream and as he filled our bowls, I swept up the broken glass, mindful of the danger to small feline paws. Of course the crumble was superb and I said so.

"So, I've avoided the wooden spoon then?" He flinched unconvincingly.

"For the moment sweetheart. For the moment." I'd never played a stern, controlling role before but venturing into it with such a willing and non-judgemental partner was more fun than I could ever have imagined.

I realised how much of a messy cook he was when I went through to the kitchen but consoled myself, as I loaded up my trusty old dishwasher, that the food was more than worth it. As the kitchen started to look more like my space, he made coffee. Every time we brushed past each other to get to a cupboard or put something away, we touched lightly, companionably, lovingly.

Fire stoked, we settled down on the sofa with the cats, sipping the strong, black coffee he'd brewed. "You do know I don't want to put you under pressure, don't you?"

I looked up from playing with the cat. "Pressure about what?"

"Well, me divorcing Marianne. It feels like absolutely the right thing to do, for her as well as for me and, hopefully, you. I mean, either we'll be together or we won't but when I think of the times we've spent - eating, drinking, sharing, making love - well, I just can't think of anything better than that." He held the back of my neck and gently pulled me towards him and we kissed tenderly and deeply.

"Now, I'm going to beat you fair and square at monopoly." He sat back and looked determined.

"You wish. You had to cheat earlier, what makes you think you can win?" We played monopoly for the next few hours; it was all comfortable and normal. I felt incredibly relaxed and yet there was that elephant in the room despite Phil's previous reassurances and much as I wanted it to leave, it wouldn't. It stayed as we played monopoly, not finishing the game so calling it a draw even though he said he was sure he'd won, it stayed as we made chicken sandwiches for supper and it insisted on coming upstairs when we went to bed.

Love-making that night was amazingly high emotion. We couldn't stop looking into each other's eyes and as we touched, fondled, caressed and kissed, we both were trembling slightly. Seconds before penetrating me he paused. "I love you Lucie." There was a note of wonderment in his voice. Ridiculously I was still aware of that dam' elephant until moments before coming, which was so powerful I could have sworn I almost lost consciousness and as the ripples of pleasure slowly subsided I clung to him and cried. He held me close, kissed the tears away, murmuring nonsense and it was hearing his voice that soothed me into sleep.

When I awoke on Monday morning we were in much the same positions as we'd fallen asleep. I eased myself from under his arm and went into the bathroom to stand under a scalding hot shower. I'd looked for the elephant but it seemed to have disappeared which was a huge relief, but I knew with absolute certainty that it would return some time. Towelling my hair, I went back into the bedroom to find Phil sleepily awake.

"Morning sweetheart." I dropped a gentle kiss as he held up his face.

I sat on the side of the bed to finish off drying my hair and started to put makeup on. "I just love watching this, this transformation."

I looked down at him. "It's not that you're not beautiful when you're all unscrubbed," he added hastily. I sat silently. "Lucie, say something."

I laughed. "Thought if I gave you enough rope, you'd hang yourself. Don't worry darling," he was looking a little uneasy, "I know that I look much better with lippie than without."

"Well, I wouldn't say that, but it's certainly a different look, isn't it?"

I was mock-indignant for a few seconds but couldn't keep it up. "Come on you, time for breakfast. Unless of course you have any better ideas?" I raised my eyebrows.

He tugged the towel away and pulled me down to him, nipping and kissing my arms as I embraced him to then move to my shoulders, neck, between my breasts and back again. I held his face, kissing and softly biting his lips, his throat and chest. He lay back with his arms behind his head and watched as I straddled him. He was more than ready and so was I, so with no more preamble, I lowered myself onto his hardness, throwing back my head and closing my eyes as I did so. I steadily rode us towards orgasm, glorying in his excitement as well as my own and when finally he came it was with a force that almost dislodged me.

Later, as we sat over breakfast of bacon and egg, we talked more about Christmas. "I need to get a few things sorted but everything should be done by Wednesday or Thursday. Ok for me to come back then?"

"Of course Phil, either day is fine with me."

It was nearly lunchtime when I all but pushed him out of the door and as we hugged and kissed our goodbyes he whispered into my hair, "This'll be the best Christmas ever, you wait and see."

I spent the next three days enjoying opening Christmas cards and hanging them on the new strands of tinsel I'd bought, wrapping Christmas presents, emailing Susie, making mince pies, cleaning the house, putting up the tree and generally creating a space for us to have a wonderful Christmas.

On Tuesday evening, Karen called round for a drink and a bite of supper. I cooked us a sweet potato and butternut squash soup which I served with garlicky toast followed by quinoa with stir-fried carrots, leeks, broccoli and a few sundried tomatoes I'd found at the back of the cupboard. "This is unusually healthy for you," Karen said through a mouthful of vegetables.

"Well, we'll be eating and drinking lots and lots over Christmas won't we?"

"I'm so looking forward to it Lucie, it'll be so good." And we went on to talk about Tony. "We're getting on incredibly well, I can't believe it. He's great fun and ..." she paused and looked at me archly.

"Say no more Karen, say no more." Of course we said a lot more over the next couple of hours and when she left I felt a surge of affection for her and, as so often, thanked God for such great friends.

I met Annie for lunch on Wednesday, she looked tired and despondent. "It's Roger. I thought things were going well but he's so moody and very often isn't very nice." She looked down. "Not nice at all in fact."

"Annie, that's not fair and quite frankly if he's being mean to you, you either need to negotiate a better deal with him or get rid." I stopped and thought for a moment. "Annie, you don't feel the same way about him now, do you?"

She shook her head. "Isn't it funny, when he was ignoring me I thought he was wonderful and so wanted him, but now we're kind of together, I can see that he's not the man I thought he was."

I reached out and touched her arm. "Annie, you deserve better than that. We all do. It's just not good enough to be treated badly."

I invited her over for Christmas but she declined. "You know, I think I'm going to have a day on my own. And actually, that feels really good. I'll have a nice, quiet day but perhaps we can get together afterwards?"

"That's a great idea Annie, I'd love to."

That settled, we went on to enjoy the next couple of hours together. I was sad to think that things hadn't worked out between her and Roger, but knew that she deserved a whole heap better and was sure that she'd find someone else once he was out of her life and out of her head.

Phil arrived late Thursday afternoon and looked round at what I'd done appreciatively. "It all looks beautiful Lucie. I can't tell you how much I've been looking forward to this." He beamed at me with such infectious enthusiasm I couldn't resist hugging him, not that that was a hard thing to do.

"It's amazing what difference a bit of tinsel, a tree and a few baubles make, isn't it?"

He laughed and we solemnly put each other's cards and presents under the tree. I'd bought him three small gifts. He brought in a very large square box topped with a huge ribbon which was so big it had to stand at the side of the tree rather than under it. He'd also brought a large carrier bag of food which he put in the fridge. "I'd like to cook for you. Is that alright?" Indeed it was, and I smiled in anticipation of an excellent meal.

After a cup of tea and mince pies which he pronounced very good, we decided to stroll into town for the last Thursday market before Christmas. The Christmas lights were on so the town looked magical, everyone seemed to be in upbeat moods and when we bought roast pork rolls dripping with apple sauce and wandered round the stalls munching them, it all felt like a wonderful new beginning. I suddenly realised that Kate had a stall covered in lovely bits and bobs so I hurried over to say hello. Phil followed me. "Kate, I didn't realise you'd be here. How are you?"

We hugged. "I'm fine Lucie, good to see you. But I'm really cold."

"I'll mind the stall Kate. You go off and get a hot drink." She hesitated. "Go. Shoo. I'll be fine here."

As she moved to the front of the stall, I introduced her to Phil. They shook hands and as she left, she winked at me and gave a thumbs up behind his back. She returned about half an hour later to see that we'd sold several pieces, mainly because Phil remained at the front of the stall and invited every passer-by to stop, look and buy. "Wow, I'll have to hire you," was her laughing comment as we exchanged places. We stayed chatting for a while longer, until we realised that many of the stalls were beginning to pack up, so helped her put the contents of the stall into boxes.

"Shall we stay here while you get your car?" Phil offered, so we did and then the three of us loaded everything into her capacious boot before waving goodbye and wishing each other a very happy Christmas.

We were making our way towards the One Elm when I heard ducks. 'Thank you. Such a great help. And I like him. Think you should keep him x' Much as it pleased me, for some reason I couldn't fathom, I didn't show him the text.

Kyle and his daughters were in the One Elm and waved me over. As we joined them and I introduced Phil, Kyle shook hands and looked at him piercingly. An hour or so later everyone was very relaxed and Kyle winked at me as if to say that he approved which made me feel very happy. Eventually we meandered back home having drunk quite a lot, so the least little thing made us giggle. The cats looked at us disapprovingly as we stumbled into the house and shepherded us into the kitchen where they showed us their bowls. I apologised to them as I gave them more kitty biscuits which made Phil laugh and we continued laughing at ridiculous little things as we made our way to bed.

We knew each other so well. Neither of us felt particularly amorous but both wanted physical closeness so we lay side by side, shoulders, elbows and hands touching, still talking nonsense. I told him about Karen's monthly gift of 'Olive', which made him laugh, and a particular article on restaurants in Wales that I'd enjoyed, so we read it together before turning to each other, kissing gently and falling asleep.

When I awoke I felt a deep sense of calm and happiness, so much so that I felt my heart swelling in my chest. He was still asleep so

I went downstairs to start breakfast which I'd decided would be bacon, black pudding and scrambled eggs. I was humming happily at the sink when I heard his footsteps and then felt his arms round me and his lips on the back of my neck. I twisted round to return his embrace and we kissed, only stopping when I heard the bacon sizzling.

As with every meal, breakfast took us over an hour to eat while we decided what to do over the next few days. We finally agreed that we would collect the goose and vegetables that we'd ordered from Aubrey Allen's on Christmas Eve and prep everything for Christmas lunch that day, so we could relax and enjoy our guests' company on Christmas Day. That sorted, we cleared the table, showered and got ready. Again he watched me apply my makeup which felt natural, comfortable and easy-going. A feeling of being very much loved and emotionally secure swept over me and I closed my eyes, revelling in the moment.

It was raining so we drove down into the town. Our first call was the One Elm yet again where we set the mood by having a glass of mulled wine. With the reassurance that we'd be back for a late lunch, we made our way to the Christmas shop where we bought two large baubles for the Christmas tree - one gold and one silver to represent our first Christmas together. "We have to play carols from now on," he asserted and told me that he'd bought two Christmas CDs that he insisted would be the only music we'd play until Christmas was over. I pretended to sigh in mild annoyance which of course wasn't the case at all.

Lunch at the One Elm could be selected from their special Christmas boards which included delicious spicy morsels of cheese, shards of smoked venison, mini croque monsieurs and smoked salmon blinis with beetroot and dill dressing which we ate, washed down with Prosecco. Because I was driving, I kept myself to just the one glass. As their Prosecco was so good, we asked if we could buy another bottle. Phil promptly bought two. "For this evening," he explained.

It was late afternoon when we arrived home, lit the fire and brewed some coffee. The two baubles we'd bought that morning were unwrapped and ceremoniously hung on opposite branches of the tree and a Christmas CD put on. All it needed was some snow to make this Christmas perfect I thought to myself as we settled at each end of the sofa legs intertwined, cats in front of the fire. As always, his touch made me tingle. I felt we'd now reached a place of peace as our relationship continued to deepen into something even more profound and meaningful.

The contents of the carrier bag in the fridge proved to be a pheasant and some winter greens which he cooked for about eight o'clock. I insisted that I be allowed to help in the kitchen. "I thought I was a good cook, but working with a professional chef is something else." He smiled modestly but I could tell he was delighted. Of course the meal was delicious. The Prosecco he'd brought back from the One Elm accompanied it superbly and as we ate, we talked. More perfection I thought and smiled.

We agreed that we'd skip dessert and take the second bottle of Prosecco up to bed which he brought up in an ice bucket with a couple of glasses. "I wonder if you'd like to see a movie," he suggested. Suddenly Richard flashed into my mind but as he loaded a DVD, I forced a smile. It was an old movie - 9½ Weeks.

"My goodness, that takes me back." I was startled by his choice.

"I rather thought it might." He smiled and returned to me.

I leaned against him as we watched the movie, felt his gradual arousal against my hip and squirmed as we watched the film unfold. The scene where Mickey Rourke feeds Kim Basinger different foods while she has her eyes closed resonated with us. I was spellbound when she was fed spicily hot chillies followed by ice-cold milk that spilled down her chin to cool the fiery heat and then watched as honey was slowly dripped into her open mouth. "I'd rather like to do that to you," he said softly as he cupped my breast. I shivered with desire.

He suddenly leant away from me. "Close your eyes now." He sounded very authoritative. I obeyed.

"Open your arms." I did so, quivering in anticipation.

I heard a clinking sound and then gasped as I felt the chill of an ice-cube being run from my hairline, down my forehead, over my nose, across my open lips, down my chin and throat and between my breasts. "Stay still," I heard as I arched my back to meet his touch. I obeyed.

I felt the slowly melting ice-cube as it was circled round my nipples, grazed down my stomach and left in my belly button. After a few moments I could feel water trickling across my waist and then his tongue lapping it up. I reached down to touch him only to have my hands gently slapped away. "I said 'open your arms'. Please." I obeyed.

"Now, open your legs." I took a sharp breath. I was now lying spread-eagled with my eyes closed, not knowing what was going to happen next. I screamed - it was a soft scream but nonetheless a scream. He'd put an ice-cube in his mouth and was licking and softly nibbling my pussy. The cold of the melting ice and the warmth of his tongue was electric and I involuntarily wriggled only to be softly bitten on the inside of my thigh. I obediently stayed still and his mouth returned to me until minutes later I shuddered into release.

I then felt him move away. "Stay as you are." I obeyed, heart pumping. I heard his teeth crunch on an ice-cube and then felt his fingers very gently pushing a piece of ice inside me closely followed by his cock. It was the most incredible sensation. I couldn't stop myself - I threw my arms around him and this time wasn't reprimanded. More shudders overtook me and I clung to him, biting down on his shoulder as wave after wave shook me. I knew that he came but couldn't have said when. I was much too deeply immersed in my own pleasure.

After I didn't know how long, I became aware that I was lying on slightly soggy sheets and cautiously opened my eyes, half expecting to be told to close them again. He was lying on his side next to me, watching me with a gentle smile. "Incredible." We both said it at the same time and our kiss was deeper and more impassioned than ever before. We slept entwined. I never wanted to let him go and knew that he felt the same way.

I was woken up in the pitch dark by a gentle shake of the shoulder and a mug of tea pushed under my nose. "Let's get there bright and early to beat the rush." I yawned and sleepily agreed. Half an hour later, we'd both had a quick shower, pulled on some clothes and were driving into Leamington. I'd even managed to put on some bright lipstick that made him smile. Although we arrived at Aubrey Allen's just after seven there were already queues but, thankfully, they were short and we were served within a few minutes. We gathered up the goose, some red cabbage we'd decided to pre-order and a couple of winter salads that I liked the look of. Next door, our vegetables were packed and ready so by half past we were on our way back into Stratford.

"I know a great little café for breakfast,"' I suggested so we parked in the market square and made our way to Maria's place where we ordered coffee and bacon baguettes. We ate the baguettes and sat, watching the town gradually come to life, and ordered more coffee. The previous Christmas Eve suddenly came into my mind and I breathed a sigh of relief that today was so, so different.

By the time we'd finished breakfast and had a final meander around a few shops, it was well after ten. I was keen to get our shopping unpacked and prepped so we could relax and enjoy the rest of the day. We made our way home talking, laughing, feeling warm and loving. I brewed more coffee and we started to unpack and get the kitchen in order. I heard his mobile ring and as I was nearest to it, picked it up and passed it across to him. He frowned and as he started to listen much more than talk, I could see his face clouding over. A full ten minutes elapsed and, for some reason, I began to feel uneasy. I didn't know why but I was.

Eventually he rang off and sat at the table, head resting on one hand. I went over to him and kissed the top of his head. "Everything ok darling?" I suddenly knew it wasn't.

He looked up. "That was Marianne." A cold feeling swept over me and I gazed down at him, trying to read what he was thinking, but nothing could have prepared me for what happened next.

He stood up decisively. "I have to go to her."

I gasped. "She needs me Lucie. She really does. She's desperate and if I don't go, I really don't know what she'll do." He held my shoulders and stared into my eyes. "You do understand, don't you?"

I stared back at him. "No, I don't know that I do even though I'm trying to." The words came out very slowly. "There's no-one else she feels she can turn to? There's no-one else who can help her? That's hard to believe." As I spoke I could see his tension rise but I couldn't stop myself, I wanted to be accommodating but this seemed a step far too far. "And what about us? What about our Christmas?"

"Oh for God's sake." Unexpectedly, and very unusually, he sounded angry. "Don't you understand? She's terribly confused and upset. She needs me." I took a breath to say something but he continued. "You'll be fine. You've got lots of friends and ..."

I couldn't bear it. "So, when are you coming back?" My own anger and resentment was beginning to build.

"I don't know. All I do know is that she needs me so I have to go. Now." He turned away and pushed past me, leaving me standing in shock and disbelief. I felt angry, bewildered and duped.

I slowly went into the hall. I could hear him moving around upstairs and moments later he joined me, holding his bag. "I'm sorry Lucie but I have to do this," and with that he went to kiss me. Automatically I leaned towards him before common sense kicked in and I stepped back.

"And our Christmas?"

He shrugged. "I don't know." And with that he was gone.

I stood in the hall, staring at the closed front door and as I did so, fat tears ran down my face as, unexpectedly, memories of last Christmas crowded into my head and fuelled my pain. The cats knew I was distraught and circled round my feet, softly mewing. I returned to the kitchen, threw the coffee away and poured myself a whisky. "Shit, shit, shit. What's with me and bloody Christmas?" I whispered to myself as more tears came. I tried Karen's landline but it went to voicemail so I put the phone down, she was probably out seeing family or Tony and I certainly didn't want to rain on her parade.

I opened a bottle of Merlot and downed a very large glass very quickly but the pain was still there so I took a sleeping pill and went to bed. I didn't want to see anyone or talk to anyone. Thankfully, I slept.

I awoke in the dark, it was just after five. I'd slept most of the day away and as memories of the morning swept over me I lay on my stomach and cried. I needed the bathroom and as I washed my hands, stared at myself. So, what are you going to do now? My little inner voice came through loud and clear. I stood, hands on the basin, leaning forward and closed my eyes while I thought. All too easily I could have given in to my feelings of sorrow and frustration but as I stood there, my head resting against the mirror, deep inside me came the clear message 'this isn't ok - this isn't reasonable - this isn't fair' and when I raised my head, there were no tears, just a look of resolution.

I had a shower, dressed in red and put my makeup on. It was clear that I had been crying. My eyes were bright with unshed tears but I felt much better. I'd left my mobile downstairs and when I looked, I saw over a dozen texts from Phil, all apologising but reaffirming that he felt he had no choice but to do what he did. Each one ended with 'I love you Lucie xxxxxx'. I ignored them.

I was very tempted to cancel Christmas but then realised that the only one I'd be hurting was myself so prepped everything ready for Christmas lunch after which I called Anita and asked if I could pop over for a drink. "Of course Lucie, be lovely to see you," was her slightly surprised response. I was in the car and at theirs within ten minutes. We sat in the kitchen and talked while they continued with their own preparation for Christmas.

"So how's everything with you?" John asked.

I took a deep breath and told them. Anita came and sat next to me, while John continued to peel sprouts. When I finished I asked them what they thought. Anita was gently angry with him for hurting me but John's view was more in line with what Kyle had said the previous week, which made me stop and think. As I took my leave from them a couple of hours later, I felt calmer and more reflective and as I drove home yet again I thanked God for the blessing of my dear friends.

I was prepared to recognise that, for some reason, Phil felt a huge sense of responsibility for Marianne and had a grudging admiration for that, but on the other hand, leaving me the way he did was, in my view, absolutely unacceptable.

I texted him later. 'I understand and accept that you feel the way you do. BUT doing what you did in the way you did it was very very hurtful and absolutely NOT ok'. I didn't send a kiss, he didn't deserve one.

He called minutes later. I stared at the phone but didn't pick up. I wasn't interested in hearing excuses or listening to him trying to persuade me to look at things from his or Marianne's point of view when so clearly mine weren't considered.

I recognised I was entitled to be a bit more selfish than that and as the realisation that we wouldn't be together for Christmas hit me, I started to cry again so the remainder of the Merlot was drunk as I sat on the sofa with my cats. Here we fucking well go again, was my final thought as I went to bed and managed to fall into a slightly bombed sleep - Christmas would happen with or without Phil.

Chapter 14 - Christmas Present

Christmas Day

I was in one those delicious transient moments between sleeping and wakefulness when reality gently nudges into consciousness. I'd just been woken up by being given the most amazing head by the most amazing man who loved me and who I loved. He'd made me one of my favourite breakfasts of scrambled eggs with smoked salmon washed down with icy-cold Bucks Fizz. He'd prepared Christmas lunch and laid a beautiful table. Naked, he'd knelt at my feet to give me a huge box which I thought was a present only to find in it a card that he'd sketched, depicting us both in a close embrace and on that card he'd written what was in his heart.

I yawned, stretched, wriggled my toes and reached over to touch him to find a cool, smooth pillow. No-one was there. My eyes snapped open. I was alone and as I slowly sat up, memories of Christmas Eve flooded back. The fabulous sex, the breakfast, the lunch prepared, the Bucks Fizz, the box, the card - they were all a dream. Not good enough. Just not fucking good enough my little inner voice told me. I closed my eyes and let the pain wash over me for a few moments while I composed myself.

I took a hot shower, dressed in white and red, put on my makeup, threw the scarf that Jean-Michel had given me over my shoulder and stood at the top of the stairs for a moment. My guests would be arriving in about three hours expecting Christmas lunch and I was going to make sure that they had a great meal and a great time. I took a deep breath and started to descend.

I was halfway downstairs when I heard the doorbell. I certainly wasn't expecting anyone, not yet, and opened the door with a small questioning frown. When I saw who it was, I gasped. "Oh my God - it's you ..."

I knew that this Christmas was so going to be good enough ...

I do hope that you've enjoyed this book — if you have, please post a review on Amazon.

Lucie's adventures will continue very soon...

(In the One Elm, July 2015)   © facebook.com/HarrietLong

This is Vivien Heim's first venture into fiction although she's been writing all her life. Vivien has spent the last 20 years running her own management consultancy business as well as hosting foreign students and teachers, teaching English as a foreign language and working as a marriage registrar. Divorced, with one grown-up daughter, Vivien lives in Stratford upon Avon with her two cats.

Made in the USA
Charleston, SC
07 January 2016